I0760584

# A Daughter of Winter

# A Daughter of Winter

THE
SCENTED COURT
· BOOK 3 ·

A.L. KNORR
USA TODAY BESTSELLING AUTHOR

## Books by A.L. Knorr

### Elemental Origins Series

*Born of Water*
*Born of Fire*
*Born of Earth*
*Born of Æther*
*Born of Air*
*The Elementals*

### The Siren's Curse

*Salt & Stone*
*Salt & the Sovereign*
*Salt & the Sisters*

### Earth Magic Rises

*Bones of the Witch*
*Ashes of the Wise*
*Heart of the Fae*

### Arcturus Academy

*Firecracker*
*Fire Trap*
*Fire Games*
*Legends of Fire*
*Source Fire*

**Rings of the Inconquo**

*Born of Metal*

*Metal Guardian*

*Metal Angel*

**Mermaid's Return**

*Returning*

*Falling*

*Surfacing*

**Elemental Novellas**

*Pyro, A Fire Novella*

*Heat, A Fire Novella*

**The Kacy Chronicles**

*Descendant*

*Ascendant*

*Combatant*

*Transcendent*

**The Scented Court**

*A Blossom at Midnight*

*A Memory of Nightshade*

*A Daughter of Winter*

*A Prince of Autumn*

To learn more visit www.alknorrbooks.com.

ISBN 5x8 Paperback 978-1-989338-55-1

ISBN 5.5x8.5 Hardcover 978-1-989338-56-8

ISBN 6x9 Large Print Hardcover 978-1-989338-57-5

# Prologue

Rayven Sabran stood in the huge empty throne room, legs shaking. Her father, Master of the Ice, had told her that the throne room had once been in the courtyard, not in this cavernous, cold space that echoed like a tomb. When she was a faeling, he had regaled her—always in secret—with whispered stories about winter sunshine and a beautiful benevolent queen holding court under an open sky, listening to her subjects' petitions, not just nobility, but farmers and peasants, too. Often, she would surprise them by bestowing generous gifts. He never called this queen by name, and would close the story by vowing loyalty to the current queen, an utterance that rang hollow, no matter how many times it was repeated. But those stories were a long time ago, embellished and romanticized, as unlikely as a fable. That fairy-tale queen had nothing in common with the sovereign seated before Rayven now.

Sylifke gazed at her, tapping the talon of her index finger on the marble arm of her throne. Her hair was a silvery waterfall of curls, her gown breathtaking, but her face was all sharp angles, craftiness and cruelty: a portrait painted by two different artists, one who valued beauty and light, the other who treasured darkness and malice.

"You failed me, Miss Sabran," said the queen.

"I am sorry, my queen." Rayven cast her eyes down. "I have given you their reasons for keeping Sasha, they are within their ri—"

"My only son is dead," Sylifke hissed, "and you want me to accept their reasons, their rights as you call them, to stand between me and Ruskin's murderer?"

"No, Ma'am." Rayven put her hands behind her back, not daring to look up.

"So they will try him at court, like one of their own citizens…" mused Sylifke.

The queen's voice slithered around the empty throne room. All things considered, she did not sound as angry as Rayven had expected, but the queen was known to hide rage—to release it later, just when you thought you were safe.

"That's what I understand, Ma'am."

"And the lady in the ice… did you know her?"

"No, Ma'am. I never met her."

"Was she fae?"

"I was told she might be half."

"I assume she had dark hair?"

Rayven felt unbalanced by this line of questioning. She wasn't sure why it mattered. Rayven had guessed the frozen woman had jilted Prince Ruskin at some point during the festival, ticked him off, maybe humiliated him. Unlike his mother, Ruskin had had no self-control whatsoever. Rayven searched her memory, but truthfully, she had not gotten a good look at the lady before or after the ice. What's done was done. But

Sylifke was waiting for an answer, and Rayven found she had a vague recollection of a dark blur inside the ice, in the vicinity of the woman's head.

"I believe so, Ma'am," she said.

Abruptly, Sylifke stood, making Rayven flinch and glance up. But the queen was not looking at her. She took the three steps down to floor level, walked some distance away, then stopped, a sure sign that she was thinking. No, not thinking. The queen did not think; she contrived, devised, machinated. She muttered something that sounded to Rayven like, 'This might work for us', but, surely, that couldn't be right. Ruskin had been slaughtered, his throat torn out. Was the queen in denial? Had she misunderstood the situation?

"Sorry, Ma'am?"

Sylifke turned back to Rayven. "What did they do with her?"

"The… woman?"

"Of course the woman," the queen snapped.

"I-I…" Rayven felt poleaxed. The queen had just lost her only son, yet she was showing more interest in the person Ruskin had attacked.

"Well?" Sylifke stomped her foot, like Rayven was a mule that needed to get moving.

Rayven expected that at any moment she would be sentenced to prison, or exiled. Or maybe the queen would just run her through with an ice-blade, right here in the throne room. Why bother with prison? She swallowed before filling the room with conjecture, hoping she might land on something the queen wanted to hear.

"I assume they'll wait for the ice to melt. They may not even understand the significance of it," Rayven guessed. "If she is a halfling, she won't survive. Then, I suppose they'll bury her, or send her back to wherever she's from to be buried. She wasn't a Solanan citizen. I heard she was from… somewhere south."

"And when is the trial?"

Rayven blinked. Following Sylifke's line of thought was like chasing a rubber ball through a labyrinth.

"Sasha's trial?"

Sylifke hissed.

"They haven't set a date yet," she blurted, heart pounding in her ears like a war drum.

"Right," said the queen, sounding like she'd decided something. "Fetch my scribe."

"Your—"

"Do it now!"

Rayven ran from the throne room, her footsteps echoing around the queen as she stood there, ticking through possibilities, weighing opportunities. A smile slid across her face, one of triumph.

"So, you think you found her, my son? If you are right, then you will be remembered as a hero. And all that remains is to finish what you started."

# Part One

## Chapter One

# Jessamine

Laec and Grex were a blur of thundering black flesh, flashing hooves, and flying red hair far ahead of Jessamine. Her mount—which she'd never ridden before, but borrowed from the stables because he looked more awake than the others—a painted gelding named Kitabee, sturdy and stalwart though he was, could not keep up with the Stavarjakian stallion. Tears streamed from Jess's eyes as she pressed low over Kitabee's neck, urging him on. Her breath was hot in her throat, her thighs screaming their own burning pain as she crouched above the saddle the way Laec had shown her.

The race had been Laec's idea. So had the ride. At another time, when things in Jess's life were humming along the tracks of routine, she would have declined his invitation. But routine had been derailed, along with Jess's peace-of-mind, not to mention good nights' sleeps. Jess had not been able to see Sasha— or Rialta—in the four days since he had fainted in the lion's den and been carried away, hidden by a crowd of soldiers, Fahyli and big familiars.

So when Laec knocked on her door—before the palace corridors began to bustle with life, before the stable hands had rubbed the sleep from their eyes—dressed in boots and riding leathers, Jess had agreed. Beazle complained that even the bugs weren't awake before tucking his wings more tightly around himself and going back to sleep.

As Solana City came into view, Laec slowed Grex to a canter, then a walk, giving Jess and Kitabee time to catch up. They caught their breath as rays of silvery sunlight kissed the highest towers, lighting the terra-cotta tiles and reflecting off stained-glass windows. Flags fastened to the tallest towers whipped and snapped. They could be heard even from where Jess and Laec stood upon a distant hill. Solana's lion's head sigil blinked in and out of sight.

A pang of loss tugged at Jess's heart as she thought of Marion, and of Greta. Marion had lived long enough to know of Jess's ascension—if it could be called that—to the ranks of the Calyx, but not the many strange turns Jess's life and talents had taken. Jess was no longer a child. This she felt within—like the hardening of candle wax once the flame was blown out—as she was forced to respond to difficult circumstances, make difficult choices. No, Jess was no longer the naïve and innocent village girl she had once been, no longer the novice Calyx who didn't know up from down.

She scanned the city walls, the towers, the incredible beauty of the wealthiest kingdom on the continent of Ivryndi. Despite the incredible power and loveliness all her mind could muster was: *Where are you?*

A visit to the city gaol—a place Jess hoped never to visit again—confirmed that Sasha and Rialta were not being kept there, which was a relief. But it had also become clear that no one was going to give her their exact whereabouts—either because they didn't know or because they were sticking to the rules. Permission had to be given by one of three people: the justice—who didn't live at the palace and whom Jess never learned the name of as everyone just called them 'the justice'—Captain Bradburn, or Ian Peneçek. Presumably, the king and queen's say-so would work as well.

Ilishec hadn't seemed to notice that Jess's focus on her work was basically non-existent. He bustled about the palace in a state of constant fretting and frustration over the way the Calyx had reacted to the quarantining of their familiars. Of Solana's flora fae familiar population, only Ania and Beazle had escaped the week-long hell of being restricted to life in a small box. Some of the insects seemed to understand and accept their fate, like Sphex, Jalla, and Amarylis's familiar, a carpenter bee named Xylo. But Bombini, Trea, and Heath's familiar, Coco, buzzed about their tiny prison walls angrily, eating hardly at all. Others fell into a despondency that would have sent their fae into a panic had the Calyx not been mystically connected to their familiars. Familiars who'd gone dormant had responded to none of the attempts to revive or comfort them: nectar, music, fragrant blooms tucked inside their boxes to be a comfort and a nourishment.

The good news though, was that four days had passed and none of the familiars were acting in the way Moony had before he died. Ilishec reminded the Calyx of this beam of light in an otherwise dark time, but the Calyx were too upset to work until the quarantine was over—and there were still three days to go.

Jess and Laec rode back to the stables and put their mounts in the capable hands of the grooms to be rubbed down, blanketed, fed and watered. They parted ways with hardly a word, and it wasn't until Jess was bathing away the smell of horse in her suite that she regretted not asking him how he was. How he *really* was. He cared deeply for Çifta and not knowing if she would survive the ice must be torture.

She chided her reflection as she combed out her hair: "You're not the only one suffering, you know."

She donned a long-sleeved woolen gown of deep burgundy, a typical winter dress for a Calyx. She pinned back half of her hair, revealing her ears, before wrapping a thick scarf around her neck and a soft fur cape around her upper body; she felt ready to go outside. Everyone was complaining that this winter was the coldest in a hundred years, but Jess was too distracted to care much about the weather. As she opened the door to leave her room, Beazle swooped from the ceiling and crawled under the hair at the nape of her neck. Jess smiled when she felt him drop off into a doze again almost immediately.

Jessamine spent most of her time in the west keep, hoping for some clue about Sasha's whereabouts and avoiding the moping Calyx in the east keep.

"But what if they're being mistreated, or not fed well, or Sasha needs to have a letter delivered?" Jess complained to Regalis as he carved a new handle for an old Kittrell blade that had belonged to his grandfather.

The Fahyli spared her a glance. "They're fine, Jess. No one is presumed guilty or treated as such before a trial. Their needs are being met. Now leave it alone. Leave *me* alone," he added with a cornerwise smile of affectionate annoyance.

Jessamine sat down on the bench beside him. The head of an eagle was taking shape under his deft fingers. It was already so like Ferrugin that Jess should have been impressed. She stared blankly at Regalis's hands as they coaxed a new shape from the wood, registering nothing.

She sprang up again. "But, *where* are they?"

"Jess, you're in my light." Regalis pushed her sideways, then blasted dust and shavings away from his creation with a quick, well-aimed puff. Condensation misted the air and dissipated on the winter wind. "Why is it important to you, anyway?"

"I told you." Jess replied a little too quickly. "We're friends."

"I see." Regalis's tone said he didn't care.

Beazle shifted sleepily, coming briefly out of his slumber with an exasperation that matched Regalis's. *You've interrogated pretty much everyone else. Why not him too?*

*Who?* Jess looked around and caught a flash of sunshine on brown hair and tanned cheeks as Digit walked by the open gate before disappearing behind the stone wall. A moment later Ania hummed by in a straight line.

"Bye Regalis," murmured Jess, her sights and hope now set on Digit.

Regalis didn't look up. "Mercy, at last."

Jess caught up to Digit as he climbed a rocky trail curving up and around the base of the castle, leading to pastureland. It passed a forested copse where animals gathered between the slender trunks for shade on hot days and shelter on windy ones. Right now there was so much horseflesh crammed into the grove that their exhaled breath hovered over them like a fog.

"Shouldn't you be on the other side of the palace?" Digit asked as she fell in step beside him.

"The Calyx are on strike," Jess replied, picking up her skirts to make for easier walking over the rough terrain.

This was not strictly true. Ilishec had—in a moment of irritation—referred to the Calyx's lack of interest in work during the quarantine as a strike, and the term had stuck, even though it was not their intention to be rebellious. Their insects were in distress, so naturally, they were also. Jess, however, had many Calyx duties she could do on her own—botanical studies, sweat sessions, even learning the new spring dances—but if the rest of the Calyx weren't working, then she didn't want to either. Jess told Ilishec that it was solidarity for her fellow flora fae. He'd rolled his eyes but let it go. Really, it was all about Sasha.

Digit looked up at the sky, calculating something, maybe the time. "I'd go on strike too, if the crofter wanted to put Ania in a box."

"Well, sure," replied Jess. "Can I ask you something?"

"I'm all ears."

"Do you know where they might keep someone… who… recently got in trouble with the law?"

Ania landed in the pillow of Digit's hair, looking like a glittering jewel in the world's softest nest.

Digit cocked an eyebrow. "Gee, I wonder who that might be? No, I don't know where they're keeping Sasha and his wolf, but I do know the palace pretty well, and they're not in it. If they were, the guard rotation would make it obvious."

Jess stumbled over a loose stone. "Not in the palace?"

"Careful." He put a hand under her elbow.

"Where then?"

"I'd guess they're in the caperlands."

The name rang a very small, very distant bell.

The caperlands referred to a run-down building on a corner of land that was totally overgrown and mostly forgotten. The palace grounds were massive, with not only huge yards, gardens, greenhouses and keeps, but also countless outbuildings, towers, stables, forges and sheds. Jess had never had a reason to visit the caperlands, but recalled seeing it marked on one of the secret passageway maps. It was positioned well away from the palace, beyond even the training yards.

"They use it as a prison?" Jess pulled up her scarf as they turned a corner and a blast of wind struck her in the face.

Digit pulled a pair of gloves from the pocket of his bulky coat. "Not usually. It's a five-hundred-year-old building that hasn't been maintained, but it's still pretty solid. They say it was the building Erasmus first lived in while Solana City was being built. Caperberries took over the land, hence the name."

"Weird place to keep him," Jess mumbled.

"Better than the gaol or the dungeons," Digit said, tugging a glove on with his teeth as he lifted his collar for Ania to crawl inside. "I heard there was a big debate about where to keep them. Laws say he should be gaoled, but many view him as a hero, so they pressured the justice to put him somewhere nicer. The justice is up for an election next year, so I guess he caved, which is just as well. Sasha and Rialta don't deserve to be thrown in with murderers and thieves."

Jess felt a renewed sense of hope. "Thanks, Digit. In that case, the caperlands makes a lot of sense."

"It's an educated guess, but I'd stay away if I were you." At her expression, he put up his palms. "Just a suggestion. It's your business, but you'd better not let Ilishec see you with that look on your face."

Digit strode away, leaving Jess standing alone with a pounding heart. What did her face look like when she was thinking of Sasha? However her love changed her features, it was recognizable as love to others, and that was a little frightening given the circumstances.

She made her way down the hill, narrowly avoiding spraining an ankle as she picked a path toward the lumpy stone structure. The trail narrowed through a patch of thick, prickly caperberry bushes—dense, with perfectly round, silver-green leaves, even in winter. Leggy tendrils curled out from a central root, catching at her skirt and boots with tiny green crochet-hook thorns. Gaby would not be pleased.

As she crested a rise, before descending into a vale, the building came into view. It might have been a majestic manor once, but time had broken its back, peeled away the plaster and tiles, leaving big patches exposed to the weather. Moss, lichens, and vines choked big gray blocks of stone, crumbling the mortar as nature made every attempt to turn the building to dust. A stream trickled somewhere in the undergrowth, and clouds hung over the hollow, filtering the winter sunlight. The caperlands building looked frozen and forlorn, and the closer she got, the less she liked it. Jess had no doubt it had been Erasmus's home in the early days of this kingdom, but as beloved as Erasmus was, it was no wonder the manor had been rejected. Though it was on palace land, it would never be embraced by Solana as it appeared to have been designed by the same architect that masterminded the Rahamlar fortress.

Two fat wooden doors barred the way in. In front of those doors stood a pair of human soldiers in Solanan livery. Digit was right, Sasha and Rialta had to be inside, otherwise there'd be no one guarding this place. At the realization that she'd found them, Jess's mouth went dry.

The soldiers were talking in the relaxed way of men who had been boys together, until they looked up and saw her coming down the trail. Then she realized that they were hardly men at all. One was short and soft-cheeked with a round belly pushing at his leathers. The other was tall and gangly, with a scrawny neck and spots on his forehead. Her confidence rose and she put on a friendly smile, picking up her gown to leap gracefully over a puddle. She sunned the boys with her most flirtatious grin. Her body tingled as she summoned a honeysuckle-scented flush to her skin.

"Hello, gentlemen."

Beazle stirred sleepily. *Why do you sound so weird?*

The guards straightened, the smiles that had accompanied their private banter were gone. The shorter one looked at her with curiosity, but the skinny one took on a superior expression that Jess immediately disliked. She hated petty authority, and this lad was full of it. Jess supposed she should be grateful he took this duty so seriously. There might be unfriendlies who wanted to get to Sasha.

The thin one spoke with a strong country accent. "No one is allowed here 'cept a few, and you're not one of 'em. Best go back where you come from, 'fore you get into trouble."

Beazle sensed her rising anxiety. *Jess. What are you doing?*

*What we're good at. Gathering intel. Go back to sleep.*

She tucked a lock of hair behind one ear, still smiling, though her heart was scampering about like a frightened mouse.

*Do we have an assignment I don't know about?* He stretched his wing, which had mostly healed from the puncture wound he'd sustained in Syrgana—though it was still stiff after a long day.

*No.*

She imagined she could feel Sasha's presence, and the thought wrestled down her fears.

"Thank you for the caution," she simpered. "It's kind of you to warn me, but I won't get in trouble. I'm Calyx and Sasha is a good friend of mine. I have permission to visit him."

"This prisoner can't have no visitors, Calyx or not," the soft youth said, looking apologetic. "Because of the trial, you see."

He stared at her with big eyes, taking in her faeness, maybe smelling her perfume.

"And if you *did* have permission," sniped the other, "it'd be in writing, and I don't see nuffink in your hands."

She twirled a stray curl of hair through her fingers, her expression delicately perplexed. "I didn't realize I had to wait for *written* permission. Of course I can get it. If you'll really want to make me walk *all* the way back to the castle." She gave an exhausted sounding sigh. "Then I'll have to find Ian, of course. He could be anywhere, and the palace grounds are huge! It could take me *hours* and I have a very busy day ahead. If you'll let me inside for a quick hello, I'll only take a minute. I promise. I'll be gone before you even know it, you won't even remember that I was here."

The spotted one narrowed his eyes and actually put his hand on the pommel of his sword. "We don't care if it takes you weeks, we can't let you in without a stamp from Bradburn or the *Honorable Crofter*." His emphasis was a none-too-subtle rebuke at her supposed inappropriate use of Ian's first name.

The soft soldier looked uncomfortable, but didn't voice any disagreement.

Jess let out a long, unhappy breath. "Very well. If I must." She brightened, as though having an idea. "Shall I bring you anything from the kitchen when I return? A cinnamon popkin, or something savory? There's hot coffee available for another hour, I could bring you some. That would help keep the cold out of your bones."

The sweet-faced one lit up like a candle, but the thin one glowered and touched the back of his fist against his colleague's chest, as though to say: *She spied your weakness, but I'll keep you in line.*

"We get three squares a day, miss," he told her in a frigid tone. "We don't need you to bring us anything."

"Thank you, anyway," the short one said, suffering a hard look from his fellow guardsman.

"Suit yourselves." Trying to hide her irritation and not totally succeeding, Jess tossed her scarf over her shoulder a little too dramatically. She turned away, rolling her eyes once the guards could no longer see her face. She raised her eyes heavenward, watching the winter clouds shift slowly across the sky. Ferrugin and Erasmus whirled briefly overhead before disappearing behind the trees. She closed her eyes as a shaft of sunlight fought its way through to touch her face, as warm as a promise. Her resolve hardened, nosing past this failure. There were other ways to surmount this obstacle.

*If they see you again, without a stamp, they might report you,* Beazle cautioned, recognizing the hope rising in her heart and not wanting her to be disappointed. *Better not to sniff around anymore.*

*I'm not going to do any more sniffing around,* Jess told him as she slipped into the palace through a side door. Warmth embraced them. *You are.*

*Am I?*

*If I can't see them with my own eyes, you can at least send me a visual. I need to know they're ok.*

*That's an abuse of power,* observed Beazle, but without any real fervor.

Jess smiled. Technically, he was right, it would be an abuse of their powers, but sneaking in to see Sasha and Rialta wasn't going to hurt the kingdom or anyone in it. Beazle was—even now—getting a thrill from imagining himself slipping unnoticed through the cracks of the old manor.

*It's a stupid rule anyway,* Beazle added. *They should be allowed visitors.*

Jess agreed. She didn't like stupid rules and felt few qualms about breaking them.

## Chapter Two

# Laec

Laec wrapped his scarf more snugly around his neck and stamped his feet on the cobbles. At least the winter temperatures had had the decency to wait until the Midwinter Festival had come to a full close before it slipped its freezing fingers deep into the streets and courtyards of Solana City. It wasn't much to be thankful for when the woman he loved—yes, now that he'd lost her, he could admit that he was properly in love with Lady Çifta—was imprisoned inside a pillar of ice, fighting for her life, if his loose understanding of Silverfall rituals was anywhere close to right. Realizing that someone could be lost forever had the effect of bringing one's feelings into sharp and central focus. Returning from the stables that day to find Çifta entombed was like a slap so hard that his entire world view had changed in a moment.

He sipped hot tea from a waterskin as he circled the ice, searching for a clear patch through which he might get a glimpse of her face, however clouded. It was not satisfying. Her face was a pale blob, her hair a black blur, her body a smudge of darkness. He ran a hand over the handle of Ruskin's sword, still wedged deeply in one corner of the block. The ice had changed not one whit since the moment Sasha had created it.

Laec had quickly realized that if they waited for temperatures to naturally rise enough to start the melting process, there might be no change until spring. It wouldn't do. He and Auvo, the artist friend that Çifta had made, were the only ones who seemed prepared to act as Çifta's advocates in this matter. The consensus had been that the ice was heavy, and Çifta was Silverfae anyway, so leaving her in the courtyard was the easiest and safest thing to do. While Auvo was too busy to get any real traction on the problem, Laec had undertaken a lively argument with the crofter and Captain Bradburn for the right to move her.

Surely—he'd argued—there was a time limit to how long she could remain frozen without expiring, especially for a half-blood. Worse, Kazery could return at any time and in her current location, she would be the first thing he saw on entering the courtyard. For her father to find her in this state reflected badly on Agir and Esha. If an attempt was not made to thaw her, the Boskayan merchant would have every right to be irate with them, and he'd be even more difficult to reason with. After all, he'd left his beloved daughter in Solana's care, and would return to find she was teetering at the brink of death.

It was when he mentioned Kazery in the debate that Laec finally convinced Ian and Bradburn that they had to move her to a warmer place. The ice was thick enough, Laec had argued, that it would not crack provided the job was done with the help of many strong men. It was those men for whom Laec now waited, with a great knot of tension filling his belly. And not only was he waiting for help, he was waiting for a reply from Queen Elphame.

Exhausted and traumatized, Laec had written to Elphame before helping Ilishec and the Calyx gather all the insect familiars into their quarantine boxes. He sent the letter using one of Esha's personal birds, the fastest and best trained bird in the aviary, according to the keeper: a peregrine falcon. Any hour now, Laec expected a response, and was hoping for insight from his queen about Çifta's predicament.

The sound of boots tramping on the cobbles accompanied by the rolling of wooden wheels drew Laec's attention to the far side of the courtyard. He fastened his waterskin to his belt, freeing his hands, as a dozen burly workmen poured through the gate. Four of them pulled a low, wheeled platform behind them, while others carried ropes and pulleys, or hefted timbers. Laec greeted them with a smile he did not feel. He just wanted to get this whole ordeal over with. In spite of his confidence that ice would not split, last night, he'd had nightmares about that very thing happening, and Çifta breaking along with it. He'd woken up to his own strangled cry.

Though many Solanans had already come to view the ice pillar with the fae female locked inside, many of the workmen had not yet seen her. Laec had to be patient while they stared at her in wonder, peering through the ice—not daring to touch it with their bare hands—and murmuring between themselves about the strangeness of it all. Then they set to work.

It took an hour to get the pulley system set up and the ropes firmly supporting the block, but once it was rigged the men were able to use one of the large crossbeams of the nearby stable to lift Çifta's pillar with ease, while others slid the platform beneath her. It was just like lifting a large marble stone from the quarry they said.

That done, they rolled her slowly and with great care across the courtyard to the mostly flat walkway that led around to the gardens on the east side of the castle. Double doors tall enough to accommodate the white pillar had been propped open to receive the strange parade. Getting her over the threshold was the hardest part, as the men had to lift the cart with their collective brute strength, but after that, wheeling it to the ground-floor room Laec had secured for the purpose was easy.

Ilishec had surrendered a small ballroom that was used for dance lessons and orchestral rehearsals. It had tall ceilings, pretty stained-glass windows full of flowers and dancing butterflies, and—Laec's favorite feature—a huge fireplace.

As the men positioned the pillar near the hearth and locked the cart's wheels, Laec was pleased to see that the firewood he'd requested had already been lined up against the wall, cords of the stuff, along with baskets of dry kindling and paper trash. Laec thanked the men, and the moment they left turned his attention to the next task. Casting off his coat, scarf and gloves, he gathered enough wood and kindling to make the largest fire the hearth could hold, feeling almost giddy as he arranged the fuel in the grate. The kindling lit like a hungry animal, snapping and crackling as it spread to the larger logs. Heat and light basked Laec's face, easing some of the tension from his bones and lifting his hopes.

A hoarse caw drew Laec's attention from the fire.

Mistik was a black fae-terran crow hybrid with a white crest on her right wing, and a green patch encircling her right eye. When Elphame wanted to reach him quickly, she sent

Mistik. Laec took it as a good sign, a sign that Elphame knew something that might help.

Mistik hopped across the floor with a few springy bounces before landing on the fireplace mantle. Laec unfastened the cylinder fixed to her leg and spilled the contents into his palm. With trembling fingers he unrolled the tiny scroll, hope burgeoning in his chest.

It deflated before it had any chance to float as he read the first line:

*Urgent! Whatever you do for Lady Çifta, do not expose her to the heat of flames!*

Before he read the rest of the letter, Laec emptied the remaining hot tea in his waterskin over the fire, dousing it with a loud sizzle. He felt immediately damp with sweat and hoped the small amount of heat the fire had kicked out had not done any damage. He cursed himself with a string of choice Stavarjakian insults, but really, how was he supposed to know not to use fire? Elphame was very old—no one really knew how old—and had gathered all kinds of obscure knowledge over her lifetime, including about foreign magic. His pulse singing all the high notes, Laec turned his eyes back to the message, grateful that Mistik had arrived before the room had a chance to heat up.

*It is not conventional ice that has consumed your friend, it is magic. The ice is a Silverfae ritual that, once begun, cannot be reversed or hurried. Even if it looks like nothing is happening, there is a process occurring that must not be interfered with. Provided she is not left outdoors in subzero temperatures, Çifta will melt in time. To use fire would be to tempt the ice, and in response it might make Lady Çifta suffer more than she needs to.*

Laec looked up abruptly at the shape inside the ice, his mind a torrent. Magical tests were not fun, not the life-threatening ones, anyway. He hoped that whatever it was she was experiencing, it wasn't too painful.

"Have courage, my lady," he said to the block before returning to the letter.

*There is something you can do that may have a positive effect, but I cannot tell you what it is. It must occur organically, or it will hinder instead of help. Think about what you know about magic. That is all the advice I can give. Otherwise, the test will come to an end in its own time, and she will be released, dead or alive. Until then, you must wait.*

*Your beloved queen,*

*Elphame*

Laec read and reread the note, flicking back to the part about there being something he could do, but that she wouldn't tell him what it was.

Yes, Elphame was a great queen, a powerful sorceress. She could also be insufferably frustrating, especially when she claimed that she knew a way to help, but wouldn't share what it is.

"Not won't, faeling," Mistik croaked, somehow channeling Elphame into the room, and making Laec jump. Only Elphame could get away with calling Laec a faeling.

"Not won't?" Laec prodded the crow.

"*Can't,*" Mistik added with the voice of a rusted hinge.

Knowing that Elphame couldn't share a thing did not improve his mood, but it did set him to thinking.

He couldn't build a fire, but he might do something to have a positive effect… how? With warm water? He thought not. But whatever it was he could do, it must occur to him naturally. He looked around the room, probing for possibilities, seeking inspiration. A few things had been left scattered about the space. Stacks of chairs the musicians used during practice, stands for sheet music, left-behind dancing slippers and forgotten notebooks. A bookshelf with titles dedicated to the arts sat to one side of the fireplace.

There was no inspiration to be found in this room.

He circled the ice, contemplating the queen's message.

Çifta was alive inside. Since it first happened, he'd believed it to his core and Elphame had confirmed it. She was alive and she was being tested, but the test would come to an end, and Lady Çifta's fate would be determined. If he was allowed to talk to Sasha, Laec could get more advice, but he'd already tried that route and been soundly rejected by a set of petty young guardsmen enjoying their newly acquired authority. Besides, even if Sasha could tell him what he might do to help, according to Elphame it would void the positive effect.

No, he had to figure it out on his own.

Laec lay his bare palm against the ice, touching it without

gloves for the first time since immediately after the ice formed. With a hiss, he snatched his hand back. That was new. It was frigid of course, but there was a more unpleasant sensation that accompanied the skin to ice contact. It had not been there on the day of her freezing, Laec knew, for he'd looked into the side of the block like a little boy drooling at sweets in a candy shop window. The sensation reminded him of stinging nettle: a half-burning, half-freezing sensation; a thousand tiny needles stabbing his hand. When Laec pulled his hand away, the pain ceased. What remained was a glossy handprint, the topmost layer of frost melted away.

*Think about what you know about magic.*

Magic had a price, that was the first rule—the universal truth—that all magical beings and those who commanded magic understood. The most benign magic simply made the bearer tired, and demanded nothing further. But other magic required payment, sometimes steep payment; and on the darkest end of the scale, some magic required blood.

Laec looked at his hand, then at the ice. "I can have a positive effect, but it will cost me. Is that it?"

Elphame was not there to affirm it, but he didn't really need her to. It was obvious, now that he'd landed on it. Melting this ice with body heat was an idea so unappealing that it would only occur to someone who not only cared deeply about the occupant, but was also desperate to help, desperate enough that they were willing to endure agony.

He closed his eyes and sucked in a deep breath, bracing himself for the pain. Then he ripped off his vest and tunic, and cast them to the floor, baring all of his torso.

## Chapter Three

# Çifta

At first there was nothing.

Then there was something: a whisper. The quietest whisper, soft as it came to her, nudged at her. Then all was quiet again. Might she have imagined it? No. There *was* something. A muted… weeping? Yes. It was like the cry of a woman from deep inside a dream. Anguished and throaty now, deep and heartfelt.

She understood the cry, what it was for, because it was universal: it was for a return of balance, for crooked scales to be righted, for injustices to be answered. It was a cry that had sounded for centuries, throughout every kingdom, and every village. It was a cry for retribution, a return of safety, of peace and prosperity. A cry for respite from the ravages of conflict and war.

It was cold. Yes, she was not uncomfortable, only very, very tired, and unable to coax her senses into full wakefulness. The stillness and the frigidity were absolute, wrapped around her like many layers of strong fabric. There was no hunger, no need, hardly even any thought. Time had no meaning.

There was only that far away voice… crying.

## Chapter Four

# Jessamine

After she'd had her last meal of the day, Jess slipped from the dining hall without a word to anyone. Going to her room, she donned long underwear, trousers, a sweater, a scarf and the winter coat she'd been issued with her Fahyli leathers. She looked like she was on Fahyli duty—though she had no assignment—as she made her way to the fields beyond the west keep and a stone wall between two of the training yards. The wall was overshadowed by many large oaks, casting it in darkness, which hid her climb up to perch and wait, rubbing her gloves together for warmth.

Beazle zigged and zagged overhead, feasting on bugs. Every few minutes he came to Jess to warm himself beneath her scarf before going out to hunt again. Slowly, he filled his belly without freezing to death.

A half-moon kissed the tops of the trees and bathed the terra-cotta roofs of the outbuildings with a misty cool light. Ice between the tiles and in the gullies reflected dimly. Distantly, a group of musicians played something sweet and uplifting from an upper floor of the palace, most likely Princess Isabey's rooms. Rahamlar's heiress had emerged from her rooms only once since she had arrived at the palace, and that was to see with her own eyes if what the servants whispered about Lady Çifta was true. She had entered the courtyard and stood like a block of ice herself, staring at the pillar without moving for half an hour. She said nothing to anyone, only stood there hugging her middle. She'd taken no notice of the servant who wrapped a shawl around her, speaking kindly to her, trying to get her to go back inside.

Jess could just make out the pale glow from one of Isabey's windows, the rest were obscured by swaying treetops. Isabey had not ordered the music, it had been sent by the queen. It was sweet of Esha to try to comfort the princess, but Jessamine knew from her own difficult days after Marion had passed away that food and music were little comfort in the face of such loss.

When Beazle was satisfied, Jess drew her gaze back to the target she couldn't quite see: the caperlands building. *We have our own concerns.* It was time to make their move. Beazle was to sneak inside, locate Sasha and Rialta, then watch them throughout the night while sharing visuals from time to time.

Beazle did not think 'you mean *you* have *your* own concerns' in such a clear and articulate way, but she was aware of his feelings all the same. He sensed her sensing his reaction and was immediately sorry. He landed on her shoulder and licked her neck.

*I love him, Beazle. I can't help it.*

*I know, and I'm ready.* He snapped at the air a few times. *This will be easy. Do you want me to give them a message?*

Beazle knew that Jess hadn't prepared a written note—it would be evidence, and might endanger all of them—but sometimes he was able to share thoughts with other familiars, even those he'd never been formally introduced to, like Rialta.

Jess's objective was simply to confirm that Sasha and Rialta were recovering from their wounds and being treated well.

*If you're able,* Jess told him, *let them know that I tried to visit, and that we're watching out for them.*

Beazle cheeped and fluttered into the night sky. Jess smiled as she felt Beazle ascend and ride the cold currents of a wintry night. Her little familiar did love to fly.

Their connection seemed to be evolving, growing stronger. Jess—if she concentrated—could now vaguely perceive what sending and receiving sonar was like for Beazle. It happened far too quickly for her to read the information her little bat took in by the microsecond, but she had a low-level awareness of his bat-vision as he navigated the night sky and all the obstacles it presented. To her, the night sky was a vast vacant place full of wind and smells. But to Beazle it was an endless sea churning with life forms, most of which were prey to him, but some of which presented dangers he knew how to avoid. Currents in the air were as plentiful as currents in the sea, and changes in temperatures could sometimes be drastic.

Beazle sent her a snapshot of the caperlands as he approached, but it was a dark blob that meant nothing to her. He landed on the stone and crawled, searching for a fissure where he could scent the air leaking out, seek the smell of wolf.

Just as the night sky was a completely different experience for Jess than it was for Beazle, so were the surfaces of a building. For Jess, the wall of a building was nothing but a barrier, for Beazle it was a vast terrain of smells, possibilities, and often food.

When he found a crack that smelled faintly of predator,

he slipped into the fissure and scrabbled his way through the wall. Crawling around chunks of broken mortar and the roots of a weed that had taken hold, he reached the interior and dropped into a column of emptiness. Possibly a stairwell. A voice murmured quietly from somewhere near the front of the building—a woman's voice, Jess realized with surprise, and a man's voice responded. Beazle fluttered silently through corridors and doorways. Among other smells, the scent of Rialta grew strong. They were close. An ache whispered that Jess was squeezing her thighs together so hard they were burning, and she forced herself to relax.

A scream pierced the darkness and Beazle squeaked in dismay. Jess sensed that something had closed around him, but not what that something was. Her heart leapt into her throat and she almost gagged with sudden fear. Was it some kind of trap?

*Beaze?! What is it? Are you okay?*

Beazle's thoughts were a shattered mess of fright and shock. *I'm caught!*

Heart surging, Jess's own vision returned as she sprang to her feet, almost losing her balance and falling off the stone wall. She cursed herself roundly as she caught at an overhanging branch, steadying herself. She was desperate to know what had happened. Now that things had gone awry, Jessamine was flooded with regret and self-flagellation. Why had she sent Beazle straight into possible danger? She thought she'd lost him once before, and she *had* lost Greta. Had she learned nothing? Why had she taken such a risk? How stupid could she possibly be?

*Stop that, Jess.* Beazle's thoughts were laced with annoyance and a touch of humiliation. *I agreed to this. I'm on my way back. I'm not hurt.*

Jess closed her eyes in relief. *What happened?*

*You'll see for yourself in a minute.*

Before Beazle's thought finished, Jess heard the sound of wings beating the air. A crow-sized bird approached, but it was not a crow. Its beak was too short, and the outline of its wings against the sky appeared too sleek and sharp to belong to a corvid. The only sound was the soft shoosh of a smooth flyer. Jess squinted into the darkness, wondering if it was Erasmus.

It wasn't though. It was a bird Jess did not know, a species that was smaller than Kite's familiar. It swooped low toward her then hovered. Unceremoniously, it opened a claw and Beazle came flapping out like a disoriented fly from a jar. The bird wheeled back toward the caperlands.

Beazle landed on Jess's shoulder, his little heart pattering. He was deeply embarrassed. *May I introduce Ratchet?*

*Who?* The bird was no longer visible. It had vanished over the caperberry plants.

*Kite's sister's familiar.* Beazle began to lick himself like a cat, a ritual that he'd picked up from palace cats because bats in the wild did not do such things. The licking was more to calm his frazzled nerves and recover some dignity than to clean his fur. *Kestrels and bats are natural enemies. They smell terrible, and now I stink.*

Jess hadn't smelled anything unpleasant, and she hadn't been aware that Kite had a sister, let alone that that sister was a Fahyli. She wasn't sure which question to ask first, and opted for: *But aren't you natural enemies with Ferrugin and Erasmus too?*

*Not so. In the wild, a bat my size is beneath their notice. Hawks and kites want larger prey, but kestrels like to eat small bats.*

*A kestrel,* Jess mused. *No prizes for guessing Kite's sister's name, in that case.*

Beazle shuddered and Jess felt his horror all the way to her own bones. *Thank goodness he was a familiar or I'd have been a meal. He caught me before I could find Sasha, but I got close enough to Rialta to hear her breathing and moving around. She must be ok.*

That was a little comfort, but Jess was still stuck on the way Ratchet had interfered with their subterfuge. Did that mean Kite's sister was a guard? Was *she* the female voice Beazle had heard?

*Could you share thoughts with him?* she asked. *Ratchet, I mean.*

Under her scarf, Beazle was licking the fur on his chest with long strokes. *No. He's not very smart.*

Jess bit back a smile. She doubted that Ratchet was dumb, especially if he was anything like Erasmus. Erasmus was impulsive but far from stupid. Besides, Ratchet had been able to communicate his name to Beazle, hadn't he? Jess wished she could hear other familiar's thoughts through Beazle, but their magic didn't extend that far and she didn't know if it could be cultivated. Panther seemed to think that fauna fae magic was limitless, but Jess had doubts.

Beazle's chagrin was fading now and he was mostly over the incident. He quit licking himself, and crawled out from under her scarf to hop onto the back of her hand. He looked up at her with shining black eyes. *I'm sorry, Jess.*

Jess dropped a kiss on the top of his head. *I'm just glad you're ok.*

His thoughts turned to the night sky. Jess tossed him up and he flew away to do bat-things. She climbed down the wall and marched back to the palace. Attempt two had failed. She hated this predicament but consoled herself with the knowledge that they had, in fact, made a little progress: they knew where Sasha and Rialta were, on palace ground and still close to her.

Just not close enough to touch or talk to.

She made her way through the mostly quiet corridors to the Calyx side of the palace, and up the stairs toward her room. Shedding her outer layers, Jess had just put her hand on the latch of the door to her suite when a voice made her jump.

"There you are! Where have you been?"

She turned to see Hob, the palace steward, bearing down on her, his eyes bloodshot and his uniform rumpled. She had never seen him looking this tired and out of sorts.

"I… well, I—" she stuttered, trying to come up with an excuse on the spot. At this hour, she had not expected to be accosted by anyone. Most people were thinking about bed.

"Never mind, never mind," he told her impatiently. "It doesn't matter. I've found you now and you will not escape me."

"I don't want to esca—" Jess felt poleaxed by Hob's brusque manner. Up until now, she'd only ever known him to be calm and professional.

He hooked her by the arm and pulled her along the hall. "No bed for you yet, Miss Fontana. You're wanted in the lion's den. Right now. I could have my ears boxed for how long it's taken to deliver you. Leave your winter things and come with me, please."

Jess left her outdoor gear just inside her room and followed Hob, bewildered by this development, and worried, because the lion's den meant an audience with authority, possibly even Esha and Agir. Ratchet and Kestrel must have ratted them out. Jess's stomach tightened up and her skin began to ooze the scent of wilted *nicotiana* and *cestrum* blossoms. Beazle felt her distress, and by the time she and Hob rounded the corridor and were approaching the closed doors of the lion's den, he had landed on her neck and crawled up into her hair.

"Wait here, Miss Fontana." Hob faced her. "I can't stay with you, I'm afraid. I have many things to do before I can go to bed."

"What's this about? Do you know?" Jess asked as he straightened the shoulders of her tunic and patted down her hair.

"You'll find out soon enough, Miss Fontana. They're eager to see you, and won't make you wait long. Forgive me. I must go."

And with that, the weary steward bustled off down the hall, leaving Jess standing before the big double doors, alone with her worst fears.

Jess tried not to allow a sense of doom to get its hold on her. Her gaze went up to the carving above the doors of the lion's den. Her heartbeat slowed and calm washed over her as her eyes fell on the largest male. His mane was beautifully rendered in wood, thick waves blowing back from his noble face and forehead as he stared sightlessly out at the real world. Trade grains of wood for filaments of light and he would be the creature Jessamine now thought of as *her* lion. She skimmed the faces of his pride: majestic females and curious cubs with round ears. One of the smallest cubs licked her own nose with a long tongue, as though having recently lapped up cream.

From his place in her hair, Beazle sensed her new tranquility. Her bat could feel her gratitude, her solemnity and wonder. Most of all, he felt her panic fizzling away like smoke from a dying fire.

*Is he the one?* Beazle wondered.

*It looks like him,* Jess replied. She weighed the presence of the carved lions against her personal experience, which she'd shared with her bat the morning after they'd taken Sasha away. It could not be a coincidence. *Although I think my lion's forehead was a little broader, his eyes a little further apart. But I don't trust my memory.*

Beazle crawled up to perch on the top of her head. *If it is, wouldn't that mean the carver met him too?*

*I don't know. I keep meaning to ask Ilishec about it but he's busy and distracted. I'm scared he'll tell me it was a hallucination, something I conjured to save my own life.*

Beazle stretched out the wing that had been punctured in Syrgana, easing it to its full length. *The lion's head is Solana's sigil. I don't think he'll tell you that.*

He darted back into her hair when the doors opened, seized by an irrational impulse to hide. Jess understood the feeling. She felt like hiding from the world these days, too. A courtier in a purple tunic lined with gold braid emerged, followed by two soldiers.

"You can go in now," a soldier told her, holding the door open.

She found Agir and Esha seated together at the table near the windows, which had been propped open a crack to let in fresh air. Esha talked quietly and the king's head was bent toward his queen, listening. A scroll with a broken seal sat on the table near her hand. There was no one else in the room. Jess and Beazle had never been alone with Solana's sovereigns before.

Because she was wearing trousers and a Fahyli tunic, she bowed. "Sire, Ma'am."

King Agir beckoned. "Come in, Miss Fontana. How are you?"

She stood at the end of the table, in the stance the crofter liked his Fahyli to take: feet set slightly apart, hands behind the back. "I'm well, Sire. Thank you for asking."

"How is Beazle?" Esha's gaze roved Jess's head and shoulders, searching.

"Better, thank you. His wing is mostly healed. How may we serve?"

"Earlier today, we received a letter from Rahamlar." The king touched the scroll, brows pinched. "Prince Faraçek has announced his intention to visit Solana tomorrow regarding a serious matter, one he does not wish to discuss on parchment."

"Oh?" Jess swallowed, her anxiety creeping skyward. It always did at thoughts of the prince.

"He has not explicitly stated the topic in question, but given the report we received from the crofter regarding the events that occurred in Syrgana, we believe Faraçek will inform us officially of the deaths of his sisters."

Jess opened her mouth to protest, but Agir put up a hand.

"We know that Faraçek is responsible for Serya's death, and we know that he believes that he successfully removed Isabey as well. We are aware that we are dealing with someone who has committed murder—which annuls his right to rule—as well as someone who is…"

"Mentally unhinged," Queen Esha provided when the king faltered.

"Yes." The king's mouth twisted. "He was never fit to rule. His own father knew it. Yet he appears to have the loyalty of Rahamlar's military, a considerable unseelie force. As you might imagine, the queen and I are… uncomfortable with these developments."

"Of course, Sire." Jess thought 'uncomfortable' was the understatement of the year.

"Rahamlar's laws state that he cannot be crowned unless and until the death of the heir—Princess Serya—is proven to be of natural causes. But if he somehow manages to circumvent these laws, we have a serious problem." The king touched the seal with a fingertip. "How we respond to him during his visit may be a critical turning point for relations between Solana and Rahamlar. We must not make a mistake."

"I understand," said Jess, solemnly, even though she failed to grasp what all this had to do with her.

"We must have more information." The queen's tone was kind, always the one to clarify things. "Starting with what you know."

Jess took a quick sip of air, surprised. "What *I* know? What I know about what, Ma'am?"

"The prince's abilities, Miss Fontana." Queen Esha leaned forward, her expression hopeful.

The king threaded his fingers over his stomach. "The gardener informed us that Faraçek is in fact flora fae, and that his powers are linked to a parasitic fungus called *cordyceps*. We understand that he used his power to exert control over Lady Çifta while she was imprisoned at Rahamlar. We cannot interview her, most regretfully, but you..."

Jess stared at them as this news registered. The prince? Flora fae? A parasitic fungus?

*That explains a few things,* thought Beazle with a shiver of repulsion.

"You faced the prince in Syrgana, alone. And you were the only Fahyli present when Sy and Mae were killed," the queen said. The corners of her mouth drew downward and she swallowed loud enough for Jess to hear. Without taking his gaze from Jess, Agir put a hand over Esha's, rubbing his thumb over her knuckles.

"So, Miss Fontana," he said. "What can you tell us of the prince's magic?"

Jess took a deep breath, clear about what they wanted, and determined to be as helpful as possible, even if it hurt to remember. "The prince does have powerful magic, Sire."

The queen's gaze simmered with grief. "Is his flora magic how he killed Sy and Mae? Sy was an excellent swordsman, I cannot believe the prince bested him without some kind of devilry."

"No, Ma'am. I'm sad to tell you that Prince Faraçek killed Sy in honest one-to-one combat. Faraçek is a master swordsman, and wields his rapier with exceptional skill." Jess's throat closed up as her mind filled with Sy, Faraçek's skinny blade protruding from his back.

"Take your time," the queen murmured.

Jess nodded, clearing her throat. "I saw no evidence of the prince's magic when he killed Sy, but he did use it on me, and on Beazle, as well."

The king's forehead pleated. He stroked his chin, waiting.

"We attacked the prince with duplicates," Jess explained, brushing at her eyes. She remembered herself and put her hands behind her back.

"At ease, warrior," Agir told her.

Grateful, she crossed her arms over her stomach, feeling sad and vulnerable. "My goal was for Beazle to distract him for long enough to give me a chance to poison him."

The queen sucked in a gasp. "You tried to kill the prince?"

Jess stalled at the shock in the queen's voice. Was there a rebuke there? Perhaps she'd admitted too much? She'd had no permission to kill Faraçek. Defending herself from unseelie soldiers was one thing, killing the prince was another. She searched for words to explain herself.

"I was… upset, Ma'am. Seeing Sy… and Mae, the way they died." She shifted from foot to foot, her gaze darting to the floor, back to their faces. "I thought… well, I wanted to avenge them."

The king's hand tightened over the queen's. "Continue, Miss Fontana. You're not in trouble."

Jess took a moment to remember what she'd been saying. For a second, she'd wondered if she might be accused of treason… again. She glanced at the queen, looking for forgiveness, or at least understanding. Esha waited for her to continue, expression unreadable.

"He… was fighting the duplicates when he changed tactics, he just… breathed at them, and they all disappeared. They disintegrated, all at the same time. I thought Beazle had been killed and I panicked. I started looking for him. While I was searching, the prince picked me up, held me off the ground so that I couldn't get away, and demanded I tell him who it was that had helped me to free Lady Çifta."

Agir's eyes narrowed. "How did he know it was you, at that point?"

"I… told him… sort of," Jess admitted.

Queen Esha put her hand over her mouth.

"Not in words," Jess hurried to add. "But I… I let him recognize me."

Agir and Esha looked even more confused, so Jess explained how she'd lost a sleeve the night she and Laec had rescued Çifta. Her sleeve had been used by Faraçek's captain to try and identify her. In Syrgana, she'd pulled her sleeve away on purpose, so Faraçek would see her bare arm and know who she was.

King Agir smothered an oath and Jess stopped talking, unsure whether he was swearing at her. "After all the gardener did to protect you?" he said. "That was very foolish, Miss Fontana. You have endangered Solana further. Now Faraçek knows that it was indeed a member of our court who insulted him. He will think we—the queen and I—are responsible for the destruction of his future plans."

"It was foolish," said the queen, putting a hand on his arm, "but it was also very brave. And I'm not sure it matters anymore." Jess thought she saw a flash of admiration, maybe even respect, in the queen's face. "Go on, please."

The king seemed willing enough to skip over Jessamine's reckless actions for now. He waved a hand, looking wearied. "Spare us no details, please."

Her face flushed, Jess cleared her voice. "I didn't give him Laec's name. He threatened to kill me, but… I thought Beazle was dead and no longer cared whether I lived or died. I've already lost one familiar. The loss of the other one…" Her voice cracked. Her eyes stung.

The king and queen waited as she composed herself.

"Faraçek breathed into my face and after that my memory is fuzzy. It's like trying to remember a dream. I do recall an irrational but powerful need to climb the highest tree, but I don't remember why. I forgot what I was doing there, I forgot about Beazle, I even forgot my own name. It was, like a spell, I guess. The next memory I have is of waking up very high in a tree, about to fall, or maybe jump."

"What woke you?" the king asked, straightening.

"This is very important, Miss Fontana." The queen looked

excited. "You broke the spell. Can you remember how? Perhaps a night sound, or Beazle?"

Jess blushed again. She had to tell them about the lion now. There was no other explanation, and they'd said it was important. If it made her appear crazy, then she'd just have to live with that.

"It was… a lion," Jess told them, watching their faces for signs that they thought she'd lost her mind in that tree.

Queen Esha made the tiniest sound of shock, covering her lips with her hand, and her eyes grew round. She whispered her husband's name—there was something desperate in that whisper, something almost euphoric.

King Agir didn't seem to notice her reaction. He squinted at Jess, the way he always did when he wasn't sure he'd heard something right.

"A lion? A flesh and blood cat?"

Esha shook her head, just a little. That tiny gesture lifted Jess's heart. It meant that Esha knew something about the transparent lion. Maybe had even seen it herself.

Jess shifted in place. "No, Sire. Not flesh and blood. It was like a… a ghost. I could see through it."

The king exchanged a look with the queen that spoke volumes. They'd *both* heard of a ghostly lion, not just the queen. Jess thought her heart might thump itself right out of her chest as she watched them absorb what she was telling them.

Queen Esha's eyes were shining. "Oh, Jessamine." It was the first time today that the queen had used Jess's first name. "Was he a big male? Like the one over the door of this room?"

Jess nodded, her heart filling with relief. The queen did not doubt her, and Jess had not realized until now just how important it was that she was believed. It was the real reason why she'd hesitated to share her experience with anyone thus far, even Ilishec.

"You believe me," she breathed.

"Of course, we do," the queen said in a rush.

The king looked like he didn't want to, but begrudged a nod of agreement.

A powerful feeling of vindication flooded Jess. It meant everything to her, the way Esha was looking at her, without a trace of doubt, and even with respect.

"I wondered if I had imagined him, afterward," Jess admitted.

Esha lay a hand over her heart. "You did not imagine him."

The king rubbed his brow, as though he was getting a headache. Esha didn't notice.

"No one has reported an encounter with Nella's familiar—at least I believe that's who he is, I couldn't say for sure—but no one has seen him in…" she paused as if casting her memory back, like a fisherman with a long line. "Decades, at least. I haven't read the chronicles in such a long time."

The king patted the queen's hand. He looked like a man who—normally self-possessed—had been knocked off balance, like he had had his world view challenged and he didn't appreciate it.

The queen glanced at him, then back at Jess. "He has always struggled with the stories."

"Now, now," Agir chided, his voice gentle, his cheeks tinged with pink.

"The stories?" Jess canted her head.

Esha shifted forward; obviously this topic was a delight to her. "It was Queen Nella who first broached peace between Rahamlar and Solana, one hundred and fifty years after Toryan's

Massacre. She was exceptionally brave. She was a fauna fae with a magnificent lion familiar, his name was—"

"My dear," the king interrupted, still gentle in his tone. "We haven't time for this now. She can ask Ilishec, or Hob, or any of the older courtiers."

The queen sent her husband a look of disappointment. "*I* would like to be the one to tell her, my love. The others might give her the wrong idea, or tell the story with skepticism, and that will make her feel alone."

Jess thought she could discern that which the queen did not voice: the queen herself had felt alone for the same reason.

Esha confirmed it by adding: "I don't want her to feel that way. So few remain that believe… she is one who can strengthen our faith. She must be told by someone who harbors no doubts."

"Very well, but some other time please. Tell us the rest, Miss Fontana." The king sat back. "The lion saved you, then what?"

Jess blinked, not expecting to have to skip over how the lion had coaxed her, loved her, and safely brought her back to the ground. But perhaps it was for the best. The experience had been wondrous, and the love Jess had felt from the creature and for the creature was so big that Jess was in some way relieved that she did not have to relay it to someone who might diminish it, even if he was her king.

She picked up the story after the stream where she had slaked her thirst. "I found Beazle and we walked in the direction of the gorge, but we were too tired to make it all the way. Tully found us and carried us back to the group. Pan told me that Serya had been killed by Captain Yorin and fallen into the gorge, and that Isabey had been thrown in shortly after. I saw Ferrugin's duplicate lift Princess Isabey out. Everyone was relieved that she had survived."

"Did you see Faraçek or any of his soldiers?" the king asked.

Jess shook her head. "They were all gone by the time I arrived."

"And did you have any lingering effects from Faraçek's magic?"

"No, Sire. I felt normal. Tired, but myself."

King Agir stroked his chin. "So, his magic *can* be overcome, to which both you and Lady Çifta can bear witness."

Jess's mouth dropped open. "The lion also helped Lady Çifta?"

"No, no." Agir waved a hand. "Çifta had no lion."

Esha explained. "Lady Çifta reported that the effects wore off after Faraçek left her room." She paused for a moment. "You should know that Solana's lions do not come when called."

Jess studied Esha as this sank in. "Lions, Ma'am? Plural?"

"Yes, the records speak of Solanans encountering more than just the big male—"

"But it helps to know that Faraçek's magic fades, as Lady Çifta reported," the king interrupted. "The gardener has confirmed that while Faraçek's magic can affect larger beings, it is lethal to insects. It is our Calyx's familiars who are in the greatest danger from the prince."

"But he wants to come here," Jess reminded them, "to the palace, where the Calyx reside."

Agir nodded. "We will take steps to ensure that none of them come anywhere near the prince during his visit, and that it is as brief as possible. It is the best we can manage. Thank you, Miss Fontana."

Jess nodded, hoping that keeping the Calyx and their familiars far away from the prince would be caution enough. She recalled Wisteria dancing with Faraçek—Moony sitting on her forehead—the same night that her butterfly had begun to act strangely. Plenty of insects had been in the ballroom that night, but no other familiars had become sick. It followed that an insect had to be directly breathed upon to get ill.

"Unless you can think of anything else, you are dismissed," the queen told her, smiling. "Thank you. You have been very helpful."

Jess bowed and began to back away, then hesitated, casting a hopeful eye between them, thinking of her personal predicament

The queen noticed. "What is it?"

Jess plunged forward, throwing caution to the wind for love's sake. "During the Midwinter Festival, Sasha and Rialta Drazek became friends of mine. I am very concerned about them. I would like to visit, but I've not been allowed."

Agir produced another scroll from somewhere and broke the seal, not looking up. "They are not permitted visitors unless it has something to do with trial preparations."

"I understand that." Jess twisted the fabric of her trouser leg, realized what she was doing and stopped. "But, I thought… if special permission came from one of you…"

The king did look up then. "The justice will permit no guests, not until a lawyer has been assigned and terms for the trial determined."

"We've yet to arrange a jury, and other things must be done, too," the queen said.

The king canted his head. "Why would a Calyx need to visit a foreigner she only recently became acquainted with, anyway? I understand that young people take a shine to one another when wine and dancing are part of the scene, but those friendships are shallow and fleeting. You'd be best advised to let them be."

Queen Esha gave Jess a kind look. "Take comfort, Miss Fontana. Sasha and Rialta are both healing well from their wounds. They are warm and being fed and cared for. You have no cause for concern."

"Thank you," Jess mumbled. She pressed her lips together and dropped her eyes to hide the rebellion she felt simmering there as she backed from the room without another bow.

## Chapter Five

# Çifta

The cry seemed to go on for an eternity. Until it halted. Suddenly. As though cutting itself off in order to harken to something new. There was a wonder in the silence, a thoughtfulness and consideration so palpable it could be smelled and tasted. It stretched out for what might have been years, decades even, until it formed a sentiment.

*You are here.*

The words were full of welcome and expectation and not quite joy, but perhaps a distant cousin of joy: a weary felicity that something long awaited has finally occurred.

It was difficult, and took what felt like months, but she summoned a response.

*I am here.*

A sense of identity slipped its fingers around the edges of her consciousness, like shadows moving across a moonlit land. Her name crept in as well, tiptoeing as softly as any spy. It was a revelation that felt as warm and good as a hug from someone who had always loved her, given after returning from somewhere far away.

*I am Çifta.*

Laughter. Womanly laughter—there was an edge to it, yet it was not wicked. This time the response was strong, and the words were clear: *You are Çifta Unya.*

Consciousness came with all the immediacy and illumination of a lightning strike. *Where am I?*

*The ice has you. I have you, my little artist.*

A mental struggle to comprehend began in earnest, as though her mind was tightly buckled inside layers of burlap and she had to get out or she'd die. The cold was everywhere. Was the cold the reason that everything was so still? Why could she not draw breath? Why were her senses not working? She had no sight, only the sensation of having blind vision, eyes that were pressed upon by the same chill that had long ago saturated her mind. It seeped through her, permeating her to her core.

*Finally you have come. I have been waiting.*

It wrapped itself lovingly around her center, not only her spine and organs, but around her very soul.

*I don't understand anything. I'm frightened.*

Light. Without source, illumination vaguely reminiscent of moonlight reflected off water. But it's not that, it's too bright, too hard, and yet somehow soft. It is like moonlight reflected off ice… fields of ice, all of it crushed and broken and jagged.

*Tell me,* the voice slid around her, through her. *What it is that you want most, child?*

The voice was next to her now, and she tried to turn toward it. And turn she did, yet it was like skating, gliding. She was sliding and the light was shifting. The sensation was strange. She was in a foreign and unfriendly place, hosted by a voice she did not recognize. The qualities of this place might come clear, if only she could regain control over her senses.

The cold pressed against her, like a cat curling around her leg. *What is it you want most?*

She had to think hard, go deep inside. She knew her name, she knew her identity, an answer to this question must also be here. She reached for it.

*I want…*

*Yes?*

The voice was eager, hungry to know.

She had the impression that, for the voice, there was nothing in the world more important than her, and nothing more important than her answer to this question.

There was a distant cracking sound, like a frozen lake awakening in earliest spring. She tried to turn toward it, and had no idea whether she'd been successful or not. The gliding feeling returned.

*I am waiting,* came the voice.

She tried to inhale, yet there was no sensation of air, or any of the satisfaction that came with breathing. She focused on the answer, because the sense of being waited upon was getting intense. She must answer, or things would only get worse.

*Love. What I want most is love.*

Laughter.

Was it derisive laughter? She couldn't tell. It was deeply amused laughter, of that she was sure. Çifta responded with a sense of shame, a sense that she has disappointed the voice, that she has answered incorrectly. Yet, it was the truth. It was her truth. Love *was* what she wanted more than anything: a deep, true and lasting love, one that transcended the short life she would have. The kind of love she had read about in stories since her youth. If it did not exist, writers would not write about it. It had to exist. She believed this deeply, and she knew that she was meant for it, and it was meant for her. *He* was meant for her.

The laughter trailed off and the voice returned. *Your priorities are mixed up. If you want to survive, we must first fix that.*

*My ability to survive?*

She was in danger. That was not in question. She felt danger all around her. It had the properties of a hooded snake rearing up, hissing, waiting for a single wrong move. The snake might strike, or it might not.

The cold corrected her. *No, your priorities.*

Çifta disagreed, yet she did not have the power to shake her head, or vocalize any of the negation she so strongly felt. She could at least return a question—that much, it seemed, was allowed.

*What should I want instead?*

The answer came instantly. *Power, of course. That is why you are here.*

A recoiling sensation rippled through Çifta's spirit, a withdrawal, a falling back. She wanted to disengage from this encounter. She did not like this voice, and she did not like the cold.

It could read her mind, though. *You cannot disengage, and you cannot run away. You are stuck with me until this is finished.*

The crackling sound came again, fissures tinkling almost musically all around her.

Çifta wilted, her dismay ran deep. Yet she felt the truth of it: There was nowhere to go. No place she could run to, no escape. She must have this encounter and see it through to its end. Above all else, she understood that she must stay true to herself, true to who she was in her deepest being. The great danger she sensed would be unleashed if she did anything other than that.

*Power is what my father wants,* she returned. *I have never wanted that. I have always wanted love. I disdain the hunger for power, it only leads to loneliness.*

*What you disdain does not matter. You must do your duty,* the cold replied. *Your destiny must be fulfilled.*

Disappointment filled her. How many times had she heard this in her life? From her sisters? From Kazery? *You sound like my father.*

*Because he is right. Smart man.*

*What if fulfilling my destiny makes me miserable? What if it makes me feel that life is not worth living?*

The voice slithered around her; at times its tone seemed biting, and other times it soothed and stroked, giving a comfort that she did not fully trust.

*That is simple. If you feel this way—and I truly hope you do not, for your own sake—then perhaps you do not deserve life. Those who only wish to serve themselves, fulfill their own selfish desires, do not deserve to live. Only those who give, deserve to receive.*

Çifta had no response for this, she felt only a deep discomfort and a sense that something was terribly wrong. She was in the hands of an authority she did not understand or agree with, and there was nothing she could do about it. She was utterly and completely under its power. The rebellion and wholehearted disagreement welling up within her was like a pot boiling over. She and the cold did not understand one other, did not see eye-to-eye, to recall a phrase her father often used.

Obstinately, she poked back. *But wanting power is not selfish? Is that it?*

*It can be, but not for someone like you. For you, having power means carrying a heavy burden, shouldering great responsibility. Someone like you is driven to wield it in a better way than your fellows, for the good of those around you. There is only so much power in the world, child. You should want more than your fair share—if you are sturdy of heart and truly selfless—so that you can change the world for the better. Do you see? Power in the hands of someone lesser than you, or worse, in the hands of someone evil, will only lead to tyranny and destruction and injustice.*

*I understand your point,* Çifta allowed, *but I am not a powerful person. Why should I strive for power over love when I have none? I cannot conjure power simply by wishing for it.*

*Can you not? You are alive, Çifta Unya. You are frozen solid, and yet you are alive. You are cognizant enough to have this conversation, and yet you complain you have no power?*

*I haven't complained…* she retorted, ire rising. *I'm only trying to explain my point of view, my desire to have love over all else.*

The laughter returned. *You hardly know your own character, and you have made such a judgment? You have judged that your life is yours alone, to be lived for yourself and the as-yet fictitious counterpart to your love.*

Fictitious counterpart? The phrase sent a shard of glass into Çifta's heart. She quailed, then rallied as a strong knowing surged in her heart. *He is not fictitious.*

*He is not the point.*

Çifta wished to differ, because her heart told her that he was exactly the point. But the voice seemed able to run roughshod over her, stifling her ability to lead the conversation.

*The point*, it went on, *is that you think you should not have to sacrifice your own personal desires for the good of your fellow creatures.*

*I do not think that,* she returned, annoyed. *I have never thought it, because, as I told you, I am not a powerful person. I am simply a pawn for the Unya family.* Self-pity crept into her tone and she was unable to stop it. *I was raised to put duty above all else, but I am just a piece on a chessboard, the lowest piece there is.*

The voice seemed annoyed now.

*Is that what you are? Hmm. I must have the wrong person. I must have the wrong idea about you… perhaps you are not the one I have been waiting for.*

Unease. Danger. And for the first time… real fear.

*What do you mean? Who have you been waiting for? Who are you?*

*Ah… there are the questions. Finally.*

She knew the answer. *You are the ice surrounding me.*

*Yes.*

But she didn't know what that meant. The ice had an identity. She could sense it. She was speaking with someone who had a past, someone who had loved and lost and grieved and fought, who had done terrible and wonderful things, someone who knew who they were and would never deviate from the traits they acquired as they grew from childhood to adulthood. All of this she could sense as well as she sensed her own identity, but she still did not know what it all meant.

*But who are you?*

Çifta sensed a smile.

*Are you sure you want to know?*

*Yes, of course. Why wouldn't I?*

*Because, once you see, you cannot unsee. Once you know, you cannot unknow. And my identity is tied up with yours. I can show you everything, but it will be hard.*

Fear. Again… but turning back was impossible.

*Do you have the courage?* it probed.

She hesitated, but it was brief, a mere moment of pause.

*Yes. I have the courage.*

*Then come…*

The sensation of cold faded away, the crackles in the background were silenced, and—frozen inside the ice, unable to move or open her eyes or even breathe—Çifta Unya received sight.

# Chapter Six

# Jessamine

Welcoming foreign royalty usually involved the Calyx, dressed in beautiful clothing and tossing fragrant blooms, both mystic and real, into the air. But for Faraçek's arrival, the only Calyx present was Jessamine, and she was there as Fahyli, wearing her dark green leathers and with her dagger strapped to her thigh. Behind the Fahyli stood six rows of ten soldiers wearing Solanan livery, at ease but armed. Near the stables, a group of stable hands waited solemnly to receive the Rahamlarin horses. No sane visitor would view this group as a welcome party. Rather it was a warning, an unspoken message: your actions have been marked, those who witnessed your crimes have shared what they saw, and we are not afraid of you.

Jess agreed this message needed to be communicated, she just wished she didn't have to be part of it. If Ian had really wanted to make Faraçek squirm, he would have included the red-headed Stavarjakian among the group, as Laec was the only witness when Yorin speared Serya, and when Faraçek dropped Isabey into the gorge. Jess wondered why he wasn't present.

She tugged at the neck of her leathers. Everything felt too tight, her braids, her leggings, her vest.

*Stop fidgeting,* Beazle sent as Jess tugged on her sleeve, which had become twisted. *I'm trying to nap. I'll go elsewhere if you don't quit.*

Jess put her hands behind her back, shifting her shoulders. *You can't. Commands from Ian include you, furball.*

Beazle changed position against her skull, extricating a claw from a braid. *No one would notice if I wasn't here. What do they need me for? I plan to sleep through the whole thing.*

Jess smiled. Beazle was just as interested in the arrival of the prince as everyone else. He claimed to be tired but she could tell when he was sleeping, and right now, he was as wired as the other familiars seated or perched next to their fae.

Iron horseshoes striking frozen cobblestones echoed through the air, preceding the Rahamlar entourage. Any moment now they would enter the same courtyard where Ruskin had been killed, and Çifta frozen. Evidence of both events had been erased.

Two-dozen riders, led by the prince himself, trotted through the gates. Jess hardly noticed Yorin or the unseelie soldiers, her gaze was glued to her enemy. Prince Faraçek rode a big red charger wearing a brown leather headstall and collar with orange birds embroidered around the edges. The prince wore a matching vest and a hat with a long pheasant feather fixed to the band.

*There's a lot of them,* Beazle thought, *but at least his party doesn't outnumber ours.*

*He wouldn't have been allowed past the city gates if it did.*

Prince Faraçek did not look around, did not look at the Fahyli, not even impressive Tully. Jess felt like the air was sucked out of the courtyard as the one who had killed Sy and Mae came into the Fahyli's presence. She stiffened and fidgeted, drawing another rebuke from her bat.

A two-horsed chariot brought up the rear of the Rahamlar party, driven by an unseelie soldier who pulled it to a stop at the bottom of the steps. It couldn't have been easy to get that chariot over the mountain pass full of steep switchbacks, and littered with stones and boulders. The driver hopped down and was joined by another well-muscled unseelie. The two of them hefted a trunk from the back of the chariot, their shining black talons curled around the wood, and carried it up the steps.

Faraçek waited until the trunk was halfway up the stairs before dismounting in one smooth motion. A stable hand took his horse away—careful of the charger's huge hooves—which triggered a storm of grooms to attend the Rahamlar mounts, taking them away for food and water.

The unseelie wielding the trunk, Faraçek, and Yorin made their way up the steps to where Captain Bradburn stood waiting to escort them inside. Every Rahamlarin rider followed, their dark eyes darting as they took in the wealth and beauty of the palace. As the last of the Rahamlarin party disappeared into the foyer, the crofter sent a signal that the Fahyli and Solanan soldiers should follow.

King Agir and Queen Esha were waiting to receive the prince in a small ballroom positioned behind the three staircases leading up to the second level. It was a room rarely used because it couldn't accommodate the large numbers that attended Solanan balls. Prince Faraçek's soldiers, Solana's soldiers, and the Fahyli almost filled the space.

The Fahyli split into two groups, then skirted the room to stand on either side of the dais where they had a clear view of everything going on. Tully and two large mastiffs sat obediently in front of their fae, while winged familiars—including Ratchet, Ferrugin and Erasmus—found perches on crossbeams or light fixtures.

Prince Faraçek approached the dais alone, as though his men were instructed never to get too close to him. He doffed his hat and bowed as deeply as any peasant paying homage to his lord, his nose nearly touching a knee. His black hair was smooth and glossy, tied back with an orange bow. His goatee had been trimmed to a sharp point, and his cheeks shaved so that his facial hair looked like a clawed hand grasping his chin. His rapier lifted into the air behind him as he bowed, pointing almost at the ceiling. The prince straightened, a smile on his face.

"Your Majesties, I bring a token of my esteem."

Two soldiers moved forward, carrying the wooden trunk between them. Captain Yorin stepped aside as they approached the dais and set the trunk down on the marble floor. Yorin lifted the lid and laid it back on its hinges. Inside, glittering under the etherlights, was a small fortune in jewels and gold coins. The trunk must have been extremely heavy, yet the unseelie carried it like it was full of feathers.

Jess thought that Agir and Esha must be surprised by Faraçek's gentile display and extravagant gift—she certainly was—but they revealed nothing. In the style of seasoned monarchs, they'd stowed all emotion beneath cool, authoritative exteriors. If their lack of reaction discomfited the prince, he did not show it either.

Finally, King Agir lazily raised a finger from the arm of his wooden throne. "Prince Faraçek, well come."

"Well found." Faraçek returned the Solanan greeting in the traditional way, smile broadening.

There was a momentary break in the counterfeit pleasantries, where the crowd was quiet and the outer doors not yet shut. A breeze swept in from outside, blowing dead leaves across the marble floor with a dry rattle. Someone closed the front doors, but just before they clicked shut, a high whistle echoed through the room, like the strangled cry of captured prey. The mulchy scent that accompanied the sounds made Jess suppress a shudder, as the memory of Faraçek breathing into her face rose in her mind. She wasn't the only one who felt uncomfortable. Others shuffled in place until a hiss from Bradburn made them still.

Faraçek held his hat over his chest, the feather bobbing as he spoke. "Thank you for receiving me on such short notice. Both our kingdoms have experienced misfortune of late, binding us together in sorrow. News of the tragedy that befell the Silverfall prince has reached my ears. We rode out together several times during the Midwinter Festival; he seemed like a good man. Please accept my condolences. If any help is required from Rahamlar, we will not hesitate to give it."

So the prince knew about Ruskin. Did he also know about Lady Çifta? Unease burned in the pit of Jess's stomach. She dropped her gaze to the handle of his rapier, the weapon that had whispered the life from Sy's body. Her throat felt like it was lined with bark.

If Faraçek noticed the discomfort in the room, he pretended not to. His smile bared very straight, very white teeth, set in a too-gray face under oil-slick black hair. The effect was more feral grin than smile. In Jess's opinion, the prince's countenance edged toward gruesome.

"The purpose for my visit is the tragedies that have befallen my own kingdom. So close upon the heels of the death of my brother, Ander, and that of my father—a great king—proved too much of a weight for my sisters to bear. Thank you for your generosity in allowing us to search your land. We did find them, but we were not able to save their broken minds nor their broken hearts. Alas, my dear sisters—so attached to one another, as close as if they were the same person—have taken their own lives. Their suffering and sorrow is over now."

His eyes shone with a hungry light that chilled Jess to the bone. He was outright lying, bold-faced and without fear of contradiction.

King Agir's brows contracted in an expression of concern that every Solanan knew was fake.

"What a shame, Prince Faraçek. We are deeply sorry to learn this. We had received our own reports, which differed a little. In truth, more than a little."

Prince Faraçek dropped his chin in a deferential nod. "I humbly ask for any report regarding my sisters' suicides that has not come from my lips, today, be disregarded. I alone hold the truth of the matter, because I myself was present."

Jess staggered mentally. How did he think he would get away with this lie? The Fahyli had been in Syrgana that night, they had converged upon the gorge not long after the crimes had been committed. Faraçek's daring had startled the Solanans into a state of shock. Jess snatched a glance at Ian and saw that he was staring at the prince in open horror. Queen Esha visibly stiffened. Behind Jess, someone sucked in a breath.

Undaunted, Faraçek continued, his voice as sweet and calm

as a rural morning. "My lawyers and ministers are, as we speak, preparing the legal documents and necessary amendments to make way for my coronation. Without a king, Rahamlar will soon falter. I have a responsibility to ensure that does not happen."

Agir narrowed his eyes.

"I have come to you out of respect,"—Faraçek swept his arms wide, his hat in his right hand—"to deliver this news personally. You'll agree it was too important to trust to a messenger. I have also come to request your presence at my coronation." Here he paused for long enough to allow for a reaction that never came. "Time is required, as the legalities are complicated, so a date has not yet been set. King Agir, Queen Esha, I feel that a powerful alliance should be forged between our kingdoms. Your presence at my coronation will be seen as a sign of your approval and support, after which new terms of partnership can be discussed."

Faraçek brought his hat back to his chest and fell silent.

The hall went quiet. The crofter exchanged a look with Bradburn, a look that said the scent of smoke was in the air but they weren't sure where the fire was, this kingdom or that one.

King Agir's voice was soft with restrained rage. "And if we are not able to attend?"

Prince Faraçek looked composed. He had expected this. "Then your decision will have been made, and I shall proceed in a new direction, with a new understanding."

King Agir blinked. "What new direction would that be?"

Faraçek gave the king a smile so patronizing that Jess's hands curled into fists, her nails biting into her palms.

*Easy,* Beazle murmured. *He's just playing games.*

"I can hardly say," said Prince Faraçek in a way that suggested that the opposite was true. "I am ever hopeful for a strong and lasting friendship."

The prince was full of bold lies. Jess was sure that he had contingency plans for either outcome, depending which way his neighbor leaned. She released a long slow breath. She could hardly be surprised, given what she'd experienced of him herself, but she was one insignificant cog in the great wheel of Solana. How Faraçek behaved toward her was without consequence, but how he behaved toward Agir and Esha did have consequences. They were not to be toyed with—a fact reinforced by the presence of the Fahyli and their animals. Solana's human soldiers were not so menacing as Faraçek's unseelie thugs, but Bradburn's men were accomplished swordsmen, his ranks thick with deadly archers, all well trained to follow orders. That was their magic. Yet in the face of all of that, Faraçek lied and threatened.

"I shall send a formal invitation when a date has been chosen," Faraçek was saying, "Until then, my best wishes to you and your kingdom. I hope the inconvenience of the unfortunate incident concerning the Silverfall prince is resolved quickly, and with minimal discomfort for you. Thank you once again for allowing me an audience." Prince Faraçek bowed deeply once more, straightened, and—before he turned around—placed the hat on his head, the jaunty feather curving to the rear. The unseelie entourage prepared to move.

Queen Esha's voice rang out. "Prince Faraçek?"

He turned back, his expression all keen interest. "Ma'am?"

Her lavender gown shimmered as she stood. "When will the funerals be held for the princesses? May we expect invitations to *those* as well?"

Faraçek's lips peeled back from his teeth. "Of course you

may. How kind you are to inquire." He turned on his heel in one smooth motion.

The crofter gave a signal that the Fahyli should escort the Rahamlar party out and Jess fell in step with Panther as the whole procession was reversed.

The courtyard filled with bodies as grooms returned the Rahamlar horses to their riders. The Fahyli stood to one side of the gate, Bradburn's soldiers on the other. The prince mounted and walked his horse to the gate. As he did so, his gaze fell on Jess… and stuck. His eyes widened enough to let her know that he was surprised to see her. She stared back, boldly, enjoying the first look of uncertainty he'd shown since he arrived. Faraçek stopped and all his soldiers halted too. Captain Yorin squeezed his mount through to the prince's side.

"We meet again. How unexpected," the prince said. He was close enough now for her to grab his boot. "Forgive me, I never caught your name. The last time we saw each other, you were bawling like a baby ripped from her mother's teat."

Heat rushed to Jessamine's cheeks. He spoke loudly enough for all of her companions to hear. It took great effort not to drop her gaze. Beazle gave a throaty growl, so small only Jess could hear it.

A cold smile crept across Faraçek's face, worse than any glare. "I wouldn't normally care for the name of someone so beneath me, but you've now escaped my men twice and me once. That makes thrice, so I must take notice. What is your name, child? I must know."

The Fahyli shifted, looking to the crofter for guidance, disliking this open threat to one of their own. But the crofter gave no orders. Jess could sense Ian and Bradburn and all the Solanans within earshot, listening closely to this exchange.

*Do not be ashamed.* Beazle emerged and crawled up one of her braids. He stopped at the crest of her forehead, looking boldly at the prince. *It's what he wants. To make you feel small and weak.*

Faraçek's gaze narrowed briefly on Jessamine's bat, recognizing him, too. The prince's hand went to one ear, moving the hair enough for Jess to see a scar there, from one of Beazle's duplicates. Her bat was tiny, but the courage he displayed filled not only Jess, but all the Solanans around them, with pride. Panther and Kite moved closer, one on either side of her, glaring up at the prince. From somewhere above, Erasmus screamed loud and long.

"My name is Jessamine Fontana," Jess said with a steady voice. "I am a Fahyli of the Kingdom of Solana, and you… Prince Faraçek of Rahamlar, are a murderer and a liar."

The unseelie soldiers within earshot stiffened, exchanging looks of unease, and amusement.

Captain Yorin yanked on his reins, making his horse toss his head. "Watch your mouth, brat, or you'll find yourself without lips!"

Ignoring Yorin's threat, Jess kept her gaze glued to the prince. "And your magic is not as powerful as you think it is."

There was a flicker of something ugly in the prince's eyes.

"Miss Jessamine Fontana, a Fahyli of the Kingdom of Solana," Faraçek mimicked with a sneer, "you and I are destined to meet again. I do so enjoy a challenge."

He spat a wad of saliva that landed in the middle of her chest.

Beazle bared pin-sharp teeth and screeched at Faraçek. The piercing cry spooked the prince's horse, making it toss its head and prance in place. It was the loudest sound her familiar had ever made, and it was chilling.

The prince got control of his horse, then passed through the gate and out of sight. Yorin glared at her as he followed. Behind the Rahamlar captain, the whole entourage picked up speed, thundering down the high street with a fearsome clatter.

Jess's heart was pounding like the battle drum of a man-o-war as Fahyli closed in around her, muttering words of support and pride. She heard none of it, and felt capable of nothing except replaying, over and over, Faraçek's promise that they were destined to meet again.

## Chapter Seven

# Laec

Laec was tugging a fresh tunic over his damp hair when a sharp rap sounded at his door. He let the shirt fall down over his hips and the red rash covering his torso. Pressing his skin to the ice was painful, but there was a kind of meditation to be found within the pain, a catalepsy that he found mentally comforting. It took several long minutes to stop feeling the acidic burn from the ice—maybe it was just when his skin surrendered and went numb, but Laec speculated that it was deeper than that. He liked to think that he was being helpful to Çifta, even though he didn't know what form that help was taking, only that it was important he keep doing it.

Laec tugged the neck of his tunic, hoping no redness was visible. Raking his messy locks away from his face as he crossed the room then opened the door to see Ian waiting in the hall, with his usual half-awake expression. Laec had learned that the expression was a ruse. Ian was always fully awake, missing nothing.

"Crofter," he said, surprised.

"Fairijak," Ian said. "Sorry to disturb, but I need a word."

Ian had never searched him out before. Laec was surprised the crofter even knew where to find him, especially since he'd moved from the violet suite to the ground floor to be closer to Çifta. Ilishec had arranged the move for him. Now his room was a single, sparsely furnished box with narrow windows, a low ceiling, and not a stitch of purple wallpaper in sight. He had to use the toilets down the hall that the cooks used while on duty, but overall Laec preferred it.

"A moment, please." Laec closed the door.

He wasn't about to invite the crofter into his room. He and the Fahyli captain had never been on friendly terms, and he didn't want to invite questions about his new apartment, either. He tied his hair back, tugged on his boots and went out into the hall. They meandered in the direction of the main palace foyer, which was a very long walk from Laec's room, but apparently the crofter was in no hurry. The crofter put his hands behind his back and strolled like he was enjoying a summer day.

"What might I do for you, Crofter?" Laec crossed his arms over his chest, jamming his hands under his armpits as they walked, trying not to scratch the itch his latest session had raised on his skin. The worst of it was in the very beginning, when he first pressed his torso to Çifta's ice, and the fifteen minutes after he'd stopped. Hot water didn't help, in fact, it was beneath the heat that his skin itched the most. If fire was this magical ice's enemy, then he supposed it followed that hot water was not favored either.

Ian turned toward Laec. "I have a request concerning Princess Isabey. Have you seen her since we returned from Syrgana?"

"No." Truthfully, Laec had not spared the Rahamlarin princess a thought since the events in the courtyard. A spear of guilt went through him at this neglect. He'd never even checked on her, and should explain himself, but he wasn't about to admit to Ian what he'd been up to, so he gave the vaguest excuse possible. "I've been busy."

Busy was not the right word, he knew. Obsessed. He had one woman on his mind, and until she had thawed, until she looked at him again with those ethereal eyes, smiled at him with those petal-pink lips, Laec could think of little else.

During his "meditations" he'd convinced himself that this had to be why Elphame had sent him. This was the darkness his queen had foreseen, this cold unyielding magic that had swallowed all the happiness and joy from his life. This was why he was here, to sacrifice his own comfort to ease Çifta's journey. It was never anything to do with Faraçek. Hang Faraçek. Let Rahamlar's people take care of Rahamlar.

At Laec's lame excuse, the crofter shot him a disapproving look.

Laec put on his usual mask of detached hauteur. "Why?"

Ian looked annoyed that he had to explain it. "Because Isabey is in trouble."

"Because she is in mourning?" Laec allowed a contemplative frown, pretending to be confused by Ian's meaning. "I wouldn't call that trouble. Her brother doesn't know she's alive, that's a blessing. She can weep and wallow until she feels better, then take her murdering brother by surprise. It's perfect. Except for the mourning part. That part does stink."

The crofter's eyes rolled heavenward.

Laec knew he got on the crofter's nerves. It was in Laec's nature to goad those who disliked him, exaggerating the characteristics that he knew were annoying. It was fun. Rather, it was *usually* fun. There wasn't much joy in it lately.

"It is not perfect," Ian replied with a tone of thinning patience. "She hardly eats, and she goes to bed but no one knows if she is sleeping. It doesn't seem like it, because she looks like death and doesn't speak. The servants have to pull her to standing in the mornings, they have to dress her, even force her to bathe, for pride's sake. Esha is worried that she may have come unhinged."

"Well, sure. Serya was not only her sister, they were best friends. Of course, she is traumatized."

Ian exhaled through his nose, then spoke like he was addressing a halfwit: "The problem is that Isabey is royalty. She is not given the same allowance that regular folk get. She has a kingdom to tend to, and a murderous brother to displace."

Laec arched a brow. "Sorry, but why do you care about Rahamlar's situation, exactly?"

Ian replied hotly, a flush crawling up his neck. "I only think about our neighbor insomuch as it affects us. The lot of them can slide into the Tadylat, for all I care. But this does affect us, it affects us greatly. We need the princess to pull herself together, and quickly."

"What does that have to do with me?" Laec asked.

*I'm busy enough with my own problems*, he wanted to add, but that would be extra selfish, even for him. His house arrest had been lifted. He'd been given a second chance thanks to his actions in the forest. He should *want* to help. He should want to give the crofter—who had secured the acquittal for him—any aid the Fahyli leader required. The problem was that Laec couldn't find the energy to care. Any matter outside of the woman from Boskaya was not a matter that interested him, and he couldn't pretend it did. It just took too much out of him.

Ian stepped in front of Laec, in the middle of the hall, and took him by the upper arms. Instinctively, Laec leaned away, disarmed by the need in Ian's face, the desperation. The last thing Laec wanted was to be relied upon by someone of the crofter's stature.

Ian's expression bordered on pleading. "You are one of the few faces that Isabey recognizes and trusts. I would rather make this request of Lady Çifta, but for obvious reason, I cannot. So I am asking you, Stavarjak. *You* rescued Isabey in the forest, *you* were with her when her sister was murdered. She looked for *you* after she was rescued from the gorge, and it was *your* horse she chose to ride home on, *your* arms in which she found comfort."

Laec glowered, trying to pull away, but Ian's grip was strong. "Will you stop saying *you* and *your* like that? I know all that. I was there."

The crofter ignored his protest. "I would like—" He stalled, shaking his head, hands almost bruising Laec's flesh. "No, I *need* you to talk sense into her. We all know she is sad, that won't change, perhaps for many years to come. We all have experienced loss, we all have had grief in our lives, but this is more important than her personal sadness. She needs to be reminded of that… gently, and by someone she trusts."

Laec felt the weight of this burden settle over his shoulders, a freshly hewn yoke. Ian's plea did make sense, and he could not refuse. But, would he succeed? Convince Princess Isabey to take up her own mantle of responsibility in spite of her grief? The irony was not lost on Laec. Laec had shirked his own responsibilities in Stavarjak many times. He had wallowed in self-pity for months on end, drinking himself into oblivion.

Yet now, somehow, *he* was the one being chosen to convince a critical chess piece—the true heir and queen of Rahamlar—to snap out of it and put her kingdom first? It would be laughable if it was not so sad, so serious.

Laec turned away, finally breaking Ian's hold on his arms. It was on his lips to agree, but the words did not want to come. The crofter saw his inner quarrel, Laec's crumbling resistance. He pushed all the harder.

"Who else should we ask? Princess Isabey doesn't know anyone here. Queen Esha has tried talking to her, royal to royal. Isabey listened politely, then asked if she could talk to Lady Çifta. For the hundredth time, she was reminded that Lady Çifta is inside the block of ice that she has already viewed. She barely seemed to have heard the queen, and after Esha left, the servants heard the princess weeping." The crofter let out a weary sigh. "Just do your best. You're the only one for this task in all of Solana."

"It must be terrible for you," Laec muttered. "Asking me for help."

"It is, believe me," Ian said with passion. "So will you do it?"

"I'll try. That's all I can promise." He was still supposed to be Elphame's eyes and ears, he was still supposed to be here as a favor to Esha. He was supposed to be helpful. He could at least include Isabey's status in his next report to the queen, even if he failed to stir her loyalties.

The crofter's dark eyes flared with hope, then a desperate kind of fury that Laec wanted to draw away from. The big man put a hand on Laec's shoulder and pressed down a little too hard. For a moment Laec got the impression that it was Kashmir the bear standing over him and compelling him to act, not the crofter.

"Go today, please. Now. Prince Faraçek is scheming, and we are running out of time. The best chance we have to thwart his plans lies on that young woman's shoulders. She *must* step between her brother and the crown. Do you understand?"

Laec put his hands up. "I said I would try. Don't hang all your hopes on me, though. It's not wise."

Ian nodded and then turned away, muttering, "Don't I know it."

Laec made a face at Ian's back as the crofter headed for the west keep, then asked the nearest passing servant where Princess Isabey's rooms were and learned that she was staying down the hall from Laec's old suite.

He took the stairs up two at a time, stopped in front of a mirror to straighten himself and make sure his rash was covered, then knocked on her door. Beside the door, fixed into the stone wall, was a copper plaque announcing that this was the Dahlia Suite. No one answered, so Laec knocked again. When no one came, he depressed the latch and pushed the door open enough to peek inside. He said he'd try, and try he would.

"Princess Isabey?"

Laec didn't see anyone at first. He took a few steps inside, boots silent on the plush red carpet. The room was a mirror layout of the Violet Suite, only this one was done up in shades of pinks, oranges and reds. Bits of yellow were splashed about: a decorative pillow here, a piece of art there, frilly curtains. He supposed the queen chose this suite for Isabey because it was cheerful, but the overall effect made Laec feel queasy. He was of the opinion that what might actually help someone in mourning would be to be surrounded by dark colors and dim lights.

He caught sight of Isabey's long dark curls. She was sitting out on a balcony overlooking Mount Vargon. Perhaps that had been a strategic choice by the queen also. Beyond Vargon was Rahamlar, and Isabey would be reminded of it every time she looked out a window.

Laec approached the arch leading to the terrace, stopping just inside. "Princess Isabey?"

A breeze lifted her hair, throwing it back over her shoulder. He could see her profile, the curve of her cheek and the sweep of her neck. She turned her head a little in his direction, but did not look at him.

"Laec," she said, her tone flat.

"Yes, princess. I came to see how you are."

"I don't want you here," she said.

"I understand that—"

"I don't want anyone here, but I especially don't want you." Her tone was sharp.

When she looked up at him, he recoiled from the hatred he saw in her face—it felt like a punch in the gut.

"Princess, I don't understa—"

"You could have saved her," Isabey said.

Laec needed a moment to adjust to her new attitude toward him. In the forest, she had leaned on him so heavily, wouldn't leave his side. Not because he wouldn't allow anyone else to take her, but because it was what she wanted.

He swallowed, recalling the moment of Serya's death. She'd been far from them, and he had only a sword. He failed to grasp how he might have prevented the older princess's demise.

"You could have done *something*," she whispered, a tear streaking down her cheek. She brushed it away and looked at the horizon again. "Instead you put your efforts into stopping me from going to her."

"I was trying to keep you from sharing her fate, Princess. I failed, I know. I am sorry…"

"Everyone is sorry," she said. "But no one knows what it is to be me. No one knows how I feel. No one has suffered as much as me." She swiped at her cheeks again.

"I'm sorry," Laec repeated, feeling stupid and inadequate. Why had he let the crofter convince him to come? He was only making things worse, only upsetting her further.

"I know why you're here," she said.

"Well that's a comfort," Laec said, trying to lighten the mood. "I hardly know myself."

"You want to remind me who I am. King Agir and Queen Esha think I have forgotten my heritage, but I have not. They want me to forget my losses, claim my birthright."

"They don't expect you to forget your loved ones," he said, feeling relieved. At least he did not have to explain anything to her. "But yes, Princess. And will you claim your birthright?"

She shot him a look filled with acid. "I used to want it. But now? I have never wanted anything less than to sit on Rahamlar's throne. I am broken. I'll never be whole again. I can never be queen."

All of Laec's relief drained away. "Princess, you cannot mean that. Surely you cannot wish to give your kingdom and your people over to your brother, a murderer."

"Show me a king who has not murdered, a queen who has not been treacherous."

He didn't know what to say to that.

"I will go south," Isabey said, sounding far away. "I'll change my name, seek citizenship in Archelia, or Tryske. Faraçek thinks I am dead, and it is better that way, for me and for the people of Rahamlar. They have no love for me. Even so, they deserve more than a shell of a ruler, for a shell is all that I am, and all I'll ever be."

Her words sent a chill through him. "In time, you will feel differently."

But his words sounded so hollow, even to him.

"Get out, Laec. I can't bear being in the same room as you."

"As you wish."

He bowed—which she did not see, as she had returned her gaze to the mountains—and backed away.

Isabey was broken, sure, but did that give her the right to wield her grief like a lance, cutting whoever crossed her path? Her accusation pricked his heart. He had done all he was capable of doing for Serya and Isabey. Without his magic, he was a lesser being, a lesser fae.

Laec left the dahlia suite and returned to his room. He was too tired to make his report of failure now, he would do it tomorrow. Esha did not have to worry that Isabey was unhinged. As far as Laec could see, the princess of Rahamlar was in complete control of her faculties. She was of a sound mind and had explicitly and intelligibly made her choice.

## Chapter Eight

# Çifta

Tundra, miles and miles of it, sped by as though viewed from the back of a great bird with the smoothest wingbeats and the steadiest course the world had ever known. Awe grew within her breast. Who had ever viewed the world from so great a height? What non-winged creature had ever been carried so high, and above such beauty? There was no fear that she would fall or be dropped. Çifta did not feel wind or have any sense of being borne up against the downward forces that press upon every living thing. This was something utterly new, utterly foreign. No wind, no cold, only the vantage point of some great and unknowable goddess.

*Where are we?*

*Further north than you've ever been, young one.*

Çifta had questions, but there was no room for them as a land of a thousand lakes opened up before her, all reflecting a perfect sky of brightest blue. A pack of something… wolves perhaps, it was difficult to tell at so great a height, moved smoothly across the land, weaving between the waters, before falling behind, and finally, out of view.

*We approach the northern coast of the Ivryndian Sea, in another time.*

*The past?*

*Naturally. Everyone must deal with the past before reckoning with the future.*

The lakes grew skins of ice. Snow rippled in waves across those skins. Flocks of long-winged, long-necked birds, all white, flew low over the tundra, heading in the opposite direction. The snow increased and soon the lakes froze solid, no longer reflecting a blue sky but a dull gray one. Ahead was an endless expanse of broken ice and sea, a jagged coastline full of rocky outcroppings. They turned to follow the coastline, passing frozen beaches scattered with driftwood. Tough northern shrubs and grasses clung to the sand as a winter wind battered them down.

A small ship appeared, a chain stretching down from its hull and holding it fast to its anchor. That ship fell away, but soon there was another, and another. A town materialized, a rickety outpost, really. The great invisible bird descended. This forlorn and nameless speck, perched on an endless frozen coast like a tick on the back of a beast, was their destination.

No smooth roadway connected this place to inland communities. Only rough and narrow trails snaked from its heart, suitable only for hooves or boots. The place reminded Çifta of Cardagenya—only built on flat land rather than cliffsides—with many tall and narrow wooden buildings, crooked streets bustling with merchants and villagers, stevedores and sailors. Many ships were anchored out in the deep-water harbor, and many small boats taxied back and forth from those ships to the busy dock.

Çifta hung in the air over a busy main street until a man wearing a wide hat with a glossy black feather appeared below. They followed him, staying at his back as he strode up the dirt street with a powerful stride. He had business in mind, climbing a stony hill and dodging those coming down. Someone greeted him and he cheerfully returned it, his voice mellifluous and hearty, one she would know anywhere. He moved nimbly, dodging frozen puddles and loose rocks. From her vantage point, he was only a hat, broad shoulders and thick long legs, but Çifta would know him anywhere.

*Father.*

*Yes, it is he, one Kazery Unya,* the ice confirmed.

Now she just needed to place when they were. She studied him from top to bottom. *He looks young and has no belly. This must be at least twenty years ago?*

The ice did not confirm or deny this, but Çifta felt certain she had to be within five years either side of twenty years ago. She had either not yet been born, or was a babe. Her sisters were certainly all alive.

Çifta relished the look of her father in his prime. Kazery's black hair flowed thick and beautiful over his shoulders. He was slim and cut a fit figure, walking like a man who did not yet know the stiffness of age in his joints. He came to a tall house of three stories. It had a red door with narrow windows on either side. Sad scrubby plants in garden boxes had long ago given up the ghost, mostly buried under snow. The house was so close to the street that there was no room for a real garden, or even the need for a proper walkway. Instead, there was a frozen puddle, which Kazery skirted. He entered without knocking, calling into the house.

"Evelin?"

They followed Kazery into the house, his broad back before them until he doffed his hat and turned. His black beard was close-trimmed to hug his jaw. His eyes glittered like obsidian as he looked around the room. On his lips hovered a half-smile of expectation. Whoever was in the house, he was eager to see them. He tossed his hat on a nearby table already hosting an unlit lamp and a small book. A fire crackled in the grate, a fresh log had been added not long ago. A long pale cape with a fur collar hung on a peg, the kind a woman would wear.

"Evelin? You here?"

An answer came, a quiet croak from an upper floor.

Kazery cocked his head, smile falling away. He ran for the steps, bounding two at a time until he came to the second floor and a single bedroom—with a double bed, a wardrobe and a fireplace licking with flames—vacant of life.

He called again. "Darling?"

His face now taut with worry, he took the narrow stairs up to the attic. He had to duckwalk, shoulders stooped forward and head to the side to avoid bumping it. He emerged in a single room with a low A-shaped ceiling.

On the floor lay a figure draped with a woolen dress the color of goldenrod. She didn't so much wear the dress, as was engulfed by it. Her back was to the stairs and she seemed to be swimming slowly inside the gown, or perhaps she was struggling. Her head hung forward as she leaned on one elbow, trembling visibly.

"Who are you?" Kazery barked.

She turned her head toward him, showing her profile.

His voice fell to a horrified hush. “It cannot be… Evelin?”

He knelt, reaching for her but afraid to touch her. When she looked more fully at him, he gave another cry. The woman’s face was ravaged by time. Deep seams had carved themselves into her cheeks. Her eyes were like small stones caught in tangled nets of wrinkles, but the expression in those eyes was one of deepest joy. Unbelievably, she was smiling.

“Kazery,” the wizened woman said, slowly and with great effort. “Help me, my love.”

“Evelin, what… I don’t understand. You… you’re…”

The brokenness in her father’s voice sent a crack through Çifta’s heart.

As gently as though handling a newborn, Kazery put his arms beneath the woman’s knees and around her back. He rose with her, taking no effort. Her knees tented the fabric like two sharp, tiny mountains. Her skeletal hand lay against his upper arm. The veins in the back of her hand looked like purple worms beneath thin skin, and the bones there were as fine as spider legs. Kazery lay her on the single bed against the wall. As he bent, Çifta saw a basket on the floor, and the shape of a bundled babe inside it, nestled in white knit blankets.

“Bring her,” the old woman rasped as she lay her head back on the pillow. Astonishingly, she had aged even further since Kazery had found her. Her eyes had turned cloudy.

“I don’t understand,” Kazery cried, even as he picked up the baby. “How is this possible? Evelin, I do not understand.”

“Bring…” the woman gestured with a withered hand.

The baby was so tiny in the big merchant’s hands: a baby with blue-black hair, and fae ears. Her cheeks were full and flushed with good health, her dark lashes lying against her pale skin. She was sleeping. She was beautiful. She was Çifta.

The grown Çifta reeled from the realization that the wizened woman was her mother. The portrait she had of her dead mother looked nothing like this aged shell of a woman. Only the pointed fae ears were the same. The woman in the portrait had blue-black hair, ice-blue eyes—like Çifta's own—and porcelain skin.

*He told me her name was Maisa.*

*He lied to keep you safe.*

*The portrait, was it of this woman?* Çifta had no doubt the ice knew. There was a sense that the ice knew everything.

*Yes. Your father had the color of your mother's hair altered. Another way of wiping away the clues that might lead to your true identity.*

Çifta's gaze went to the woman's hair, of which there was hardly any left. Her scalp showed through patches of dried white fluff, and on the floor of the attic lay long locks of white hair. Her mother's hair had been white.

Her father lay her infant self against the woman approaching the door of death.

"They found her," the woman rasped, her gaze directed lovingly down at the baby, but her eyes were glassy and unfocused. In the last few minutes, she had gone blind. "But I saved her," she croaked, voice dry as paper. "The spell…" she lifted her unseeing eyes to Kazery, and—even blind—they gleamed with triumph.

"It was meant for her. They failed. Do you see?" She laughed, a sound like a handful of thin dry twigs breaking.

Kazery sat on the side of the bed, very slowly, so his weight did not jar her. He put his head in his hands. "I only left for one hour. A single hour, and this… They…" He gulped and began to weep.

Çifta had never before seen her father weep. To her, this man was entirely different from the one she knew, the man she had last spoken with in the alcove in the palace. She had no doubt that this moment had been a defining one for Kazery, one that had hardened him, scarred him and made him resilient. He had lost Alana before this. She wondered if she was seeing the reason that her father had never taken another wife. Losing two had been enough—even if he and Evelin had not been married, he had clearly loved her.

"Now, love," the woman comforted him with soothing words that husked from her throat. "Better me than her. I am happy. I knew this day might come."

Kazery lifted his face from his hands, wincing visibly as he did so. "Your life… Evelin. It is gone. You are only twenty-three. You are but a babe yourself."

"Yes." She smiled and a thousand wrinkles marred her face. She coughed and lifted a trembling hand to spit into it. She dropped something to the floor and Çifta quailed, realizing what it was: a tooth. Evelin paid it no mind. "And because the spell struck me instead of our daughter, it was a life well lived and well used. I would change nothing." She inhaled and something in her chest rattled. The words were costing her. She had no time left. "You must take her with you, Kazery. Protect her. Hide her. Raise her as a daughter of Alana, alongside your other daughters."

"No one will believe…"

Evelin found enough energy to protest with passion. "They will believe what you tell them, and if they do not, it does not matter. They will have no idea of her heritage."

For a moment Çifta imagined she could see the young woman inside the old woman, the young vital fae whom Evelin had been but an hour before. Çifta considered with solemn reverence just how brave, how strong in spirit and in love, her mother must have been to take the curse and be glad for it, even as it drained away her life. It made her feel like weeping. She had known nothing of this. She had been told her mother was too ill to travel, and passed away after Kazery had returned to Kirkik with Çifta.

Kazery put a hand on the baby's wrapping, feeling her breathing in and out. "Will they not know their spell failed?"

A troubled shadow came over Evelin's face. She took a long time to answer. "That is why you must take her. They will know. Elvio is strong. He will know his spell failed. There is little time, my love. You must remove her from here. Take her…" she sucked in a breath, the rattle was worse now. "Take her to your home. Raise her, love her, keep her safe." Evelin gestured that Kazery should pick up his daughter. "You must go. Now."

"But, why? I don't understand why she is so hated. She is but a child." The pirate-merchant put his hands beneath the sleeping girl and drew her to him, cradling her protectively against his chest.

"Tell her…" Evelin lost her sentence in her struggle to breathe.

As Kazery watched, most of the rest of Evelin's hair fell away to lie limply across the pillowcase and the shoulders of the dress made for a fuller, younger woman's body.

"Tell her, her mother was pleased to protect her. Promise…"

Kazery held his daughter and wept quietly, tears flowing down ruddy cheeks and into his black beard. His face was wrecked by sorrow. "I promise, Evelin. I promise. I love you."

"And I… you."

Evelin let out her last breath, and died with a smile on her face.

Çifta felt her mother's presence depart, at first filling the room and engulfing Kazery and her tiny young self with love, before attenuating like fog and vanishing entirely from the realm of the living. Kazery stared at the corpse as if in a stupor, until shouts in the street jarred him back to the present. He looked down at his child, kissed her forehead, and headed for the stairs.

## Chapter Nine

# Jessamine

For all that Jess knew every last passageway and secret corridor within the walls of the castle, she couldn't find any passages linking the caperlands building to the palace. She'd found faint old lines on maps, leading in the direction of Sasha's prison, but no access point. Perhaps there had been subterranean routes connecting them, but they'd caved in or been walled up. In her search though, Jess found a crumbling balcony with an unobstructed view of the trail leading to the caperlands. She sat there alone—while Beazle was out hunting—drinking hot tea and nibbling a crumpet she'd taken from the dining room.

Only the top of the building was visible, and the pathway leading down to its front door. Yesterday she had seen traffic along the cart track, people delivering food and goods, and Bradburn escorted a man wearing a funny cap with tufts of white hair sticking out from beneath its brim. Jess guessed he was the justice. Questions stormed around her mind. How was

Rialta's shoulder? She had taken a deep cut. How was Sasha's eye, the one that had been puffed closed? When would the trial begin? What if they were found guilty? She put her head in her hands, trying not to cry.

"Are you trying to show solidarity for the frozen lady?"

Jess looked up as Digit came onto the old terrace and leaned against the railing, his back to the view. He wore a snugly fitted jacket with fur around the collar. His cheeks, the tip of his nose, and his fae ears were pink. He wore a thick scarf, but no gloves.

"It's not that cold," she murmured, looking away.

"It was a joke. A bad one, but a joke nonetheless." He crossed his arms. "What's got you all mopey and tied up in knots?"

"What do you mean?" Jess forced herself to pick up a crumpet and take a bite.

Digit's hair flopped over his forehead as he considered her with his dark gray eyes. "You can talk to me, Jess. I'm good at keeping secrets. I swear."

Jess looked away, uncertain. She liked Digit, but she didn't know him that well, not the way she knew Rose and Aster. But she couldn't talk to the Calyx because they were still preoccupied with the quarantine. What was her separation from Sasha in comparison to the potential death of a familiar? Thank pride, the quarantine ended tomorrow. She couldn't talk to Laec because he'd only minimize her feelings, tell her that some people had real problems. Look at Çifta's predicament, for example. He'd warned her to stay away from Sasha in the first place, and she couldn't bear to see his smug I-told-you-so face.

"No, really. I mean it," Digit said, seeing that she was considering opening up to him. "Think of me as a fixture of the palace, like a pillar or a lamp post."

Jess laughed. "You're not a fixture, Digit. You're Fahyli, which means you're sworn to the king. Your loyalties are to the crown, not to me. Whatever I say, you might have to report."

Digit smirked. "You'll be surprised to learn that I've never taken the Fahyli vow."

She looked at Digit in shock. "How is that possible?"

He shrugged. "When you're the crofter's son, you have a unique position."

Jess felt like she'd taken a smack to the forehead. Snapshots of Digit and Ian came together like the squares of a quilt. Ian hugging Digit in Syrgana, the two of them riding side-by-side, conversing easily, like they were equals. She had thought it all odd at the time, but now she realized it wasn't odd at all. "You're the crofter's son, I should have realized."

He smiled. "I have favor by default, but once in a while, I'm looked over. My father never wanted me to take the vow, or he would have pressed the matter. Whatever you say, it'll stay between us."

Jess shook her head. "Why didn't you tell me?"

He tucked his narrow hands under his armpits. "I assumed you knew. Everyone else does. Besides, it's not important."

Jess recalled Digit saying he had wanted to be Calyx when he was young, but it hadn't been in the cards. "It was your father who didn't want you to join the Calyx," she surmised. "He didn't want his son working for Ilishec."

The last part was just a guess. Ilishec disliked Ian. Jess wasn't sure if Ian returned the feeling, but maybe he did.

Digit told her: "I was upset at the time, but I'm much better suited for Fahyli work, even though I can make a nice bouquet of foxglove in whatever colors you want, including some that don't exist in nature. Father and I fought over it when I was young but, as usual"—he shrugged—"my father was right. I don't have the constitution to be a powdered courtier who dances and sweats and makes small talk. I like politics too much for that, not to mention danger." He gave a sly smile. "Plus, that rule about not being allowed to have relationships with courtiers? Ridiculous. Calyx are missing out on the best part of being at court. But you never heard it from me."

Jess chuckled, then much to her dismay had to stifle a sob that came out of nowhere. She put her hand over her mouth, her eyes watering.

Digit's expression slid from rakish to concerned.

She looked away, fearing that if she did not share her problems with someone that she might burst.

"I love him."

"Sasha?" Digit asked softly.

She nodded, grateful that he was taking her affection for the Silverfae foreigner seriously. "We didn't mean for it to happen."

"No one ever does," he replied, his expression full of empathy.

She looked at him curiously, wondering if he meant to imply that he too had fallen in love with someone he shouldn't have.

He added, "You're not just worried about a friend, you're dying to see your lover."

She nodded again. Lover. She liked the word very much. She liked it even more when applied to her and Sasha. She liked the way Digit used it, like he assumed that she and Sasha had already been intimate. Best of all, he didn't look even a bit scandalized.

It dawned on her that the no relationships rule wasn't that strictly observed, she'd just been too naïve to realize it. Rose had warned her not to be transparent about her feelings, but had also added the qualifier "at least not in public." Now, Digit had insinuated he'd had forbidden relationships, and he'd called Sasha her lover without batting an eye. All of it made her feel less alone, less like she was the only one breaking rules.

Digit looked toward the caperlands, then he looked at the sky. He moved away from the balcony, heading back into the corridor. "Follow me."

She trailed him to the bottom floor where a narrow door spilled them onto the double-track road that circled the training yards. Soldiers went about their business, Fahyli passed by, deep in conversation with one another, one of them had a possum on the top of his head. When Digit headed for the caperlands, Jess began to feel nervous. They were almost clear of the low stone wall curving around the front of the building. Those on duty would see them in a matter of seconds. They would see *her*.

She slowed down, then stopped altogether, before coming into view of the guards. "What are we doing?"

Digit came back to her and took her hand. "I'm going to help you get in to see your lover. It's easier to do it now than when the familiars are on duty after suppertime."

She let him lead her. As they approached the gates of the building, the guards stopped their game of dice and got to their feet.

The thin one, who had been there for Jess's first attempted visit, spat off to the side, then smirked. "Took you a while. Did you get permission?"

"Of a sort," Digit replied, stalking straight up to the guard. He put one bare hand up in front of the guard's face. Soft waves of magic wafted from Digit's palm and a smell came into the air, vaguely familiar, and not entirely pleasant.

*Digitalis.*

Jess almost grabbed Digit by the arm. She knew very well that foxglove—while its effects were different from her poisons—was just as deadly as her nightshades. Digit could not possibly mean to kill these men. He'd be the one in gaol in short order, son of the crofter or not. Trust made her wait, though her blood was positively zooming through her veins.

At first the guard looked puzzled, then annoyed. He made to knock Digit's palm away, but then his eyes rolled up and his chin hit his chest, teeth clacking together. He slumped to the ground as though boneless.

"Behn?" The other guard sprang to his friend's aid, checking for a pulse. He found it, because when he looked up at Digit, he looked more confused than anything. "He's asleep. What did you do to him?"

"He'll be fine." Digit put his hand in front of the second guard's face, and that guard slumped on top of his friend. The one on the bottom emitted a soft snore.

Jess stared, stunned and impressed.

Digit grabbed the top soldier by the wrist and dragged him closer to the wall, hidden under a caperberry bush where he wouldn't be seen. He looked up at her as he moved the guard's legs into the shadows, noticing her consternation and letting her see his. If Jess had thought this was easy for him, she was mistaken. There were beads of sweat on his brow and he was pale.

"A concentrated dose of *digitalis* causes instant heart attacks," he told her quietly as he moved toward the second guard, "but a mild dose just relaxes the nervous system. You've got roughly twenty minutes. Don't be here when they wake up. They won't remember us, and they won't admit to anyone that they fell asleep on the job. But if they see your face when they wake, it'll all come back to them. The amnesia only takes root if there's nothing to trigger the memory when they become conscious."

Jess's heart was thrumming as Digit dragged the second guard out of view, hardly believing what he'd done. He arranged the guards' limbs to make it look as though they had curled up for an intentional nap before slipping the keyring from the belt of the skinny guard and holding it out. Numbly, she took it, staring at it like she'd never seen keys before.

Digit snapped his fingers in front of her face. "Wake up, Jess. You're wasting time. You have to have that back on his belt and be long gone before those two wake up. Find me later. And obviously, this stays between us. Okay?"

Jess watched Digit sprint up the path. He hadn't even waited for an answer from her. His faith in her surprised her.

She shook herself, turned and put the key in the lock. The bolt sprang back as though freshly oiled. Jess slipped inside the cool darkness of the caperlands building, closing the door behind her.

She found herself in a small square foyer with a hallway stretching straight ahead. The walls were lined with peeling plaster, the hall was lined with doorless doorways, yawning their shadowy interiors. The smell of old wood, must and mildew was strong. Damp had soaked through every surface of this building. Water damage left dark stains, and the floorboards were soggy beneath her boots. A soft whine echoed from down the hall.

Sasha's incredulous voice came out of the gloom, just above a whisper. "Is it really you?"

His voice was a lit match to the tinder of her heart.

She surged down the hallway toward him. Ahead, on her right, a set of pale fingers poked through a door made of metal bars. Behind the bars stood Sasha, gripping the iron tight with disbelief. When she came into view, his expression shifted into such delight that it made her eyes prickle with tears. She put her hands over his knuckles, shining all her love up at him. Seeing him again turned her heart inside out.

"Jess," he breathed. "It really is you. Rialta told me but, I had a hard time believing it." He added under his breath, "Sorry, girl. I should know better. You're always right."

His puffy eye was mostly healed. When she'd last seen him, it had been a glittering slit surrounded by blue bruises. While shadows remained of those bruises, his eye could open fully.

Jess could not bear the bars that separated them, and fumbled for the keys.

Sasha's eyes widened when she began trying keys in the lock. "What are you doing?"

"This isn't a jailbreak," Jess told him, trying another key. "The guards are asleep. Our time is short."

Sasha pointed. "It's the larger one, with the rectangular head… that's it. How are they asleep?"

She didn't waste breath explaining, the single word "magic" had to be enough, because the lock sprang, and with it, her heart. Jess was in Sasha's arms in a moment, dropping the key-ring on the floor. He enveloped her inside the cocoon of his arms, holding her tight against his chest. He kissed the top of her head. He smelled of his surroundings—old wood and must and damp—but underneath all that, he smelled of Sasha, and Having his scent in her nose made her bones melt. Hearts throbbing, they stood like that for as long as they dared.

When Jess withdrew, her eyes were blurred with tears of relief. Sasha wiped her lashes with his thumbs and kissed her softly.

"You're a wonder. Have I told you?"

She smiled, touching his cheek. "Once or twice. I don't feel like a wonder. I feel like a shipwreck. How are you? Any broken bones? Are they feeding you well?"

He chuckled softly, wrapping his big hands around both of her small ones and putting them against his chest. "Do I look broken or scrawny to you?"

She shook her head. He was bruised, yes, but he stood as tall and straight as ever. He had not lost weight, and best of all, he looked unafraid. For all his blows, Prince Ruskin had been largely ineffectual at doing serious damage, for which Jess was grateful.

"Rialta had the worst of it," he told her.

"How is she?" she asked. "I heard her when I came in. I'm sorry they separated you."

"At least we are close enough to know the other is alright. This is more difficult for Rialta than it is for me. She's a wild creature. She's never liked kennels, or even being indoors. At least she is healing. The crofter's wife has been looking after Rialta herself."

Jess was jarred. The crofter had a wife? Maybe she shouldn't be surprised, after all, the crofter had a son. Why shouldn't he have a wife?

Sasha gazed at her like he would never look away. "I still can't believe you're here."

"I wish I could come every day," she told him. "Have they told you how long you'll be kept here?"

"No. The justice said that I'll be given a lawyer. I'll have to tell my story. Some time after that will be the trial. It could be weeks or months. I really hope it's the former."

Jess took a shuddery breath. Thoughts of the trial always made her mouth go dry. "They cannot possibly find you guilty. So many witnesses saw what happened. Rialta was only defending her fae. Any familiar would have behaved the same." Of course, most familiars would not have ended the prince's life so efficiently.

"Exactly."

Jess walked into the space Sasha was being kept in, footfalls soft on the threadbare carpet. Fire threw heat into the room from a worn stone fireplace that had once been beautiful, with flowers and vines overarching it. The peeling wallpaper might once have been red, but was now dark maroon. A single cot sat against one wall, beneath a bookshelf with a couple of books on it. Two barred windows let in light. Every surface was cracked, crumbling, and coated with dust. Beyond the carpet's edges was a hardwood floor crisscrossed with scratches, dents, and holes. Dominating the room was an old broken desk. Jess peeked behind the door in the corner and saw a bathing room, though it was the size of a closet.

Jess looked at Sasha, surprised. "It's… an old office?"

"I know. Strange, isn't it? They didn't want to put me in the gaol, nor in the dungeons beneath the palace. I suppose nobody knows what to do with me." Sasha chuckled and ran a hand through his hair, which had lost its wave and hung scraggily on his shoulders. "At least there is running water, and no annoying cell mate. I've been in a dungeon before and this is much better, so I can't complain."

"Many are calling you a hero," Jess told him. "Especially anyone who knew Lady Çifta."

"That's nice." He held a hand out. "I can't stand you being so far away. How much time do we have left?"

Jess went to him. "Ten more minutes."

He wrapped his arms around her, his eyes dropping to her lips. Her heart felt like a hyper bunny, cavorting wildly around in her chest. The heat in his gaze made her feel self-conscious, shivery and excited all at once.

She started to babble. "I tried to get permission to see you but nothing worked. I even asked the king and queen but they said no. A friend of mine, a Fahyli, although he's got the characteristics of a Calyx, put the guards to sleep with his botanical."

"Really," Sasha murmured, still gazing at her lips. His mouth moved toward hers.

It struck Jessamine what an enormous risk Digit had taken for her, but as Sasha's lips touched hers all thoughts of Digit blew away like cotton fluff. It was the first kiss they had shared since the day she'd played that ridiculous game with those ridiculous courtiers. Jess came alive as his lips moved over hers, his hands pressing into her lower back. Her hands crept up his arms to his shoulders, then to either side of his bristly jaw.

Another whine from Rialta startled Jess and she broke the kiss. She thought of how reluctant Beazle was to accept Jess's feelings for Sasha, and wondered if Rialta harbored any similar emotions.

Jess withdrew. "Is she… upset?"

Sasha looked confused. "You mean, about us?"

She nodded.

His confusion turned into a smile. "Of course not. She wants me to be happy. She's just… sore."

"Oh."

Sasha went to the cot and sat down, patting the coverlet, inviting her to sit down. But the idea of being on a bed with Sasha, even a single cot inside a rotting old office, and even if they were only sitting, made her stomach do flip-flops and her hands shake. She cleared her throat and put her hands behind her back.

"Everyone is worried about Lady Çifta. Will she survive?"

Sasha rested his elbows on his knees, his eyes turning serious. "I don't know. At least inside the ice, she has a chance. You remember the night we met, I told you that Silverfae have magic that is hard won?"

She nodded, recalling the sparkling jewel he'd made by coating her flower with ice. She had kept it as long as she could, but it had melted and turned to mush in less than an hour.

"The ice is how it happens," he said. "Silverfae are not born with power, they have to be tested. Many Silverfae do not choose the ice, because so many do not survive. Those that do freeze are faced with a challenge that is unique to them."

Sasha had Silverfae powers, so he was speaking from first-hand knowledge. A shadow crossed his face. Jess suspected he was remembering his own test.

"Why did *you* choose it?" She moved closer.

"I didn't." He looked up, taking her hand. "I was forced. My situation was unusual. My father is… was a powerful sorcerer. At one time, he was Queen Sylifke's most trusted advisor, but when he disappointed her, she took me as payment. The queen was certain that I, too, would become a powerful Silverfae, doubly so because I had Rialta. She can force a freezing upon young fae if she wants, killing many."

"But you survived," she murmured, her heart swelling with pride and gratitude. Now that she knew Sasha, she couldn't imagine a world without him in it.

"Yes, I survived, and I was given winter magic. Only someone who has survived the ice can trigger the test for another Silverfae, and when I saw Lady Çifta, and Ruskin's face, I understood he would kill her. He didn't care who saw it, or what it might do to Silverfall and Solana relations, he just wanted her dead. There was no time for anything else. She had the Silverfae eyes, so I just"—he spread his hands and shrugged apologetically—"went for it."

Jessamine thought of the way Çifta's delicate womanly form had looked inside the ice, swallowed up by all that frozen water. She remembered the way Laec had peered inside like a child at a store window.

"So… Lady Çifta is alive inside the ice, and if she passes this test, she lives. If she fails, she dies?" The idea was daunting, and Jess was glad that flora fae magic did not require such a risk.

Sasha kissed the back of her hand. "In a way, our predicaments are not dissimilar, Lady Çifta's and mine. We both must be tried, and an outcome will be decided, one way or the other. The difference between us is that a positive outcome for her is up to her, but a positive outcome for me is up to someone else."

Jess's mind snagged on what he'd said earlier about his family. "I'm sorry about your father, Sasha."

"Thank you. He's not dead though. I say 'was' because a curse backfired on him, and he hasn't been the same since.

He fell from favor, but he is still alive. And honestly, I barely know him. He was not allowed at court, and I've never been allowed to visit him."

A dark thought blew into Jess's mind. "Speaking of fathers, they say Çifta's is expected to return any day. If she dies, he may hold you accountable."

Sasha thought about this before admitting, "I hope he does not, but if he does, there isn't anything I can do about it."

Jess nodded, her eyes tearing up at the thought of anyone seeing Sasha in any way that contradicted the way she saw him. He caught the glisten in her eyes and stood up, opening his arms to her.

She stepped into his hug, but said, "I have to go. I don't know if my friend will help me see you again. It has to be his suggestion, because it's too much to ask. I don't want to get him in trouble."

He kissed her cheekbone, the tip of her nose. She turned her face up and he kissed her mouth, holding her to him. It was a goodbye kiss and Jess savored every second: the contact of his body, his scent, his warmth, his lips. Nothing would ever feel more right than being in Sasha's arms.

He drew back. "Perhaps Beazle could sneak in some time? I miss the little guy, and seeing him would let me know you're alright."

Jess rubbed her nose, wrinkling it with embarrassment. "We tried, and failed."

"You did?"

"Two nights ago. He was caught by a new familiar. Erasmus or Ferrugin would never have stopped Beazle. They're friends, and what he was doing wasn't *so* wrong."

Sasha nodded. "Sometimes they use Fahyli at nighttime. A couple of them are nocturnal, so it's easy for them."

"More fool me," Jess grumbled.

He touched her face, then took her hand and they walked toward the door. "I love that I've seen you, Jess, but I don't want you to worry about me. I'm not being mistreated, and I'm not afraid of the trial. I acted as my conscience dictated, and I would do it all again. I do regret Ruskin's death, because we were close once—"

There was a whine from down the hall at these words.

"But I do not hold it against Rialta," Sasha added hastily. "If someone had been trying to kill her, I would have protected her any way I could. If I ended up killing someone"—he shrugged—"it would be worth it to keep her alive. I don't blame her."

They hugged one last time before Jess picked up the keys, slipped from the room and locked the door behind her.

"Let me just—" She ran down the hall to the next room and peered in. Rialta was lying curled up on the floor right in front of the bars. She lifted her head, her ears perking when Jess appeared. A clean bandage had been wrapped around her shoulder, although a thin line of dried blood had soaked through. Nearby was a bowl of water and an empty plate with the residue of a meal. Rialta's room was smaller, more of a parlor, with old wainscoting and a lopsided frame hanging on the wall. At least there was a carpet for her to lie on.

Jess knelt, looking into Rialta's beautiful blue eyes.

"Thank you," she whispered, wrapping her fingers around the bars and trying to put as much gratitude into her whisper as she could manage.

With a groan, Rialta pushed herself up to sit on her

haunches. She licked Jess's knuckles, and Jess reached through the bars to stroke the soft fur on the top of Rialta's head. Rialta's ears went flat and her nose went up, a submissive gesture. She licked her lips and her tail thumped on the floor a couple of times.

"I'll do whatever I can for you." She kissed her fingertips and touched Rialta's nose.

Jess returned to Sasha. They kissed through the bars, then she retreated to the door, holding her breath and hoping the guards were still asleep. The sound of snoring had ceased. She peeked out, catching a glimpse of relaxed limbs sprawled on the ground.

Quietly she locked the door, then crept to the guard who had been carrying the keys and returned them to his belt. Her heart was pounding so loudly that she thought for sure his eyes would flare open. But that didn't happen, and after she got the keys back in place, she scampered up the trail, giddy at her success and the kisses she had shared with Sasha.

## Chapter Ten

# Laec

Laec had just finished pulling on his tunic when the sounds of celebrating echoed down the hall. His skin still numb, and with a last glance at the latest mark he'd left on the ice with his body heat, he crossed the ballroom and poked his head out the door. Cheering and shouting, the happy crowd sounded like they were in Ilishec's workshop. Curious, Laec passed the empty lecture rooms, and through the Calyx library to the rear entrance of his uncle's office, more of a greenhouse, really. The door stood open. The cheering had ceased, but excited talking and laughing now ensued. Stepping through the doorway, Laec looked around.

The gardener's office was crowded with Calyx, talking, hugging, laughing, some of them were actually bouncing up and down. A pile of small glass boxes sat heaped upon the workbench and the air was filled with insects. They zoomed around above the heads, the way cats go crazy at midnight, on the edge of losing their minds. Bees, butterflies of all colors, shapes and sizes, wasps, hornets, moths, and some insects Laec didn't have a name for. He inhaled deeply, chest expanding. It smelled of a summer garden in full bloom, in total contrast with the bleak winter scene outside. The quarantine was over.

A rush of guilt rose in his chest. Laec had promised his uncle he would be there when it was time, but no one had come to get him, and he'd completely forgotten. He shouldn't have. Seven days was not exactly difficult to keep track of. For a few minutes, Laec stood unnoticed near the doorway, absorbing the scene. The flora fae wore fine dresses and tailored suits for the occasion. Their hair was done, their skin was flushed. Though they were not as elaborately dressed as they were for banquets, Laec thought he'd never seen them look more beautiful. Even Peony, who was usually deadpan unless performing, talked and laughed with Gardenia and Dahlia. Everyone held tall slender glasses filled with clear nectar and bits of colorful fruits and herbs. Platters of fresh fruit sat about the room, and the Calyx speared melon slices and berries, munching as they chatted. Pollinators feasted on their own tiered displays of fresh fruit, flowers, and shallow dishes filled with brightly colored nectars.

Standing at the head of the table, basking in the happiness all around him, stood Ilishec. He spied his nephew and brightened, not a single sign of disappointment in his face, and waved Laec over. Laec squeezed through the press of fragrant bodies.

"Congratulations, Uncle." He clapped a hand on Ilishec's back.

"Thank you, nephew." Ilishec looked fit to burst, his eyes fever-bright, his cheeks pink. Even the dark shadows that had gathered under his eyes had diminished. The lines of worry that had continually marred his brow were now smooth. He looked like he'd shed ten years.

"It's a relief," the gardener said, putting a hand on his heart. "The prince can shove his nasty magic up his own backside. We didn't lose a single one."

"More than a relief. That's a triumph!"

Ilishec nodded. "You are right, it is a triumph. I was so afraid. I don't think I have ever been more afraid than I was this past week. But look at them now. Smell the air. They are magnificent again. I wondered, really doubted, you know? We've never been through anything like that before, and they are so fragile."

"Perhaps they are stronger than you think, Uncle."

Laec was happy for the Calyx, happy for the gardener, and sad for himself. Would he get a chance to celebrate the survival of his own loved one?

He looked around for Wisteria, the flora fae who had lost her familiar, Moony, to the prince's parasitic magic—not that he expected to see her—and was surprised he found her just behind him, talking with Jessamine, Aster, Rose and Snap. She looked fully recovered from Moony's death.

Laec turned to Ilishec, leaning close, keeping his voice low. "Wisteria seems fine."

In the middle of taking a sip of his celebratory drink, Ilishec lowered it, nodding, eyes twinkling. "She received a new familiar yesterday, a gorgeous little *Sphingidae*."

"Sounds… wonderful," Laec said. "*Sphingidae*?"

The gardener scanned the flying creatures until he spied a moth perched on the petal of a lily, and pointed. "There. Isn't he beautiful?"

"Oh, yes," Laec agreed. "Exquisite." It looked like an overgrown garden-variety moth.

The gardener either missed or ignored the sarcasm, and

Laec supposed he should be grateful. Sarcasm would only mar the joy of the day, and make him sound jaded. When the moth took flight, Laec felt ashamed. The *Sphingidae* really was beautiful. In flight, it looked so much like a tiny hummingbird that if Laec hadn't just been told it was a moth, he would have taken it for a bird. The creature hummed over to Wisteria, and hovered in front of her nose.

Enchanted in spite of himself, Laec watched as the moth touched the tip of his fae's nose. She closed her eyes and pushed her face out, looking in love. He fluttered up the skin of her cheek until he found her eyebrow. There, he clung, waving his antennae. Wisteria opened her eyes and smiled at Jessamine and the others around her.

"I'm so happy for you, Wisty," Rose told her. "He is absolutely gorgeous. The only one of his kind in Calyx history."

Wisteria put a hand up to her new familiar and he clung to her knuckle. She looked down with eyes full of love. "Thank you. No one can replace Moony, but this little beauty is making a pretty good run at it."

Laec had to disagree, it looked as though Wisteria's new moth had filled the hole in her heart that Moony had left behind. He turned to the group more fully, looking at Wisteria. "What did you name him?"

Happy for the opportunity to talk about him, Wisteria set down her glass. "I wanted to call him Sphinx, due to his belonging to a family of sphinx moths, but Peony said that was too close to Sphex."

Jess rolled her eyes, exchanging a look with Aster and Rose that said volumes about what they thought of Peony.

"So I decided to use the full genus nomenclature, and name

him Hemaris." She searched Laec's face for approval. Naming a familiar was a big deal, he supposed. "Do you like it?"

"Very much," Laec told her, even though he thought it sounded better suited for a female.

"The gardener is extra happy," Wisteria stole a glance over Laec's shoulder at Ilishec, now deep in conversation with Proteas and Asclepias. "He was worried that no new familiar would come. That sometimes happens you know, when a familiar is killed, and a flora fae can lose their magic. I was so sad, and so scared my time here was over. And then Hemaris came, yesterday morning, just after breakfast." She sunned Laec with a smile so bright it made him blink. "It's my new lease on Calyx life, and especially wonderful because the queen loves wisteria. My stuff is everywhere."

"That's true," Laec murmured politely, captured by the idea that Hemaris had just come out of nowhere. It was winter outside, so where had the moth come from? When he asked Wisteria, she shrugged.

"No one knows. Familiars are drawn to their fae by magic, whether they are animal or insect. No one knows whether they materialize from magic, or if they are born or hatched somewhere to Terran parents, or from an egg. It's just a mystery."

"Isn't it wonderful?" Aster said, twinkling up at him.

"We really needed something good to happen," added Jessamine, taking a sip of nectar. She looked feminine in a gown of soft gray that matched her eyes. Tiny gray pearls gleamed from her earlobes, and Beazle—nested in the coil of hair at the top of her head—had a tiny gray bow looped around his neck. The bat met his gaze, his ears going flat in a subtle expression of embarrassment. Laec had to suppress a smile, guessing the bat wasn't so fond of his bow, but he would endure it for the party.

"Everyone, everyone, let's calm down," called Ilishec, clapping his hands to get attention.

Conversations trailed off and the Calyx shuffled around to face their leader. He got up on a stool so everyone could see his face.

"Some of us were unsure this day would come, but it has arrived"—he spread his hands to indicate the familiars nibbling on fruits and flowers around the room—"and all is well. Eat and drink as much as you wish. Stay up as late as you want. Celebrate your reunion and the good health of your familiar."

There were a few whoops and whistles.

"But tomorrow…" Ilishec raised a finger. "I expect a return to our usual routine."

Heads nodded in agreement, and faces expressed an eagerness to return to normalcy.

Bolstered by the looks on his Calyx's faces, Ilishec plowed forward with relish. "The melt will see the return of many of our favorite courtiers and royals, visitors from afar, come to enjoy our early spring. For those of you who have finished fragrances, I expect you to provide as much stock as you're able to manage, for our store inventory. For those of you who have not yet refined a sale-quality scent, I expect you to spend the next few months with that as your main goal. And I expect all of you to learn the dances that have been choreographed for the coming season. Olinya and her staff are swamped with ideas for new costumes, and desperate for time with you. A week has been lost. Let's make up for it. Let's show King Agir and Queen Esha that the Calyx can rebound from difficulty to be stronger than ever."

Laec yawned, tuning out. As Ilishec continued to set expectations, a pageboy edged his way into the room, searching for someone. Laec recognized him. He ferried messages and fetched people for the crofter. There was only one person that a Fahyli pageboy could be looking for here, among the Calyx. Laec put up a hand to catch the pageboy's attention. When the boy looked his way, Laec pointed down at Jessamine, and was rewarded when the pageboy rolled his eyes with relief, mouthing thank you.

Ilishec finished with his speech as the pageboy squeezed in next to Jess and touched her elbow. She looked down at the young lad, who had to raise his voice to be heard over the conversation blossoming up around them.

"You're always so difficult to recognize in your Calyx clothing, Miss Jessamine," said the pageboy, cheeks flushed and nose glistening with sweat.

"Hello, Graf," said Jessamine, but her smile diminished.

"I've been all over the palace looking for you," Graf panted. "If I'd known today was the day… anyway never mind, I've found you. You are required in the presence of the king. I'm to see you to the lion's den myself."

Jessamine's face fell further. "The party is just getting started."

Beazle hooked a claw under his bow and tugged it loose, shaking himself free of it.

"No rest for the wicked," murmured Laec.

"Very funny," said Jess, nettled. "Feels like I'm always being summoned late—" She cut herself off with a shake of the head—perhaps realizing how unprofessional she sounded. She set her drink on the nearest surface. "Should I change?"

"I don't think that will be necessary," said Graf, looking for a way to the exit.

Laec frowned about Jessamine's complaint. She was being summoned often lately? He'd had no idea. It sounded like things were afoot. He was an approved emissary from Elphame, he should be present if important things were being discussed. He waved goodbye to Ilishec.

Catching up with Jess and Graf, he touched her shoulder. "I'll come with you."

She brightened. "Really? I thought you'd lost interest in lion's den meetings. It'll be nice to have you back."

"I can't have them thinking that I've been neglecting my duties," he told her.

"Have you?" Jess cocked an eyebrow.

Before he could answer, her gaze flicked to his neck, then down to his collarbones. She frowned. "Are you having an allergic reaction to something?"

"No," said Laec tugging up his neckline again. "No, to both."

They were still close enough to hear Ilishec gleefully shout, "Spring is just around the corner, my fae!"

Thinking of Çifta, Laec begged to differ. As far as he was concerned, winter had only just begun.

## Chapter Eleven

# Jessamine

"You want us to spy on Faraçek?" Jess repeated. "In his own kingdom? Inside his own fortress?"

The lion's den was as quiet as a tomb as she absorbed the scope of their new mission, unable to believe her ears. Beazle stirred against her collarbone, sharing in her disbelief. She stared at the crofter, then at Bradburn, then at the king—who had yet to say a word. She imagined she could feel Laec's quiet shock from where he stood behind her.

Her first thought had been that it was a joke, but Ian and Bradburn were not joking types, and the lion's den was not a place for such tricks. Her second thought was that it was a good idea. They needed to know what Faraçek was up to. There was also a sense of pride that it was she and Beazle they were asking, not one of the more experienced Fahyli. Trepidation was pushed out by excitement, and a sense of approval that finally they were doing something, being proactive.

From the window, the crofter turned to face her, expression impassive.

"You're the natural choice, not only because of your bat, but because you've been there before, and under cover of night. It's not an unknown to you."

Jess wondered if she should remind him that she'd also been caught. But she knew what Ian would say: she'd managed to free herself with her poison and her wits, and that she could do it again if she needed to.

"If ever there was a time for you and Beazle to shine,"—Bradburn rapped his knuckles on the wooden table—"it's now. You must not be discovered."

*No guff,* Jess thought, recalling Faraçek's threat. *We might be the natural choice, but there is more risk for us than there might be for someone like Kite or Regalis.* Even Ratchet could never be as invisible as Beazle, nor could he get into the places that a bumblebee-sized bat could.

The king spoke for the first time, elbows resting on the arms of his chair, his hands dangling toward his lap. He looked pretty relaxed for someone asking his subject to risk her life.

"I would never make such a request unless it was of dire importance, and it is comforting to know that we would be sending someone who has already done it successfully."

It hadn't been so long ago that she'd been chastised for sneaking into enemy territory. But of course, she wouldn't be so cheeky as to remind the king of that.

"Yes, I've done it before," she said, "but we can't use the underground passage this time. They've stationed a watch at their end, the same as us on our end. Even if the passage were clear, the stairs at the other end are broken. There's no way out."

Bradburn grunted. "Go on horseback, over the mountain."

"Stay off the fortress road," the crofter added.

The king was nodding. "There's always soldiers going up and down that way."

"And you want me to do this alone?" For Jess this was the scariest part. What if something went wrong?

"You can take one other with you, except for Digit, as he's assigned elsewhere," Ian told her. "But their job will be to accompany you until you are close to the fortress, then wait in the woods while you sneak into the fortress to do the spying."

*These men underestimate us.* Beazle's confidence flowed into her mind like warm water.

*It's better than being overestimated.*

*There's no need for you to go behind fortress walls at all. You'll stay in the woods and I'll do all the spying. Even our superiors don't know our skills like we do.*

Jess almost smiled. She didn't mind being given instructions, even if they were obvious. It helped her understand how the crofter thought this mission should go down. As long as she delivered the information they wanted, they wouldn't care how she got it.

"What if it takes me days, or even weeks?" asked Jess.

"It won't," Bradburn replied. "Faraçek is as eager to be crowned as a whore is for nightfall."

The crofter shot the captain a withering look. "Really, Reznik? So unnecessary."

Bradburn paid the reproach no mind. "He's already got plans in motion, and mark my words, he'll send us an invitation leaving as little preparation time as possible."

"Is there anything specific—aside from his coronation plans—that you are hoping to learn?" Jess put a hand up to Beazle. He walked into her palm and wrapped himself around her thumb. Absently, she ran a finger along his soft fur, down his spine.

*Do you mind?* Beazle thought, pushing into her finger in spite of himself. *We're getting instructions here.*

*Sorry.* She stopped, noticing that the gray bow was missing from his neck.

The crofter began to pace. "Osvitan was a decent neighbor, but Faraçek is not like his father, and Rahamlar hasn't had an unseelie monarch in generations. We need to know what his goals are, what he wants out of his relationship with Solana."

Bradburn took a small tin out of his breast pocket and snapped it open with his thumb. He grabbed a pinch of shredded brown stuff that Jess recognized by the smell. It was the dried leaves of one of her botanicals, *nicotiana*. The captain stuck the wad between his lip and his bottom teeth, speaking around the bulge.

"We have all kinds of agreements, from the use of common land near the borders, to trade and the use of certain bridges and roadways. We can't have any of that jeopardized. He won't likely talk about those things in detail, but whatever new information you can glean will be of value to us."

"We may be able to extrapolate his plans from what he says to his captain or his colleagues," the king added. "We are not asking you to sneak into his rooms and rifle through his things. Just… listen to him."

Bradburn turned to her with a shrewd look. "How close do you and your bat need to be to one another to exchange information? Perhaps *he* can go alone. You wouldn't have to make the trip to Rahamlar at all!"

Beazle cringed. *Ok he does overestimate us in some things.*

*That'll never happen,* Jess reassured him. It didn't matter to her if she and Beazle discovered that they could communicate from the Ivryndian shore to the Valdivian one. They would never be far apart enough to even try.

*That's right, you paunchy tobacco-chewer.* Beazle scratched at an ear with a claw.

"Where Beazle goes, I go too," Jess said plainly.

The crofter lay a hand on the back of a chair. "Which of the Fahyli shall I ask to accompany you?"

"I'll go with you, Jess," Laec murmured quietly at her shoulder.

Jess shot him a grateful look, but she did not miss the look of disapproval the crofter sent her red-headed friend. She loved the idea. Laec wasn't Fahyli, but he'd already proven himself handy with a sword, brave and trustworthy. Her second choice would be Panther, but even though Tully could scout the mountain terrain ahead of them, it wasn't like she could sneak into the fortress unseen, stealthy as she was. Jess really just wanted someone to watch her back, and she liked Laec's company. Plus she had a feeling that Laec needed to get out of the palace. He looked sad all the time now, even when he was smiling, and there was nothing he could do about Çifta's situation. It would be good for him to focus on something else for a night or two.

"Laec and I get along," she said to the crofter. "He knows Rahamlar as well as I do."

"Better," offered Laec. "Not to brag, but I impersonated a guest and wandered many of the hallways in the fortress when I was looking for Lady Çifta's room."

Jess nodded. "And I understand he's no longer under house arrest…"

The crofter looked taken aback. "I said *Fahyli*."

King Agir interjected. "But if she wants him, why not let him go? Mother luck was on their side the first time, and obviously they have good chemistry, plus it's *her* mission."

The crofter huffed. "No, it's fine. I thought you might want Regalis, or Kestrel. She has a clever bird named Ratchet."

*Not that clever*, Beazle thought.

*Clever enough not to rat us out,* Jess pointed out.

Beazle grumbled but agreed. If Kestrel had wanted to report that her bird caught Beazle trying to sneak into the caperlands building, she'd have done it by now.

"I'm happy with Laec, sir," Jess told the king.

"That's settled then," said Agir, slapping both palms on the arms of his chair.

"Very well," grunted Ian. "Both of you, meet me in the maproom first thing tomorrow. We'll discuss your approach and search strategy. You're free to go."

Jess and Laec bowed and backed away. When they got out into the hallway and the door was shut, she surprised him with a hug.

"You didn't have to do that."

"I know, but Ian would never have let you ask me, so I volunteered. It'll be faster with me because we already know what's what." Laec tugged at the neck of his tunic. "And anyway, there's no way I'm letting you have all the fun."

The journey over the Vargon—with Beazle scouting ahead and coming back for frequent warm up sessions under Jess's hat—had been largely uneventful. Even after they'd crossed into Rahamlar territory, where there were often patrols, all had been quiet. They'd gone off the road so Grex and Kitabee's hoofbeats would be muffled by snow and mulch, but this wintery terrain was rough going even for seasoned horses. They had no choice but to go slow or risk an ankle or leg injury.

When they reached the base of the mountain's far side, close to the twin rivers, Jess left Laec with the horses and went ahead on foot. He would feed and water them, with supplies they'd brought from Solana, in the shadows of a hollow while waiting for her and Beazle to return.

She got close enough to the fortress to hear activity from a courtyard, climbed a tree and got comfortable, wrapping her cloak around herself. Jess kissed Beazle on the head and tossed him into the night sky. *Be careful, little love.*

Her familiar winged his way silently toward the fortress, disappearing quickly into the darkness. Night sounds closed in. A raven screamed from somewhere behind the walls and Jess stiffened. A raven was not a direct threat to Beazle, but they could be trained to behave like a watchdog, screaming at signs of trouble.

*He's tied up in the aviary and unhappy about it,* Beazle told her. *Don't worry.*

Jess smiled at Beazle's reassurance. She looked after Beazle, but he looked after her even more.

He sent her a snapshot of the courtyard as he flew over. Fellow bats swooped about, doing their nighttime hunting. Beazle arrowed for an open window, one he'd visited before.

She recognized it too. *Lady Çifta's room.*

He telegraphed his view of the room from the windowsill. *Looks like it'll soon be someone else's room.*

Unseelie males carried wooden trunks into the room, while a servant girl lit a fire in the hearth. Beazle moved to the next window, then to the next, and the next. As he hunted for signs of the prince, Jess's mind wandered back to Laec's predicament.

They'd caught up on their way over the mountain. At first, Laec had needled her for information about Sasha, dropping hints that he knew that she harbored deep feelings for the young Silverfae. When she surprised him by admitting it readily, Laec had gone quiet. An hour later, he'd admitted without her having to needle him back, that he too was in love with someone. Jess told him she knew it was Lady Çifta and asked where she'd been moved to, because the last time she'd seen her, Çifta had still been in the courtyard. Laec described the ballroom that had become her temporary home.

"I know the one," Jess told him. "The Calyx use it to learn dances."

As she always did now, when palace layout was brought up, she recalled the secret corridors that skirted the entire ballroom and smiled, remembering the time she'd used the secret door to join a lecture she'd been late for.

"What are you smirking at?"

Jess told him the back of the fireplace had a secret door and enjoyed the resulting expression of surprise on Laec's face.

"How do you know that?"

"I know the palace pretty well, my friend," she'd bragged, then lost her smile as a chilly breeze froze her cheeks. She shuddered and shrank down behind her scarf, mourning that if they had kept Sasha somewhere in the palace instead of the bloody caperlands, she'd be able to see him regularly. She'd never get in a second time without Digit's help, and even with his help, it was too risky. How many times could guards fall asleep on the job before they got suspicious?

*Got him.*

Beazle's message jarred Jess back to the present. She closed her eyes in time to receive vision as her bat crawl-hopped along the wall, following their target.

Prince Faraçek was descending a circular stairwell, taking the steps two at a time. He carried something soft in one hand. At the bottom of the stairs, he entered a long well-lit corridor, and Jess could see that it was a set of gloves and a hat. He also wore a hip-length, fur-lined cape that swayed as he walked. His rapier was strapped to his side, his hair was tied back in the usual queue. His gray ears, slicing up and back from his head, were tipped with pink. As he strode, he pulled on the pair of gloves and the hat. He emerged in a courtyard where a groom held a saddled horse by the bridle. Two unseelie guardsmen were already mounted. Prince Faraçek swung up into the saddle and urged his horse into a canter. Beazle fluttered around high above, sending Jessamine a dizzying view as the group moved through the streets of Rahamlar. The moon was not quite full, but very bright, casting a cold light over the scene.

*They can't be going far,* thought Beazle. *They've got no saddlebags, no waterskins.*

The unseelie contingent passed through a gate and into the countryside that was home to acres of farmland. Jess recognized the section of road where she'd been abused by unseelie guards, but the group headed away from the river. Beazle stopped sharing his vision, and hunted bugs for a while, climbing the updrafts as he followed the riders.

A half mile into the farmland, Beazle sent Jess the blurry image of another group coming up the road, headed toward the prince. She counted six males surrounding two other figures: one with narrow shoulders wearing an elegant cape, surely a full-grown female. The other looked small enough to be a child.

While the Rahamlar group wore tunics and hats, the woman and child were cloaked, updrawn hoods casting shadows over their faces. Faraçek's group stopped at the crest of a hill, horses puffing and stamping, jetting steaming breath into the cold nighttime air.

Prince Faraçek spoke to the two who were being escorted, making it clear that this was an arranged meeting. But Beazle was too far up and the wind too brisk for him to hear anything. The two parties became one and traveled together back to the fortress, Faraçek riding at the front. Jessamine shifted positions, trying to alleviate some of the pressure on her spine. Trees were only comfortable for so long.

Once in the courtyard the horses were taken away and the soldiers dispersed while Prince Faraçek and the two smaller figures went inside. Beazle zipped in through the open doorway and followed them until they came to a large room with a long table, and a cluster of antique furniture near one end. Paintings of human and unseelie fae bearing noble expressions and fine clothing lined the walls. A fire crackled, throwing a warm glow across an elaborate carpet embroidered with a typical Rahamlarin design: cowbirds flying above stalks of wheat.

Beazle hid just behind the tapestry above the fireplace, peeking out from behind one edge, sending Jess a view of the room.

The woman tugged back the hood of her cloak, revealing that she was a young unseelie with sharp ears, auburn hair and a pale complexion. She unsnapped the brooch at her throat—a cowbird—and the cloak fell away, revealing a simple homespun dress. She lay her cloak over the arm of chair then reached to undo the child's brooch.

Faraçek stepped between them. “I would like to do it.”

“Of course, Your Grace.” She stepped away.

“My princeling.” Faraçek’s voice was warm as he crouched before the young one. “Welcome home. Let me look at you.” The prince drew back the hood from the child’s face, allowing firelight to illuminate every feature.

Jess gasped. *The prince has a son?!*

Even Beazle was dumbfounded.

The child was so much like his father that there was no mistaking his parentage. Sitting on the nearest chair, Faraçek drew the child toward himself. The boy had short black hair and the same widow’s peak as his father, the same up tilted eyes and cutting cheekbones, the same long neck and ears like blades.

Faraçek smiled into the boy’s face. “How was your journey, my lad?”

“Very easy, father.” The boy had a sweet, high childlike voice. Jess guessed he was eight or nine, but small for his age.

*This is huge news,* thought Jess. *The unseelie female must be the mother, but she does not seem important to the prince. He has hardly looked at her.*

“I have longed to have you here with me, in your rightful place,” Faraçek told his son.

“Me too, father.” The boy looked up with worshipful eyes.

The unseelie female stood back, observing with pleasure on her face. “I have been longing for this day too, my prince.”

Faraçek did not look at her when she spoke, but something unpleasant flickered across his face. It looked like he’d forgotten she was there, and she’d just reminded him of her presence, which was a bothersome thing that had to be dealt with. After a moment, Faraçek did look at her.

“Thank you, Reina,” he said. “You’ve brought him all this

way, you've raised him and cared for him. Your part is now done. Prince Toryan and I have much to discuss."

Ice formed along the corridors of Jess's heart. *Toryan. Faraçek named his boy after the murderous Rahamlar queen from centuries past.*

Reina backed up a step, obviously hurt. "Am I to stay in my usual…?"

He waved a hand dismissively. "It's been prepared. You may go."

"My prince will come… later?"

He turned back to his son. "Perhaps."

She bobbed a curtsy that the prince did not see and glided from the room, taking her cloak with her. The boy's gaze followed her, a pinch of concern between his brows.

Faraçek reached for a low stool, setting it in front of him and indicating the boy should sit on it. "She is not going anywhere, do not worry. We must talk of very important things, my boy. The thing that I told you that I was working so hard for has finally come to be. Your father will soon be king."

The boy gazed at him solemnly. "Mother told me. And I will become a prince… officially, recognized as your legitimate son."

"Not a prince, but *the* prince, and legitimate, yes," he nodded. "It won't happen right away, but soon. You have much to learn and much growing up to do, but you will be prepared to rule after I am gone. We have not seen as much of each other as I would have liked. Your father has been busy, and has had much responsibility."

"Mother also says that." The young Toryan shuffled his backside more firmly onto the stool and then slouched his shoulders forward, like a sleepy child preparing for a nighttime story.

"Sit up straight," said Faraçek, kindly but firmly. "When you are awake you are not to relax, you must always be alert. You must be ready for anything, not only in your body, but in your mind. Fight the body's urge to slacken. Rahamlar royalty are not lazy, not ever. We are of special blood, and we must strive to fulfill the destiny of that blood, always. You are unseelie."

"I am unseelie. I am ready for anything," Toryan whispered, eyes big, as though it was a hallowed utterance. He straightened, mimicking his father's perfect posture.

"Good lad. You will not suffer what I suffered when I was your age. I swear it."

The boy looked confused and Faraçek noticed the worry lines on his son's brow. "Listen. I was the oldest of four children. Did your mother tell you that, too?"

The boy shook his head. "She said you would tell me yourself."

Faraçek looked pleased. "Reina is a good girl. I chose well. Yes, I was the firstborn, which, in most kingdoms, comes with the promise of inheritance. Do you know what that means?"

The boy nodded.

Faraçek brushed Toryan's black hair away from his brow. "What does it mean, son?"

The boy's small hands grasped the fabric at his knees, tugging and pinching. "It's… what you get from your pa, I mean… father, the responsibility you are given when he is too old to do it anymore. But you are not old, father."

Faraçek put a hand over his son's, stopping him from fidgeting. "And we will have many long years together, with me ruling and you at my side. But one day, it will be your turn to rule. I will either pass on or I will step aside. It will depend on what is best for our kingdom. This is a future decision, so you do not need to worry about it right now. Your main concern is to learn how to be my son and a prince of Rahamlar. As I was saying, the eldest born would usually inherit; however, Rahamlar's laws were changed long ago to prevent this, to prevent our kind from ruling."

Toryan looked worried again. "What's wrong with our kind, father?"

This unseelie father sitting in a quiet room with his son did not sound like the Faraçek that Jess had come to hate. He looked like any father, in any room, in any kingdom.

Faraçek touched Toryan's rounded cheek. "Nothing, my lad. Nothing at all is wrong with our kind. Some say that unseelie are bent toward the darkness. Some say that the seelie, and even humans, are better than us. Do not believe it. Each of us have strengths and weaknesses, but we are not inferior or superior to one another. However, every species feels a kinship with those like himself, and we are no different. You see this everywhere in nature. Bees go with other bees; they do not make their home with horses. Where would they build their nest? In the horse's mane? Surely the horse would be stung. Can you imagine?"

Faraçek tutted and Toryan giggled.

"But many centuries ago, a foolish ruler decided that unseelie should not rule Rahamlar if it could be helped. He made a law that said that the only way unseelie offspring could inherit was if there were no human offspring left. Human monarchs have first right to rule Rahamlar, according to this law, but that ruling human must marry unseelie. This was done in an attempt to placate the unseelie who were upset by the decree. Our kingdom has been kept from unseelie rule for over five-hundred years." Prince Faraçek took his son's hands. "This is a very special time, because finally… finally, unseelie will return to Rahamlar's throne. I have seen to it myself. I was the eldest, but at every turn I was marginalized and insulted. The biggest horses, the best armor, the best cuts of meat, the nicest wine, and the best place at the table, it always went to my brother Ander. I bore it all patiently, never showing how insulted I was, how unfair I believed it to be. I even loved my family, those who did this to me. But I also believed that one day I would undo these unjust laws. One day, unseelie rule would return to Rahamlar. Either by my hand, or by my son's hand."

The boy's eyes widened. "Me?"

"I have already done it, my lad." The prince's eyes looked dewy and he spoke with suppressed passion, almost a religious fervor. "It has been managed, and fate was with me. Do you know our motto?"

Toryan nodded and took a breath, speaking slowly in that sweet, boyish voice. "*Quae providentia initiat, promovemus.*"

"Well said, little prince." Faraçek put a hand on the boy's head. "What does it mean?"

Toryan looked up at the ceiling, thinking. "*What providence initiates, we advance.*"

Faraçek looked positively rapturous at his son's perfect recital and Toryan glowed under the warm rays of his father's approval.

"Mother told me many times," the boy explained proudly. "She wanted me to remember, for you."

The prince stroked the boy's cheek. "My clever lad. Sometimes we must wait for providence to provide an opportunity, a strong wind. It always comes. A ship of many tons can sail against the strongest gale if the sails are set right. Your life is that ship, providence is the wind, but the sail-setting is up to you. If you are patient and set the canvas right, you cannot be stopped. Do you understand?"

Toryan nodded vigorously. "I understand. I have seen sailboats."

Jess's heart thudded so hard that every nerve ending tingled, every mental road inside her head felt clogged with traffic. *We thought we knew him. We didn't know anything. Not a thing.*

Beazle agreed.

"When destiny is with you, you will find that providence presents many open doors. These doors require courage to walk through, many require sacrifice, sometimes even the death of those we love. When you are grown, you will understand this."

The boy looked worried again.

"You come here at a critical time, Toryan," continued Faraçek, explaining as patiently as the most time-tested teacher. "My coronation is but months away. There is much paperwork to attend to, and my ministers are working as hard as they can to set the sails for me. When my coronation comes, we will see who is loyal, and who is not."

Toryan struggled to understand, his brow drawn. "How will we know which is which, father?"

"I will invite nobles and royals from our neighboring kingdoms and lands. If they attend my coronation and come bearing gifts, it will be a sign of their allegiance. If they do not appear, my captain—you will meet him soon, his name is Yorin—will make a mark next to their name, a mark that means they are against us. Once we know who is loyal and who is not, we make a plan."

"Plan," Toryan echoed.

Faraçek nodded. "First, I must return Rahamlar to its original state, the state that your namesake intended all along."

Toryan brightened. "You mean Prince Erasmus's lands?"

Every hair on Jess's arms went stiff.

*Uh oh.* Beazle's claws tightened with worry.

Pleased that his son knew this, Faraçek touched Toryan's nose. "Yes, exactly. I see Reina has taught you some of our history. The land that was once ours, which was so foolishly given to Prince Erasmus, must be returned to us. Right now that land is called..." Faraçek paused to see if Toryan knew the answer.

"Solana," the boy said without hesitation.

"Correct." Faraçek brushed his palms together like rubbing off dust. "Solana will soon be no more. The land will be annexed—that means returned to us—and Rahamlar's original borders will be reinstated, all the way up to Kittrell, near Silverfall."

"But, King Agir... he will not agree," Toryan said.

"He may, he may not," the prince returned, his voice mild.

Jess blinked, wondering how Faraçek could come to the conclusion that Agir might actually agree to give Solana's lands back to Rahamlar.

"My hope," Faraçek continued, "is that when I offer him a generous lordship and a beautiful estate in the countryside not far from where he currently resides, he will not challenge me. My hope is that this annexation will happen peacefully and without bloodshed. If King Agir and Queen Esha attend my coronation, it will be a signal, an open door. They may be willing to listen."

"And if they do not come?" The boy yawned, but fought it hard, trying to keep his teeth together but failing.

"They have much pride in what Erasmus of old built there, and it is beautiful. It belongs rightly to us, however, and if they resist, then we must be prepared to take it by force. I do not wish to kill or destroy. Unfortunately, Agir is stubborn. I am not sure he'll see things my way. Once a man has power, he is loath to let it go, and Agir is Erasmus's direct descendant, he will claim that the land is his by right."

Toryan rubbed a fist into his eye, struggling against weariness. "You do not like him?"

Prince Faraçek knocked his head once this way, once that. "Like, do not like. It matters not. I want an alliance. He has forces I would add to ours, unique warriors of high quality, but I am prepared to destroy those forces, if I must. It is for Agir to decide."

The boy looked nonplussed. "Why is it his decision?"

Faraçek straightened, smiling with arrogance and self-righteousness. "In the end, I cannot have the citizens say that I was not gracious to their former monarchs. I must give them every opportunity to choose peace." Prince Faraçek put his hands on the boy's cheeks. "You are very tired. We have time to talk tomorrow, and every day after that, now you've come to live with me. Finally."

Faraçek pulled his son into a long hug, wrapping his arms around the tiny frame in a tender gesture of paternal love. Then Faraçek stood and took Toryan's hand. Leading his son from the room, he murmured about the size of the bedroom Toryan had been given, all to himself, and which was not far from his father's.

*Do you think that's the information that Bradburn and the crofter were looking for when they asked us to spy?* Beazle postulated.

Jess blinked away the scene of father and son hugging, putting a hand against the rough bark beside her until the vertigo passed. She tilted her head back and looked into the sky where the moon had begun to lower itself to the horizon. Her mind whirled and she put a hand to her temple. She couldn't wait to share this with Laec, and then the king.

*I think it's a whole lot more, Beaze.* She began to climb down. *Let's go home. We have big things to share, and I'm exhausted.*

*They're not going to like it,* Beazle thought as he slipped out of the fortress and winged his way back to her.

*No,* she agreed. *They're not going to like it one bit.*

# Part Two

## Chapter Twelve

# Çifta

THE ICE TOOK Çifta over Silverfall City.

*The city is very beautiful, no?*

It was. Many slender spires in shades of white, gray and soft blue thrust themselves into a perfect cloudless sky, reflecting arrows of sunlight. Narrow winding alleys, broad straight streets with lamps of pale-blue fire, amber light emanating from windows, hinting at the coziness within. The pale stones and narrow spires called to the artist within Çifta.

Visible beyond the main palace courtyard stood a cultivated forest of snowdrop trees, which the ice brought her attention to. Silverfae moved among the trees in pairs. One used a wooden mallet to pound a small bronze spigot through the white bark, the other hooked a silver bucket to catch the sap that began to flow.

*It is the beginning of sap season,* said the ice. *Soon the lifeblood of the snowdrop trees will flow, and the Silverfae will make their secret elixir. It keeps them warm, strengthens the heart, and—some believe—*

*enhances the magical potential of young fae who wish to be frozen. The sap of the snowdrop tree is pale green,* said the ice, speaking somberly. *It is a color of value, and why the Silverfae love tourmaline stones above even rubies, sapphires, or emeralds. The brighter green the syrup, the more potent it is. Already some of these trees have begun to give forth.*

Spigots spilled a pale-green water into the buckets. Silverfae stood nearby, drinking from steaming mugs as they kept an eye on the buckets, switching them before they overflowed.

One of the older females laughed at something a colleague said, drawing Çifta's attention. Her hair was bundled up in an elegant wrap, and she wore a waist-length, pale-green cape over her shoulders. All the harvesters wore an article dyed that pale green color.

*It marks their occupation,* the ice told her. *They are servants, but they have a position of honor. Under Karinya's reign, the harvesting and processing of sap is something to aspire to. They live in the palace, and are served and cared for almost like royalty, although they are of no special bloodlines. They were selected by the ice—*

Çifta was startled by this phrasing. *You chose them?*

*When frozen, a fae meets their version of the ice. The test is personal. These came out of the melt—rather than with winter magic, like most survivors—with a talent for the snowdrop trees and processing the elixir. Some even hear the trees whispering.*

*This elixir,* Çifta wondered, *I should have heard of it before. My father transports all kinds of rare things all over the continent and beyond. But I have never seen it among my father's inventory.*

*It is forbidden to trade or even to take it outside the kingdom's borders. To do so is to be exiled, a fate worse than death in the minds of most Silverfae.*

The ice took her beyond the city walls, past icy roads and smoky villages, over snow-covered forests.

*Where and when are we now?* Çifta wondered. *Is this happening at the same time as my father fleeing with me as a baby?*

*We have gone further back.*

When a small, lonely figure came into sight they slowed to keep pace, and drew close.

A Silverfae female wrapped in thick furs and with a hunched back, stalked over crunchy, rocky terrain. Two thick white braids hung from beneath her hood. Her furs looked warm but old, worn down to near baldness in places, and dirty at the hem. The ruff of animal fur draped around her torso made her hunch appear like an animal riding beneath her cape. In spite of her rounded back, she moved with the grace and strength of the young, and walked alone. The thick fur trim of her hood covered her forehead and overshadowed her eyes. The ground was uneven and rocky. In some places there were cracks, deep and dark, like they might drop into the center of the earth. Her breath curled in front of her face as she panted, walking fast, her boots making the crystalline snow squeak. The sky was a blaze of blue so intense that it could hardly be endured, and not a cloud marred the arrows of sunlight that reflected off misshapen blocks of ice on the horizon. They were smooth and white, and veins within them glittered like marble.

Frost coated the bare branches of the occasional trees that popped up like lonely sentinels across the terrain. But it was the trees with their white bark and snowflake-shaped leaves of palest blue and green that caught Çifta's attention. The leaves danced and flashed in the sun, the only trees in sight that did not lose leaves in winter.

*Silverfall is beautiful. Harsh, but so lovely, especially those trees.*

*Observe the fae woman, child,* the ice chided.

She walked with her head down, watching the treacherous ground before her. After ascending a steep hill, slipping occasionally on patches of mirror-like ice, she stopped to catch her breath. She drew back her hood with a pale bare hand, sucking in deep breaths as she scanned her new vantage point.

Çifta studied her face. Sharp, aquiline, and as pale as any Silverfae. Her irises were icy green, and hair as fine as spun silver. She had thick, dark-blond brows that sat low over her piercing eyes. She did not look kind, no, but she did look determined. Determination and desire, she had in spades. Though her colors were cold, her eyes burned with the passion of intention and need. Something stirred within Çifta as she gazed upon this Silverfae.

*She is up to something*, Çifta thought. *Something dangerous.*

*Why do you think she is alone, way out here in hostile lands?* The ice conveyed what Çifta took as a deep sadness, as though it wished it had power to make time redo itself. *Look ahead now. What do you see?*

Çifta pushed her gaze outward. Beyond the Silverfae woman was a jagged wall of ice, or perhaps ice over stone. Either way it was a sheer cliff that some tectonic force had split, leaving a space wide enough to drive a four-horse carriage through. But the way had filled in with rubble, and was not nearly smooth enough to allow wheeled passage. Hanging over the gorge was a skeletal shape, dark and angular, and alien to this terrain.

The hunched female stalked toward it, the way being easier now that she'd crested the hill. There was no path, but somewhere along the way a second set of footsteps joined the ones she was creating. Çifta couldn't tell from which direction the other footprints had come.

The strange shape hanging over the gorge became clearer and Çifta's heart balked, for now she recognized it well enough to give it a name. It was a creature she'd only ever seen in illustrations and paintings: a dragon—or rather, what remained of one—lay wedged above the split in the rock. The bones of its wings were bent at unnatural angles, its spine twisted, its great horned head hanging down over the entrance to the gorge. She could picture it struggling to free itself, in great pain from a broken body.

Çifta almost felt sorry for the long dead titan. *When did that happen?*

*Centuries ago,* the ice replied. *It isn't important when it happened, but that it happened. Her death changed this place forever. Do you see how her head hangs down over the entrance? Do you see how she died with her jaws open?*

*I see.*

The great fangs were easy to make out now that they were so close. The immense vertebrae and one enormous wing jutted upward, like the mast and sail of a ship. Half the beast's remains had been swallowed in ice, so that the creature appeared to be part of the mountain. Frost crawled up the pale bones, glittering under the sun. The empty eye sockets—large enough to fit wagon wheels inside with room to spare—were packed with snow and ice.

*It took Sharlyk a long time to die. She bled her life into this place, filling it with her magic and the last of her vitality.*

*Sharlyk,* Çifta echoed. *She fell from the sky?*

The ice's words slithered around Çifta, whispering first from one side, then the other.

*She fell in battle, child. Every Silverfae child is told the myth of Sharlyk and Minyar, the matriarchs of the age of the ice drag-*

*ons. It is said that, as she lay broken and dying, that she—like all valiant creatures who have lived lives of violence but without fear—welcomed her own death. She used the last of her energy to pour herself into the ground, to make her spirit and her magic available to those whose fearlessness and valiance matched her own. This place has been forbidden to Silverfall citizens for centuries, and remains so, even to this day. Many do not believe it exists.*

As the ice told Çifta the story, the figure of a male—straight-backed, tall, and swathed in pale gray robes and a hood—emerged to stand just inside the shadow of the gorge. Putting a pale hand against the rock, he waited for the female in stillness. Only the edges of his cape fluttered softly in the breeze.

*They were his footsteps. He got here first.*

*Yes,* the ice murmured. *A powerful sorcerer.*

Çifta sensed a welling up of intense dislike from her host toward this male.

*Who is he?*

*No one dares walk on this ground but these two. They are not relatives, but they might as well be. They are of a kind.*

The female approached, letting her hood fall onto her shoulders. The sun lit her hair. Out of breath, she looked at the man, defiance mingled with hope.

"You came." Her voice was deep for a woman, and resonant. "I wasn't sure you had the courage to visit Sharlyk's ground."

She was speaking a language that Çifta did not understand, the language of Silverfall. Yet, by some magic, the words registered perfectly in her understanding.

The man removed his hood but remained in the shadows. He too was Silverfae, with white-blond hair that winged out at his temples. A stubble of pale beard peppered his lean cheeks.

His eyes were piercing, his thin upper lip had a hint of curl, giving his face a handsome arrogance, perhaps even cruelty.

"Sylifke," he said, ignoring her insult but looking at her with open dislike.

Shocked, Çifta's mind gaped. *This is the Silverfae queen? She looks like a deformed peasant.*

"Only those who fear this place have reason to stay away." He spoke lazily, with the sing-song quality of a storyteller or minstrel. "I came out of curiosity. I thought to myself: what could she possibly want badly enough to send such a cryptic summons, and to such a place as this?"

Sylifke lifted her chin. "I do not fear this place either, Elvio, and I could think of no other who might be willing to help me, let alone powerful enough to do what I need done."

His eyes narrowed and a small smile touched his lips. He inclined his head, appraising her from head to toe. "I'm listening, though I am doubtful that you are able to afford my services."

"We'll get to that." She braced her hands on her hips. "I intend to challenge Karinya for the throne."

All arrogance disappeared from Elvio's face, and incredulity took its place. Heavy silence passed as he assessed her seriousness. It was apparent that Sylifke was not joking, yet in spite of that, he began to laugh—a dry sound, without humor.

"You make me rise early and leave my warm bed for this… this foolishness? You cannot even *dream* of victory over Karinya. She is the most powerful queen Silverfall has seen in two-hundred years."

"I am powerful, too." Sylifke narrowed her eyes. "I will challenge her, and, with your help, I will prevail."

His laughing ceased as abruptly as it had started. He shook his head sharply. "You are mad, and this is treason."

"It is not treason to challenge the throne. Every citizen has a rig—"

"It is treason to discuss it," he snapped. "And it will be treason if you lose, *when* you lose."

"I won't if we—"

"There is no 'we'," he sneered. "There is you, and you alone, you foolish faeling. Go back to your village. Marry a fae who can tolerate you and make babies for him. Maybe one of them can dream of challenging a sovereign, if you're lucky enough in your match. But not you. You have some talent, yes. I was there when your ice thawed and saw what you could do. But this is Karinya you wish to unseat, she is a tempest of frozen blades. She is your death, not that I care. You mustn't think of it any further. Take my advice and forget that we ever met. If you are civil, and stay out of my way, I will forget this exchange as well."

Sylifke spread her hands wide, eyes glittering like cut diamonds. "Look at where we stand, Sorcerer."

A crackling sound echoed through the canyon as she spread her fingers out. A wind kicked up, sending snow swirling into the air. New frost crawled along the inner walls of the gorge. A ball of white swirling fog formed between her hands as she brought them together in front of her heart, palms facing each other. Light flashed within the sphere, snapping with electrical charge and blowing the fine hairs around Sylifke's face back, baring her forehead. Inside the ball, two dark shapes appeared, mere shadows, but as they twisted around one another in a deadly aerial dance it became clear that they were dragons fighting in mid-flight.

"She bled for *me*, sorcerer," Sylfike said, her eyes alight with power. "Karinya has ruled for thirty-two years without challenge; she is strong, but her rulership has made Silverfall soft. In spring, our rivers run clear, our forests drip with water. Green dares to poke its head from the ground, and winter fae turn their faces up to the sun to feel its heat. I will be like the queens of old. I will bring the glory of winter back to our lands. I will fill our kingdom with powerful Silverfae who survive the ice, afraid of nothing. And if you help me now, you will rule at my side. My kingdom will be your kingdom. Your word will be second only to mine, and all of Silverfall will quake at the sound of your name. Join me, Sorcerer."

Lightning flashed in the churning ball, backlighting the dragons and making their silhouettes stark: sharp edges and whipping tails, glinting teeth. Cracks formed over the globe as one dragon struck the other a deadly blow to the neck. A reptilian scream seemed to echo from the gorge.

Elvio, pale now, with a dewy brow, clearly affected by Sylifke's speech, looked up into the mouth of the dead Sharlyk. He looked back at the female, eyes wide.

A skin froze over the sphere, turning it opaque. It dissipated into a mist of white and gray, sparkling for a moment before vanishing.

"You see?" she murmured. "I have more magic than I let anyone believe. What say you now, Sorcerer?"

Elvio stared again at the ancient jaws, the prehistoric brow, the time-worn bones of the beast. He closed his eyes as if listening, his chest rising and falling. Then he lowered his face and opened his eyes.

"You would risk death for the throne, faeling?"

"I am not afraid." She watched his face with a veiled apprehension. "To die at Karinya's hand is preferable to a life of wishing. Silverfall has many fae who dream of challenging Karinya, but that's all they'll ever do. I was not born for a life of dreaming."

A grudging respect crept into his eyes, but it was tinged with revulsion. Whether that distaste was for her, or for himself, it was impossible to say.

"It will take more than winter magic," he said. "Those who have survived the ice know better than any that sacrifice is required. Are you prepared for that?"

Sylifke undid the bronze clasp at her throat and shucked her robe, casting it aside. A shock went through Çifta, sharp-tipped and cold, taking her breath away. The hunch of Sylifke's back was not a deformity but a sleeping faeling. Tiny, surely less than six months old. Strapped just beneath the faeling was a short but wicked looking dagger. Both its blade and handle were scarred with intricately carved runes.

When Elvio saw the top of the faeling's head, and the dagger, his eyes widened. Sylifke reached behind herself and unsheathed the dagger, bringing it in front of her.

*He said sacrifice. No,* Çifta tried to withdraw from the scene. *Please tell me this is not what I think it is?*

*She was willing to desecrate her very soul,* whispered the ice.

Elvio inhaled, and Çifta felt sure he would rebuke Sylifke one final time and end this damned conspiracy. But he did not mention the faeling. His eyes fell to the blade, as though the babe was not of concern to him.

"Where did you get that?"

"Does it matter? It was fashioned from Sharlyk's bone," she paused and added with a downward tilt of her chin, a gesture full of caution and meaning. "You know I am not lying. You can feel it."

Çifta looked at the fearsome skeleton, trying to imagine how anyone could even reach it to make anything of it.

*Sharlyk's bones were petrified long ago. For centuries they have been too hard for any tool to carve or cut. This dagger is very, very old. It could only have been made during a brief time following Sharlyk's death.*

Elvio uttered something under his breath, eyeing the dagger. He seemed to have changed his mind about Sylifke's chances, yet was hesitant to admit it. He said nothing until Sylifke held the dagger out, the handle balanced on one palm, the blade on the other.

Elvio shook his head. "You ask much of Sharlyk. For this she demands that you make the cut yourself."

Sylifke grasped the dagger in one hand then twisted the sleeping faeling around in its cloth cradle until it was strapped to her chest. Sylifke put a hand to the knot that held the babe in place, ready to undo it.

"Tell me what to do."

For a moment the Silverfae just looked at one another, their expressions heavy with the knowledge of what they were about to do.

Then the vision was over swept by fog, their silhouettes swallowed up by mist.

*I will not defile your mind by making you watch,* the ice told her in the darkness. *The details are not important, only that you know it happened. We go now to the court of Silverfall, mere days after this encounter in Sharlyk's gorge…*

## Chapter Thirteen

# Jessamine

"This is outrageous!" Flecks of spittle sprayed from the king's mouth, landing in his neatly clipped beard. His eyes were huge and filled with rage, caverns lit from within by a holy fury. A vein throbbed in the middle of his forehead, cords stood out in his neck. It was as though a furnace had gone out of control and there was nothing to do but let it burn out.

Beazle cowed in Jess's hair. *So angry.*

*Not with us. He just doesn't like the news we bear,* Jess returned. *Don't take it personally.*

*Hard not to.* Beazle's thought was little more than a wisp.

The lion's den was packed, yet silent, save for Agir's livid huffs and the creaking of the dais as he stormed across it one way, then back the other. The crofter stood near the row of windows, Captain Bradburn beside him, taking in the news. Four senior officers who Jess did not know were also in attendance, along with Regalis, Laec, and a few human advisors in official looking robes.

"Darling." Queen Esha spoke in a soothing voice, rising from her seat to put her hands on Agir's arms. "Sweeting, be calm."

He walked away from her. "I won't tolerate this… this insult… this treachery! I will not have it!"

He ripped the cape from his shoulders and tossed it over his seat. Esha stepped nimbly to the side to avoid being side-swiped by flying metal brooches. The king adjusted his tunic with sharp, angry motions, shooting Jess a look that could wilt an oak. He stepped off the dais.

"He has no right," Agir growled.

It took everything Jess had not to take a step back. "Yes, Sire," she murmured. "I mean, no Sire. No, he doesn't."

"This land was legally given to Erasmus, *my* ancestor." Agir jabbed himself violently and repeatedly in the chest with both thumbs. His gaze flashed around the room, looking for his own righteous anger reflected back at him.

"Yes, Sire. It cannot be borne," said Captain Bradburn.

Bradburn, who somehow projected being both hard and strong while also being a little pudgy, looked at Jessamine. "That was clever spy work, Miss Fontana. We knew he was up to no good, but this… I never imagined."

"We are all sufficiently outraged, I am sure." Queen Esha returned to her seat and settled, her hands in her lap. "The question is, now that we know about this ridiculous plan of his, what do we do about it?"

"This is where you all shine." Agir swept a pointed finger around the room. "Speak up. I have my own, very violent, ideas about how to thwart Faraçek, which means I need to hear yours." He beckoned with both hands in a gesture that said *let me have it*.

"He cannot be allowed to crown himself, surely," ventured Laec. "We were lucky to learn that his plans are far more devious than simply murdering his siblings and usurping the rule of Rahamlar."

"First of all, his coronation is not legal," Regalis said. For once, Ferrugin was perched on his forearm. "He must, by law, make every effort to recover the legal heir's body. It must be shown there was no foul play before he can legally be recognized as heir. If he were to be accused of murder, everything would halt until a trial was arranged."

The king removed his circlet and tossed it on the table near the windows and his hair flopped over his forehead.

*But the solution is simple,* Beazle thought. *Is it not?*

Jess wasn't sure what he was talking about, then she was. *Assassinate him?*

*Naturally. He assassinated Serya. He tried to kill Isabey. He doesn't even know that he failed. It would solve everything to just… get rid of him.*

Things were so simple when looked at with bat logic. Beazle had the ability to analyze consequences in the heat of battle, where things changed by the second. But he didn't have the skills for analyzing longer term consequences. The world of fae politics was too complicated, and the nature of humans and fae too unpredictable.

*That would trigger a war,* Jess replied. *The Rahamlarin guard would know that it was us, assuming the assassin was even successful. It might solve the present problem, but it would result in a much bigger problem.*

*Why assume the future problem would be bigger?* Beazle wondered. *Future problems can be solved as they come. Besides, the king looks ready to kill.*

He did. King Agir now looked like he'd been electrocuted. His curls frizzed out in a cloud around his head, sweat ran down the sides of his flushed face. Perspiration dampened his tunic under the arms and at the chest.

"It seems to me"—the crofter began hesitantly—"that we should exhaust all legal recourse before considering any further actions. The prince, much as he might wish to, cannot just wave a hand and change laws that have been in place for five-hundred years."

The king nodded. "How do we involve ourselves in the process, though? Rahamlar ministers are beyond my influence."

"He has a son that he has not claimed, perhaps there is an opening there," Bradburn offered.

King Agir snorted. "Yes. Toryan. Can you believe it? Such an insult. No wonder he's kept the boy a secret all these years."

The queen lifted her chin. "I don't think we know enough. We must put our lawyers on it. We have to understand what their laws do and do not allow. Prince Faraçek cannot simply sire a bastard and then claim he is legitimate years later."

"Our lawyers are busy preparing for Sasha's trial," the king pointed out.

"Yes," the queen agreed. "And we must see to it that he and Rialta are acquitted. We all know what happened. They should not be put into Silverfae hands. It would be the end of them."

"Ideally, yes," Agir told his queen. "But we must also do things properly, or we may have problems from the north as well as from the west."

Jess's pulse sped up. Esha believed in Sasha's innocence, but Agir was more concerned that the trial followed convention?

"Which brings us to another conundrum," said Esha.

"They do seem to pile up," King Agir added with passion.

"Queen Sylifke has written," Esha told the room.

Jess shivered and crossed her arms. The name of the winter queen drove a spike of worry into her heart, mostly because of the dislike Sasha had expressed about the northern sovereign.

Agir crossed to the table and snatched up a scroll, then waved it in the air. "The queen of Silverfall has sent us a politely worded letter with a request to attend the trial."

Jess's jaw dropped; at a curious look from the crofter, she snapped it shut again.

King Agir continued, not noticing. "You see? *This* is how a true royal behaves. She requests—*requests*, mind you, not demands—to be permitted to provide six of the twelve jurors, as well as the prosecutor. She elects Rayven Sabran, a female whom we already know behaves with decorum, even when she was denied her petition."

An unpleasant vibration began to hum deep within Jessamine's core. Queen Sylifke wanted Sasha's enemy to be his prosecutor? And to put six of her people in the jury? Surely Agir could not, would not, agree.

But, incredibly, the king continued. "It is only fair. Quite reasonable, given that her son was killed here, her only heir. She does not request anything outrageous."

"Will you allow it?" the crofter asked, appearing mostly unbothered by the news. "I do not trust her."

"You do not have to trust her," Agir said, raking a hand across his brow. "The trial is under our control, not hers. She may not like how things turn out, but it will go the way it will go. I will allow the request. I have to, otherwise we risk not only great insult, but looking like we have something to hide, which we do not."

"But, Sire," Jess blurted, struggling for words. It was painfully obvious to her that the Silverfae should not be involved. She felt stunned that she had to explain why, and it seemed impossible to convey her adamance about it without exposing herself. "T-to put Silverfae among the jury and allow a Silverfae prosecutor… it will only muddle the trial. Do they even understand how Solanan trials are run?"

"Do *you*, Miss Fontana?" the crofter asked.

"In theory." Jess flushed, but gave Ian a look of rebellion all the same. She had, in fact, spent a few hours in the library, combing over legal textbooks in a desperate bid to understand what they were about to face. But it was dry reading, full of big words. Jess had to keep referring to a dictionary, but knowing the definitions of words only made things more complicated. Nevertheless, she was right about this, and her knowledge of legal proceedings had nothing to do with it. Involving Sylifke would be unfair to Sasha and Rialta.

"All Ivryndian trials are basically run the same way," King Agir told the room. "Including six Silverfae jurors does not mean stacking the deck against Sasha. Not remotely. If anything, it makes the trial more equitable. If it were a Solanan on trial, the prosecutor would be provided by us—a representative of the crown upon whose property the alleged crime took place. But a Silverfae prosecutor makes more sense because it is their kingdom that sustained the loss, not ours. They attempt to prosecute, while we provide a Solanan lawyer for Sasha's defense. And I wish to act as judge in this case, as is my right."

"Makes sense," murmured Ian, and Jess wanted to punch him.

"Besides, what reason could I give for denying such a fair request from a bereaved mother. Not only a mother, but a queen?" King Agir glowered. "I only wish Faraçek would behave in such a straightforward manner. We've all heard unflattering things about the Silverfall queen, but perhaps we should credit them to the wagging of tongues." He waved Sylifke's letter again for emphasis. "I will not deny her request. Neither will I deny her right to be present at trial."

Esha noticed Jess's stricken look, and said gently, "We must not forget that a life was ended."

Jess stared at the queen, who had only moments ago sounded like an ally, but who now sounded like she actually endorsed this lunacy.

"Sylifke's suffering must be very great." Esha shook her head in sympathy. "To have the right to attend the trial of her son's killer will give her closure, and may go some small way toward easing her grief."

Jess bristled. "It was self-defense, not murder."

"That remains to be proven in court," the king muttered, tossing the letter on the table. "Who can say what passes between a fauna fae and their familiar? It is wise to have dissenting views among the jury. We do not know Sasha and Rialta. Miss Sabran can furnish us with testimony from those who have known him since childhood. That is a good thing. It is proper, right, and makes good legal sense."

Jess opened her mouth to protest but was silenced by a hard look from Ian. She felt rooted to the spot by the horror and anxiety. Her heart felt as though it had slid several inches downward in her chest, and was hanging somewhere near her navel, like a sad bird with broken wings. The conversation in the room returned to the problem of Faraçek, but she barely heard anything that was being said.

Queen Sylifke. Here for Sasha's trial.

Beazle felt her mounting worry. He crawled out of her hair to snuggle against her neck, giving her a couple of licks. *He is innocent, Jess. Everyone knows it.*

At another warning look from the crofter, Jess realized she was wringing her hands like a fraught old woman. Not something a competent Fahyli was to do in the presence of the sovereigns. She forced herself to put her hands behind her back, entwining her fingers so tightly it hurt. She could manufacture an appearance of calm, enough to satisfy Ian, but no one could stop her and Beazle from conversing silently. Jess was grateful for that. What life must be like for those without a familiar. So lonely.

*Why must she involve herself?* Jess fumed. *Sasha doesn't like or trust his queen, and Rayven Sabran seemed to fear her. What if she messes with the trial? Plants evidence, or bribes witnesses, or something like that?*

Beazle rubbed his face along her neck. *We'll just have to make sure that she doesn't.*

*Times have grown treacherous, Beazle. Not only for Solana, but for us personally. We are no longer children. What started as an exciting adventure is feeling more dangerous by the day.*

*We are spies,* Beazle reminded her. *Danger is in the job description.*

Jess took a breath. Sasha's beautiful face rose up in her mind. How she missed him. How she longed to see him free, to hold him, to kiss him.

*Love has changed everything, Beaze. Love makes everything complicated, more… painful and frightening.*

Beazle did not know what to say to this, all he could do was press his warm body against her and remind her that he was present, and that he loved her too.

Jess struggled to bring her attention back to the debate taking place, as it sounded like some action had been decided upon while she'd been mired in her own thoughts.

"Crofter, you are to send representatives to all of our nobility," Agir was saying. "It is important to do this in person, not by letters. We must know how many of them have been, or will be, invited to Faraçek's coronation and how many of them plan to attend."

"And what they think of him," added the queen. "We must know their opinions."

"Yes," agreed the king. "We must know who is aware of his duplicity, and who plans to support him. Only then can we understand what kind of strength we might have access to beyond of our own forces. What of Isabey? Any change there?" He looked at Bradburn, then the crofter.

"None, Sire," said Bradburn shortly. "I fear we cannot rely upon her. Unsurprising of an unseelie female, of course."

"It is worse than that," Laec added. "She is considering changing her name and going south to seek citizenship and protection in foreign lands, where she intends to build a new life. Presumably, never to return."

The queen paled. "Ignore her heritage? Flee responsibility? This cannot be. A peasant has the right to do so, but not a princess!"

"It may just be the ramblings of a heartbroken young fae, Ma'am," said the crofter, "but in case she is serious, we should prepare ourselves to lose her."

"And along with her, our best player and chance to keep Faraçek from the throne. If she leaves, we will have no leverage, no power to remove Faraçek once he has been crowned."

"You had no luck with Princess Isabey?" the queen asked Laec. "I certainly had none."

"No, Ma'am." Laec looked uncomfortable. "Whatever affinity the princess had for me in Syrgana, it's no longer there. She blames me for allowing her sister to be killed." His expression turned bitter. "The worst part is, that had it happened in my own land, I *would* have been able to do something—magic that is not accessible to me here…"

"No one is interested in your excuses, Stavarjak," said the crofter.

"No," Laec murmured, looking at the floor.

*Let me do it,* Beazle told Jess.

Jess turned her attention to her familiar. *Do what?*

*See Isabey.*

*But what can you do, little love? You cannot speak.*

*She liked me.* Beazle added an audible squeak to his request. *Just ask!*

"Ma'am?" Jess put up a hand, her face flushing. "Beazle would like to try…"

Queen Esha cocked her head. "Try what, Miss Fontana?"

"Visiting Isabey."

Everyone looked confused except for Laec, who perked up. "Why didn't I think of that?"

"Time is ticking," muttered Agir. "What's this about?"

"Isabey likes Beazle," Laec told the king. "If he wishes to visit her, let him try. There is no reason not to. In the meanwhile, I'll write to Queen Elphame. See if she has advice."

Agir waved a hand, grumbling, "Fine, fine. All of that is fine."

Ian shrugged. No one looked as hopeful as Laec, but at least Beazle had got what he wanted.

*There you go,* Jess told him. *Permission granted.*

Beazle didn't reply but she could feel pleasure radiating from him.

The meeting was adjourned and Jess left the lion's den. Her brain felt like it was filled with miles of knotted rope.

## Chapter Fourteen

# Jessamine

Jess squeezed herself into the narrow passage behind a wall of Isabey's suite, grimacing at the dirt and dust. At least there was fresh air. The secret throughways around these rooms allowed only the smallest of spies. Narrow slits between the outer stones let in mote-laden shafts of moonlight, but the stones were cold and the air coming in, icy. Jess squinted, watching Beazle crawl from crack to crevice, sniffing and exploring. He found something tasty and snatched it up.

Ahead, the corridor widened enough that she no longer had to slide through sideways. Jess shivered and pulled her collar up around her ears. They passed one of the half-finished maps and found a small square opening with a stone where Jess could perch. She brushed away the dust and did her best to get comfortable, leaning her head back against the wall and closing her eyes, tuning in to her familiar.

Beazle could smell Isabey, that warm spicy scent that he'd

grown fond of during that short time he'd spent in her palm back in the swamp. Squeezing through narrow fissures that looked too tiny even for him, he fashioned a crooked path, past crumbling mortar and pebbles of plaster, to emerge on the other side: the interior of Isabey's apartment.

Incense drifted lazily through the air from a stand near an open door. Beazle had entered near the head of a large four-poster bed, perfectly dressed and over-draped with gauzy fabric. The room was chilly, even though a fire crackled in the grate. Isabey had folded herself upon a divan near an open window, and sat with her elbows on her knees, her chin in her hands, her face pressed into the night breeze. She wore only a pale nightdress with long sleeves and elaborate frilly cuffs, but it was open at the throat and so thin that her silhouette could be seen through it—not suitable to withstand the frigid breeze. Isabey had either an incredible natural store of body heat, or she was so lost in thought that she couldn't feel the cold. Given the circumstances of the princess's life, Jess didn't doubt the latter.

Beazle landed on the top of the window frame and sent Jess a better look at the princess, whose eyes were closed and cheeks were wet with tears. Her lashes lay in damp spikes against her pale gray skin. She sniffed and finally moved, palming away her tears. Beazle crawled down and dangled upside down inside the window frame. When she still didn't open her eyes, he squeaked.

She started then looked up, spotting the bat as she straightened.

"Beazle," she said quietly. "Hello. You shouldn't be here."

He squeaked again then fluttered out the open window and off into the night.

Isabey sucked in a breath. Before he got too far, she cried out: "Wait! Don't go!"

Jess smiled, feeling Beazle's heart lift. It was the reaction he'd been hoping for. He returned, landing in Isabey's upheld hand. He wrapped his limbs around her thumb in his customary fashion. She pulled him close to her heart, stroking the top of his head with a gentle fingertip, from the nape of his neck to his stub of a tail.

"I'm sorry. I really am glad you came," she told him. "It's easier to be with you than it is to see a… person, and nice to see someone who doesn't want anything from me."

He licked the pad of her thumb and peered up into her face with those soulful, ink drop eyes, projecting all the compassion he was able to—and a considerable amount of empathy. Jess often wondered if others saw what she did when she looked at Beazle, or if they just saw an ordinary, excessively tiny, flying mouse.

*I'm safe to talk to princess,* Beazle thought at Isabey, though he knew she couldn't hear him. The next thought he directed at Jessamine. *I know she can't understand me, but I want her to feel…*

*Safe. I know,* Jess sent with a smile. *I'm not judging.*

For a long time, Isabey just stroked Beazle while gazing out the window. She wore her grief like a gown. It pulled at her shoulders and made her beautiful fae features obviously melancholic. Her oversized eyes were so full of grief that—even through Beazle's poor vision—Jess thought she looked like a painting, a caricature of sadness.

"I can't do what they want me to do, little one," Isabey whispered, after several long moments. "I know they want me to rally, to confront my brother, to be bold. I don't have it in me. My heart is not just broken, it's shattered, as withered as Toryan's breast. I feel like a dead woman rotting in a grave, experiencing every bit of putrefaction as it takes over my body."

Jess blinked at this horrific description.

Beazle let his eyes droop closed as her thumb caressed his fur—shutting out Jess's view of the princess as well—but his mind was alert and he sent everything he heard with all of his telepathic might. For Jess, it was as though Isabey was speaking right next to her. She could hear the princess breathing softly, the heaviness in her voice, the depths of her sadness.

"Ander was such a wonderful brother," she told Beazle, although there was a sense that she was now speaking more to herself. "He was never anything but kind to me. He was so handsome and so brave. He knew it too. He had a smile for everyone. I suspect he made a game of smiling at women, just to see them melt. He would have made a wonderful king. Ander was the first person I ever lost that I was close to. I never knew loss could be so… so crippling. Grief comes in waves, you know. One moment you think you're okay, you'll survive this. Then, when you least expect it, a wave crashes over you, pulls you under. I wasn't recovered from Ander's death, if full recovery is even possible, and suddenly, we were running away." Isabey's voice took on a lulling quality, a wonderment as she relived her recent past. "Hiding like fugitives from our own people, our own soldiers. I think… maybe that was our mistake. I didn't want to run, but Serya and Shade, they said it was for the best. 'Because that rock that almost killed Serya in the garden, it will be something else next time—and next time, it won't miss.'" She mimicked Shade. "Maybe it would be poison in her food, or a shove down the stairs from invisible hands."

Isabey fell silent, stroking Beazle. She had to be freezing.

Beazle could feel the chill in her fingers, but she seemed not to mind.

"Then my father. I didn't get to say a proper goodbye to him."

Beazle opened his eyes and the view of Isabey swam into Jessamine's mind. Isabey didn't notice Beazle's loving expression. Her frozen stare was fixed out at the night. Her breath drifted out the window in puffs.

"I knew he was dying, we all did, but… I thought fate would never take him while we were gone, trying to figure out how to come back. But fate was that cruel, and he was gone too. And then Serya…" Isabey's face crumpled, fresh tears streamed from her eyes. "She did not deserve that. I cannot believe that Faraçek…" She sniffed and wiped her nose. "Do you know, he was a good brother to us too? Just as good as Ander. Oh, we knew he had darkness in him, we knew he had power. We knew. He's unseelie after all, but, so am I. So am I. I have Daryli's blood in me, I have my mother's unseelie nature, but I would never…" she shuddered, and wept again, great heaving sobs.

Beazle gave a low chitter of sadness.

*This is killing me,* Jess thought, wiping away her own tears. *The poor woman.*

"I would never," Isabey hissed, sounding angry now, "kill my own. Not for any reason. He's so much worse than we knew or understood. I wish he *had* killed me. I wish I had not been rescued. It would be easier to be dead. I would not have this sorrow, eating through my insides. No one even knows the worst part of it, the hardest part. Not a soul knows."

Isabey wept for a while, before choking down her sobs.

"Shade," she whispered. "He was my everything. My heart, my soul, my forever-love."

Jess's eyes flew open with surprise at the princess's confession. She pressed her hands over her eyes and, with effort, pulled Beazle's vision back into her mind.

*Shade.* Beazle recalled the handsome young man with the dark golden hair. *The Rahamlar soldier? The human?*

*Yes,* Jessamine confirmed. *The one that told Çifta to leave Rahamlar. No one found his body.*

*I remember.*

"He and I, we… we fell in love. More than five years ago now, and we kept it a secret all this time. Now he's gone too… and I don't even know how he died… and I can tell no one." Isabey's words came out between sobs. "It's too much. I could live without Serya, I will always miss my sister, but I could go on without her. But Shade… how do I go on without him?"

Tears leaked from beneath Jessamine's lids as she heard the desolation of the princess's heart. Unable to stop herself, she conjured up something of what she would feel if she lost Sasha. It was unbearable. For five years, Isabey and Shade had hidden their love. Jessamine and Sasha had only known each other for a few weeks, but already Jess couldn't picture life without him. Isabey had suffered loss after loss after loss, like great peals of thunder that wouldn't quit crashing over the skies of her life.

*Poor princess,* Beazle thought. His fur was damp from the tears dripping from her chin.

Isabey's weeping went on for some time. When she drew in shuddery breaths that signaled an end to her sobbing, Beazle crawled up her arm to her shoulder, then to her collarbone, where he cuddled against her, hugging her in the only way he could. He let out a long, low whistle. The sound was so plaintive and empathetic that Isabey smiled, wiping at her nose again.

"You are so sweet. Now you know why I can't tell anyone

the depths of my devastation. Royals have to follow many stupid rules. We're not allowed to be with whoever we want. I'm supposed to marry someone noble, ideally from Archelia or Tryske. The further away the better, so that Rahamlar has allies far and wide. It doesn't matter what a princess wants. If my father, or even my brothers, had found out about Shade and me, they would have banished him. I would never have seen him again, but at least I would have known that he was alive."

The wind picked up and Beazle pressed closer to Isabey's neck. He was cold now; his damp fur might gather ice soon.

*She's going to catch her death if she sits there like that any longer,* Jess thought. *And so might you.*

*Maybe that's what she wants,* Beazle returned.

*Fair enough,* Jess admitted. Perhaps she wouldn't mind freezing to death either, if she lost Sasha.

There was a mental start from Beazle as he read this thought, followed by a wave of sadness. He didn't fully form the question *I'm not enough?* but Jess sensed it.

She rushed to make sure he understood. *I'd want to die if I lost you, Beazle. You are part of me, my heart, my blood. Sasha… he means a future for us, a future with a larger family.*

The bat shivered as the wind lifted his fur and got to the tender skin underneath.

*I won't thank her for letting my bat catch a cold, though,* Jess thought grumpily.

Beazle shuddered in an exaggerated fashion. For good measure, he added the clacking of his teeth. Chattering teeth was not something that bats did, it was a human and fae characteristic, but he hoped Isabey would pick up on its meaning.

"I'm sorry, little one." Isabey tugged the window shut. "Come let me warm you by the fire."

Isabey sat in a rocking chair in front of the fireplace and stroked Beazle until her head fell back against the wood and her eyes drifted shut. Once the princess was fully asleep, Beazle flew to the crack in the wall. Both Beazle and Jess were quiet as they left the secret passageway and took the corridor leading to their rooms. Beazle was thinking about Shade, wondering what had happened to him, and Jess was thinking about Sasha, knowing what had happened but not what was to come.

*I think you made her feel a bit better*, Jess thought, *but it's not like she's ready to strap on a sword and take on her brother.*

*No,* Beazle agreed. *If anything, I can see why she wants to flee.*

*I guess we keep her secret? We just tell them that we also failed?*

Beazle was quiet, noncommittal. Jess could sense that he did not know the right path. And Jess also felt too tired and cold to decide what to do with what they'd learned.

*Let's think about it*, her bat sent, crouching against her neck, still cold.

Jess nodded as she opened the door to their suite and fell into her room.

## Chapter Fifteen

# Laec

Laec sat cross-legged on the floor, stripped to the waist and leaning against Çifta's pillar of ice, a half-full glass of moireberry wine in his hand. After the meeting in the lion's den, Laec had written to Elphame with the latest news and sent it with Mistik, who'd been waiting for his report since the day his queen had warned him not to use fire to melt Çifta. That done, Laec bolted some food and went to the ballroom, which he was beginning to think of as Çifta's tomb.

The room drifted lazily back and forth in his vision. He barely felt the sting of the ice against his back. He took another sip, tilting his chin up and up to look at the block of ice behind him. He had worn one side of the block smooth with his body heat, but Çifta seemed no closer to the open air than she had been when he'd first begun. He let out a long sigh and looked down at his topless torso. His skin was marbled with red and white. Slowly, he lay himself down on his side, pushing the glass away. He was sober enough to care about not accidentally spilling the wine and staining the parquet.

Letting his eyes drift shut, he thought it wouldn't be so bad to fall asleep here, to stay all night. A whistle of flapping wings pried his eyes open. Mistik squawked as she landed beside his head, sharp talons scraping against the hardwood. She ruffled her wings and closed them.

"Already?" Laec murmured, hope rising in his chest. "That was quick, she must have sent you with magic. This is bound to be good."

Pushing himself upright, he put his hand under the bird. Obediently, Mistik stepped onto his wrist. He took the little tube from the crow's ankle and the bird hopped onto the floor, bounced once and then took flight, circling the room before landing in the rafters. Laec unrolled the parchment, blinked blearily at it, then rubbed his eyes. The room was dim and his vision was not at its best.

Squinting at the message, he read the two lines, then blew a raspberry and collapsed back on the floor, letting the letter tumble out of his hands.

"How very obvious and uninspired," he murmured to the absent Elphame, thankful that the crow could not repeat his words back to her. His eyes drifted shut and, for half an hour, his snores echoed around the room. He jerked awake when Mistik croaked.

Feeling a less dizzy, Laec got to his feet and grabbed the scroll, taking it with him to his room. He checked the time, blinking owlishly at the clock hanging over the small fireplace. It was not yet midnight. There was a good chance the sovereigns were awake.

Grabbing clean clothes, he went to the communal wash-room and bathed in steaming hot water. He cleaned his teeth and got rid of any telltale sign of wine on his lips. Then he dressed in the best clothes he had, combed and tied back his damp hair. Making sure the scroll was in his chest pocket, he headed for Esha's parlor.

He found the room locked and unguarded. At this hour, if the queen wasn't in her parlor, she had either gone to bed or was in the banquet hall talking with courtiers. Hoping for the latter, Laec hurried to the courtiers' dining hall. The double doors were open and the smell of food struck Laec square in the face as he entered. Most of the food had been taken away, but a few courtiers sat nibbling desserts and sipping wine. Some looked up when Laec entered, acknowledging him. One of the local spice merchants beckoned him over, but Laec just waved and headed for the dais, where Esha and Agir were chatting with Lady Lecta. The three of them looked sober and spoke quietly.

He bowed before them. "Sire, Ma'am. Seeking a word."

"Nice to see you Mr. Fairijak," said Lady Lecta. "I'm sorry I can't stay and chat, these old bones grow weary. I'll take this opportunity to excuse myself." With a shallow curtsy, she floated away.

Esha gestured that Laec should take a seat near her. King Agir nabbed a grape from a platter and offered some to Laec, who took a few before sitting down.

"I've received a letter from Elphame," he told them, handing the scroll to Esha.

The queen held it open and read aloud: "My best advice to my dear cousin is to keep the northern queen in her own lands. We have shared a border for over forty years, and in that time, she has done little of which I approve."

"Keep Sylifke in her own lands?" said the king, raising his brows. "Why?"

Laec swallowed the grape he'd been chewing, feeling like he had to apologize. "Elphame is accustomed to being obeyed without questions. She believes that Sylifke cannot be trusted."

"That's it?" Agir spluttered. He looked at Esha. "No offense to your cousin, my dear, I know you respect her, but I do not know Elphame, and I am not one to venerate based on reputation alone. If she cannot give us a good reason, something more concrete than personal opinion, I'll change nothing. Besides, I have already sent my reply with permission to come."

Queen Esha's voice was soothing. "Darling, you know that my cousin had a premonition about our kingdom. What if Queen Sylifke has something to do with the danger she foresaw?"

King Agir wagged a finger. "No. No. That is not right. Elphame had a premonition, yes, but she was not clear whether it was about you, someone in your care, or about our kingdom." He spread his hands wide. "What kind of warning is that? It is too vague. If I were to give it as much credence as you do, I would be fearful to get out of bed in the morning. Queen Sylifke's only son was killed on our doorstep. It is not right to deny her, and I won't do it."

Esha shot Laec a look that said, *help me!* For all that Esha could steer matters by gently pressing on her husband, who obviously loved her, there were times when Agir dug his heels in.

"Sire," Laec rolled the grapes in his palm. "I apologize for the vagueness of my queen's note of warning. However, the speed with which she answered indicates her level of concern. Most of the premonitions she receives are indistinct, but they always manifest. Elphame is accustomed to her word being sacrosanct, and she also sees Queen Esha as more than a distant relative. She wants the best for Solana. May I suggest that offending Sylifke might be a more prudent course of action than allowing her to come here? Here, she will see where Ruskin died. Solana will be fixed in her mind as a terrible place, perhaps even an enemy kingdom, especially if the trial does not have the outcome she desires. Keeping distance between you may be better both for her and for you."

Agir began shaking his head before Laec finished, a sour look on his face. "I disagree. Thank you for your advice, Laec, and I *am* grateful to your queen for her interest in our well-being, but I cannot stomach sending an emissary to tell Sylifke that I've revoked my permission. The very thought is distasteful. Inviting Sylifke here will not only help her to heal, it gives us an opportunity to show her how sad and sorry we are that her son died. She will hear witnesses at the trial who will report truthfully that no Solanan citizen had anything to do with Ruskin's death. We are beyond reproach. The more I think about it, the better an idea I think it is. Silverfall and Solana have an opportunity to make peace. If she never came, that peace and goodwill could never be built."

"And the lad? Sasha?" Esha put a hand on his forearm. "What of him?"

"What *of* him?" Agir looked from Laec to his queen, shrugging. "I will be the judge, and will ensure the jury listens to all the testimony. I will do all that I can to ensure that his trial is fair." He narrowed his eyes. "I might take this opportunity to remind both of you that the Silverfae petitioned to take Sasha and Rialta home with them—to face execution. I prevented that, and gave them safe haven. I have done more than enough for them. Do you not think?"

"But do you not worry that Sylifke may try to influence

her jurors? Or protest the outcome if it does not go her way?" Esha responded, her brows tight with worry.

Agir scoffed. "So what if she does? What will she do? Make it snow in the courtroom? She is not like Elphame, who can make people hear and see things that are not there, or utter words that are not their own. Honestly, you two are so afraid of the winter queen, you embarrass yourselves." King Agir gave Laec a hard look. "I think you should tell Elphame, politely and respectfully, that if she cannot give a rationale for her recommendations, then we do not want them at all."

"Agir!" Esha's eyes flew wide with scandal.

"I mean it. I tire of obscure warnings and fuzzy notions of danger. It is very annoying. I also have a headache and wish to go to bed. We have enough to deal with without Elphame poking her nose in where it is neither wanted, nor needed." King Agir stood and stretched his back with an audible crackle. "Good night, Laec. Good night, my darling. I shall see you in the morning."

The king stalked away, shoulders straight and chin up, the posture of a man who feels he's done a good day's work and can sleep peacefully.

Esha, still staring at the door through which her husband disappeared, said, "Please do not repeat any of that to my cousin."

Laec smiled. "I wouldn't dream of it, Ma'am."

"Laec!" Kite's voice boomed from the doorway.

He drew away from the ice to squint at the backlit figure striding toward him. Kite stopped a few feet away, looking both appalled and mystified by the state she'd discovered him in. "What are you doing?"

Laec tried to smile but his teeth chattered as he picked his tunic up from the floor and pulled it over his head.

Kite's gaze flicked from Laec to Çifta's pillar and back again. It dawned on her, but she looked hesitant to believe her eyes. "You're trying to thaw her out with your body heat?"

In answer, he jerked the leather thongs at his neck to close his shirt. "I can't use fire," Laec grumbled, uncomfortable under Kite's direct gaze. "Someone has to do *something*."

"You crazy Stavarjakian," she said, but not without respect. "I hope I find a man who loves me that much, but it doesn't look like you're making much of a difference."

Laec studied the ice objectively. He'd been at this for three weeks now, and three sides of the block had been worn smooth, the top layer as clear as glass, the corners rounded. But at this rate, reaching Çifta would require months—and by then, he might lose a body part to frostbite. He sighed, dejected, turning to Kite.

"What do you want? You were yelling like the palace was falling down a second ago."

Apprehension stole over her handsome features. "It's Kazery. Erasmus and Ratchet were hunting and spotted him on the king's road. He's almost here. I thought you'd want to know there's a meeting in the maproom."

A prickle of unease swept through Laec, a sensation that had nothing to do with freezing himself against magical ice. How would Kazery react when he learned what had happened to his daughter?

On the way to the west keep, Kite explained that the crofter was preparing a party to meet the merchant. Soldiers would escort Kazery to the lion's den directly, and they were not to tell him why, yet to make him feel as relaxed and unalarmed as possible.

It sounded like a fool's errand. Kazery would know something was wrong. The last time he'd been here, Agir hadn't requested any audience with him. He spoke to Çifta and left, without the majority of palace residents even knowing he'd been there. Now, he was to be escorted directly to a meeting with the king? Of course it would set off alarm bells.

"I don't understand why they're doing it that way," Laec replied as they navigated the busy corridors. "If they don't want Kazery to be alarmed, they should let him come alone, like nothing is amiss. Then, when he inquires as to the whereabouts of his daughter, invite him to visit Agir."

Kite agreed with him, but explained that Bradburn and the crofter had a different concern. "They don't want to chance him running into someone who will spill things tactlessly. If they control who he talks to along the way, kind of insulate him, then he won't be shocked by some weird version—though I think the reality is worse than any exaggeration could be."

"Have they decided what they *are* going to tell him, exactly? They can't keep him from seeing her. Although at least she's no longer the first thing he would see in the courtyard."

"The truth, of course, but the king wants to do it. Agir told Ian that he won't have anyone else deliver such a devastating message. It has to come from the sovereign. He wants Kazery to know that everyone in the kingdom knows about Çifta, and everyone cares. He wants witnesses to her freezing present. That's why I came to get you, I thought you'd want to be there too."

Laec nodded his thanks to Kite as they fell in step behind

Digit, Regalis and Jessamine, all heading to the maproom. Jessamine looked over her shoulder. Her hair had been curled into spirals and was tucked behind one pointed ear. A creamy pearl earring winked out. She looked so delicate wearing a Calyx dress, a long-sleeved cream gown with a cowl neck, utterly unthreatening.

The Fahyli filed into the maproom—all the Fahyli that Laec had met and many he hadn't. Some had familiars with them, others had come alone. Outside the door lay a small doe, chewing her cud. Just inside, perched atop of a fat candlestick sat a fluffy white fox, its thick tail spiraling around its feet. Bodies pressed in, fae and mammal. Ferrugin flapped to the rafters, landing beside Erasmus, who was scratching his cheek with a talon. There was a crow, two owls, and a kestrel up there too. Something furry slipped through Laec's ankles. He looked down to see a squirrel disappear under the table, only to pop up on top a second later. Scampering across the table, he leapt to Regalis's shoulder and used him as a springboard to reach another fae. Tully disappeared under the table, Laec heard her let out an exhale as she lay down. Panther moved through the crowd until he reached Ian's elbow.

Jessamine pushed her way to the table at the center of the room, and Laec pressed in beside her. With Regalis on her other side, she looked like a baby sister between two protective big brothers. Her gray eyes were glued to Ian, who leaned his knuckles on the table as the room filled. Digit squeezed in on Laec's other side, Ania hovering in the air next to his head.

"You were there?" Laec asked Digit.

After he'd come out of the stables and discovered Çifta frozen solid, Laec had failed to notice much else—at least not until he looked up to see blood pooling in the courtyard and a dead body beneath a hulking white wolf.

"I didn't see much." Digit nodded as Ania alighted on his shoulder. Her feet disappeared beneath her, and she looked like she was sitting on tiny eggs. "There were a lot of bodies in front of me."

The crofter pounded his fist on the table and the room grew quiet. "Lady Çifta's father, Kazery Unya, is expected to arrive within the hour. He does not yet know what has befallen his daughter, and we want to break the news in the most sensitive way possible. A party of soldiers is on their way to greet him and escort him in. He'll be informed that the king has requested his presence."

"He'll ask about his daughter," Laec said.

"Yes." Ian's dark gaze swept the room. "And the soldiers will withhold all information, impressing upon Kazery that he must see the king. He'll be escorted to the lion's den, where a small party of witnesses will be waiting. No one is to speak unless called upon. You are to remain calm, but be prepared to answer questions if asked, and possibly to restrain him if Kazery reacts badly. I need three volunteer witnesses, please."

Jessamine's arm shot straight up, along with a dozen others. Laec's hand drifted skyward.

Ian quickly counted hands. "Anyone who did not have a clear view, put down your hand."

Half the volunteers eliminated themselves.

"Regalis." The crofter nodded toward the tall, long-haired Fahyli. "Thank you."

Laec could feel tension pouring off Jessamine's body as she held her hand high. She was bouncing on her toes in an effort to be seen. Jess was tall for a Calyx, but most of the Fahyli were taller and more imposing. The crofter's gaze skimmed over her.

"Kite? Where were you?"

Kite slid out from behind Panther. "I was with Regalis, Crofter. I had a clear view, but Jessamine was there as well. She was standing closer to Çifta than either of us. She should go, if you don't mind the suggestion."

Ian looked for, then found Jessamine. "Okay. So, Jess, Regalis. One more..."

"I'm not Fahyli, but I was there," Laec said, deciding in the moment that this was too important to miss, though he was nervous about it.

Ian's gaze sharpened on him. "Do you know Kazery?"

"Yes," Laec lied, responding on gut instinct and the intense desire to be included. He immediately kicked himself, but he couldn't take it back without wrecking what little faith the crofter might have in him. Besides, he had to be in that room. No matter what.

Ian nodded. "That'll do. The rest of you, thank you. You're dismissed."

Except for the chosen volunteers, the Fahyli filed out in a tight parade of fae, feathers, and fur. Laec saw Jessamine shoot Kite a grateful look. Kite winked at her. Shortly, the room was empty save for Ian, Regalis, Jessamine and Laec.

The crofter's voice softened now that he was addressing a smaller crowd. "I don't know what to expect, but for sure, Kazery will be heartbroken. At worst, he'll be openly hostile, perhaps accusing King Agir and Solana of putting his daughter in danger, or of neglecting her." He looked at Laec. "Any thoughts?"

Laec opened his mouth but hesitated. The story Çifta had

told him of Kazery's violent and piratical past surged to the foreground. If he relayed all that, Ian would not be encouraged. "Kazery can be unpredictable," he said, choosing his words carefully. "But he won't thank us for sugar-glazing the truth, or the odds of his daughter surviving the ice. And I'm sure he'll want to see her as soon as possible. Other than that… it's anyone's guess."

Ian gestured to the door. "Right, if there's nothing else, let's go. Jess, change into your Fahyli leathers before you join us. It'll be best to be seen in that role."

Jessamine mumbled, "Yes, sir," as she ducked out the door, skirts swishing.

"I'll go with her," Laec said. Without waiting for permission, he caught up to Jess and touched her elbow. "You okay, kid?"

Jessamine nodded, her brow pinched.

"I just don't want Kazery to be angry with Sasha. That's what I'm most afraid of. What if he thinks Sasha didn't have to freeze her? What if he gets involved with the trial? Leans his weight on it somehow, makes sure Sasha and Rialta are found guilty?"

Laec almost stopped walking he was so surprised. It had never occurred to him that Kazery might react that way. Upset, yes. Vindictive? It didn't make sense.

"That's a big leap, Jess," Laec told her. "Try not to imagine the worst. Before you know it, you'll be skipping meals and staring at the ceiling at night."

"Too late," she scoffed as they took the steps up to the east keep.

## Chapter Sixteen

# Jessamine

The lion's den had never been so quiet, even when she had been alone with the king and crofter. The doors were pushed open by Bradburn's soldiers, then they stood aside to let Kazery in.

He wore a red and black uniform with brass buttons running up the breast, his hat was pinched against his body under one elbow. Jess's first thought was: *he's a bear!* But her next reaction was a pang of sympathy. He had a bushy black beard and the stature of a barbarian, but there was obvious kindness in his eyes.

Two men and one woman—experienced ship's captains, with weathered faces and impeccable uniforms—entered behind Kazery. Following them were four more professionals, less decorated than the first three.

Solemnly, Kazery bowed to Agir, moving gracefully for such a large man. His party followed suit. He took the time to look around the room and acknowledge everyone present. Even Jessamine, the smallest person there, felt seen by the merchant as he made eye contact with her. Finally he returned his dark gaze to the king.

His voice was deep and resonant, a voice meant for storytelling. "King Agir, I am flattered by such attention." He inclined his head respectfully, and his words were somehow both bold and reverential. "Quite a welcome party, I must say. I do appreciate transparency, and would be guilty of opacity myself if I did not admit to a level of anxiety at this invitation. Forgive me, it is truly a pleasure to meet you all, but I am most anxious to see my daughter. May I know what this is concerning, or how I may be of service?"

King Agir rose from the stone bench. He strode forward with a hand out. "Good Captain Unya. Well come."

Soldiers exchanged uneasy looks. The king rarely left his seat during a formal audience, and never had he directly approached or touched a guest.

"Well found." Kazery put his hand out and the two clasped forearms in the way of military comrades.

Agir looked up into Kazery's eyes, not quite smiling as he released his grip. "You are most welcome to my court. I am sorry for the apparent secrecy. The news I must share is sensitive, and of a private nature. Consider who you would like to have in the room with you, Captain, for this does indeed concern your daughter."

The look in Kazery's eyes changed as a father's fear entered. Jess guessed there was nothing that could make Kazery afraid but danger to his kin. Kazery made a gesture and his entourage left the room. At a glance from Agir, Bradburn ushered out the human soldiers, leaving the crofter and the Fahyli present.

Agir gestured that Kazery should take a seat at the table under the window.

Kazery settled into one of the wooden chairs, making it creak. "Sire," said Kazery as Agir took a seat across from him. "Do not delay for another moment."

Agir wiped a hand across his mouth as he sat down, then took a second to settle himself. Jess wondered if he was rethinking his words.

"We had an unfortunate incident, on the last day of our Midwinter Festival, that involved your daughter."

All the stillness of a painted ceramic came over the merchant. His gaze remained locked on the king.

"A party from Silverfall had attended the festival, including Prince Ruskin. On the day they were to depart, Ruskin spied your daughter in the crowd. He appeared to recognize her as an enemy, drew his sword and pursued her—in the open courtyard, in front of many eyewitnesses. I'm told it was very clear that he intended to end her life."

Agir paused, giving Kazery a chance to react. Kazery said and did nothing, neither did he remove his gaze from Agir's face. It was difficult even to see him breathing. Jess's heartbeat thundered in her ears. This reaction, this nothingness was somehow worse than if Kazery had cried out or thundered a fist on the table.

Agir went on, exhibiting some nervousness at the unblinking gaze of the merchant. "A Silverfae noble, a fauna fae named Sasha, was nearby, and—believing he knew your daughter's heritage—took steps to save Çifta in the only way he could. He… froze her with winter magic. She is currently trapped inside a block of ice."

The room went silent again, everyone holding a collective

breath, waiting for Kazery's reaction. The merchant stared at Agir's face for a long time. When he lifted a hand, Agir winced. It was a tiny pinching of one eye, but Jess noticed it. She was sure everyone else had too. Agir was afraid of the merchant.

"So," Kazery growled, "she is alive."

Agir blinked and took a second to process that the merchant was still sitting before him, calm and self-possessed.

"Yes, from what we understand, she is alive. We are only passingly acquainted with Silverfae rituals, but we understand that there is a chance that she may… not survive the ice?" The king cocked an eyebrow. Now it was Agir hoping for information from Kazery.

Jess felt Laec stiffen beside her.

Kazery ran a hand over his inky black beard, stroking it thoughtfully. He didn't appear to have heard the king's question, and his gaze was unfocused. Inward. "I wondered when they would find her."

These words impacted everyone in the room. Jess and Laec exchanged a wide-eyed look. Regalis and the crofter both gasped softly. Agir's jaw sagged before he remembered himself and shut his mouth.

The king cleared his throat, looking as out of his element now as a fish on horseback. "It was not a case of mistaken identity, then? We have been laboring under that assumption because all of the Silverfall citizens were just as shocked as we were. None of them could explain Ruskin's behavior. They told us Ruskin had made a terrible mistake."

Kazery shook his big head. "No mistake. I do not know much, but I do know this: my daughter is the one that Ruskin was seeking. I have never fully understood the pursuit of my daughter by the northern kingdom—and after all these years I thought they had given up. I was wrong." His dark eyes sharpened on the king. "But this Sasha, you questioned him. What does he say?"

Agir shook his head. "Sasha was injured and lost consciousness before we could question him at the time. Since then he has been incarcerated awaiting trial, over which I will preside, and I must obey our laws and have no contact with him."

Kazery's brows shot up. "He faces trial? Surely not for saving my daughter? Ruskin would have killed her without Sasha's quick thinking. That is certain."

Jess closed her eyes, letting relief wash over her. Kazery would not blame Sasha. If anything, he was on Sasha's side. Weakness rushed into her legs, dissolving her bones. She wished she could collapse into a chair.

"Not for Lady Çifta's freezing, no," King Agir told Kazery in a rush of words. "After Sasha froze your daughter, Ruskin attacked him, and Sasha's familiar, a dire wolf, stepped in and ended the prince's life."

Kazery's expression was grave. "Prince Ruskin is dead, then?"

Agir nodded.

The merchant paled, and his voice went quiet. "What of the Silverfae citizens? What of Queen Sylifke?"

"They will attend the trial," the king told him. "Our scouts have seen a small group traveling this way, Queen Sylifke among them. They are yet north of Kittrell."

Kazery grunted and stroked his beard before looking up again. "First, I must see my daughter, then I must speak with Sasha. You are the king, you can make an exception."

Agir hesitated for a moment. "The guards are instructed to let no one inside without written permission, but I will accompany you to the door of his quarters myself. That way you won't be delayed. I'm sorry I can't go inside with you, as it could be considered prejudicial."

Kazery nodded. "Understandable, and thank you. With your permission, I will stay in Solana until my daughter melts. I can rent a floor in a tav—"

King Agir waved a hand. "You will be given a suite in the palace, near your daughter. As many rooms as you need."

Kazery got to his feet. "Most appreciated. I will have assistants coming and going. My business cannot stop, even for such a drastic development within my family."

The king tented his fingers. "Whatever you need. Your assistants may come and go as required without being delayed at our borders. We—my servants and I—are at your service. We are as hopeful for a positive outcome for your daughter as you are. The Fahyli will escort you to see her. You can ask them anything you like, as they were present and will be able to give you a full picture of events. They are yours to question, until you dismiss them."

Kazery turned to the crofter and Fahyli. "Thank you. I am most eager to see her."

"Then let us not delay," Ian said gruffly, and the party moved for the door.

It took Jess a moment to realize that she was going with Kazery, first to see Çifta, then Sasha.

Kazery stood before the pillar that contained his daughter. Everyone else stood behind him, watching and waiting. Jess noted that three sides of the block, unlike the fourth, were glossy and nearly transparent, parts of the corners were worn down. Çifta's features were blurry, but her face and hair could be seen. She looked caught in time, her clothing billowing around her.

The merchant approached the sword wedged in the ice and ran his hands over the pommel, the grip and cross guard, before flicking his thumb over the bare bit of sharp steel. When his fingers touched the ice, he snatched his hand back. Kazery murmured under his breath, nothing that could be made out by those present.

Kazery faced the king. "Sasha?"

The king nodded.

Jess's mouth felt dry and she walked at the back of the group, just in case her feelings were showing on her face. Beazle had dozed during the entire conversation between Kazery and the king. He stirred again now, in response to Jessamine's eagerness.

*What's happened?* Beazle asked with a mental yawn. *You're all excited.*

*Kazery wants to talk to Sasha. We're going there now, with the king.*

*Oh. How nice for you.* Beazle changed positions against her skull and drifted away again.

The guards—the skinny one and another Jess had not met—leapt to their feet when they saw the group approaching, led by the king himself. The skinny one recognized Jess, giving her Fahyli leathers a once over with a clear look of astonishment. She gave him a smug *I-told-you-so* smile, and he looked away with a frown of embarrassment. At a sharp command from Agir, the other guard scrambled to open the door. Agir and Kazery grasped forearms once more, then Agir left.

The guard that Jess had not seen before led them inside,

strutting importantly and swinging the keys. When they reached Sasha's room, he rattled the bars.

"Oi, you awake in there, lad?"

Jess wanted to smack him upside the head for his patronizing tone.

"No," came Sasha's ironic reply, calm and unruffled. "I'm napping. Go away. Unless you have one of those pepper seed pastries, or a bowl of mashed potatoes with butter. Anything salty would be nice, frankly."

Sasha appeared at the door, peering out through the bars. His icy gaze froze on Jess, flicked to the crofter, then to Kazery. His eyes widened and he muttered something in the Silverfae tongue.

The guard hit the bars with a fist. "Step back. No one wants your opinions."

He opened the door, giving Sasha an unnecessary shove back.

"His opinions are precisely what I've come for," Kazery boomed, holding a meaty hand out to Sasha. "And the facts, of course. I'm Kazery Unya, Çifta's father."

Sasha's expression sobered. In slow-motion, he grasped Kazery's forearm. "I'm sorry we have not met under better circumstances, Mr. Unya."

"Call me Kazery." The big man pulled Sasha close, looking down by inches into Sasha's eyes. "You saved my daughter from certain death. I am forever indebted."

The guard had enough shame to cast his eyes down, his cheeks flushed red.

"I did not know what else to do," Sasha told Kazery. "That's the truth of it. I couldn't see her cleaved in two. At least in the ice, she stands a chance. I hope she survives."

Kazery sounded confident as he shook Sasha's forearm. "She will. She *must* survive."

Kazery released Sasha and moved into the room, the rest of the party followed, coming in to lean, perch or sit on whatever broken down furniture was strong enough to hold them. Sasha sat on the pallet. Jess, Laec and Regalis leaned against the big desk. After a cursory glance outside, the crofter stood below a window, observing everything with distant eyes. Kazery tested a chair, gingerly lowering himself onto it. When it took his weight, he relaxed, folding his hands in his lap.

Jess forced herself to emulate normal behavior, mimicking Regalis, who looked completely relaxed. She felt like everyone in the room knew that she and Sasha were in love, like it was etched on her forehead in big bold letters. Her heart throbbed when she looked at him, like a swollen, aching bruise inside her chest.

"Obviously, Çifta's mother was Silverfae, as I'm sure you guessed," Kazery said. "And Prince Ruskin's was not the first attempt on her life."

"She never said," blurted Laec, before snapping his mouth shut. He rubbed a hand over his lips, looking chagrined.

Kazery studied Laec. "You are friends with my daughter?"

"Yes," Laec said. "I'm just surprised. She never said anything about anyone trying to kill her, Silverfae or otherwise."

Kazery assessed Laec a moment before answering. "She doesn't remember it because she was a child. Some days, *I* barely remember it, and sometimes think that I must have dreamed it. I was not there when it happened. Çifta was with her mother."

Kazery's eyes went unfocused, dreamlike. "We met at a northern outpost. It has a name now, Ortaka, but back then it didn't. It's a deep-water harbor where merchant ships ready themselves to cross the Ivryndian Sea. We met not long after my wife, Alana, passed away, leaving me with three daughters. Evelin was young and suspicious of everyone, including me. She never told me what she was running from, but I knew she needed help. I let her stay in a house I owned and we grew close. She wanted me to take her across the Ivryndian Sea, but that winter was long and the break-up did not happen until late spring. In the meantime, Evelin became pregnant. One hesitates to take a female who has never sailed before across any sea, and one definitely does not take a pregnant one. So Evelin remained at the outpost and birthed the babe, who I met when I returned the following winter." Kazery smiled. "Çifta was a beautiful faeling babe, with my hair and those incredible eyes of her mother. She had fae ears too, but as you'll know, she appears not to have those now. It is a spell, nothing more. One done for her protection." Kazery's gaze sharpened on Sasha. "Protection from your kind. I should have guessed that your people were the source of the danger before, but"—he shrugged his huge round shoulders—"my mind is full of my work. If that makes me stupid about other things, then that is my own failing."

Sasha's mouth pressed into a thin line. "I'd be executed on the spot for admitting it, but you are right, the spell would have hidden her ears to protect her from Sylifke."

"But why?" Kazery's face was a picture of bafflement, his shoulders lifted in a shrug of confusion. "Çifta is a soft-hearted lass. She can't even kill insects."

"Because of the prophecy," Sasha said. "Queen Sylifke is afraid that your daughter is the subject of a warning that emerged some twenty years ago. Çifta is not the only Silverfae halfling to be hunted down, others have died in Sylifke's quest to hamper its fulfillment."

"Please!" Kazery held his palms wide, his expression pleading. "Tell me everything."

"I have some of the story, but not all." Sasha's face pinched with some internal pain, it made Jess want to run to him. "I was sworn not to breathe a word about any of it, but I think this is bigger than my oath. In Silverfall, the name Drazek, my family name, has for years been uttered in the same breath as turncoat and traitor." His jaw clenched. "I fulfill their expectations now, but damned may she be for how she treated my father."

The hair on the back of Jess's neck spiked stiff, and the room went quiet as a crypt.

Sasha got up, rubbing his jaw, as if sifting through memories, wondering where to start. When he spoke again, he addressed everyone in the room, not just Kazery.

"I was raised at court, not because my family was noble, but because the queen believed we were indebted. For many years my father was Queen Sylifke's right hand because he had… powers. Powers beyond the winter magic given to those who survive the ice. When he failed a mission, something of great importance to her, she exiled him from the city and took me, his only child as punishment. She raised me at court as her own. My father and I were not allowed to see each other. I was not yet five."

"Seems a strange choice." Kazery folded his arms. "More like a reward than a punishment, to be raised at court."

"The punishment was for my father, not me. And her choice also had to do with Rialta. There were, and are to this day, no other fauna fae who reside at the Silverfall court. We are an anomaly, a novelty, not just for the queen, but all courtiers and visitors."

"So Sylifke is like your mother?" Laec asked.

Sasha scoffed. "Not remotely. She has no love for me. I would say that when we were young, Prince Ruskin and I were like brothers. But our friendship did not last, because as Ruskin grew, he became more like his mother. She formed him in her own image, cultivating him to be the type of prince she thought Silverfall needed. The change in his character happened over a span of years, but the change in his attitude toward me happened overnight. I used to think it was jealousy, but now I believe the queen told Ruskin—who was too young to remember my father's failure for himself—what Elvio had done, putting it in the worst context possible. After receiving that knowledge, Ruskin decided that I was worthy of neither his friendship nor his respect."

"I'm failing to make the connection to my daughter," Kazery said.

"It has to do with the tree," Sasha said. "The one in our main palace courtyard. Sylifke has cut off access to it, so I don't even know for sure the tree is still there, but I suspect it is."

"Tree?" Kazery murmured, sounding lost.

Laec straightened. "Everyone in Stavarjak knows how Sylifke won the war of the Silver queens. It's one of the reasons my own queen hates her. We Stavarjakian fae are not permitted to cross the border without special permission from Elphame, who wants a bloody dissertation from anyone who hopes to visit the frosted lands."

He paused to give Sasha a chance to elaborate, but when Sasha didn't, Laec carried on. "Royal succession in Silverfall doesn't work the way it does in other kingdoms. The vast majority of monarchies pass the kingdom down to their children, who inherit by right of birth. It *can* work that way in Silverfall, but it doesn't have to."

"Why is that?" asked the crofter.

Laec's gaze flicked to Ian. "Because Silverfae value power in their monarchs, above all else. Anyone who wishes to challenge the current sovereign for the right to the throne can do so, provided they are prepared to die for it, because it means a duel—a fight to the death—and they're expected to use only Silverfae magic in combat."

Sasha nodded as he sank back onto his pallet, perhaps thankful that he wasn't the only one who could help Kazery understand.

Laec gestured at Sasha. "There are some Silverfae, Sasha and Rialta being examples, who are born with hints of the kinds of magic seen elsewhere in Ivryndi. It's rare, because Silverfae keep mostly to themselves, marrying and mating predominantly with each other, but every once in a while, the winter magic manifests 'tainted'. My understanding"—he glanced again at Sasha— "stop me if I'm wrong, is that Queen Karinya was a very powerful Silverfall queen, and Sylifke emerged from nothing, a family of the outer tundra, a place poor and unknown, to challenge Karinya for the right to rule."

Ian looked shocked. "Why would Queen Karinya entertain a challenge from a peasant?"

"She had no choice," Sasha explained. "A challenge for the throne cannot be refused."

Laec nodded. "We're told in Stavarjak that Karinya was magnificent. Elphame was fond of her and treated her as an equal, which means something, because Elphame *has* no equal and she knows it. At any rate, Karinya and Sylifke dueled—and against all odds and expectations—Sylifke won. It was a huge upset, and those present claimed foul play. I recall debates among the elders when I was young, years after the battle. It is said that Sylifke was not truly more powerful than Karinya, but that she cheated, though she claimed that she was simply one of those Silverfae with tainted magic."

Kazery looked at Sasha. "Is it true? Did Sylifke cozen the battle? Cheat to win?"

Sasha put his hands out. "I wasn't there, so I can't say, but many believe so."

"That's appalling!" Kazery, threw up a hand. "Silverfall has a usurper on the throne? It is a travesty! A farce." He smacked the remaining arm of his chair and it broke off with a snap. He tossed the broken arm on the floor. "But what of this tree you mentioned?"

"The snowdrop tree," said Laec, looking at Sasha for confirmation.

Sasha nodded. "It was part of our sigil for years. Sylifke had servants just to look after it, and she liked to hold court around it. But one day all of that changed. She closed the area and put guards at the doors. No one was permitted in. There were no more balls or banquets in the courtyard. I vaguely remember my father telling me a prophecy had been given, and that it involved the tree. My understanding is that it frightened Sylifke so badly that she no longer had any desire to host parties, not until she'd dealt with the threat the prophecy spoke of."

Kazery looked pale. "You're not insinuating that this prophecy has to do with my daughter?"

Sasha shrugged. "I was only permitted to read the first line: 'Beware the blood of the dark-haired halfling.' And when I was selected to join Prince Ruskin for the Midwinter Festival, I was commanded to watch for a dark-haired half-Silverfae female. He referred to her as the daughter of winter—a phrase taken from the prophecy."

"So Ruskin saw my daughter, a dark-haired halfling, even though she did not show fae ears, and thought he would deal with her there and then, become a hero in his mother's eyes. But you can't tell me the rest of the prophecy, nor what it is they are so afraid of?"

Sasha shook his head. "I am sorry that I cannot. If I found someone of that description, I was to report her to Prince Ruskin. I wasn't told why, and I never saw Çifta until the day we were meant to leave."

"She was hiding from Prince Faraçek," said Laec, enunciating and looking at Kazery.

Jessamine suspected he'd been wanting to tell Çifta's father that his daughter was terrified of the Rahamlar prince since the moment they'd met.

Jess added, for good measure: "She had been abused by the prince, and was frightened that he would take her back to Rahamlar, force her to wed him."

"Abused?!" Kazery lunged to his feet, fists clenched, his cheeks flushed, turning to face Jess and Laec.

Laec's voice hardened. "Prince Faraçek is a villain, Mr. Unya. Çifta was afraid to tell you, afraid of what you would do if you knew."

Kazery would break his own knuckles if he clenched his fists any harder, Jess thought. Slowly, his face working, he calmed himself. Then, sorrow swept over his features and he turned away, but not before Jess saw the mist in his eyes. He put a hand over his face. "I've been a fool. I should have guessed it. My minnow is ever the peacekeeper." He turned back, his onyx eyes fastening on first Jessamine, then Laec's face. "How do you know all this?"

Laec gestured to Jess. "Jessamine and I broke your daughter out of Rahamlar, after we saw her with bruises on her face."

Kazery uttered a Boskayan curse word. Throwing both arms wide, he shouted, "I'm indebted to half of Solana on behalf of my daughter!"

"You owe us nothing," said Jess, but too quietly for Kazery to hear.

"This prince," he spat, "this beggar in royal clothing will pay."

"That's what she was afraid of," Laec reminded him gently.

Kazery grunted, sounding a lot like the crofter's bear. "I need a drink. I need to think. I need… a bed. I'm exhausted."

"I'll show you to your suite," said the crofter.

He shot a look at Ian. "Do you have any daughters?"

Ian smiled grimly. "No, but I have one son, and they're almost as much trouble."

Kazery grunted again. "There is more that needs to be discussed," he said. In charge of himself now, in control of his temper, he turned to Sasha. "Thank you, young man. Where is your wolf? I would like to thank her too."

"Down the hall," Sasha jerked his thumb in the direction of Rialta's parlor.

Kazery blinked. "A dire wolf, in this building? That is madness! One does not keep any wolf locked up! I understand there is protocol before a trial, but come,"—he looked at Ian reproachfully—"can they not be given more comfortable quarters? The wolf kept outdoors?"

Sasha looked at Kazery like the sun had risen behind his head.

"I'll see what can be done," Ian said.

Kazery crossed to Sasha, boots clomping on the hardwood floor. Sasha rose to meet him and the two grasped forearms.

"We shall speak again soon," said Kazery.

"As you wish," Sasha replied. "I'm certainly not going anywhere."

Kazery clomped out the door, muttering, "I've never needed a drink so badly."

Jess lingered as the others left the room, she and Sasha looking at one another with such longing that Jessamine's face filled with heat. She chanced a moment when no one was looking to reach her fingertips toward him. He brushed her hand with his, smiling. She left as slowly as she could without raising suspicion, her heart crying out as the bars were closed once more upon her love.

## Chapter Seventeen

# Çifta

We are thirteen *days after the blood ritual that took place in Sharlyk's gorge,* said the ice as they skimmed across the majestic buildings that made up the capital of Silverfall, enclosed by white marble and topped with walkways, much like Solana's walls, only without any of the greenery.

They approached the palace, a structure of pale smooth-cut white marble, with a rooftop courtyard at the back of the palace, overlooking sprawling gardens.

*The sovereign keeps court under her glorious winter sky. She is the most powerful queen in recent memory. Even the weather bows to her. Observe the winter court in all its glory… before it is felled by treachery.*

Çifta's focus narrowed on a single point in the courtyard below.

Queen Karinya sat on a throne of white marble threaded with reflective silver veins. The throne itself was a sculpture: a muscular white horse rearing up on hind legs, pawing at the sky. Its nostrils flared, its teeth bared, and its long mane eternally flying like a pennant of war. The tail arched from muscled hindquarters to spill its curls to the courtyard floor where it became one with the stone, carved from a single monolith.

*A Silverfall pony,* the ice told her. *A much-coveted breed, even abroad.*

Çifta thought "pony" was comically understated for Such a majestic animal. Just beneath and slightly forward of the hindquarters was the sovereign's seat. Karinya sat under the shelter of the sculpture's massive front hooves—some ten feet above her left shoulder.

As for Karinya herself, beautiful was too dim a word to describe the monarch of the winter kingdom. Waist-length white hair, thick and spiraling, spilled over one shoulder. Overlarge fey eyes of lavender ice took in her subjects with affection, glimmering like opals. Long lashes made spiked shadows on her cheeks, and her pale pink lips held a relaxed smile of generosity. Curvaceous and clad in a satin gown of seafoam green, she bore an intricate silver crown decorated with clusters of seed pearls and green tourmaline.

A subject stood before the queen, in the wide space reserved for those making a petition. Between the throne and the subject's feet was a patch of smooth ice, with something long and narrow frozen deep inside. A semi-circle of marble pillars, each as tall as a man and topped with the carving of a unique snowflake, acted as a border behind which other citizens waited their turn.

Everyone wore thick, well-made furs and soft leathers, the majority of which were white or shades of palest blue, green or purple. Some wore turbans, others wore slouchy knitted caps that drooped, or stiff caps with fur trimmings. Most had white, or a-shade-near-to-white hair peeking out from under their headwear. Some soldiers wore metal helmets, but most wore only a thin knit cap.

*Pale colors are valued in Silverfall,* the ice explained. *You see those in the crowd wearing browns, tans and tawny colors?*

The fae in these shades stood out like starlings on a snowbank.

*The colors identify home regions. The darker their winterwear, the further away they have come from. Look at Sylifke, in her tawny colors. She is from Outer Dharkan.*

Sylifke stood quietly, not talking to anyone, nor sipping from a steaming cup. Her gaze was locked on the queen. Çifta's heart sank as the queen signaled a guard and Sylifke was allowed to enter the courtyard.

Çifta quailed. *I do not know if I can watch this.*

*You must,* the ice chided. *Do not desert the murdered queen by turning your eyes away, child. This is also your story.*

Çifta shuddered as Sylifke strode forward, dreading what she understood would shortly come to pass. She braced herself, determined not to look away no matter what. This *was* her story.

Çifta could now identify the item frozen inside the pool of ice: a sword pointing toward the throne. Its details were obscured, but it could not be anything else.

Sylifke knelt at this oval pool. She lay her hand flat on the ice and looked up at Karinya.

A hush fell over those who could see, which then swept through the entirety of the crowd as the message was relayed. Someone had knelt before the sword. There was a press of bodies as fae jostled for a better view.

Without taking her eyes from Karinya, Sylifke sent a wave of magic into the ice. With a single loud crack, followed by many crackles and snaps, the pool turned to liquid. Sylifke's slender white hand slipped into the pool up to the elbow. Fog gathered as Sylifke straightened, the sword gripped in her fist.

Queen Karinya watched, her expression losing its gentle benevolence. A frown of annoyance marred her perfect face, but she was unafraid. Experience had hardened her and her confidence in herself was as easy to read as the pages of any book. Sylifke was but an irritating insect, an unpleasant flaw in an otherwise perfect day.

As the fog cleared, Çifta got a better look at the sword in Sylfike's hand. Fashioned from a single piece of silver and decorated with tourmaline stones, it was a ceremonial piece, not suitable for true combat. Sylifke held it point down at first, but as she stared her challenge at Karinya, she lifted it, slowly, until the point was up and the base of the blade was in front of her face. Sunlight licked along the metal.

"You're not only an outlander, you're a fool," said Karinya in a loud voice, tapping her fingers against the armrests. "What is your name, Fool?"

All talk ceased. It was as though Sylifke and Karinya were the only living beings present.

"I am no outlander," called Sylifke. "I am Sylifke Agorek of Outer Dharkan, a Silverfall citizen born to many generations of pure-bloods, and a great-great-granddaughter of Queen Devan, for whom this sword was forged. I challenge you this day." She sucked in a breath and raised her voice so her words would not be mistaken. "I, Sylifke Agorek, invoke the ancient covenant of our ancestors. You cannot refuse me. Stand, and it shall be decided whether you shall remain as queen, or fall."

Çifta wondered vaguely if it was possible to faint while having an out-of-body experience like the one she was having.

Karinya's upper lip curled in a sneer, a tiny movement that changed her entire face from feminine elegance to a scorn so deep that it made Çifta quake. The queen's hands tightened, bending her fingers from graceful curves into angles of rancor. A wind kicked up, making the snowdrop pennants snap. Snow swirled around Sylifke in a tornado, touching, licking, tasting her. There was nothing natural about that snow. It circled the queen's enemy, starting at her feet and wrapping around her legs, her waist, her torso, then her neck and face. Sylifke's head snapped back and she gasped, her pain apparent. Two cuts appeared across her cheekbones—one after the other, as though delivered by a whip. Silver blood ran down her cheeks and dripped from her chin.

Karinya stood, her magnificent gown frothing across the marble. Her smile was as terrifying as the scream of a predator on a dark night. "I don't care whose granddaughter you are, or where you are from. Too late to back down now, Fool. Today you die."

She walked forward, skirts billowing. Hands flexing like the talons of a raptor, they swept behind her hips then snapped forward. A blast of sorcerous wind crossed the courtyard, and glittering arrows formed themselves from the snow. Elvio had referred to Karinya as the tempest of frozen blades, and Çifta could see why. Icy projectiles pelted straight at Sylifke, still wielding the sword. Silver blood caked her cheeks and soaked into the ruff under her jaw.

Sylifke backpedaled, holding the blade up in defense like

a well-trained warrior. The blade flashed as she knocked some arrows away, and shattered others. But she could not stop them all and screamed in agony as she was pierced. An ice-arrow struck her upper arm, grazed the side of one thigh, and punctured straight through her calf. She stumbled, but somehow kept to her feet, favoring her wounded leg.

Karinya stood with her hands at her side, stiff and ready. Ropes of snow curled around her, orbiting her fists, writhing like a nest of white snakes.

Sylifke dropped the sword with a clatter and staggered back. Bracing against a pillar, she summoned her own sorcery. Crackling filled the courtyard, punctuated by sharp claps of high-pitched thunder. A whine, like a sound of pain from deep within the throat of a great beast, a dragon perhaps, began low and soft. It built to a pitch so unbearable that those watching clamped their hands over their ears and cringed.

Undaunted, Karinya bared her teeth. Bracing her legs apart, she summoned more of her power, back bowing, arms swirling. All the air seemed to suck into the queen. Sylifke's clothing and hair blasted inward, to the central point of some building terror. Citizens clutched at fixed objects to keep from being drawn toward the queen, and all the while the unbearable pitch built and built. But the sound of Sylifke's magic distorted as the queen drew energy toward herself. With an outward flip of her hands, Karinya sent one powerful blast at her opponent.

For a moment Çifta thought the ice had taken her away from the scene before the fight ended, because everything went white.

Then she caught faint glimpses, shapes in a storm. Snow swirled and blew, filling the air with an angry torrent of blinding whiteness. The sound was a living thing, an ongoing roar that rose and fell, the screaming of a hurricane. Flashes of light sizzled and popped like fireworks, as magic clashed with magic, sonic blasts, the vibration of energy roiling everywhere, bouncing off pillars, flagstones, walls, trees, churning like an angry sea. Çifta was shocked to her core by the power of it all.

In a moment, it all ceased. The bellowing and crackling, the shifting effluvium of magic, the supernatural snowstorm riddled with electricity… it gave a harrowing final scream before it was abruptly cut off. As quickly as the melee had begun, it ended. Snow continued to swirl, but softly and with hardly any sound. The scene cleared. Silverfae helped each other to stand, brushing each other off, looking around dazedly, questions in their eyes. What happened?

Someone gasped; another gave a cry of sorrow—the first of many as the fae saw the place where their queen had stood moments before. The artificer of their sacrosanct winter magic, powerful and terrible in her fury, undefeatable, incorruptible, unassailable Queen Karinya of Silverfall, was gone.

In her place…

A snowdrop tree—trunk thick and twisted, roots thrusting through the stones of the courtyard, lifting and breaking them; branches sinuous, jointed, and bare; twigs like broken fingers, thick and warped—naked and humiliated, with no glittering foliage to hide its bones. It filled the air over the courtyard to scratch at the underbelly of the sky.

Sylifke pushed herself away from the pillar. Limping heavily, she went forward, eyes huge and hollow in her face. She stared at the tree with almost as much shock as the citizens. She reached for it, laying her palm against its trunk.

Someone found the courage to approach, then another, and another. Five citizens touched the tree, as though checking to see if, instead of smooth bark, they might feel the silk-clad body of their monarch. A faeling, likely not yet twenty, put a finger in a crack. Horror dawned on her face as she withdrew her finger and looked at it. She screamed and staggered backward.

"Blood! It's Queen Karinya's blood!"

A disturbed murmur swept through the crowd. Those who dared look for themselves, muttering and nodding to their neighbors as they touched the oozing liquid that—not green, but silver—looked so much like Silverfae blood.

Çifta's mind stretched. *Karinya is inside the tree? Or she became the tree?*

The Silverfae maiden who first discovered the blood-like sap cried: "This is not winter magic!"

Sylifke, who up to this point had looked as though she was in a dream, intent on the tree, stepped back at these words. She moved away from the tree.

"I am now your queen," she said, hunched sideways in her pain. Silver blood ran down her wounded leg and oozed from her arm. "You must honor the accord." She took a deep breath, struggled to stand upright, then screamed: "I am your queen!"

The Silverfae murmured, uncertain what to do. Karinya was no longer there for them to look to for wisdom… only this outlander, whom they did not know. Karinya had called her a fool. Worst of all, she had destroyed their queen with strange magic.

Sylifke bent and Çifta saw why she'd shuffled, crablike, scaring back a circle of fae who were afraid to let her too near. Sylifke snatched up the silver sword she had dropped, wielding it with her unwounded arm. Çifta was not practiced in the art of swordplay, but even she could see that Sylifke had as much facility in her left arm as she had had in her right.

The crowd had formed clusters, their voices rising in protest.

"You did not uphold the covenant, stranger!" someone called.

"You said you were pure, but this magic is not!"

"Winter magic cannot do this thing!"

"Mine can!" Sylifke's impassioned gaze swept the crowd, searching for the ones who had spoken. "I say it again… I have winter magic. Snowdrops belong to the winter, and I have done this with my own sorcery. I have earned the right to rule this kingdom. You will pay homage to me. I am a descendant of Queen Devan. I have a right by heritage, and I have proven in front of all that I also have right by might. You must honor me, as the covenant dictates. This is the way of the Silver." She brandished the sword and turned in a circle, limping less now. Perhaps she was less aware of her pain because with each passing moment, it seemed she was getting stronger.

Angry and rebellious grumbles increased. A few Silverfae reached for their swords. Even the guards looked mutinous. Things did not look good for the usurper, but Sylifke just gave a terrifying smile. As her cut cheeks oozed, her expression was grisly.

"Who defies me?"

A brave male yelled, "What if we all do?"

Sylifke did not lose her grin. "Then I shall subdue you all. Do not tempt me. What you just saw was merely a taste of my winter magic."

"It was *not* winter magic!" someone shouted.

"What have you done with our queen?" cried a young female, her voice tearful and afraid but defiant, taking courage from her fellows.

"We will not bow to a usurper!"

"You have not won legitimately!"

"Blood magic is forbidden! The punishment is death! You must submit to questioning!"

Sylifke turned, the tip of her sword up and steady, rotating like the point of a compass.

The crowd grew bolder. A young male was the first to draw his blade.

"Kill the witch and Karinya may be released," someone hollered. Others agreed, calling that they would never follow this cheating traitor. There were nods of agreement everywhere.

Sylifke waited, expression unchanging, blood crusted on her cheeks. The faeling, emboldened by the crowd, strode forward. He lifted his sword, pale eyes full of murder. He bared his teeth and came at her, his own bearing telling of some years of training.

Sylifke met his steel with her silver, and the sound of the fight galvanized the crowd as they shifted for a better view. They screamed support for the young male.

Wounded, yet rising above her agony, Sylifke moved her booted feet across the stones in the ancient deadly dance of swordplay. At first, the two looked well matched.

Çifta's heart guttered like a candle though, as she could see that the young male was no match for the wounded Sylifke. She was hardened, fearless, determined and driven by madness. She countered every blow, parried every thrust, simply fending the youth off for long enough for him to tire. He did tire, and danced back to take a break, chest rising and falling rapidly. Fear had entered his eyes.

"You have a chance to walk away, stripling," she said. "To the stones with your knees, and my punishment for your rebellion will be light, a mere whipping."

Her words infuriated the youth. Ire renewed, he leapt forward again. Metal clanged, and Sylifke defended and defended while he attacked and attacked. Only a half-second's worth of delay finished the fight. His weariness rose, his muscles slowed. Sylifke lifted the blade and brought it down in a killing blow, cleaving the young male between the neck and shoulder.

*Take me away,* Çifta begged the ice as the youth's body slumped, lifeless, and pearly blood flowed across the stones. *I cannot watch this. I do not want to see any more.*

*Just a little longer, child,* the ice said. *There is something more coming.*

The crowd's fury was a tinderbox, and the faeling's blood was the spark. A dozen Silverfall soldiers surged to the fore, unsheathing their swords and coming for Sylifke, who stood over the boy, her sword lifted.

Some signal must have been given, though Çifta could not tell what it was.

A deafening battle cry rose from beyond the courtyard. Those advancing stopped in their tracks, looking around. Fae in tawny-colored boiled leather poured over the walls and swept into the courtyard through the gateways.

"For Queen Sylifke!"

"For your honor, for Outer Dharkan."

"For your queen!"

Karinya's citizens and soldiers rallied, all weapons out. Those who were not trained to use a sword, male and female alike, grabbed whatever was near. Those in pale colors and white turned to face those in browns and tans. The courtyard became a fray, a brawl of sudden violence. Çifta mentally recoiled, wishing she had eyelids she could close against his scene. But after a few moments of watching both sides punish the other, it was clear that death was not the desired outcome for either party. Rather, it was to subdue, to bring the opponents to their knees. Blood was spilled, much of it, but killing blows were few.

*Please,* Çifta begged. *It's enough. I know that Sylifke wins. She is the present queen.*

The scene began to fade.

*Yes. She is the present queen,* whispered the ice. *And now you know how she did it.*

Çifta was grateful that the melee before her dimmed, first to shadows, then to nothing. She'd been spared the details and could now process what she'd seen.

Laec had told her he suspected her of having Silverfae blood, and now she knew he was right. Surely now the ice would show her the link between these events and her mother's death.

*We go now to a few years after this battle. Are you ready?*

*I am ready.*

She was not, but what choice did she have?

## Chapter Eighteen

# Jessamine

Jessamine spent the early morning producing nightshade poison for Vivian's assistant to pick up. She had not seen the faceless manager or her scarred henchman in weeks. She assumed the raw materials she made once a week before dawn, with Beazle flying overhead to ensure no one was around to get inadvertently poisoned, were of satisfactory quality. Beazle went for an early-morning hunt while Jess cleaned herself up, putting her poison-soaked clothing into a bundle for special cleaning. She had just finished washing all the toxins from her body when her bat fluttered in through her open window.

*He's been moved,* Beazle told her triumphantly. *All it took was a request from the continent's wealthiest merchant.*

Wrapping a towel around her dripping form, Jess left the bathroom in a rush, skidding on the wet marble floor. She cast her gaze about, forgetting where her clean clothes were in her excitement.

*Where to?*

*He's in the East Keep. Not in the dungeon, but on the way.*

Jess rifled through her wardrobe for clean leggings and a tunic, then hopped around struggling to pull the clothing over damp skin. She knew which room Beazle referred to. Near the maproom was a corridor leading to a deep square stairwell. Halfway down the stairwell was a landing and a room that was normally used to store training equipment; it had a wooden door with bars on the judas window. It was dank and smelled of sweat and mildew.

*That room isn't any nicer,* she complained to her familiar.

Beazle perched on the top of the mirror, watching her dress. *The crofter had it cleaned, and at least he's in the palace, now.*

Jess braided her wet hair, fingers working quickly. She looked at herself in the mirror. Her eyes were bright with hope, her cheeks flushed. She whirled, looking for her ankle boots, and spied them just under her bed. She dove for them, ramming her stockingless feet into them.

*Did they move Rialta, too?*

*Yes. She's in an unused stall beside the fallow fields.*

Jess wrapped a tie around the end of her braid. *Chained?*

*No, but they reinforced the walls. At least she's outside and can stretch her legs and breathe fresh air.*

Jess nodded, thinking of Sasha again. *There's no direct access to that room from the hidden passage, but there's bound to be crumbling mortar—that whole hall is crumbling.*

Beazle stretched out his wings and yawned.

Jess strapped on a belt, glancing at the lightening sky out her window. The majority of palace residents would either be looking for their breakfast, if they were awake at all, or serving it.

*I'll make a way in, even if we can only talk to each other. Now's the best time to try.*

Beazle tucked his head under a wing. *I'm going to nap.*

Jess grabbed her Fahyli cape on her way out the door, stowing it beneath her arm until she got to ground level. The palace corridors were warm and lit with etherlamps, but even in the height of summer, the passages beneath the palace were cold. At this time of year, they'd be frigid. She made her way to the maproom, greeting those she passed with a succinct nod, just as she might if she was on official Fahyli business. She'd decided that her excuse, should anyone ask, would be that she was looking for a piece of equipment. Once she was between the walls, she wouldn't have to worry about being caught.

She heard Digit and Panther's voices through the open maproom door and stayed out of sight until she heard them leave, then slipped inside. Maps embroidered into tapestries covered the walls. The largest tapestry looked as though it had been stretched over a wooden frame, but this frame was a panel that slid aside. She slipped into the passageway and closed the paneling behind her.

Jess followed the narrow and dark corridor—barely wide enough to pass through without turning sideways—to where a torch hung in a claw holder. She lit it with a match from her pouch. An uneven stairwell with deeply worn treads dropped into darkness. Jess took these until she estimated she was near Sasha's room. She went still, listening.

Muffled male voices came through the wall. She crept on as the voices grew louder. When she heard Sasha's voice, her stomach gave a flutter. Setting the torch in an iron holder, she perched on a step and began to follow the mortar with her fingers, testing it for unfilled crevices.

The older passageways had many unmortared stones, behind which were always little hidey-holes, sometimes arm-deep. Other times stones could be removed to provide a spyhole into another room, often from behind a painting with a small hole in the canvas. When she found what she was looking for, she shifted a couple of stones out of place, setting them on the steps beside her. A waft of cool, musty air drifted out. She wrinkled her nose, peering inside the hole, and saw a faint outline around another loose stone.

Once she heard Sasha's guard lock the door, she shifted the stone inch by inch from the hole. Setting it on the step next to the others, she looked inside. A pale, startled eye peered back at her through the hole.

"I must be dreaming," Sasha whispered, disbelieving. "Jess?"

Heart in her mouth, she reached into the hole and felt Sasha grasp her fingers. They held hands for a few moments, but while she was touching him, she couldn't see him. She withdrew so they could see one another in the torchlight. His face was awash with shadows and his breath lifted the dust in the cavity between the walls.

"At first, I thought you were one hell of a big rat. Then I looked under the table and watched a stone being pulled backward. Rats don't do that." He grinned. "If this is a jailbreak, then you should know I'm not going to fit."

She laughed, so happy to see him again that she didn't notice all the dirt and dust that had fallen into her hair and down the back of her neck.

"I know all the secret passageways," she bragged. "There are loose stones all over the palace."

With a grunt, she shifted another out of the way. With a little more effort, she might have enough room to wiggle through.

When Sasha told her to move back, she did so, holding the torch near the breach for light. He put a hand in the hole and the temperature dropped suddenly and drastically. A series of cracking sounds echoed within the wall.

Jess jumped. "What did you do?"

"The mortar is crumbling and there's a lot of damp down here," he told her, knocking more stones out of place and setting them on the floor in his room. "There's enough water inside to bring down this whole wall."

The light around Sasha increased as he pulled away more stones. Soon, there was enough room for her to pass through.

Jess put the torch back in its holder. The walls were thick, and the hole was jagged, but going slowly, and squirming on her belly, she emerged into the former storage room, head first and close to the floor, like a baby born from a rock womb. Sasha cradled her upper body as she came through, helping her to her feet. Stones, dust and pebbles littered the floor around them. For a moment they just looked at one another, then she threw her arms around his neck, standing on tip-toe. Sasha buried his nose in her hair with a sigh.

When they separated, Sasha put his table back in front of the hole, covering most of the debris. Jess looked around, noting the judas window was currently closed. All the equipment had been taken away, the room cleaned and simply furnished. There were no windows, nor any fireplace, but there was a brazier filled with glowing coals. He'd been given one table, two wooden chairs, and a proper bed with a mattress, quilt, and two pillows. A stand near the door held a jug and ewer containing fresh water.

Now that she'd reached him, Jess felt suddenly shy. It was difficult to find words, especially with the way he was looking at her. He took her hand, stroking her knuckles as they sat on the side of his bed. Their knees touched as they turned toward one another.

"You know where Rialta is?" Jess asked.

"Yes, she told me. She is glad to be outside. Jess, listen, I love that you're here, but you'll be in big trouble if you get caught." He touched her cheek. "You're amazing to have got in to see me twice, but you're taking such a risk."

She flushed. She didn't feel amazing. She was abusing her position, taking advantage of her secret knowledge for her own benefit. But at this point, she hardly cared. It was too painful to be separated from Sasha for so long, and with a trial coming.

"How is Lady Çifta?" he asked. "Any change?"

She shook her head. "Why? Should she have melted by now?"

He shook his head. "The ice can take weeks, even months."

She looked at his long fingers, intertwined with hers. She remembered seeing magical mist drift from his hands as he froze her flower into a jewel. She recalled the blast of cold air as he froze Çifta. Yet, his hand felt warm to her touch, full of strength and life.

"You could break out of here," she murmured. "If you can break stones apart, why couldn't you break the door, too?"

"Then I would be a fugitive from your people, as well as mine."

She looked up. "Are you afraid?"

"Of the trial?" He almost smiled. "Why should I be? I'm not guilty. I didn't ask Rialta to defend me. I have to trust the court will uncover the truth. I would rather be acquitted and show my face than flee like an outlaw."

Jess loved him for his nobility, but… "I don't want to worry you…"

"But?"

"But your queen wrote to King Agir. She is coming for your trial."

Sasha went still as this sunk in. "I am not surprised."

"No?"

He released her hand and shifted back on the mattress, crossing his legs. He wore only socks, no shoes. "Ruskin was her only heir, and I am the son of someone she hates. I would have been more surprised if she didn't try to interfere. I am surprised she asked. Sylifke usually demands."

Jessamine pulled her legs up, wrapping her arms around her knees. "It's worse than just being present for your trial, Sasha. She's allowed to put six Silverfae in the jury, and Rayven is to be your prosecutor."

Sasha rubbed the back of his neck. "I should be flattered to get such attention. Don't be afraid, Jess. If I was at home I'd be dead by now, Rialta too, and killed in the most gruesome way Sylifke could imagine."

Jess was not comforted. He could see that and reached for her. She swiveled so she could lay her head against his chest, thinking how ironic it was that he was comforting her while he was the one in such trouble. He stroked her back and kissed the top of her head, asking her about all the goings on outside his cell.

She brought him up to date about the Calyx and told him what she and Beazle had learned about Faraçek's intentions to annex Solana. Sasha listened quietly, tracing her spine, as she went on to relay Isabey's tragic story. His embrace tightened as she told him about Shade and how devastated the princess was. As Sasha murmured soft sounds of sympathy and asked her thoughtful questions, she found herself helpless to keep anything from him. One topic spilled into the next, and it was the most natural thing in the world to tell him about the lion, and how she hoped to one day get some time alone with Esha to learn more about him. Sasha was quietly amazed, but expressed no doubt at her story, suggesting that it must be a sign that she was someone special to the kingdom of Solana. Jess doubted it, since others had had similar experiences, but told him that he was sweet to think it.

Realizing that she had been talking for nearly an hour, she pulled back and looked at him, enjoying the look of his face in the shadows. "I've been going nonstop. I'm sorry."

He smiled, flattening his palm against her lower back. "Why sorry? I like knowing what is happening. It's not like there is anything exciting going on in my life at the moment."

She curled a lock of his hair around her finger, enjoying the silky feel of it. "But here you are locked up, waiting for judgement, and all I've been doing is talking about my problems. So let's talk about you for a while."

He shrugged. "But you said it yourself, Jess. I'm just waiting. There's nothing else to say."

"There is though. There is a lot you could talk about."

He arched a blond brow. "Such as?"

"Well, for example, you had to go through whatever it is Çifta is going through, in the ice."

"And?"

She canted her head. "And… what was it like?"

He looked startled by her question, and maybe a little embarrassed. He was quiet for several moments before glancing covertly at the door. He shifted on the bed, then he moved forward, looming over her, whispering.

"I came to my senses, only to find I had been tied down on a bed."

He slid his hands under her hips and shifted her to the middle of the coverlet before gently pushing her back. Jess's pulse picked up speed.

"Really?" she breathed.

"Really. My hands were tied above my head, with rope. Like this." He took her wrists and lifted them, holding them over her head. Jess's mouth went dry.

He moved closer, hovering over her, his face close to hers. Their bodies were touching now, from chest to feet, their legs tangled together. Desire warmed her whole body, making her feel weak. She swallowed, feeling her hands shake in his grip.

"The ice tied you down?" she husked, head whirling.

His lips neared enough that she could feel his breath. His hair dropped around them, shrouding them in shadow. His white gaze scalded hers, then dropped to her lips as he held himself up on his free elbow. His mouth was so close, soft and waiting. She couldn't stop herself, and rose to kiss him. Only when he smiled against her mouth did she realize he'd been teasing her.

"Sasha!" she cried against his lips, laughing and blushing. "You're such a liar!"

He released her wrists, but she slipped her arms around his neck, not wanting him to move away. He kissed her cheek, her neck, her jaw, her lips again. He pulled back and looked at her, serious again.

"Silverfae don't really… talk about what happens in the

ice. It's considered private. A wedded couple might share their experiences, but…" he shrugged.

Jessamine's cheeks flushed. "I'm sorry."

"Don't be silly. How could you know? It was an excellent opportunity to get you horizontal." He brushed a lock of her hair away from her forehead. "Which was pretty easy, I have to say."

He muffled her squeak of indignation with another kiss, blowing her thoughts apart.

A sound from the hall had them bolting from the bed in a panic. Sasha gestured for her to crouch under the table beside the hole, then straightened the tablecloth to hang down and cover her and the pile of stones. He was back on the bed just as the judas window slid open.

"Drazek?" said the guard through the window.

"Hmm?" Sasha put on a groggy voice, like he'd overslept.

"Someone here to see you."

Sasha swung his legs off the bed, sounding more alert now. "Who is it?"

The window slid shut, and a moment later the bolt was drawn back and the door creaked open. Jess couldn't see anything, but she heard the heavy steps of what had to be a human as he crossed the threshold. Fae did not clomp around like that.

"Good morning, Mr. Drazek," came a thready male voice. "My name is Bertrand Bedar. I've been assigned to your case."

Sasha got to his feet. "Assigned?"

"I'm your lawyer." Bertrand thumped into the room. "You can leave us now," he told the guard. "We'll be an hour or more."

"Knock if you need anything," the guard said before shutting the door and bolting it.

"Defense lawyer?" Sasha sounded pleasantly surprised.

"Nice quarters," Bertrand said. "Not bad for an accused murderer, I say. I'm sorry I haven't been 'round to see you sooner. I was actually notified a while ago, but I've been so busy that I've only been able to get away from the office for the first time today. My apologies."

"That's alright," replied Sasha, pulling the chairs toward the brazier. "Have a seat. I wondered why they gave me two chairs. Now I know. It's nice to meet you, Mr. Bedar, and it's nice to have a… defender."

"Of course." Bertrand plopped into the creaky chair. "No one defends themselves in Solana unless that's their preference. My fee is even covered by the state. Now, I've been told a lot about your case, but it's been rather boggling. I'm eager to get the facts as you know them."

There was a snapping sound as the lawyer opened a case. A paper drifted to the floor. Jess saw pudgy fingers poking about as the lawyer couldn't quite reach it. "Tell me about that day, then we'll go back to how you came to be in Solana in the first place and connect any dots."

Sasha picked up the page and handed it to Bertrand. "That day… the day my familiar killed Ruskin, you mean?"

"Ah, ah, ah," the lawyer chided. "Never admit that your dog killed the prince. He was acting in defense of his… person. He was protecting you."

Jess closed her eyes, shaking her head.

There was a long beat before Sasha replied. "Familiars are always the opposite gender of their fae. I guess you didn't know… being human and all."

Bertrand hesitated, then spoke quickly. "Yes, I did know that. I'd just forgotten. She… she was protecting you."

"Rialta."

"Right." There was scribbling as the lawyer made a note. "At least I knew your familiar was a dog, although I forget the breed."

"Rialta is a dire wolf," Sasha said, his tone flat.

"Really?" Bertrand sounded mystified. He rifled through more pages. More of them drifted to the floor, one of them sliding close to where Jess was hidden. "Hmm… That was not in my briefing. Apologies. It appears I was given bad information."

"That's alright." Sasha let out a long slow breath of tried patience and retrieved the pages. "You should meet her for yourself, since you'll be defending her as well."

As Sasha bent down, he exchanged a quick look of dismay with Jess.

"Of course, of course. Forgive me, lad. I've just come off a case of fraud. My mind is muddled." Bertrand flipped through a notebook, scribbled some more. "Take me through the day from the beginning. Please don't leave anything out."

Sasha took a breath and began to talk.

## Chapter Nineteen

# Çifta

The clouds shifted and daylight moved rapidly into night.

*What am I supposed to see?* Çifta wondered as she floated high above Silverfall City.

Her host did not reply. It was silent but felt, like the presence of someone standing at the foot of one's bed in the dark.

From this height, it was impossible to make out individuals or details. But it was apparent that time was speeding up. The sun and the moon traded places. Day became night and back again in dizzying succession. Fighting vertigo and a desperate wish for eyelids she could clench, Çifta focused on the clouds, which boiled like a tempest. With each passing day, they grew thicker, darker; pregnant with snow. Precipitation released from time to time with blasts that turned Silverfall into a blur, softening the edges of everything. As the cycles continued, the clouds thickened further. Weeks turned into months, but the clouds did not break, nor did they rest in the spewing of snow and sleet.

*The people must be suffering with so little sunlight,* Çifta thought. *The winter must break soon, surely?*

*Winter has never broken, child,* the ice told her. *Sylifke secured her reign, and with it, the weather. Fae have been born beneath this gloominess, a whole generation that does not know the sunlight of their forefathers and mothers. The city is full of faelings who do not know that the sky can look any different.*

They descended through clouds so thick and heavy it was like being swaddled in a wet woolen blanket. The flashing of days slowed, then ceased all together as they broke through the bottom of winter's shroud. The tallest spires pierced the overhanging gloom as the sky spewed snow and ice. Pennants looked like shredded tissue, destroyed by the driving ice. Figures moved across a courtyard, swaddled with garments. Ponies kept their heads down against the wind, their eyes and foreheads enveloped with protective headgear. Lamps sat in windows and dangled from posts, but the illumination they provided was scant. Ropes had been installed along the outer walls of the buildings, strung from ring to ring, giving fae something to grasp if weather blinded the way.

*What happened to the beautiful winter kingdom that Karinya reigned over? I do not recognize this place.*

*That is the power of an unseelie monarch, my child. It reflects her nature with constant darkness and cold. Look ahead.*

A tall, slender tower loomed, lined with small, dimly lit windows. They swept in through a crack in a stained-glass window to a spiral staircase. The figure of a bare-headed Silver-fae female made her way down the steps. The lighting was poor, but Çifta recognized her short cape as the kind the harvesters had worn. They emerged from the staircase into a long, well-lit corridor, and she looked up. In the better light, Çifta could see that the cape had changed color. No longer was it pale green, now it was a watery shade of yellow-brown.

*We saw her working in the snowdrop grove.*

Instead of a turban, the fae's hair hung over one shoulder in a fat, white braid. Strands that had slipped loose curled around her pointed face. Her expression was solemn.

*Yes. This is Salme Sariatha,* the ice told her. *Your maternal grandmother.*

Çifta felt winded. *My... grandmother?*

*After the battle of the Silver queens, Salme remained a servant in Sylifke's court. She lost many friends, and her husband, in that fight.*

Studying her, Çifta noted the bright blue-white eyes, the wide mouth, the lines at the outer corners of her eyes, the high curve of her cheekbones and strong chin. There was a kindness in Salme's face that could not be overshadowed by her apparent weariness. Çifta's heart softened toward this female, filling with a sense of kinship.

Salme approached an arched double-door. She paused, her hand resting against the wood, seeming to brace herself. Then she pushed through into a huge open space with a high tented ceiling supported by thick timbers. Skirts swishing, she walked along one wall, gaze flashing up and about as though watching for someone she wished to avoid. In the center of the open space stood a single snowdrop tree, its trunk twisted in a familiar way, its branches gnarled and bare.

*This is the courtyard!*

A massive tent had been erected over the courtyard, but there was no mistaking the flagstones or the marble pillars topped with snowflake sculptures. The pool was again frozen, the blade visible in the ice.

*Sylifke had the courtyard covered so fae could gather here without suffering from the weather,* the ice told her. *She wanted them to never forget how she had defeated their former queen. For the Silverfae who harbor loyalty in their hearts to Karinya, it is a kind of torture. A reminder that Karinya's rule and life were cut short. Never again would she inspire the sun to shine, or bestow gifts upon her subjects. For Salme, this is a place of faith and reverence.*

*Faith… Faith in what?*

*That this story is yet unfinished.*

Figures walked reverentially around the tree. Talking was done in whispers. Tears ran down the cheeks of some, while others gazed up in silent contemplation, stoic expressions veiling their thoughts. Salme waited until all present left the courtyard, looking around to make sure she was alone. She approached the tree and laid a palm gently upon the bark, observing the pearly fluid oozing from its cracks but not touching it. Salme closed her eyes for a time, then looked covertly around again. The room was still empty.

"My queen," she whispered, "you are sorely missed. Your people suffer, but your servant abides. My family is well. My sons are growing like the ice of the Arroyo. They eat everything in sight and I must work doubly hard to ensure they have enough. I enjoy the work, though the elixirs are poor and bitter these days. Harvesting keeps me moving…"

She was quiet for a full minute before speaking again, her words still soft. "I believe you are in there. At times, I think I can feel you. They are fleeting moments, but… I'll not give up, my queen. You were good to us, and it is not in my heart to love to another, especially her."

A sound from the doorway made Salme recoil, then lift her scarf to cover her face. She walked with her head down, in the way of the others who had been there, toward the nearest doorway. A couple entered, dropping silver coins into a marble vessel before beginning their own turn about the room.

Salme slipped from the courtyard.

Çifta and the ice stayed under the tent. Time passed, sconces were lit and extinguished, fae came and went. Salme was among them, always alone, only staying until other fae entered. Always, she put her hand on the bark, looked at the pale blood glistening between the cracks. Always, she spoke to Karinya. Salme became pregnant, and the bump grew. Time marched on. Her visits stopped, then resumed again, now carrying a swaddled faeling.

*My mother?* Çifta gazed with wonder at the infant cradled in her grandmother's arms.

Salme began her next visit the way she always did, laying her hand against the bark. She bounced the sleeping faeling and whispered to Karinya. Then she stopped abruptly. Tentatively, she poked a finger into a crack and withdrew a droplet of clear moisture on her fingertip. She held it up where more light could fall upon it. The sap was no longer pearly and blood-like. It was pale green.

Salme stared at it as though she did not trust her eyes. She showed the droplet to the faeling.

"Look, Evelin," she whispered, her voice full of amazement, "The tree no longer bleeds. What can this mean, my love?"

Her pale eyes flicked between her offspring and the droplet, her expression growing thoughtful.

Salme's visits became even more frequent. With the help of one other harvester, who stood at the door to warn her of approaching fae, she harvested sap from the snowdrop tree in secret. So as not to create a hole in the bark that would be noticed, she wedged a tiny spigot into a crack, gathering only a little sap at a time, holding a small vessel beneath the drops. Every time she finished, she took the spigot with her, leaving no trace of her activity behind.

Time passed as Salme faithfully gathered the pale-green liquid, bit by bit.

In a blur of advanced time, Çifta found herself in a small suite of rooms with stone walls and wooden floors. A tapestry depicting a forest of snowdrop trees in full foliage hung above a bed, displaying more shades of green than Çifta had ever seen in a single piece of art.

Across from the bed, a cordoned off section of the room had been set up like a makeshift kitchen. The counters were cluttered with objects: vials, distilling equipment, books, jars of dried herbs, and other substances less easily identified. A window stood open. At the counter, Salme performed a delicate operation. Picking up a steaming copper vessel with a pair of tongs, she began to transfer its contents into a glass vial held upright by a clamp and stand. A thin stream of syrup the color of sparkling tourmaline poured out. A feverish smile lit Salme's face as she filled the vial to the neck. Letting out a sigh, she set aside the copper pot and tongs. She placed her hands flat on the countertop, staring at the green elixir, expression exultant.

Then she closed her eyes and whispered, "I have done it, my queen."

Her face momentarily cramped with sorrow, a tear slipping down her cheek. She wiped it away, then called in a casual voice, "Evelin? Come here, darling."

Evelin came from an adjoining room. She could not be much older than four. She was a beautiful faeling, with soft curling white hair as fine as silk, round cheeks and iridescent eyes. She wore a knee-length dress with embroidery around the neckline and hem: dancing leaves the same shape as snowflakes, snowdrop foliage.

Salme beckoned, crouching down on her haunches and opening her arms.

"Come, Evelin my love. I have your inheritance."

Evelin had clearly been told previously about this inheritance. She came to her mother without question, although the youngster looked less excited about it than her mother. Evelin lay her head on her mam's shoulder and Salme stood, holding the child to her bosom. She kissed the top of Evelin's head and set her bottom on the countertop.

Plucking the elixir from its cradle, she showed it to her daughter. "What is the most important thing about this, Evelin?"

"It's secret," said Evelin, looking mesmerized by the play of light through the green syrup.

"Good girl. Almost since you were born, I have been working toward this day. This"—she put a finger against the glass—"is like the ones we used to make, but even brighter, more vivid. That means it is the best elixir I have ever made, and it is all for you, Evelin Sariatha."

Evelin gazed lovingly at her mother and the vial, taking it all in. "Me?"

Salme nodded solemnly. "Whatever magic is contained within will one day manifest in you. You will become great, perhaps even as great as Queen Karinya was. That is my hope."

Evelin held out a chubby hand for the elixir.

"Wait." Salme opened a drawer and fished out a spoon.

Carefully, she poured some into the spoon, then held it to the child's lips. Evelin slurped the syrup, swallowing and smacking her lips. Eyes wide with pleasure at the taste, she lifted her gaze to her mother's face and opened her mouth for more.

Salme laughed. "Yes. It is delicious. That is the taste of seelie magic. But too much all at once is not a good for a wee faeling. You may have one spoonful every month until it's gone. I will make more, but it will be another four years before I'll have enough to fill this vial. In the meantime, this is not to be shared with anyone. Not a word of it."

Evelin looked disappointed but did not protest as her mother stoppered the elixir. Salme put it in a cupboard, cradled in a specially made holder behind jugs of oil and containers of dried grains and lentils. She closed the door and locked it with a silver key.

"Will it really make me like Queen Karinya?" the child asked, watching her mother wash her hands.

"I don't know exactly what it will do, darling. Elixirs do different things for different fae, but I know for sure that it will do something good." She kissed the child and helped her jump down. "Go and play. Better yet, work on your runes."

Evelin ran off to the other room.

Salme closed her eyes in a moment of prayer.

"Maybe…" she whispered, "just maybe, wee one, you will one day return our kingdom to its previous greatness."

## Chapter Twenty

# Jessamine

By the time Bertrand left the cell and she'd said goodbye to Sasha—with a promise to visit Rialta with as many of the expensive oysters, Rialta's favorite, as she could pilfer from the kitchen—nearly three hours had passed. Jess's stomach was rumbling, and she had only twenty minutes left before the servants cleared the morning meal away.

Her torch in the passage had long since guttered out, so Jess was replacing the unmortared stones in near darkness when she heard the sound of wings above her head. She paused, listening as the creature landed above her. The wings ruffled, then folded, and all went silent.

"Who is there?" Jess asked. "Erasmus?"

The answer came in the form of a raspy croak that didn't sound like Erasmus. Jess finished replacing the stones, picked up her dead torch and felt her way up the stairs. The bird slipped out over her head as she emerged in the maproom, fluttering to the back of a chair. He watched her with one beady eye as she slid the secret panel closed.

"Ratchet." Jess glowered.

A form appeared in the doorway and leaned on the jamb. Kestrel—Jess assumed—crossed her arms, looking at Jess with disapproval.

"You've been trying to contact the prisoner for weeks, and now you've done it. The complacency and dullness of human guards never fails to amaze me."

Jess shook her head and a bunch of dirt and dust landed on the floor with a spatter.

"I don't know what you mean. I was returning a parchment I had borrowed when your bird…" She swallowed. It was no use. If Ratchet and Kestrel shared even half the telepathic ability that Jess and Beazle shared, Kestrel knew everything. "What are the odds that we can keep this between us? You kept it quiet the first time."

"The odds are zero." Kestrel replied blandly. "I didn't report you the first time because you didn't succeed. And there are no favors big enough to make me commit treason. I have to report you to the crofter. I'm sorry."

Ratchet let out a piercing shriek to punctuate this threat. Jess winced, squeezing her eyes shut. The maproom was too small for the full-throated scream of a raptor, even one as small as Ratchet. By the time she opened her eyes, Kestrel and Ratchet were gone.

Jess dashed to the door, catching a glimpse of Kestrel's booted heel as she turned a corner, headed for the dining hall. Jess skidded to a halt at the entrance just as Kestrel marched up to where Ian sat in conversation with a group of Fahyli at the end of a long table. Jess followed Kestrel at a slow walk, heart pounding and mouth dry.

Kestrel stood at attention until Ian noticed her. He signaled for the conversation to cease, and the Fahyli looked at Kite's sister expectantly. Jessamine approached as Kestrel began to talk.

"We caught this person"—Kestrel pointed at Jess, her arm and finger as long and straight as a poker—"sneaking out of the prisoner's cell."

Everyone went still. Ian looked at Kestrel with a blank face, one hand still wrapped around his mug. "Sneaking *out* of the prisoner's cell?" Ian parroted. "Not *in*?"

"That's correct. We intercepted her familiar, the bat, trying to make contact several weeks ago, when the prisoner was still in the caperlands building."

"Why did you not report her a few weeks ago then?" asked Ian calmly.

It was Kestrel's turn to go still. "B-b-because we-we… we prevented them from making contact. Those were our orders: keep the prisoner isolated and ensure that no unauthorized individuals contacted them."

The Fahyli were watching this exchange with interest. Ania, who had been perched on Digit's head, zipped into the air, orbited once, then hummed from the room at high-speed. Jess watched the hummingbird go, then looked at Digit. He winked, though he didn't smile.

"What do you say to these accusations, Miss Fontana?" Ian sounded toil-worn.

"Well, um…" Jess crossed her arms. More dust fell from her sleeves. "It's true. I have been trying to contact Sasha because I've been worried about him."

Ian's eyes bored through her. "You understood it was forbidden? Our laws decree that those who are to stand trial are not permitted visitors."

She swallowed. "Yes."

Pan and Regalis exchanged a look. Kite was positively glaring at her sister. Digit hadn't moved, but Ania came humming back into the room and landed on his hair, followed by Bombini, who droned across the table and landed on a tapestry with red flowers cavorting across it. Movement drew Jess's gaze to the door, where a small crowd had gathered. Slowly, as though trying not to wake a sleeping bear, they moved into the room. Rose was among them. Jalla buzzed into the room, landing on a chandelier. Then Sphex flew in, followed by Peony. The normally speedy kitchen staff moved leisurely about their cleaning activities, not wanting to miss the unfolding drama.

Ian ignored the gathering crowd. "So you knowingly flouted the law, Miss Fontana. Why? Why take such a risk? You thought that we would starve him? Or beat him, perhaps?"

Jessamine's heart sank like a pebble in a well.

Ian crossed his arms. "Or perhaps you were recruited to spy on the situation?"

Jess recoiled. "Of course not. I'm not a traitor! I just love him."

There was a collective murmur, many sounding sympathetic. It was out, now. There was no going back.

Ilishec appeared in the door, scoped out the situation, then approached the table, brow creased as he looked from Jess to the crofter and back. "What's happening?"

"I'm sorry, Gardener." Jess felt tears prick her eyes, but she refused to cry in the presence of her Fahyli friends. Her Calyx friends would understand, but the Fahyli thought the

Calyx were weak and emotional. She was loath to prove them right, even though she felt like a sharp word from Ilishec might shatter her.

Ilishec sounded frightened. His voice shook. "Why? What have you done?"

"I love Sasha, and he loves me," Jess blurted. Then it all came pouring out in a tumble. "We didn't mean to. It all happened so fast. We can't be separated, it is too painful. He has no friends here, only me, and he's not a murderer. To not be allowed to see him, to talk to him, it's unbearable. So I snuck in because, otherwise, he's all alone. It's not right, especially not after what he did for Lady Çifta."

More murmurs and exchanged looks. This time, there were no sounds of disapproval, which was a little comfort to Jess.

"Oh, Jessamine." Ilishec rubbed his forehead and closed his eyes, as though asking some deity of patience to bless him with restraint. "Why must you insist on breaking the rules? We have already bent them for you once. You are forcing my hand."

A tear slipped down Jessamine's cheek and she brushed it away. *Beazle? Where are you? I need you.*

Beazle jerked awake at her call. He dropped from the rafters in her room and fluttered around in a frenzy. *I'm coming! I'm coming!*

"Let's not be hasty," said the crofter, rising. "First of all, it is not against Fahyli rules to have relationships with courtiers, only the Calyx are restricted in this matter. She will not have consequences from me for falling in love. I've never believed that such a thing could be prevented with decrees anyway—all it does is force young people to do things in secret. And why should we care who falls in love with whom?" Ian's words were heavily loaded with criticism; it was clear he disliked Ilishec's rule. “What the Fahyli get up to on their own time is not my business. Jessamine will be punished for sneaking in to see the prisoner, but since it is clear that she was not operating against the king, it is not treason, only rule-breaking.”

Jessamine looked at Ian with glassy appreciation.

Ilishec glared at the crofter. “The Calyx are the lifeblood of this kingdom.”

Ian gave Ilishec a heavy-lidded look of annoyance. “Are they?”

“Yes,” the gardener snapped. “The reason we are the wealthiest kingdom in Ivryndi is thanks to their near-deified status. People come from hundreds of thousands of miles, not just to buy their perfume, but to worship the Calyx, to dream of obtaining them. If it was known that the Calyx could be *had* by anyone, their mystique would be destroyed, and Solana would become something less. I do not expect someone like you to understand how important it is to keep the Calyx sacrosanct.”

The crofter rolled his eyes. “I tire of your pretentiousness, Gardener.”

“Ian!” Ilishec looked surprised and hurt. “I do this for the kingdom’s sake, not for my own glory. I cannot, I will not, allow the reputation of my Calyx to be tarnished. You are Jessamine’s senior in all things Fahyli, you can do as you wish to correct her. But I have no choice but to dismiss her, as much as it pains me to do so.”

Jess covered her mouth, but not before a sob escaped. Beazle zipped into the room and plopped on her shoulder. *I’m here. Oh my. What’s happened?*

*I was caught with Sasha.* Jess squeezed her eyes shut, tears spilling down her cheeks. She was helpless to prevent them.

The humiliation, the heartbreak, Sasha, Faraçek… it was too much. *Ilishec… he's dismissing us.*

*Oh, Jess.*

Beazle did not berate her with words, but she knew his heart and understood his feelings. He was disappointed in her. She had known what she was doing was against the rules, yet she'd done it anyway, risking their position and the trust of their superiors. *She* had done this to them. Knowing how Beazle felt was worse than Ilishec's judgment, and more tears ran down Jess's face. She palmed her cheeks, trying to get herself under control, but her heart was breaking.

*I'm not angry with you.*

But he was angry. She could feel it, and it hurt. Worst of all, he was justified in his anger. This was their home. The Calyx was their family. They'd been happy, and Jess had ruined it all and taken Beazle down with her.

*We'll be fine,* Beazle told her. *Remember? As long as we are together…*

*In life and in death,* she returned, sniffing.

Peony's voice penetrated their silent mourning. "I'm in love with Pan."

Jess gaped as Peony stepped from the crowd of Calyx to stand apart. She lifted her chin and crossed willowy arms. Sphex landed on the side of her neck and buzzed his wings.

The entire hall fell silent. Not an insect moved. The kitchen staff were frozen in a tableau of activity. Eyes were round. Mouths were open. Peony stood like a queen, then looked at Panther.

Panther, beaming like this was the proudest moment of his life, got to his feet. "It's true. We've been together for over a year. We met before Peony was offered a place in the Calyx."

Ilishec had gone pale, but at least now his attention was off Jessamine and on his star fae.

"I've been seeing Lord Gillner for three years," said Rose, stepping forward to stand elbow to elbow with Peony. "We plan to marry when my time as Calyx is over."

Ilishec made a sound of scandalized outrage.

Jess's jaw dropped. *Rose? Seeing a courtier for three years*?

Beazle's response was a squeak of surprise

Ian just raised his eyebrows.

"Me and Regalis are also in love." Gardenia floated over to stand behind the long-haired Fahyli still seated at the table. She put a hand on his shoulder. He didn't look up, but one corner of his mouth lifted and a faint blush rose in his cheeks. He lay a hand over hers.

"You dirty dog, Regalis," sputtered Digit with a laugh.

"Digit," muttered Ian reproachfully. "This is serious."

"Sorry." Digit wiped the smile from his face, but it immediately returned.

Jessamine could hardly believe what she was hearing. The Calyx were standing up for her. Tears stopped leaking from her eyes.

Ilishec exploded, throwing up his hands and glaring around at the Calyx. "Anyone else? Would any others like to confess an illicit relationship? Don't spare on my account!"

Proteas wrapped his arms around one of the servant girls, who looked up at him with adoration. "Wren and I are pregnant."

There were multiple gasps of delight from around the room and several Calyx moved toward the couple to hug and congratulate them.

"Great," Ilishec said sarcastically.

"I'm in love with Kite," blurted Snap.

Kite closed her eyes and pinched the bridge of her nose. "We're not together, you idiot. You just have a crush."

Snap looked hurt. "It's not a crush. I love you."

Ian gave an irritated growl. "Even I'll admit this is ridiculous."

Ilishec looked furious, his face the color of plums.

"You can't dismiss everyone, Gardener," said Rose softly, huge eyes shining. "Maybe it's time to rethink your rule?"

"That's enough, Rose." Ilishec put up a hand. "I'm so disgusted that I can hardly speak. I'll be in my workshop. If anyone needs me… too bad."

The gardener stalked out of the room. Everyone watched him go.

*I think they just saved us,* thought Beazle.

*I think so too.* Jess smiled blearily at her friends, beaming her thanks at Peony. Her prickly frenemy had risked the thing she valued most in the world—her status as Calyx—for Jessamine. She begged with her eyes for a moment to talk with her, but Peony was whispering with Panther. He wrapped his arm around her and kissed her full on the mouth. It was jarring to see them behave so affectionately, but Jess had to admit, they looked good together.

"Miss Fontana," said Ian, as the crowd began to disperse. "Come with me, please. I'm uncertain whether to assign you to stall cleanup, or weapons repair."

As she followed Ian from the room, Jess saw that Kestrel looked dazed, like she'd just been engulfed by a tidal wave and wasn't sure which way was up.

Jessamine completed her final day of penance: four hours in the tack room attached to the stables, cleaning sweaty, smelly tack for Ian's inspection. Exhausted with only half the day gone, Jess took a quick bath to clean off the smell of horse, donned a dress, then picked up her lunchtime elixir from Mrs. Tierney's kitchen. She was guzzling it in big gulps when Snap came up to her.

"Where have you been? I've been looking for you for the past two hours!" He rolled his eyes and grabbed his hair with both hands, pulling it outward in frustration.

She swallowed the last of her drink and put the goblet in the bin for dirty dishes. "I was in the stable—gah!"

He grabbed her hand and yanked her along behind him.

"Snap!" She whacked him, trying to tug from his grasp. "You're giving me whiplash!"

"Ilishec canceled all post-lunch activities and called a meeting," he said, ignoring her complaints. "Every Calyx has to be there, no exceptions."

They joined the flow of Calyx making their way to the lecture hall and took seats at the back, near Aster and Dahlia.

Beazle flitted through the open door and landed on her head. *What's happening?*

*Calyx meeting,* Jess told him, her stomach a ball of nerves. *Ilishec has never canceled anything for a meeting before.*

The gardener appeared at the front of the room and watched as Calyx slid into the seats, all of them choosing to sit at the back. He beckoned with both hands. "Everyone move up. This is important and my eyesight isn't what it once was. I need to see your faces."

Reluctantly, the Calyx shifted to the front of the room, moving in clumps of twos and threes. Giving Jess a questioning look, Rose slid in beside her. Jess shrugged her shoulders, though she was pretty sure this was about all the illicit relationships that had been confessed to three days ago.

Ilishec waited until everyone re-settled. Hazel came in and leaned against a wall, crossing her arms.

"Many, if not all of you, will know what this is regarding." Ilishec put his hands behind his back and paced slowly back and forth on the dais. "For clarity's sake—and I will try to make myself as clear as possible—this is about several of you breaking my rule that Calyx are not to have relationships with courtiers, Fahyli, or servants."

The Calyx murmured, some of them shrank down in their seats. Jess saw the back of Peony's head, two rows in front of her, ever proud, defiance clear in her posture.

*She must really love Pan,* Jess thought, still amazed by Peony's public confession. *She risked everything for him. Her position here, her future afterward, everything she loves.*

*So have you, Jess,* Beazle reminded her.

*But I tried to keep it all hidden. She admitted it in front of everyone.*

As though Peony felt that Jess and Beazle were exchanging thoughts about her, she looked over her shoulder and caught Jess's eye. Jess gave a little smile. One corner of Peony's mouth twitched before she faced front again.

*She's far braver than I am. I wish now that I'd just been honest with Ilishec and taken whatever came. Now, I've disappointed him. How long will it take before he trusts me again?*

*I guess you've learned something, then,* Beazle replied.

Peony raised her hand, and Ilishec noticed. He wagged a finger.

"I know what you are going to say, Peony. You, of all the Calyx, are more a stickler for fine print than anyone. The rule is not in the contract. You never agreed to it in writing, therefore it should not be grounds for dismissal. Am I right?"

Peony withdrew her hand, nodding.

"You are correct. The rule was only spoken. How foolish I was to think that my Calyx might respect it, based on your regard for me and recognition of the great privilege you have."

The rebuke in his words stung, and the flora fae wilted like flowers in a sun-scorched garden. Someone began to cry softly. Gardenia, whose emotions were always so close to the surface.

"There has never been a rule against Calyx having relationships with Calyx," said Ilishec, his tone gentler now.

Upsetting the Calyx worked against his overall goal of fine fragrances for sale. How tricky it must be for him to reprimand his charges without spoiling the raw materials they were to produce in the coming days. Jess might have felt sorry for him, or at least appreciated what a fine line he walked, but she was too worried about what was still to come. He had threatened dismissal, and would have likely done it already except for the show of Calyx solidarity.

"In fact," he was saying, "though I don't outright approve of it, because any relationship is a distraction from your work, I would never forbid it. Calyx with Calyx usually means flora fae offspring, which ensures a strong future for the retinue. But I have requested that Calyx who fall for one another keep it private." He paused, letting the tension build. "I haven't slept well the past couple of nights. My own rules stipulate that I levy some kind of punishment on at least six of you for the crime of falling in love with the 'wrong' people." He took a deep breath and let it out slowly. "Hazel has helped me to see that my rule, while created with the best of intentions, goes against nature."

More murmuring, but less fearful.

"She reminded me that we too were young once, and that we fell in love while in the employ of the kingdom. As you know, Hazel was never Calyx, but she reminded me of something that I discovered firsthand in those days: Calyx who are in a loving and stable relationship produce finer fragrances."

Something loosened in Jess's chest.

Ilishec held up a finger. "The key word here is *stable*. Calyx whose relationships are filled with drama, who are heartbroken, jilted, or otherwise hurt by their lover—breakups happen to most of us at least once—produce poor raw materials. All it takes is a lover's passion to grow cold, and you may find yourself without sufficient magic. Consider yourselves warned."

He let this hang in the air. No one made a sound. It seemed like they'd forgotten how to breathe as they waited for the gardener's final judgment.

"So"—he templed his fingers—"I have decided to lift the rule. Your royalty payments will dictate whether your private behavior means you leave here wealthy or disappointed. I continue to frown upon outside relationships, and I continue to insist that—should you embark upon such a foolish endeavor—you remain professional at all times. No one at court is to know that you have *lowered* yourself in such a manner, made yourself available as it were, lest other courtiers get similar ideas. The last thing I want is to encourage more of this behavior."

Jess shrank down in her seat, buffeted by a whirlwind of feelings. She was elated—she could be with Sasha openly—but she was ashamed that she had disappointed Ilishec. There was nothing she could do about the way the gardener felt though, and she could no more change her feelings toward Sasha than she could make the moon stay longer in the sky.

The Calyx whispered among themselves, and all strain had evaporated from their faces. Gardenia stopped crying and wiped her eyes. Ilishec's warning may as well have fallen on deaf ears. Jess could see that the gardener was disappointed by their lack of solemnity about his warnings, but her own feelings of relief and joy bubbled up like sparkling wine.

Ilishec sighed, seemingly resigned to the fact that young fae had to learn for themselves.

The Calyx were quiet again, though there was a new energy in the room and a glorious floral perfume seeped into the air.

"Questions?" Ilishec looked around the room with an exhausted expression. He hadn't smiled once.

*He's upset with you,* Beazle told her. *Especially you. Don't you think?*

*Yes,* Jess returned. *Though I don't understand why. Peony and Rose have disappointed him in the same manner. They're more important to the retinue than me.*

Beazle was quiet, then: *It's because you're like a daughter to him.*

His suggestion jarred her. She shook her head. *Why would I be?*

*You're rare, and you're an orphan. Remember how upset with Ian he was when you were bruised from your Fahyli training?*

Jess remembered, but still didn't think that she was more special to Ilishec than any other Calyx. Her brow creased and Beazle felt her doubt.

*Everyone has favorites, Jess,* he told her. *Even Ilishec.*

When there were no questions, Ilishec dismissed everyone

with a final, ineffectual, "Please consider my words this afternoon. Whether you have admitted your relationships or not, I expect you to have a serious conversation with your partner about what you risk. Schedules resume as normal tomorrow. Good day."

He turned away, having never once looked in Jessamine's direction. The Calyx trickled from the room, talking quietly in their cliques. Beazle was right, everyone had favorites.

"You coming?" Snap asked, eyes bright. "I'm starving, and I want to celebrate."

Jess slid from her seat. "I just ate, but I'll come with you since our afternoon is free."

As they walked toward the exit, Rose turned to Snap. "It doesn't mean Kite will suddenly want to be with you, you know. Don't get your hopes up."

He dimpled. "Maybe not, but I don't give up easily."

Jess and Rose exchanged a smile. Snap had matured since joining the Calyx, but he still seemed like a boy. Kite was a warrior, better paired with someone older, stronger, experienced in battle. Someone like Regalis, or… Jess frowned as she remembered Sy and Mae. Sy had been strong, brave, handsome and kind. He would have been a good match for Kite. She missed him and his bandit-eyed familiar. Swallowing down the lump in her throat, Jess looked away so Rose and Snap wouldn't see her misting up and saw that Ilishec and Hazel were talking quietly near the wall.

"I want to speak to Ilishec," Jess told them. "You go ahead."

She approached Ilishec shyly, clearing her throat. He looked at her, his cool gaze making her shiver.

"I was wondering if I might have a word."

"I'm very busy, Miss Fontana." Ilishec sniffed.

Jess's stomach turned inside out. He never called her Miss Fontana; it had always been Jess or Jessamine. She twisted the fabric of her skirt, feeling vulnerable. Beazle snuggled against her, letting her know he was there.

"Queen Sylifke and her entourage arrive in a week," he continued. "I have preparations to make. I expect you to perform perfectly at her welcome banquet, regardless of any personal feelings you might have about your… lover's… situation."

"I know, Gardener." Jess felt like she was shrinking. The way Ilishec referred to Sasha seemed so cold. "Of course, but—"

"Good day, Miss Fontana." He gave her a polite nod before stalking toward the door.

Jess looked at Hazel, who gave her a sympathetic look and patted Jess on the arm.

"Give him time, dear. My husband is a proud man, and he has had to go against his conscience in order not to lose you and the others."

"Also because it was the right thing to do, I hope," Jess replied, hating the tremor in her voice.

"Right thing, wrong thing." Hazel shook her head. "One can debate the value of such a rule forever. Ilishec believed it was beneficial, and still does. He is afraid that the reputation that he has worked so hard to build will crumble little by little. But he fell in love with me, a common gardener, while he was Calyx. If it weren't for that, he would have been harder to convince."

"He does not wish to be a hypocrite," Jess said. "I understand that."

"There was no rule at that time, and we were young. He didn't have a philosophy about it then, didn't know he would become Royal Gardener. Like I said, give him time. He's hurt, and disappointed that his Calyx are not as invested in the Scented Court as he is."

"But it's not true." Jess touched the back of Hazel's hand, desperate to make her understand. "I *am* invested in the Scented Court. I want it to be just as magical as Ilishec expects it to be, and I don't believe that who I love will diminish my performance. My time at the Scented Court is finite, but I'm hoping my relationship will last a lifetime."

Hazel nodded. "Of course, my dear. I don't disagree with you."

Jess felt a fraction better. It was good to have the understanding of Ilishec's wife, even if the gardener himself was bitter.

"Is all well with you and Sasha?" Hazel asked.

Jess's body flushed with heat at just the sound of his name, spoken aloud by someone important, who knew that they were in love. At times love felt a galloping horse she was clinging to. It was scary, it was fun, but if she thought that she was in control, she'd be lying to herself.

"Other than the fact that he is awaiting trial," she replied, "all is well."

Hazel shook her head. "Oh dear. Trial? That does sound serious. Well, you'd best run along. The court awaits a queen, which is not an event we have every day." She turned away.

Jess's stomach lurched. "Uh, Hazel?"

The woman turned back, face blank. "Yes?"

Jess lowered her voice. "Is it true that Ilishec thinks of me like… like a daughter?"

Hazel looked confused. "I'm sorry, my dear. What did you say your name was?"

Jess blinked. The reminder of Hazel's condition was like a

slap in the face. One moment she was lucid and articulate, the next, she didn't recognize who she was talking to. It had to be devastating for Ilishec and Jess was guilty of forgetting that. She felt speared with shame. Why was it so hard for her to think of anyone but herself these days?

"I'm Jessamine. Jess Fontana." Jess tried to smile.

"That's a lovely name," Hazel touched her shoulder. "How pretty you are. Are you new?"

"No, ma'am." Jess suppressed a cough. Her throat felt so dry. "I'm still in my first year, but I can't say I'm new."

A shadow of vague remembrance crossed Hazel's face. "You had a question, darling?"

"Never mind." Jess waved a hand. "It's not important, Hazel."

Hazel smiled and her concern melted away. "I must get back to the dance hall. Today we are learning new steps to perform for Queen Karinya. She is coming all the way from Silverfall. It's very exciting."

Jess's mouth opened, but she said nothing, recalling that Ilishec had told her that being corrected only upset Hazel.

*Sylifke, not Karinya,* Jess thought, letting out a long breath as she left the hall.

## Chapter Twenty-One

# Çifta

Salme looked older now, moving stiffly through the trees as the harvesters tapped them at the start of another season. They did not have the joy on their faces that they once had, and even the hope that had been there in the early years following the battle had vanished.

Salme crunched across crusty snow, her feet breaking through, jarring her body with every step. She was out of breath when she reached the pail. She lifted it and sniffed, wrinkling her nose in distaste.

"You'd better not let one of the Dharkans see you make that face," warned the female harvester who had once stood by the door of the courtyard to warn Salme of incoming fae. "Or worse yet, the queen."

Salme replaced the bucket with an empty one and carried the full one to a silver drum sitting on the back of a cart. As she poured out the sap, Çifta could see its color: not green, but a cloudy topaz. Salme turned her face away so she wouldn't smell it as it tumbled into the drum.

*The color of the elixir changed from green to pale amber in response to the unseelie age now ruling the winter kingdom,* explained the ice.

"They pretend like it's the most potent, the most vibrant, the most delectable our kingdom has harvested," she grumbled, adding the empty bucket to the stack to be rinsed.

Her companion switched out a bucket before trudging to the cart. "I don't think they're pretending. They prefer the unseelie version because they are unseelie, most of them. Naturally, it is to their taste."

A young female just coming into her teen years ran across the snow toward them, weaving between the trees.

"Evelin!" Salme brightened. "What are you doing here?"

"Hello Erya," said Evelin to Salme's harvesting companion.

Erya smiled at the girl. "Hello, dear one. Staying out of trouble?"

"Sometimes." Evelin dimpled and went to her mother's side, looking like she had news.

Erya moved away among the trees, giving Evelin and Salme a moment of privacy.

Salme brushed her daughter's long white locks back from her face. Çifta felt a tightening sensation in her heart as the planes and curves of Evelin's face were easy to see. She could see her own countenance there. Evelin was paler, her ears pointed, and her face framed by that bright Silverfae hair, yet Çifta felt she could have been looking at herself around the age of twelve.

Salme cupped her daughter's chin gently in her fingers. "Finished your exams already?"

Evelin beamed. "Finished, and I mastered them, Mam. They were easy, especially the language exams. Professor Velmat says I have a gift for foreign tongues."

"Well done, child."

"Do you think…" Evelin lowered her voice, stealing a glance around before continuing. "Do you think it might be the gift, from the… stuff? A gift for languages? I like them so much, and I'm so good at them, I'd like to become a translator."

Salme gave a sad smile, releasing her daughter's chin. "No, darling. As I've told you before, your gifts will only manifest after the ice ritual. You seem determined to forget this simple fact. Why is that?"

Evelin's joy fell away. She went quiet, her fingers twisted together. She spoke just above a whisper. "I am afraid, Mam."

Salme went to the nearest bucket, switching it out with an empty one before returning to the drum. Her expression had tightened. She was struggling with patience, this obviously being a conversation they'd had before, perhaps many times.

Salme poured out her bucket before turning to her daughter. "All Silverfae fear the ice, Evelin."

Evelin's eyes shone with unshed tears. "Not as much as me. I have… bad dreams…"

"I know." Salme sighed. "The dreams are normal too."

Evelin's chin trembled as she grew more distressed. She whispered, "Don't make me do it. The ice will kill me. I know it."

Salme rested her hands on her daughter's upper arms, looking Evelin full in the face. "You have Karinya's elixir flowing through your veins. You will not die."

"I will," Evelin replied, her voice rising. "I will. If you force me, I'll die, and that will be on you! Is that what you want?"

Salme grew alarmed. "Keep your voice down. What is wrong with you today? Did someone say something? One of your unseelie classmates? I've told you not to listen to them."

Evelin looked angry, her forehead knitted, her fine white brows pressing together. She glared at her mother and hissed, "It's not them who upset me, it's you!"

"Evelin," Salme replied reproachfully.

Evelin pushed away, stomped a few feet in the snow before turning back to hurl: "You put unreasonable expectations on me, and you don't care if I die. I hate you. Do you hear me? I hate you!"

Hurt transformed Salme's features. She reached for her daughter.

"No." Evelin yelled, and ran away, feet light on the crust.

Salme stood for a long time, distressed, shocked. Her hands were shaking as she reached up to her harvester's turban, topaz colored, like her cape. Dry snow swirled through the trees as the wind kicked up. A shiver wracked her body, and she tugged her cape closed, staring forlornly after her daughter.

Erya's footsteps made Salme turn, forcing an expression of calm. "I suppose you heard the yelling?"

"All teenagers yell," said Erya gently. "Remember when you were her age? Evelin is a mild-mannered youth, but even she must pass through this difficult stage of life. Times are not easy. Especially for the young Seelie."

"Evelin does not have the luxury of behaving like a spoiled brat," Salme snapped, then sucked in a breath and put a seeking hand toward her friend. "I am sorry, Erya. I am not angry with you. I am disappointed in my daughter. She is no ordinary Seelie, so I do not have ordinary expectations for her."

Erya's brows lifted. "You think Evelin of higher value than

other faelings of her age? Worth perhaps more than my Terrinia, or Septyna?"

Salme closed her eyes, her cheeks flushed with shame. "No, of course not. I apologize, my friend. I am just… upset. I did not think. I am a stupid old seelie, pay me no mind."

Erya came to Salme and took the older female in her arms, simply holding her for a while. When Erya pulled back she smiled at Salme. "Apology accepted. We all feel that way about our offspring, even when we haven't snuck them contraband that we feel sure will make a difference." She glanced up, measuring what little diffused light managed to come through the cloud cover. "Come. We have much to do and the day is late."

Day and night marched on for Silverfall. The cloud cover never lifted, the weather never improved. The best the Silverfae could hope for was a day without wind to blast snow and ice into their faces, and make even easy tasks difficult.

Salme stood before the snowdrop tree, her expression fraught. She had new lines bracketing her mouth, and puffy pockets had sprouted beneath her eyes. Years had passed, years that had stressed her, aged her.

"I don't know what to do," she whispered, putting her forehead against the trunk and squeezing her eyes shut. "I have failed you, my queen. All the years, all the effort, all the risks I've taken, the hopes… it is all for nothing if Evelin won't go through with it. I have begged her, cajoled her, she still simply refuses. There is nothing I can say to change her mind. What should I do?"

A male voice made Salme jump back from the tree, her face full of guilt.

"Were you talking to the tree?" A nobleman dressed in a white quilted tunic and a thick topaz-colored belt approached, long hair tied back exposing a high forehead. He sauntered nearer, moving with all the confidence of a courtier who had the world laid before him on a platter.

*This is Vin Sabran*, the ice told Çifta. *Master of the ice in Sylifke's court.*

*What does that mean?*

*He oversees all those who undergo the ritual.*

"What is your name, harvester?" Vin asked.

"Master Sabran." She dipped into a curtsy so low that it took effort for her to stand again. "My name is Salme."

He gazed at her with curiosity. "Why were you talking to the tree?"

"It may have looked that way, Master Sabran, but I can assure you that that was not, in fact, what I was doing. My legs are not what they once were, and I was leaning against the tree to take a rest. And as I did so, I was talking to myself."

"Touching the tree is not encouraged, you know," Vin told her in an oily voice. "Gazing upon it and admiring the queen's triumph, and the unique magic she retains, is expected. But do you really think you should treat such a trophy with so little respect? As a support for your weakness?"

Salme looked down at the flagstones. "No, Master Sabran. I beg your pardon."

It was apparent to Çifta, and therefore to Vin, that Salme was extremely uncomfortable and wished more than anything to be dismissed. He stared at her for seconds without responding. This was a trick Çifta knew from her father, a simple but effective way to winkle out true motives from someone who had something to hide. Stay silent, and their own discomfort will bring words to their lips.

"If Master will forgive his servant," Salme said, "I have much to—"

Vin interrupted her—not something Kazery would have done—and put on an air of contemplation. "I'm sure someone mentioned you to me once before, now that I think of it. It is not the first time you have used this sacred place to mutter to yourself about your problems."

"I apologize again, Master."

"No need to apologize." He waved a hand and gave Salme a smile that left few of his gleaming teeth covered. "Perhaps I can help. What troubles you?"

When Salme hesitated, he pursued her with all the passion of a religious zealot. "Come, do not hide your problems from me. I am not just master of the ice, I am also to help the queen's subjects where I can. Let me help."

A change came over Salme, as subtle as a new leaf uncurling in the spring. Çifta could not put her finger on what changed, but something had shifted in her grandmother's mind as she looked into Vin's face.

"It's my daughter, Master Sabran," simpered Salme in a manner so unlike her that Çifta was filled with sudden dread. "I worry about her. That is all. Every mother in the kingdom can relate to my problem. It is not uncommon."

The master took in this information with interest. "Who is your daughter? Would I have seen her at court?"

"Not likely, Master. She is too young for court. Her name is Evelin."

"And why does she trouble you?"

"She…" Salme paused as though reconsidering what she was about to say.

*Here,* the ice whispered. *Watch.*

Salme plowed forward. "She does not wish to undergo our beloved ritual, and it is a source of shame to me."

"Ah." Vin's expression expanded with sympathy and understanding. "As you say, that is normal. Every faeling is anxious about the ice. I was, too. Of course, if it were up to Queen Sylifke, all faelings would undertake the test. But I have told her many times that some are simply not suitable. Someone needs to keep our bellies full, our clothing washed, our boots polished. Try not to be too hard on her."

"I agree with you, Master," said Salme demurely. "It's just, mothers often have a sense about their children, and I know Evelin could be great." Salme looked him in the eyes and lay a palm over her chest. "I know it in my heart. I do not wish the kingdom to be deprived of the wondrous magic that my daughter will surely acquire."

Vin's gray-white gaze bored into hers. "Many mothers will say with their lips that they wish their children to undertake the test, but in their hearts, they do not mean it. No one wants to lose a child. I may be male, but I have seen enough mothers to understand that most of them would rather have a living faeling without magic than watch their child fall from the ice, lifeless and cold. But you… you seem genuine in your desire for Evelin to undertake our most sacred ritual. Are you?"

Salme kept her eyes on his. "I am genuine, Master Sabran. I wish for it, most fervently."

Vin didn't say anything for a long time, but neither did he dismiss her. When he spoke again, it was in a low voice. "If you really mean it, I will mention your daughter to the queen."

"Oh, Master!" Salme's face filled with hope and gratitude, and fear—yes, lots of that. Çifta could practically smell the concern baking off her grandmother. She had not forgotten Evelin's words, the child's fear that she would not survive.

Vin stepped closer, his mouth near Salme's ear. Other Silverfae had entered the courtyard and were making their slow circles, noting the presence of the master as he conversed with a harvester. "You understand what it would mean? Were I to do this favor for you? There will be no going back."

"I understand," Salme whispered. "It will be for the best."

*Queen Sylifke can force any subject into a freezing, and she does so frequently. Of course, many die. But some survive, and with magnificent magic, magic that she considers hers, because without her it would never have manifested.*

Horror, like moonlight rising over an open grave, dawned on Çifta. *If the master brings Evelin to Sylifke's attention...*

*Evelin will have no choice.*

*But this is a betrayal!*

*Yes, Salme's allegiance to the former queen is greater than her allegiance to her daughter. A rare Silverfae indeed.*

Before Çifta could rally a response, the scene melted, spinning away like a snow devil until it reformed on a place Çifta had never seen.

A river of dark water with a strong current carried a small boat beneath an arch of unhewn rubble. Roots jutted through the stones, twisting along the cavern walls like tentacles. Two lanterns, one fixed to the prow and the other to the stern, provided light for the boat's occupants. Inky darkness went on forever ahead of the boat and lay out behind it just as endlessly. A slim male figure in a cloak stood at the stern with a bargepole, pushing the wooden vessel through the water, though the current was strong enough to carry it alone. A second figure, but female, was swaddled in a cloak as well, hood up. She sat stiff and upright, looking straight ahead.

A fresh gust of air made both fae take deep breaths.

"We are almost at the end of this cavern," said the male.

The female drew her hood back, revealing long, curly white hair. Evelin had become truly beautiful, with clear bright eyes visible in the torchlight. When the night sky opened over the couple, she looked up at the stars. She wiped away the tears streaming down her face.

"Hey, now," he said gently. "We can go back. It's not too late. You've only been gone for one day."

With both palms against her cheeks, she shook her head. She sent him a look of misery before facing front again. "No. Thank you, but I cannot."

"Aren't you Evelin Sariatha? Why did you tell me your name was Merya?"

Evelin's face cramped with terror. She yanked her hood up.

"Don't worry," he told her in a soothing voice. "Your secret is safe with me. I'd be in almost as much trouble for helping you as you would be if they caught you. I'm not going to tell anyone, no matter what your name is."

She nodded but didn't look back again or take her hood down. They continued in silence. A forest rose around them, thick and gnarled and impassable on foot. Dark treetops, jagged against the cloudy sky, closed in on either side of the river, like black sawblades.

"You were supposed to freeze," he said quietly. "That's why you're leaving."

"No, that's not it," she answered quickly. "At least, not entirely."

"I don't want to freeze either," he told her. "You'll have

no judgment from me. I don't know why they pressure us so much when the outcome is mostly bad. It's better to be alive and without magic, if you ask me."

Evelin gripped the sides of the boat with white fingers. "That's not even the worst of it."

He almost laughed. "What could be worse than dying from a failed experiment, and all for the queen's entertainment?"

"It was my own mother who brought me to the queen's attention." Evelin began to weep silently again. "My own mother. She thinks…"

The young male looked shocked, his eyes like saucers. "Does your mother hate you?"

"No. She loves me. She's a wonderful mother, actually." Evelin sniffed and got herself under control again. Wiping her face, she turned to look back at him. "She thinks that I will become something I'm not. Destined to… return the kingdom to its former glory."

He rolled his eyes. "Reasonable expectations, then."

Evelin's focus went inward, far away from this boat she shared with a near stranger. "I used to believe it too, when I was small."

His brows hiked up. "Why would you? She told you stories when you were little that you were something special?"

"Not exactly. My mother is a harvester, and… over the course of years," Evelin turned to face front again, "she secretly gathered sap from the snowdrop tree in the courtyard."

Evelin did not see the impact her words had on the lad, how his face changed, but Çifta saw it. He lost his expression of solidarity and instead absorbed the news with a new light coming into his eyes, one of amazement. She told him her whole story, and he listened in silence.

When she finished, Evelin waited for a response, but when he didn't speak, she said, "Don't tell me that you would do it, if it were you?"

He looked doubtful, then let out a long sigh as he steered them around a curve. The forest was thinning and the banks climbing, leaving them in a gorge. Overhead, the sky was gray with approaching dawn, the clouds threatening to dump snow.

"I don't know… maybe…"

She looked aghast. "Really?"

"Well, it's bigger than you. Isn't it? Something like that… it's about all of us." He looked afraid of offending her, but also like he wanted to be honest.

She went quiet for a while. Then, "I shouldn't have told you. You think less of me."

"Oh no," he protested. "I don't."

She turned, sending a pleading look his way. "You'll not tell a soul? You promised!"

"I'll not tell," he told her. "Like I said, my skin is also on the line. You're not like the others, just a faeling who wants a different life—a life in a place with a change of seasons—you're… you carry the elixir of Karinya's snowdrop in your veins. If they find out I helped you, I'm dead."

"I'm sorry, Millen." She faced front again. "It just felt good to share it with someone. I've been carrying this burden since I was four, almost my whole life."

"No doubt," agreed the lad. "We will join the Tadylat soon and that's as far as I can take you. If you hike up the eastern bank, you'll come to a harbor. From there… a pretty thing like you can hitch a ride to anywhere."

"Thank you, Millen." She adjusted her hood over her hair, then reached into her cloak and pulled out a small bag. She leaned back and dropped it into the middle of the boat. "There's a little extra in there, for your ear and your discretion."

Millen looked at the sack, a deep sadness stealing over his features. He swallowed but said no more to Evelin. Not even when he helped her get out of the boat. He only nodded, head down, when she said goodbye.

Evelin watched Millen trade the barge pole for oars, perhaps waiting for him to look at her, standing on the bank with her runaway sack. But he only bent his strong body to the oars for the long journey upstream, back to their homeland.

## Chapter Twenty-Two

# Laec

Three days before Sasha's trial, Sylifke arrived with a small entourage, explaining to Bradburn that she'd had to leave part of her escort behind to deal with the sleighs when an unexpected storm struck. They would arrive a few days later. Laec had no plans to attend her welcome banquet until he found a hint that he'd been invited; a fine new outfit hanging in his room. So, that evening he donned the clothing—oyster-gray leather leggings, as soft and buttery as kid gloves, a smoke gray quilted vest and a wool jacket with tails—and made his way to the ballroom. The moment Laec got a glimpse of mystic blooms spinning in the air, he retreated to the third-floor balcony for a better view. He spied Jessamine easily, wearing an ice-blue sheath dress that glittered in the etherlights like sunlight on freshly fallen snow. Winking and sparkling as she moved, the gown highlighted her lithe body and contrasted with the tan skin of her hands, collarbones and neck. Her sublime expression gave nothing away of her personal feelings about the being they were performing for.

Ilishec and Olinya had chosen a winter theme, naturally, and the Calyx were beautiful in whites and pastel hues. With all that glittery white makeup, they looked like dolls dipped in icing sugar, even the males. They swirled gracefully around the dance floor, spewing transparent blossoms from their fingers, and sprouting real ones from pots of soil that had been dusted with white powder to look snow-covered. Fragrance filled the room, and the Silverfae seated among the locals looked reluctantly impressed. Queen Sylifke—seated in a position of honor, to the right of the king—wore layers of silky fabric. Her head was covered by a pale purple veil that looked brown in the etherlight. Her gown and cape were also purple, darker than the veil, the color of ripe eggplant. No part of Sylifke was uncovered, not even her hands, which were encased in gloves as white as bone. She was unseelie. There would be talons at the end of her skeletal and obscenely long fingers beneath those gloves, and probably short fangs in her mouth too. Behind her stood two of her Silverfae escorts, both staring at the Calyx.

The sight of this merry-making while Lady Çifta stood trapped in her frigid prison, her life hanging in the balance, filled his mouth with ash. He was about to turn away when his gaze hooked on Kazery, standing just inside the doorway, looking around with his mouth slightly ajar. He looked more perplexed than impressed, but when he was approached by Hob and invited to sit, he followed him through the crowd—trailed by two of his assistants, who stared at the Calyx like they thought they'd died and these must be angels.

Laec couldn't go down there and pretend to have a good time or pretend to care that the talents of the Calyx or the palace chefs mattered to him. He couldn't dance with Çifta, either, so pretending gaiety would feel like a betrayal.

He returned to Çifta's ballroom through hallways that were mostly empty. He stripped off the tails and tunic, staring up at the ice. The freezing, burning sensation that stung him when he contacted the ice had become a meditation he welcomed now. He hoped it was helping Çifta—there was no way he could know for sure—but strangely enough, it was helping him. In spite of the rash, in spite of the pain, every time he did this, he felt closer to her. There were times he imagined he could hear her breathing, her heart beating. It was ridiculous, of course, but people tell themselves all manner of lies in order to get through difficult times. Lies had become his friend.

He put his arms up and stepped forward, placing his torso against the frozen pillar. He closed his eyes as a thousand tiny needles stabbed into him, piercing, burning, itching. He had begun a second round once all the block's faces had become translucent, but the sensations had not eased with the loss of the frost.

A soft sound from the door made Laec turn. A few Fahyli and servants knew what he was doing and took pity on him sometimes, bringing him soup and bread. They'd even sworn themselves voluntarily to secrecy because they thought it was both romantic… and insane.

Kazery stood in the doorway, his fine hat pressed against his chest, his gaze locked on the scene before him, face utterly unreadable. Bafflement stole over his features, followed by a flash of annoyance, then something positive, something like… pleasant surprise, maybe.

"Did you see them?" the merchant asked. His boots were loud on the parquet flooring as he crossed it.

Laec stood like a cornered rabbit, uncertain how to feel aside from ashamed. His clothing lay in a gray puddle on the floor, his pale skin already a flushed and splotchy red. "I… sorry, who?"

"Those puddings dressed in lace and tulle," Kazery growled. His gaze drifted over Laec, taking in his state of undress, then to the ice, and back again.

"The… Calyx?" Laec felt confused. Kazery had just been in the ballroom. Laec had seen him talking with Hob, settling in for the show and the meal. How could he be *here*?

Kazery waved a hand. "Not them; they're just doing their job. I mean the rest of them. The powdered poofs who've never known a day's hard work in their lives, laughing and simpering." He gave a high-pitched giggle, followed by a moue of disgust. "How can they pretend like everything is fine? Like there isn't a girl fighting for her life in here, a lonely corner of their castle. Forgotten."

"I can't pretend everything is fine," Laec said slowly. "I haven't forgotten." He watched Kazery, who looked as though he might charge like a bull if too sudden a movement was made.

One bushy black eyebrow lifted like it was tied to a puppeteer's string. "Apparently, not. I mostly bring up the others for lack of something else to say besides, what do you think you're doing? I would wring your stringy little neck with my bare hands if I didn't suspect your bizarre and inappropriate behavior might actually be helping her."

Laec crossed his arms defiantly over his chest. "I couldn't think of anything else."

"There's a huge fireplace, and enough firewood to get through ten Boskayan winters." Kazery gestured to the cords that Laec had ordered what felt like eons ago.

"That was my original plan." Laec wasn't about to plaster his body against Çifta's pillar while her father was watching, so he picked up his vest and pulled it over his head. He tugged his hair out from under the collar, uncomfortable under the merchant's steady gaze. "Turns out fire is no good in this situation."

"Your original plan…" Kazery considered him. "Who are you, exactly?"

"We met—"

"I know we met. You're Laec Fairijak of Stavarjak, representative of Queen Elphame of the spring kingdom. I never forget a face or a name. I can't, not in my business. What I want to know is,"—he took a step closer—"who are you to my daughter?"

"I'm a friend," Laec said, keeping his shoulders square to the merchant-pirate.

"A friend." Kazery pointed a sausage-sized finger at the ice. "That stuff burns when you touch it."

"I know."

"*I know, you know*. What I'm saying is, you must be more than a friend."

Laec wasn't sure what to say to that. Kazery studied the ice, the smoothed translucent patches versus the opaque frostiness of the bottom of the pillar, around Çifta's legs and ankles, that Laec had not touched.

"I do believe you're making a difference, albeit a small one," the merchant muttered, laying his palm flat on the ice. His jaw flexed as he grit his teeth against the pain of it. When he pulled his hand away, there was a new expression in his gaze: respect.

"You're mad," the merchant said. "But I thank you. It's more than anyone else has done."

Laec blinked. "You're… welcome."

"Keep it up. You'll have no complaint from me, Stavarjak." Kazery patted Laec's shoulder, almost sending him sprawling. The merchant turned toward the door. "Just don't think that I'll be giving you her hand in marriage because you were willing to get a rash."

Anger surged through Laec. "Still planning to wed her to that madman, I see?"

Kazery stopped and turned, his eyes big. "Of course not! What do you take me for? An Archelian slave-merchant? I love my daughter! If she had told me the truth—"

"—you might have sparked a war," Laec seethed. "That's why she never said anything. And, by the way, she tried. Before we rescued her, she wrote to you, telling you she wanted out. The prince burned her letter and forced her to write another, one full of lies claiming she was happy. Did you even look into the prince's character? Check what kind of person you were saddling your daughter to? Or did you just see cheap passage on the twin rivers, and a rich ally with a big military?"

"How dare you!?" Kazery thundered forward, eyes narrowing.

He knocked his hat off, which fell to the floor, and swung his arms up, hands fisted and ready for a fight. It was like being approached by a mountain, but Laec lifted his chin and balled his own fists, ready to punch back, even if it was the last thing he did.

Kazery stopped in front of Laec, looking down with fire in his eyes. "I'll not have judgment from you, you carrot-topped little fairy! You know nothing of me, where I came from, who I am. You know nothing of how I raised my daughter, what I sacrificed to keep her safe. Or… who I lost. Don't presume you know anything about our family."

Laec lost his vitriol at the mention of what had to be Çifta's mother.

"Did you know the prince was controlling her with parasitic magic? All he had to do was breathe on her"—Laec pursed his lips and blew into the merchant's face—"and his poison shut down her mind. If I hadn't gotten her out of there, she'd be married to the devil… and you wouldn't even know it."

Çifta's father blinked, obviously disturbed by this, though trying not to show it. He took a step back.

"I'm not saying I've been perfect," he said, his voice low, "but I love my daughter. I'm grateful that you saved her and I'm sorry I didn't understand the situation better—though looking back, I don't know how I could have. Osvitan was a good man, and Ander was a good son, a prince with a bright future. How was I to know Faraçek was anything other than good, too?"

Laec nodded, eyes glittering. "Yet here we are. She is just as much a prisoner as she would have been in Rahamlar, in spite of either of us."

"Yes," Kazery growled. "Here we are. Just don't forget that she is my daughter, and when she comes out of that ice, she'll be coming home with me, to marry a man of my choosing, no matter how many inches you melt away with your bare skin."

Laec was winded, and at a loss for words as the merchant stalked away.

If Çifta had been just a friend, Laec could have found an easy comeback; it would have been waiting at the tip of his tongue, the way comebacks always were. But he loved Çifta, was in love with her, and harbored secret dreams—hidden so well they'd hardly been known to himself—that she might one day be his. She used to look at him like she harbored those dreams too, since that time at the Hashe estate when they'd cuddled kittens and laughed over newborn calves together. And now, in one moment, with a single sentence, her father swung words like an axe and splintered those dreams like kindling, before they'd had enough time, enough air, to grow into something more than a wisp of hope.

Laec looked at the door long after Kazery vanished, feeling despair wash over him, along with memories of the woman behind him: How she had looked up at him when she had stepped from her carriage in Cardagenya. The way she'd stood on top of her luggage in the unnamed forest, fearlessly yelling expletives at thieves. The way she felt in his arms as they'd danced, her breath against his neck. He could see in his mind's eye her black-lashed ice-blue eyes gazing at him with such longing that his insides flushed with warmth.

He turned and looked at the woman-shaped blur inside the pillar, immovable, unalive.

"Even if you can never be mine," he said quietly, "I will go on. My physical pain is nothing compared to my mental anguish while you're inside that thing. I'll never stop, never give up. And I don't just mean about this." He lay his hand against the ice, feeling the burning itch razor into his palm. "I mean about love. I let someone go once before, and maybe we weren't right for each other, but I'll never know, will I? I don't want to spend the rest of my life wondering—we fae live too long for that. No matter what your father says or does, it's not his word that matters. It's yours. So I'm just going to do the only thing that I can to make sure that you will speak again."

With that, he tugged off his jacket and vest and went back to work.

## Chapter Twenty-Three

# Çifta

Çifta recognized the makeshift buildings, the dirt roads, the deep-water harbor full of sailing vessels, and the icy tundra. They were in front of the street side property where her mother had died, but instead of Kazery going in, he was coming out, and kicking someone else out ahead of him; a portly man with crumbs spilled down the front of his jacket. The man sprawled onto the street, narrowly avoiding being run over by a carriage.

"Good riddance!" Kazery's young face was twisted with anger as he yanked the door closed behind him.

An assortment of furniture, crockery, and some dingy bed linens had been given the same treatment as their owner. A tin cylinder rolled down the street, spilling grain as it went. Clothing lay scattered across the walkway. What might have once been underwear, but now resembled a rag, had landed on the nearby white picket fence. The woman in the neighboring yard flicked them off with the end of her pruning shears, shooting both men a look of disgust.

Kazery didn't notice the neighbor or the skivvies that went flying into the street. He bared his teeth in a sarcastic grin. "You know what, Janus? I'm *glad* you were late with the rent for the fifth month in a row. You're a slob and a lecher. I doubt I'll ever be fully rid of your stench."

"But if I could only have one more day," Janus pleaded, gathering bits of wardrobe from the street. "Two more days. I know you can manage it. Ye're a kind and patient man."

"Too kind. Too patient." Kazery locked the front door with the twist of one meaty fist. "You don't know how lucky you are. Six years ago, I gutted those who ignored their debts. Someone else can teach you how to be an adult, Janus. I'm finished giving chances."

"But where will I go?" the man whined, clearly disbelieving Kazery's claim about previous treatment of those who owed him money.

"I care not," Kazery growled. He stalked down the street toward the town center, dropping the key in an inner pocket of his jacket, then buttoning it up for good measure.

Dirty clothes and other items piled in his arms, Janus stumbled after him. "But there's no vacancies in town…"

"You should have thought of that before."

Kazery sped up, pulled his hat down around his ears as the wind whistled between the narrow buildings, throwing dirt and snow into the air. He graciously acknowledged passers-by as though he wasn't being followed by a man carrying an armload of dirty laundry.

"Good day to you, Captain Kleck," Kazery called to a man in a military uniform standing outside a storefront. A wooden blade sign pronounced in a crooked handwriting that it was the home of the Postal Service. The military man lifted his hat to the merchant but did not smile. Whoever Captain Kleck was, he wasn't someone Janus wished to be seen by. Kazery's over bright greeting was enough to send him scurrying into a side street.

Kazery went into the building and waited in the small space while a young woman was served ahead of him. Long white curls spilled out from beneath her knitted cap and he seemed captured by her hair, the way it gleamed like spun silver. While her hair was glorious, her clothing was not: a too-large homespun dress that had been patched in various places, and one of her boots had a hole in the toe. Her jacket of brown oiled canvas swam around her torso, the sleeves rolled up so they didn't cover her hands. The only part of her outfit that was the same as the last time Çifta had seen Evelin was her gray scarf. The rest looked like hand-me-downs.

Evelin had one hand flat on the countertop, pinning down an envelope, while the clerk had hold of the same envelope, patiently waiting for her to relinquish it to his care.

"You're absolutely certain that this letter will go directly to the addressee, and to no one else?" Evelin asked sternly, her expression concerned.

"Yes, milady," said the young clerk earnestly. "For the most part, that is what we do."

Evelin frowned. "But, you see, when you say 'for the most part,' I get a sick feeling in my tummy. 'For the most part' is not acceptable."

Kazery's lips twitched.

"This letter," Evelin continued, "is going to my mother, you see, whom I have not seen or spoken to in years. It is of great importance that it be put into her hands, and her hands alone."

The clerk let go of the letter and gestured with both hands to a white canvas bag held in a wooden frame. It bulged with mail. He spoke patiently, gently, taking her concerns seriously. "Miss, after I put the envelope into the mailsack, it goes into the care of another postal worker. I don't see it again after that, so I'm afraid I can't give you any personal guarantees. However, I am told that we offer excellent service, and I can assure you that it will make it to the Silverfall border to be handed off. As I'm sure you know already,"—he gazed pointedly at her hair—"they prefer to handle their own mail."

Evelin snatched the letter back. "I'm so sorry to have wasted your time."

The clerk looked troubled, and a red flush crept up from under his collar. "But you don't have anything to worry about. Who would wish to interfere with a letter from a young fae to her family?"

Evelin tucked the letter into a pocket. "I'm so sorry. My mistake."

She turned and ran straight into Kazery's barrel chest. Bouncing off him, she almost fell. He grabbed her elbow to steady her. She looked up with those oversized Silverfae eyes shining with unshed tears. Her lower lip was trembling.

"I beg your pardon, sir. I am full of mistakes today."

"Not to worry, Miss." Kazery smiled at her. "We all have those days."

Evelin nodded, brushing at her eyes. She slipped around him and out the door. Kazery watched her go, bemused.

The young clerk straightened his uniform. "Help you, Mr. Unya?"

Kazery finished his transaction and stepped outside. Scanning the street, he spied Evelin walking slowly up the road, shoulders hunched against the wind. He hurried to catch up to her, dodging potholes and dirty snowdrifts.

"Miss?"

She turned, expression fraught, tears lining her lids.

"I couldn't help but overhear your conversation with the clerk." He fell in step with her. "Maybe I can help?"

She looked down at her toes, slowing a little. "That's nice of you, but no thank you. I'm not in the practice of accepting assistance from strangers."

"Wise of you to be cautious," he told her. "I am raising my daughters to be just as careful; however, sometimes we find ourselves in difficulty, and its only acceptance of kindness from a stranger that relieves us."

She looked away, biting her lip.

Encouraged, he said, "If it's so important to get a letter to your family, you don't have options aside from the Ivryndian postal service."

"I'll think of something." She kicked a stone out and shrank down inside her hand-me-down coat.

"I keep a small aviary on my ship," Kazery told her. "I need them for communications when I'm at sea. I have four well-trained birds. Two are pigeons from Archelia—well known for their excellent birds—the other two…" He gave her a cocky smile. "Well… they're fae species and never fail. You'd be welcome to use one to get your correspondence to your family."

Evelin looked up, wide-eyed. "Why would you help me?"

He lifted his shoulders. "Why wouldn't I? I have been helped by many strangers. Life provides opportunities to return favors, and this is one such opportunity for me. You have need of a trustworthy delivery, and I have birds that have never failed."

Her eyes narrowed. "What do you want in return?"

He looked thoughtful. "I'm in need of someone to clean a rental property before it goes back on the market. It isn't a very big house and shouldn't take long. I would have one of my sailors do it but they're all needed at the docks. I would do it myself, but frankly, I hate cleaning and I'm not very good at it. I'm likely to make it worse."

Evelin's caution eased. "I'd be happy to do that in exchange for the use of a bird."

Kazery held out a hand. "We have an agreement, then, Miss…"

"Paula," she lied, shaking with him. "You?"

"Kazery."

She nodded. "Very well. Where is this house?"

He released her hand, eyes sparkling. "Tell you what, I have an errand at the harbor. We can go to my ship first and get that letter of yours on its way, then I can take you to the house. I will provide the supplies you'll need. If you can have it in shape by nightfall tomorrow, I'd be happy as a gull with a sardine."

Evelin agreed, and they headed for the harbor.

Çifta kept her sights on Kazery and Evelin, her parents, as the ice withdrew her from the scene, pulling back and back.

*My father lets her stay there.*

*Yes. They fall in love and Evelin becomes pregnant with you. The moment you are conceived, something extraordinary happens back in Silverfall.*

The misty darkness before Çifta slowly cleared as they descended into the heart of the Silverfall courtyard and approached the snowdrop tree. It was deep in the night and the palace was quiet. The white bark of the tree's trunk was etched with elegant patterns, like frost: curlicues, feathery fronds and fern-like designs.

*So beautiful*, thought Çifta. *There is nothing like these trees in Boskaya.*

*They are exclusive to the winter kingdom,* returned the ice. *Are you watching?*

*Yes.*

At first, there was nothing to see but bark, then, slowly, slowly, a line of darkness seeped into its surface, stretching out from a central point, up the bark and down, until it became half the length of a palm, then stopped growing.

*A flaw appeared in the bark when I was conceived?*

*Not a flaw. You cannot yet see what it will be, but its presence will change the kingdom. Let me take you forward to the moment of your birth. Watch.*

Night and day sped by in quick succession. Figures moved about the tree, noticing the line, studying it, discussing it, arguing over it. Çifta recognized Salme, but her grandmother came and went too quickly to register her reactions. As time passed, more lines joined the first, each spaced at a short distance from the last, like the notches on a cell wall from a prisoner counting days. Some of the lines were slanted, but most were upright. Then a second row appeared below the first. Pale-green sap oozed from the cuts, but as it dried, it darkened to a stark red.

Sylifke appeared, first on her own, then again with a male. The queen seemed fascinated by the marks, pointing to them the way one might when discussing a piece of art.

*Do they know what it means?* Çifta inquired.

*Not yet,* the ice responded. *This is the day of your birth.*

Çifta's heart fluttered as they lurched forward in time. Horizontal marks now connected the vertical one, making letters. Three lines of unfinished text had emerged:

BEWARE THE BLOOD
BEWARE THE INN
BEWARE THE TE

*It's a message,* Çifta marveled.

*Not a message,* whispered the ice. *A prophecy. One that speaks of you.*

Disbelief flooded her. *It cannot be about me…*

Yet… Yet, she knew that, in fact, she was the only one it could be about. It emerged the moment of her conception in the fae who had taken elixir distilled from this very tree. Even the ice did not bother to counter Çifta's denial.

*At this point, the prophecy is not yet finished, but Sylifke knows it is a warning. Her attitude toward the tree changed overnight. Before, she was fascinated, but now she is fearful. She cuts off all citizens from this tree. She used to want them to visit, to be reminded of her victory. Now she wants to hide it. She believes it is Karinya, threatening her from the realm of the dead. From this point on, only a select few are permitted to enter the courtyard. The citizens know that something has changed, but they do not understand what.*

A loud crash returned them to the scene. Doors were flung open and two Silverfae entered the courtyard. Sylifke, and someone that Çifta had not seen since Sharlyk's gorge: Elvio the sorcerer.

Trailing Elvio was a faeling and a white pup. The lad's face was soft with youth, his cheeks round, his large pale eyes luminous. His child's voice was a pleasant contrast to the heated discussion the adult fae were having.

Elvio bent to the boy, putting a hand on his shoulder and speaking sternly. The boy nodded solemnly and went to the nearest wall, calling the puppy, who frolicked, clumsy and long-legged, with paws too big to manage.

*That's going to be one enormous dog,* Çifta thought, absently.

*That's no dog,* returned the ice with some amusement. *That boy is Elvio's son, Sasha, and the dire wolf pup is his familiar, Rialta. It is Sasha who will allow us to meet, and Rialta who ensures that Ruskin will never be able to harm you… or anyone, again.*

Çifta became fascinated with the toddler and his familiar. They tumbled together as though Sasha was also a pup, wrestling and rolling like den-siblings, yet so quietly that the adult Silverfae did not notice them. Neither did they pay any attention to the adults.

*They are lovely, are they not?* the ice said, with real warmth in its tone.

*So adorable,* Çifta agreed.

But the ice's statement struck her as odd. Until now, it had not expressed any personal feelings about what it had shown her. Sometimes she thought there might be sentiment under the surface, but it was not until it showed her Sasha that it expressed affection. She was about to ask the ice about this when it pulled her into the conversation taking place around the tree.

"What say you, Sorcerer?" Sylifke's eyes glittered with expectation as she crossed her arms and stood back.

Elvio moved closer to the tree, studying the words in the bark, touching the sap which oozed from it, and examining it under the light. His expression remained neutral. "Only in the fullness of time will we understand what, or of whom, it speaks."

"Who!" Sylifke almost yelled. "You admit it refers to a who!"

"These things usually do, my queen," he replied in a patronizing tone. "It is a warning. When it is finished, it will speak of a person, perhaps Karinya herself, reincarnated."

"Do not speak her name," Sylifke spat, patches of fury blossoming on her lean cheeks. "And do not pander to me."

Elvio looked at her with something like pity, but, as always, his expression was tinged with superiority. "You were not afraid when you sought me out for blood magic. I told you the cost is never apparent at first. This is the way of dark sorcery. It deceives its own users, for it cannot deny its nature, bent toward treachery. Did I not warn you? Yet you insisted."

"That is enough!" She sliced a hand through the air. "I'll not be chided by you. I gave you your position. Never forget that. You rose to power because of me. Your former queen did not even allow you to show your face in her presence. Do you remember? So do not speak to me as if I am an ignorant faeling. I know what I did. I know what you did. This,"—she jabbed a finger at the bark—"is a problem for both of us."

Elvio lifted his shoulders in a gesture that suggested obvious powerlessness. "What do you expect of me, my queen? I cannot fight an opponent without a face or a name…" He trailed off as her expression grew thunderous, then softened his tone in an effort to placate her. "Why not allow more time to pass? Letters appear daily, now. We will soon have enough information to take counsel, to form a plan."

Sylifke circled the tree, thinking. "There is someone who

may know something. A harvester who—before I closed access to this place—was here every day, sometimes more than once per day. She believes she moved about concealed, but I am always watching. Her behavior was secretive and raised suspicion. Reports of her frequent visits reached my ears again and again. Some reported of her talking to the tree. I should have put a stop to it, and nearly did, but when she brought her daughter to Master Sabran's attention, I believed her loyal to me. No one forces the ice upon their children, unless they really love me."

Elvio looked doubtful but intrigued. "Who is this harvester, my queen?"

"Her name is Salme." Sylifke turned to him. "Question her. Find out what she knows. Her daughter ran away, determined to avoid the ritual. Since then, Salme has kept to herself. Rarely does she speak, even with her fellow harvesters, even those with whom she had friendships. She is ashamed. Perhaps she would like to purge that shame by serving us, but even if she does not, use whatever means necessary to ensure that she hides nothing from us."

Elvio nodded. "I will question her. I will leave no stone unturned."

Sylifke lifted her chin. "Good. Because I will hold you personally responsible. Until my son is old enough to be my right hand, the position falls upon you. Should you fail me, betray me, or founder upon rocks you should have foreseen,"—she pointed at the faeling now sleeping on top of the wolf pup near the wall—"I will take the most precious thing you possess."

Elvio's expression shifted, his cheeks drained of color, his arrogance wiped away. "My queen… no sorcerer is infallible."

"*You* are," she retorted. "*You* must be, for you are the sorcerer of Queen Sylifke of Silverfall, a kingdom I alone was able to return to the ways of the ancients."

"Other kingdoms have relinquished the old ways." Elvio's voice was gentle, but his eyes were desperate. "And they have prospered for it."

The queen snapped, "Other kingdoms soften and grow weak. Other monarchs lose their magic because they give in to base desires, their lust to mate with those who are weaker, lesser. This will not happen to Silverfall, not while I am queen. Winter has returned and is full of wrath because of Karinya's neglect. When its vengeance is satisfied, we will see the return of a winter sun. I, Sylifke of the Outer Darkhan, will bring this about."

Elvio was staring at her in outright horror.

"Do not look at me so," she snarled. "Do not fail me, Sorcerer, and you will have nothing to fear. You and your kin will have protection and honor, as long as you do my will."

The queen marched away, leaving Elvio standing under the snowdrop tree, staring at her back with fear and loathing in his eyes. The queen spared a cool glance at the sleeping faeling and the wolf pup before she left the room, closing the doors behind her.

Elvio sequestered himself in his rooms in the highest tower, so high it was completely swallowed in dark clouds and daytime looked no different from night. Ice had turned the exterior stones white with frost, and the windows were so caked that they couldn't be thawed. Over the course of the next month, Elvio barely slept and did not take time for proper meals. He nibbled bread or chewed jerky while poring over books and manuscripts. He did not allow servants to enter to clean. He kept his own fire lit, but his room went from orderly to disastrous. Pages were strewn about, maps and scrolls pinned open to pages of importance, dirty mugs stacked in towers, crumbs and dust covering every surface, and Elvio's clothing lay in corners and draped over furniture rather than hung in his wardrobes. He was frantic, his every motion propelled by anxiety and desperation, but as days went by, he found something encouraging and his manner became increasingly pacified. Finally, he washed himself, combed his hair, put on his winter boots and his sorcerer's mantle, and left his room.

He went to the snowdrop grove, spying on Salme as she moved through the trees and went about her business. Her complexion was chalky, her body bent with sorrow. She had lost weight and her topaz colored uniform hung on thin shoulders. She looked a broken fae, all former resiliency and youth drained away, leaving in its place an aged female. When he'd looked his fill, Elvio approached her, a warm smile on his face.

"Salme Sariatha? I was told I could find you here."

She looked up, not returning his smile. "Where else would I be, Sorcerer? I do nothing but harvest, for I serve the winter queen," she droned.

"As do I. In fact, I am on an important mission for her now, one that has led me to you."

Salme barely looked interested.

"I have secured permission to remove you from your duties." With a half-bow, he gestured toward the palace. "Would you accompany me to my study, please?"

Salme put down her bucket and went without protest or suspicion, moving like she was in a dream. As they approached the castle entrance, she roused enough to look at him with a flicker of interest, as though only now realizing who he was. "You are Elvio Drazek. What business does the queen's magician have with a humble harvester?"

Elvio chuckled, touching Salme's lower back as they went inside. "Humble harvester? You have the most important role in the kingdom, do you not? What else can better prepare our faelings to face the ice than your elixirs?"

She murmured something inaudible, stepping through a narrower wooden door that opened to a set of spiral steps. "You said we are going to your study?"

"That's right," he replied. "Have you ever looked from the tallest tower?"

"No." And neither did she sound excited by the prospect.

Elvio followed Salme as she took one laborious step at a time, lifting her cape so she didn't tread on it.

The stairs took them up and up before spilling them into a wide stone gallery. It was lined with pillars of ice sitting atop blocks of marble. Salme recoiled when she saw them, dropping her gaze to the floor before moving down the center aisle. They passed dozens of frozen youths, their forms more amorphous blobs than anything recognizably fae.

Elvio spoke casually, pretending not to notice Salme's discomfort. "You were meant to have a daughter among these, were you not?"

"Yes," Salme murmured, without lifting her gaze. She brushed at her eyes and held her fingers at her brow. Her hand trembled.

Anger stirred in Çifta's heart as the sorcerer intentionally poked the most tender place in her grandmother's heart.

Elvio led her from the gallery and through another doorway leading into the broader staircase that led up to his rooms. "What went wrong?"

"She ran away." Salme's tone was flat. "You already know this. Everyone knows."

"Yes." Elvio put on a grotesque mask of fake sympathy. "You must be devastated."

Lit torches cast flickering shadows, leaving long black tongues of soot up the wall of the staircase. Salme trudged in front of Elvio until they reached a landing with three closed doors. He unlocked one and let her inside. His study had been tidied and now looked like a proper sorcerer's quarters.

"Have a seat." He closed the door. "May I offer you tea, or some other refreshment?"

"No, thank you. I'd just as soon get this over with and back to work," Salme replied, then added as an afterthought: "If you don't mind."

"Understandable." Elvio stoked the fire, and Salme watched him without much interest. She wrapped her arms around herself and shivered.

"Yes, it's cold up here. They cleaned but let the fire go out." Elvio tsked. "Tell me, Salme. You have two sons and a daughter, the girl being the youngest. Am I right?"

"Yes. What of it?"

Elvio stood behind the chair across from her, leaning his elbows on the leather. "I understand your husband was killed during the battle of the Silver queens, and that afterward you had a short relationship with another male, the relationship which produced Evelin."

Salme stiffened.

"I'm not implying anything and have no judgment. I merely would like to know the identity of Evelin's father. Not even his full identity. I would like to know if he was Silverfae, or some other race. It would help explain some of your daughter's fear. Do you not agree? Halflings may survive the ice, of course, but we know that many of them do not."

Salme looked annoyed. "Of course he was Silverfae. I would never dally with another species. I am a northern female. Whose wagging tongue suggested otherwise?"

Elvio frowned in disbelief, but before he could answer, a knock came. He excused himself to answer.

A soldier in a surcoat with a sword strapped to his hip stood on the landing. When he saw Elvio, he snapped his heels together, pushing his chest up and out. "I serve the winter queen."

"Yes, yes. I know." Elvio flapped a hand as though batting away an insect. "Did you find anything?"

"Yes, Sorcerer." The soldier produced a small envelope from beneath his coat and held it out.

Elvio snatched it up. "Anything else?"

The soldier flicked a glance at Salme, now seated in front of the smoking fireplace. "She has equipment to distill elixirs within her chambers."

Salme—who had been staring at the frost-covered window—snapped her attention to the door, eyes wide.

"I do not know the rules the harvesters abide by." Elvio spoke to the soldier while opening the envelope and sliding out the folded contents. "Is this forbidden?"

Salme sprang from the chair and took a few steps toward the guard. "You were in my private quarters?"

"Sit down, Salme," Elvio said. "It's alright. I'll explain in a moment."

"Not forbidden," the guard told Elvio, "just unusual.

No other harvesters do this." He snapped off another salute. "There's nothing else to report."

Salme did not sit. She looked at the envelope and letter in Elvio's hand, recognizing it. "That is my property. What is going on?"

"You will sit," Elvio commanded, speaking sharply this time, as he shut the door.

Salme backed up and plopped into the seat, crossing her arms like a petulant child. "I've done nothing wrong. I don't know why you want to read my private correspondence."

"I'll decide if there has been wrongdoing," Elvio replied softly, unfolding the letter. "Give me a moment."

Salme looked mutinous as Elvio paced around the room, reading. When he finished, he took the chair opposite Salme, placing the letter face up on the small table at his elbow. It lay there like an accusation. "So, your runaway daughter has forgiven you for some indiscretion."

He folded his hands and crossed a leg, waiting.

Salme glared at him and said nothing.

Elvio's tone turned as slick and smooth as oil. "What did you do to your daughter that required forgiveness, pray tell?"

"You're the queen's sorcerer, aren't you? If you think about it for a while, I'm sure you'll figure it out." Salme's expression was full of rebellion.

Elvio tsked as though chastising a child. "Such a tone with the queen's second can earn you stripes. Yet you court punishment so blithely? Have you lost care of your own well-being since your daughter left you?"

Salme looked down, face tightening. Finally, she sighed, her shoulders drooping. "She was angry with me for bringing her to Master Sabran's attention. She did not wish to take the ice trial because she feared death. When she learned that she was among the group to be forced, she ran away. She has found it in her heart to forgive me, and now you know as much as I do."

Elvio folded his hands in his lap. "She now understands that you only wished her to aspire to something greater, and that you are not to be blamed?"

"But I am to be blamed," Salme returned. "I should not have put any expectations on her. My parents did not put them on me. I was not raised to be ambitious. I was wrong to do it."

Elvio shrugged. "*You* took the ice and became a harvester. I'm told you can even hear the trees talking. Why should you not want something like that for her?"

Salme sighed and looked away. "It doesn't matter. Now you know my shame. I don't know why it's important to the likes of you. May I go?"

"No," he said softly, and threat crept into his tone. "We are not finished. I wish to speak of the snowdrop tree. I am told that you spent a lot of time in its presence over the course of many years. More than anyone else."

Fear stole into her features for the first time, real fear.

When she didn't respond, he added, "I would like to know why."

Salme cleared her throat, but her voice wavered, betraying the tension within her. "At that time, we were freely allowed to visit the courtyard as much as we wished, to praise and honor Sylifke within our hearts for her valiant triumph."

Elvio watched her steadily. "And that is what you were doing? Praising and honoring Sylifke within your heart for her valiant triumph?"

Salme threaded her fingers, clenching so tightly that her knuckles bled white. "Of course. What else?"

Elvio slid forward, templing his fingers. His eyes turned hard and bored into hers, his jaw flexed. "Let me be very clear, Harvester. You are nothing. I have the permission and the power to torture the truth out of you. I do not speak of the barbaric devices the queen keeps in the dungeons, reserved for traitors. I speak of torture by magic. You will not withstand it, I promise you. I have been polite; I have even been kind. But I know that you are hiding something, and I will have it out. It is your choice whether you give it to me of your own free will, or you choose the way of pain."

Salme shrank back, her eyes glazing over. She swallowed, her hands clutching at the arms of her chair.

Çifta felt sorry for her grandmother.

Finally, Salme seemed to come to a decision. She straightened and let go of the armrests, folding her hands once more in her lap. She held Elvio's dark gaze.

"I am a mother, Sorcerer," she told him plainly. "A mother's love is greater than your magic, greater than any pain. Do your worst. I'll tell you nothing."

Çifta's heart swelled with pride. *She was so brave.*

*Yes. Salme was a brave soul. Pain she could have withstood. Had she known that Elvio was operating under threat of losing his only child, she might have chosen another way.*

The scene flickered and faded.

*I will not subject you to the hours which passed after that conversation. You already know the outcome.*

*She told him,* Çifta guessed. *She must have.*

*Yes. Elvio was right. He could and did get the information he wanted. By the time he was finished with her, she did not even realize she'd told him. She died believing that she had won, which was a mercy for your grandmother. But for Evelin, the damage was done.*

A dingy pub with low ceilings and rotting floorboards materialized around Çifta. The ice let her look around, perhaps sensing her fascination. This was not the kind of place the merchant's daughter would ever have visited. Wealthy young women of station did not associate with low characters, risking their reputation, and potential for a good match.

A fug of wood and pipe smoke filled the room with a haze that would have burned her eyes had she been present in body. Several of the patrons released hacking death-coughs that rattled from their chests and made those nearby shift their chairs away. Suspicious-looking characters sat around small crooked tables talking in low voices or drinking alone and glaring at everyone else. A squat woman with frizzy hair and a scar down the side of her neck pumped foamy ale from a tap and yelled at someone to ladle a plate of stew. Balancing a tray of six mugs, she waddled from behind the bar. As she passed the front door, it opened. A gust of snow twisted her skirts around her legs, nearly tripping her. She swore a blue streak, which her patrons seemed to appreciate. One of them applauded with a hand and a stump where a hand used to be.

A caped figure entered, ducking under a blackened beam, then straightened as he pulled back his hood. Elvio looked about the room, lip curling faintly with contempt. He arrowed for a table in the corner where a young fae male sat, half a glass of ale in front of him. He shoveled in mouthfuls of stew, glancing up as the sorcerer approached.

He was not Silverfae, for he had copper hair, pale, freckled skin, and brown eyes. He wore a sleeveless tunic of thin brown leather but a thick fur coat lay beside him on the bench. A small sleek bird with a short, sharp beak perched on his bare shoulder, looking around the room with quick jerks of her head.

Elvio frowned as he slid onto the bench across from the male, who grunted in greeting. "Hirundo? I was looking for a Silver fauna fae."

"Your information was bad. I'm not Silver, obviously," muttered Hirundo, his tone gruff. He slurped up another mouthful of stew and swallowed without chewing.

Elvio tugged off his topaz colored gloves and lay them on the table, signaling the matron for a mug of ale. "All the better, you won't have loyalties I'll have to worry about."

"*My* information was not bad, on the other hand," Hirundo said around a mouthful. "Just surprising. You really are him. Drazek, I mean. The queen's warlock."

"Yes, that I am."

"I take payment up front."

Elvio lay his hands flat on the table and eyed the fauna fae. "How about half, and the rest when you succeed? If you fail, you keep the deposit."

Hirundo agreed, and the two fell silent until the matron delivered Elvio's ale and took away Hirundo's empty bowl.

Elvio eyed Hirundo's bird with a frown. "I was told she was among the fastest."

Hirundo crossed his muscled arms and scanned the room, taking note of everything and everyone. "Caith is a stormbird. She's small, but she can fly between here and the Outer Islands in less than a day, in any kind of weather and with zero visibility. Stormbirds spend most of their lives aloft. Even now, she is irritated to be sitting here, waiting for you to get to the point. As am I."

The bird cheeped, and Elvio relaxed.

*For your information,* the ice told Çifta, *the Outer Islands are more than three-thousand miles away.*

Çifta's mind staggered. If the bird could do that, then she could fly like lightning.

"I was also told," Elvio said, lifting a brow of inquiry, "you and Caith have made duplication your life's work. An art, some say." He blew the foam off his drink and took a sip.

Hirundo sat up straighter, cracking his knuckles. "Most fauna fae have to be under stress to trigger duplication, something to do with a hormone they release when threatened."

"Adrenaline," murmured Elvio. "I'm familiar with it."

"That's the one. I learned it but I always forget the name. Strange word." Hirundo covered a soft belch with a fist and muttered a barely audible, sorry. Caith cheeped again, an aggravated sound, then flew into the rafters over the bar. "Caith and I don't need it. We can hold a duplication for days."

"Impressive." Elvio pulled a scroll out of an inner pocket and lay it out on the table, using the mugs to pin down the sides. He also produced a folded bit of parchment, which he unfolded and handed to Hirundo, who peered at it with interest.

"Here's the job."

"Pretty Silverfae." Hirundo said appreciatively, then looked up. "She in trouble?"

"Not at all," lied the sorcerer. "She is important to the royal family. She ran away, and we wish to rescue her and return her to her family, who are distraught, as you can imagine."

"What a shame," Hirundo replied flatly. He did not appear

to believe the lie but was willing to play along. "You want us to find her."

"We only need her location. That's it. I'll take care of the rest." Elvio put a finger on an X marked on the map. Beside it, a handwritten flourish said: *Silverfall City.*

"We know that a boy helped her take an underground river that runs this way, toward the Ivryndian coast. Elvio's finger laid a trail. He says he dropped her off here, not far from the barges, which may have taken her to any one of several outposts."

Hirundo was following along. "How long ago?"

Caith returned to Hirundo's shoulder and crooked her head to look at both the map and the drawing of Evelin.

"That's the problem." Elvio folded his fingers, looking contrite. "I'm sorry to say it was close to five years ago. In this drawing, she's only eighteen. It's the most recent image we have of her. She will have matured in the time that has passed, as she is now 23. She may have even changed her appearance, cut her hair, or dyed it, though I doubt it. Silverfae females are notoriously precious about their hair."

Hirundo looked at Elvio with open skepticism. "She's important to the royal family, but you're only *now* looking for her? Years after she ran away?"

"No." Elvio slowed down, his tone becoming sterner. "We looked for her immediately, but only now has the boat boy come forward with information about the direction she went. I suppose he had a crisis of morality. I care not. I care only about the girl."

"Right." Hirundo waved a hand, as though to brush aside Elvio's embroidery. "So you know that someone took her to the barges on the Tadylat, and you believe she may have gone to one of the outposts on the Ivryndian seacoast. But in five years, she could have gone anywhere. She could have hopped a merchant vessel and sailed to Archelia or Tryske. She could be across the Valdivian by now."

"She could be, but we do not think that is the case. The girl is attached to her mother, and in written correspondence, expressed a desire to maintain contact. She will not have gone far."

"Why not use the mother as bait, then? Why hire me?"

Elvio's mouth twitched. "I wanted to, but her mother… passed away recently, sadly."

"I see." Hirundo rubbed his chin as he scanned the map, and memorized the young runaway's face, Evelin's face. "This is a difficult job, even for us."

"I expected so." Elvio crossed his arms. "How much?"

Hirundo chewed his bottom lip. "It'll take time, even for the fastest bird."

Elvio nodded. "That's why we came to you. You are the best. We spare no expense when one of our own may be in peril."

Hirundo gave Elvio a price, enough gold to purchase a four-masted vessel outfitted with guns, but the sorcerer did not balk.

"How soon can you begin?"

Hirundo rubbed his hands together, clearly eager to get started. "I need a quiet place where I won't be interrupted. The inn at the edge of town has a loft. Rent it for a week. It may not take that long; then again, it may take longer. Five days is a good estimate."

Elvio raised his eyebrows, and Hirundo mistook the expression for disappointment.

The fauna fae flushed, perhaps annoyed. "If you have other magic to find this girl that is faster, use it. I won't begrudge you walking away. We have plenty of paying customers, and we tire of Silverfall. The weather here is cursed."

"No, no." Elvio waved a hand. "A week is fine, faster than I expected. Yes, I'll rent the room, and another for myself."

"You?" Hirundo canted his head. "You're the queen's warlock, yet you want to oversee this yourself? It will be very boring for you."

"I have other things I can do while I wait," replied Elvio.

"This female must be important."

"She is, and I would prefer you did not fail. I've no wish to lean upon more distasteful methods."

Hirundo patted his stomach and signaled the matron, who scrawled the bill on a yellowed pad, her tongue poking out of her mouth. She brought it over and put it on the table in front of the fauna fae.

"Thank you," said Hirundo, pushing the bill toward Elvio. "The stew was good."

He rose and reached for his furs. Underneath his overcoat was an overstuffed packsack and a dagger in a well-worn scabbard. Fixing the scabbard around his hips, he hiked the pack over his shoulders and pulled on a hat and thick gloves.

Elvio paid the matron, put on his winter gear and followed Hirundo out of the pub. Caith slipped into the sky the moment the door opened. The fauna fae and the sorcerer stepped into a winter storm that buffeted them so hard that they could not speak.

The snow swirled, and the scene dissolved and resolved before Çifta's eyes.

She was now inside the bedroom Elvio had rented. Elvio was stoking the fire as the fauna fae prepared himself and Caith for their task.

"No one can enter except for you," Hirundo commanded. "You must be silent at all times, and keep the room warm. If I get too cold, it will break our connection. Stay out, except to do the fire. Put one of your men to guard the door, otherwise the inn's staff will come in to clean. You'll have to field questions, but you know how to deal with those."

Elvio nodded. "What about food and water?"

"I'll take none." Hirundo checked the windows, then drew the curtains. "Only water, and broth, upon finishing."

Elvio dropped his chin. "None at all?"

"Not until after. Caith will take water and hunt. It is enough to sustain me, for a time."

Elvio looked impressed, and Çifta was too. She didn't know much about fauna fae magic, but she had heard that duplication was not easy, and it was difficult to maintain for long periods of time. She'd never heard of a familiar able to keep its fae nourished. No wonder Hirundo had many customers.

Hirundo kicked off his boots and stripped down to thin shorts, then fluffed the pillow. Getting into the bed, he drew the covers up to his chest and lay his arms along his sides, flexing his jaw open and closed.

Caith gave a scream from somewhere outside. Elvio peeked out but turned back in time to see the fauna fae's body go stiff. His head pressed back into the pillow. Outside, a flock of stormbirds exploded into the sky, flying in all directions. Their fauna fae lay twitching on the bed as the birds whirled, organizing themselves before spreading out over the landscape in search of the missing faeling.

# Part Three

## Chapter Twenty-Four

# Jessamine

The courthouse was a quarter of the way down the main throughway from the palace. Its impressive pillared front sat high above the street, and two flags hung from the top of its triangular face: the blue and green Solanan flag with the wreathed lion's head, and a red flag announcing that a trial was in session. At trial's end, that flag would be changed depending on whether Sasha was acquitted (yellow), or found guilty (iron gray).

A murmur of suppressed conversation filled the courtroom. Dressed in her Fahyli leathers and with her hair in braids, Jess squirmed on her wooden chair in the front row of the public seating section. Digit sat beside her. Ania was perched on his head, and several other familiars sat up in the open-beam rafters, including Erasmus, Ferrugin and Tully. If she hadn't been so anxious, Jess might have marveled that the big cat had been able to get up there in the first place. The Fahyli were distributed in and around the courthouse.

The jury—six Solanan citizens and six Silverfae, as expected—trooped single file up the right-side aisle. Panther and Regalis stood behind the judge's bench, along with two Solanan soldiers. They watched as the room filled with citizens, and the jurors took their seats.

The citizens who wanted to watch had already passed through a security checkpoint. Sasha's courtroom was at the rear of the courthouse, chosen because it was the largest courtroom in the building.

A hush fell over the room and heads turned. As Queen Sylifke entered, Jess felt like she couldn't breathe. All necks craned to watch the Silverfall queen—covered by a sheer gray veil—make her way to the second level. No one aside from her and her retinue were allowed up there. She was followed by two Siverfae females. One managed the queen's train, the other carried a cushion. A single chair had been placed near the front of the balcony for a good view of the proceedings. The cushion was settled on the wooden seat, and the queen sat down.

Jess felt Digit take her hand. She looked over to see his encouraging smile. She tried to smile back and managed a grimace.

Rayven Sabran strode up the aisle, carrying a folder and rifling through pages. She wore fitted pale-blue trousers, tall gray boots and a dark blue jacket with a stand-up collar. A dense line of silver buttons ran up the front. Her hair was tied back and fastened with a black bow. She looked masculine, solemn, and confident. An assistant, cradling more folders in his arms, trailed Rayven to the prosecutor's table where he dumped his load.

When the door behind the defendant's bench opened and Sasha emerged between two Solanan guards, Jessamine clutched her stomach. His expression was dispassionate, but his eyes were alert. He took his seat and scanned the crowd, finding Jess. The corners of his mouth turned up in the faintest smile and he blinked owlishly.

Digit leaned over and whispered in Jessamine's ear, even though others were mumbling in normal voices. The courtroom was abuzz with speculation and opinions.

"Where's Rialta?"

"Sasha doesn't want her exposed to this," Jess replied, repeating what Beazle had told her as she gestured to the crowd.

Digit frowned. "She stands accused too and knows it. I can't imagine you not wanting Beazle with you if it were you up there in that box. I'd never be without Ania if it were me."

"Beazle's different," was all Jess could think to say. "Not from Ania, but from Rialta."

Digit raised a brow. "How, exactly?"

Footsteps drew focus to the center aisle. Bertrand Bedar made his way to the defendant's desk, dropping papers along the way that fluttered to the carpet and left a trail. Apparently, he didn't have an assistant, at least, not one who was present. He looked at Sasha, nodding as he set whatever he hadn't dropped down on the his desk before going back to pick up everything. Then he went over and spoke quietly with Sasha. Preparatory words, Jess hoped they were encouraging for Sasha.

Digit was still looking at Jess expectantly. "Well?"

Jess momentarily forgot what they were talking about. She searched for words that wouldn't make it sound like she thought Beazle was superior to every other familiar, even though that was how she felt. She was biased, of course. All the Fahyli were.

"She's more vulnerable, you know?"

"Than a bat? Really?"

"She's big, yes, but Beazle is not easily caught. Rialta could be subdued and imprisoned."

Digit cocked his head. "You mean Sasha doesn't trust her to behave herself?"

"I don't think it's that, although…"

Digit had a point. Rialta had already proven she had a mind of her own.

"I think he doesn't want her to be stressed," Jess muttered, hoping Digit let it go. She didn't want to converse: she wanted to listen and watch.

Digit looked skeptical but didn't pursue it, as King Agir had just come through the door behind the judge's bench. He wore a simple silver circlet on his head and a black gown with a red stripe encircling each cuff.

"All rise," shouted a soldier. "Court is now in session. Honorable Judge Agir presiding."

The room got to their feet as the king settled behind the bench.

Agir looked out at the packed room, waiting until the audience settled back into their seats before proceeding. "Good morning. Representatives in the case of the crown versus Sasha & Rialta Drazek, are both sides ready to begin?"

Rayven Sabran was still on her feet. "Prosecution is ready, Your Honor."

Bertrand nodded, returning to his table from Sasha's box, and putting on a pair of bent wire spectacles. "Defense is ready, Your Honor."

King Agir looked at the dour-faced human standing near the jury's box. Jess thought he looked mostly asleep, even though he was on his feet.

"Clerk?"

The clerk faced the jury and spoke in a monotone. "Please stand and raise your right hand."

The jury did as asked, giving Jess time to look them over.

One side of the box was filled with white-blond Silverfae, four broad-shouldered males and two females. The other side held citizens from Solana, both human and fae. Jess recognized none of the Solanans. Most of them were dressed the way villagers in Dagevli dressed, in simple homespun clothing. A couple looked like they'd rather be anywhere else, but the rest looked bright-eyed, keen to experience this new and rare thing, a high-profile trial for a foreigner.

Jess's eye was drawn back to the Silverfae jurors again and again. They had to be among the most attractive specimens that Sylifke could provide. Was she trying to engender sympathy with a pretty group of fae? They weren't just as good-looking as Ruskin's entourage had been. They were fit as well, straight backs and strong shoulders filling out their jackets. Not a single silver hair was out of place, and their eyes were ghostly-pale but for pinpricks of black. They sat as still as reptiles, their gazes flicking around the room.

After the oaths were said, the clerk collapsed into his chair.

"Ms. Sabran?" Agir sat back, threading his fingers together in his lap.

Rayven moved to the front of her table and faced the jury.

"Your Honor and members of the jury, my name is Rayven Sabran. The defendant,"—she gestured to Sasha—"has been charged with the crime of murder. The evidence will show that Mr. Drazek not only had the motive and the means to end Prince Ruskin's life, he had the wherewithal to make it look like a spontaneous act of self-defense. The evidence I present will prove that Sasha is guilty as charged."

She returned to her seat, chin high and expression sanctimonious. Jess crossed her arms and slouched, glaring at the back of Miss Sabran's head.

Bertrand stood and smiled at the jury. He spoke between puffs of air, though he'd been sitting down for several minutes already.

"Your Honor, ladies and gents of the jury; under the law, my client is presumed innocent until proven guilty. During this trial, you will neither hear nor see any true evidence against Sasha, because there is none. You will, however, endure much bluster, insinuation and hearsay. What you will learn is that Sasha acted quickly to save a life, one that was in imminent danger, and in the process endangered his own. In her turn, Rialta stepped in to defend her fae, as any good familiar would do. Her actions ended the threat against her fae's life, but also ended the life of the prince, against the expressed wishes of the young Mr. Drazek. This event was witnessed by hundreds of courtiers, servants and citizens. The defendant is not guilty and should not only be acquitted post-haste, but hailed as a hero."

Jess sat up straighter. Bertrand hadn't stuttered, stumbled, or sounded in any way anything but confident. Perhaps she'd misjudged the lawyer. She stole a glance at Sasha, who was not quite slouching, but his big shoulders were relaxed. Hope rose in Jessamine's chest like a dove in flight.

King Agir pronounced, "Miss Sabran, you may call your first witness."

"Prosecution calls Eldred Sakkinen to the stand."

The room rustled as a distinguished-looking Silverfae male rose and made his way to the witness stand. He was sworn in, then looked at Miss Sabran expectantly.

Rayven turned her back to Eldred and gazed at the back

wall of the courtroom as she asked, "Mr. Sakkinen, you were a member of Prince Ruskin's entourage, were you not?"

Eldred looked perplexed. He leaned in his chair in an effort to see her face. "Miss Sabran?"

Rayven turned. "Yes?"

He spoke in the halting way of the deaf. "I am very hard of hearing, Miss Sabran, but I'm an excellent lipreader. Could I ask you to repeat the question facing me?"

"Ah," she said as though enlightened.

Jess rolled her eyes. Her theatrics were annoying.

"You are deaf!" Rayven raised her voice. "Jury, please note that Mr. Sakkinen is almost completely deaf. Mr. Sakkinen, I asked if you were a member of Prince Ruskin's entourage."

"Oh." Eldred smiled. "Yes, Miss Sabran. I was."

Rayven began to wander around in the front of the room, her hands behind her back, keeping her face to Eldred. "And were you in the courtyard on the day in question?"

"Yes, I was there."

"Would you tell us what you witnessed the day the prince was killed? Take your time. It is important we hear all the details."

Eldred's voice was the only sound for the next twenty minutes, as he took to heart Rayven's permission to take his time. In the beginning, his descriptions were accurate, but Jess's heart sank when he got to the moment Prince Ruskin unsheathed his sword. Leaving out the prince's aggression toward Çifta, Eldred went straight to when Sasha froze her solid, then ran away as the prince pursued. When describing the critical moment of Prince Ruskin's death, Eldred told the room that he saw Sasha's lips moving right before Rialta appeared to deliver the killing bite.

Rayven pounced. "His lips were moving, you say?"

Jess glanced at Bertrand, who sat with an elbow on the table and his chin in his hand. He looked half-asleep.

"Yes," said Eldred.

"What did he say?"

"It was difficult to tell because there was blood on his face, but I believe he was calling to his familiar for help. Straight away, Rialta appeared. Fauna fae telepathy in action."

The room rumbled and King Agir used his gavel. "Order in my court, please."

The room went quiet.

Rayven gave the jury a meaningful look. "So, in your estimation, Sasha was using telepathy to order Rialta to kill the prince?"

"I can't see it any other way," Eldred said. "Everyone in Silverfall knows of Sasha and Rialta."

Rayven's voice was like warm honey. "What do you mean, Mr. Sakkinen? What does everyone know?"

"They're rare, you see." He looked at the jury. "You have many fauna fae in Solana, but we have only a few, and only one pair at court: Sasha and Rialta. Everyone knows they speak to one another silently, and Rialta—for all her intimidating size—is really a sweet overgrown dog. She would never attack or kill anyone, except at Sasha's command." He shrugged as though it should be obvious to the jury.

"Objection," said Bertrand, finally coming to life. "This is hearsay, Your Honor. To say 'everyone knows something' is to assume. It's meaningless, especially in a murder trial."

"Sustained," said the king. "Keep to the facts, please, Miss Sabran."

"Move faster next time," Jess whispered at Bertrand.

"Let me clarify then," said Rayven. "Mr. Sakkinen, you can read lips well, we've already established that."

"Yes," he replied.

"And you swear that you saw Sasha's lips moving just before the dire wolf appeared?"

"Yes."

Jess clenched her teeth. Sasha's face, bloody or not, had been covered by his arms. Only one eye had peeked out, and just for a second, as he'd taken blow after blow from the enraged prince.

She leaned toward Digit, hissing. "He's lying."

Digit nodded. "Obviously. The questions now are: how many lies will they tell, and how big will those lies get?"

Not only that, thought Jess. Would the jury see through the lies?

Jess stole a look at the queen, but it was impossible to see her expression beneath her veil. All she could make out were long white talons tapping out a slow rhythm on the railing of the balcony. Jess blew out a long breath and faced front, wishing the king had heeded Elphame's advice.

## Chapter Twenty-Five

# Çifta

W*E'RE NOW SIX days after Hirundo went into his trance,* said the ice. *True to his word, he's allowed no one into the room. While Elvio slept, a soldier stood guard, but as soon as Elvio awoke—always in under four hours—he took over the job again himself.*

Hirundo still lay on the bed, stiff and twitching. His eyes remained closed, as his head turned this way and that, quickly, just like his bird, as he received visions from Caith and her duplicates.

As they watched Elvio wait for Hirundo to awaken, the ice explained to Çifta that the sorcerer had always been envious of fauna fae, which was what had drawn him into a romance with Sasha's mother, Halyn.

*She was from a small village outside the city and had a cottontail familiar named Walloon. Halyn and Elvio's affair had been kept secret from everyone, including the queen, who—thanks to a little incantational trick from Elvio—never pressed the sorcerer about the identity of Sasha's mother. Elvio had no desire to answer questions about lowly Halyn, a peasant.*

*He never married her?*

*No, and when it came time to reveal that Elvio had a son, no one at court even blinked. The bastard of a courtly sorcerer was not a shock to anyone.*

*I suppose they'd be more surprised if he'd had none at all,* returned Çifta wryly.

*Too true,* the ice agreed. *Soon after Sasha was born, Rialta arrived out of the winter wilderness like a fluffy apparition, drawn to the fauna fae infant. Elvio had been delighted. No one and nothing captured his heart the way Sasha and Rialta had. When Halyn asked Elvio to take their son into the city and give him an education and opportunity, he'd been glad to do so.*

*I suppose it never occurred to him that Sylifke might use the boy against him,* wondered Çifta.

*That's right,* the ice whispered. *She values winter magic above all, but she also values those with other kinds of magic, too. To this day, Elvio berates himself for allowing Sasha to mingle with the offspring of Silverfae nobility. When Sylifke threatened to take Sasha, it was as close as Elvio had ever come to having his worst fears realized. He long ago decided that love made people weak.*

*Yet, here he is,* Çifta mused, without much sympathy, *utterly devoted to his son, and therefore utterly devoted to the destruction of my mother.*

Elvio stared at the floor outside Hirundo's door, chewing a thumbnail down to the quick.

*Awful scenarios are playing out in his imagination,* the ice told her. *Sasha being ripped from his arms, crying, as they hook Rialta with a noose and drag her away, yelping and whining, powerless in her puppyhood to defend her fae.*

Elvio stared at a scroll containing the queen's seal. Its tattered state made it obvious that he had read it many times. As Çifta observed over his shoulder, he opened the scroll once more, unwittingly sharing its contents with her.

The message explained that more finished sentences had appeared in the bark of the snowdrop tree, and what they said explained Elvio's unease.

BEWARE THE BLOOD OF THE DARK-HAIRED HALFLING,
BEWARE THE INNOCENT ONE,
BEWARE THE TEARS OF THE DAUGHTER OF WINTER,
YOUR ENEMY'S RAGE...
YOUR KINGDOM...

Elvio sat outside the room, muttering to himself, "Dark-haired halfling... Daughter of Winter... Dark-haired... Halfling..."

The target was not Evelin after all.

The sorcerer was raking his silver-gray hair into knotted spikes when a loud thump—something heavy but soft hitting the floor—came from Hirundo's room. Elvio sprang to the door, throwing it open. The fauna fae lay on the floor beside the bed, trying, yet not succeeding, to lift himself up.

Hirundo's formerly muscular body had wasted in the days that had passed. His arms trembled from weakness. Elvio lifted him, wincing at the feeling of loose bones and stringy muscles. Hirundo uttered a strange whistling sound as Elvio settled him back in bed. The sorcerer went to the nightstand and poured water from the carafe into a glass.

"Welcome back." Elvio tilted the glass for Hirundo. "Did you find her?"

Hirundo sipped and swallowed, coughed and lay back, too exhausted to speak. A thin film lay over the fauna fae's eyes, pale and milky. He looked like he had a serious case of cataracts. Elvio waved a hand in front of Hirundo's face, but the fae did not blink or react.

For the next twenty minutes, Elvio gave Hirundo small sips of water, cradling his head with tenderness, like Hirundo was his own son. When Hirundo opened his mouth, only chirping sounds came out. He closed his eyes and lay back, breathing deeply. He put a palm on his concave stomach and let out another short whistle, but this one ended in a human-sounding grunt.

Elvio told him. "I've sent for the broth, as you requested."

When the broth came, Elvio fed it to Hirundo. The fauna fae still chirped and squeaked like a bird, but the milkiness of his eyes had already faded, and the bird sounds were now interspersed with Hirundo's own gravelly voice. He worked to clear his throat, taking his time. By the time he finished the broth, his eyes were clear and focused. Elvio helped him to a more upright position, resting against a stack of pillows.

Hirundo grunted his first intelligible word, "Caith."

Hearing the stormbird's wings fluttering against the glass, Elvio went to the window and opened it. Caith zipped inside and straight to her fae, landing on his stomach. He cupped his bird and smiled blearily.

"Well done," he croaked, then coughed and coughed until Elvio grew alarmed.

"Shall I send for more broth?"

"It's normal," wheezed Hirundo. "I'm fine."

Waving Elvio away, he relaxed again. Caith chirped and settled into Hirundo's hand, shaking her feathers. She tucked her head under a wing and went to sleep, apparently just as exhausted as her fae, only not half-starved.

Elvio left the pair to rest while he took a meal of his own in the tavern below. When he returned, Hirundo looked stronger, eager to talk. Caith was still sleeping.

"How do you feel?" Elvio asked, pulling a chair close to the bed. "You look better. Skinny as a twelve-year-old, but better."

Hirundo flashed crooked white teeth. His voice was only a little hoarse now. "I'll gain the weight back. My body benefits from these fasts, though it doesn't look like it while it's happening. We found her."

"So I surmised." Elvio hid his feelings about this information. "Her family will be grateful."

"Her family will be more than grateful. Your pretty female is at the top of the Ivryndian coastline, and she is a mother."

Elvio stiffened, absorbing this with visible shock. "A mother?"

Hirundo nodded, looking smug.

"Did you see the babe?"

Hirundo nodded again. "She is very young. I'm not good at placing the ages of children, but I'd guess she's not even half a year old."

"She… a daughter."

The ice echoed: *A daughter. A daughter!*

"A girl, yes. She's a half-breed."

*A halfling…*

"She has Silverfae eyes but black hair, and curly."

*A dark-haired halfling.*

Elvio rubbed the heel of his palm into the muscle over his heart, like it was aching. Beads of moisture gathered across his brow. "Did you get a name?"

Hirundo wiped dry lips with the back of his hand, making a scraping sound. He licked to moisten them. "Her name was never said in our presence. We found them only yesterday and Caith was fatigued. She loses her ability to convey language when she is tired. Could I have more broth?"

"Of course." Elvio tugged the bell pull near the bed.

While they waited, Hirundo gave Elvio more details. Elvio brought the map over to the bed and had Hirundo mark the location of the outpost on the coastline.

It was as plain as day to Çifta that the sorcerer was disturbed, reeling over the news that Evelin had given birth. His awful task had become even more terrible. Evelin was no longer the target. The baby was—she, the innocent dark-haired halfling.

Çifta processed the same information and was having almost as difficult a time with it. She felt numb.

*I can't be the daughter of winter*, she protested

*Why not?*

*Because I'm no one. I am nothing, just a merchant's daughter. I've never felt anything remotely like magic within me.*

The ice seemed to sigh as it took her out of the inn and over the cold dark Silverfall terrain.

*What do you think all of this is for, little halfling? I show you your true history to prepare you to step willingly into your destiny.*

Frozen forests sped by below them.

*What happens if I cannot?*

After what seemed like miles, her host replied, *What do you think will happen?*

Çifta had seen the fear in Evelin's face. She'd seen the icy pillars of frozen Silverfae in the gallery. She knew that many fell from the ice lifeless. Even so, the answer came as a blow.

*I'll never wake up. I'll never feel the sun on my face or smell the sea air. I'll... expire, like so many others.*

Cloud cover grew thick, and the wind picked up, howling. A forlorn sound that perfectly expressed the way Çifta felt.

*But it's not fair, nor is it right,* she cried out mentally. *It means that, in fact, I have no choice at all. You ask if I will step into my destiny willingly, one that looks more and more with every passing scene, like a direct conflict with Sylifke, a fight to the death. How can I accept that? You're asking me to either die inside the ice or die at Sylifke's hand. What choice is that?*

*The prophecy—*

*Hang the prophecy! The prophecy doesn't say anything other than for Sylifke to 'beware'. There's no guarantee of anything.*

*Isn't there?*

Çifta felt the stirrings of anger as the walls of Silverfall City appeared below, and the ice swept her toward the courtyard. She grew tired of this place. But something was different now. Time had passed, and before the tree stood someone who looked exactly as she had seen him when he had advanced upon her with his sword drawn.

Prince Ruskin.

Ruskin and his mother stood before the tree.

In the time that had elapsed, someone had tried to deface the snowdrop. The bark had slashes and cuts in it, chunks removed. But it had not worked. The words showed just as well through the scars as they had when they'd gleamed from white bark.

BEWARE THE BLOOD OF THE DARK-HAIRED HALFLING,
BEWARE THE INNOCENT ONE,
BEWARE THE TEARS OF THE DAUGHTER OF WINTER,
YOUR ENEMY'S RAGE IS HER SUM.

YOUR KINGDOM, SHE'LL RAKE,
YOUR RULE SHE'LL TAKE,
AND ALL YOUR POWER SHE'LL SPLINTER.

Çifta stared at the full prophecy, returning to the finality of the last line. *And all your power she'll splinter.*

The ice whispered; *What do you think now? Does the prophecy not guarantee your triumph?*

Çifta was unable to muster an answer.

Salme, the grandmother she had never known, had died for this, been tortured for this. Her mother had died protecting her, taking a curse meant for Çifta. In spite of Sylifke's efforts, in spite of Hirundo and his exceptional magic, in spite of Elvio—the greatest sorcerer in the north—Çifta had thrived. She'd been protected and sequestered in Kazery's care, without any clue about who she really was.

She wished Kazery was with her now. He always knew what to do. Her father, the pirate-merchant, was afraid of nothing. Others feared him instead. Would she ever see him again? Both of her parents had been brave in their own way, and through her veins flowed their blood, blood the prophecy spoke of: beware the blood of the dark-haired halfling.

Yet she balked. The task the ice had revealed as her destiny was impossible. What was she meant to do? Show up in the courtyard and challenge Sylifke? She didn't even know how to melt the ice around the ceremonial sword she was supposed to wield when issuing her challenge.

It was insane. Foolish. She'd never succeed.

She couldn't fathom a way in which she could ever conquer this queen, prophecy or no.

## Chapter Twenty-Six

# Laec

There were two Lady Çiftas encased in two pillars of ice, sitting side-by-side. Laec squinted at them, slouched in an upholstered chair that he'd dragged from a neighboring salon just before he'd begun drinking. The skin of his chest and back throbbed and itched.

A yell of frustration had brought a servant scurrying into the room, hunched over like a frightened mouse. Laec had taken the opportunity to ask for a bottle of plum wine, which had thoughtlessly been delivered without a glass. Once he'd finished that bottle, drinking from the neck, Laec had analyzed the ice again, and felt certain that Çifta's melt might well be imminent. He suspected that it was the plum wine making him optimistic but didn't care. He was just happy not to feel so hopeless.

He'd fetched two more bottles of plum wine—himself this time, pilfering from the cellar near Mrs. Tierney's elixirs kitchens—and set them on the side table he'd found. He couldn't find wine glasses anywhere in Tierney's shelves, especially in the dark, since he hadn't been able to find a switch to the etherlamp. So one of the elixir glasses the Calyx took their strange concoctions in would have to do. It was like a champagne flute.

Laec talked to Çifta while he worked his way through the wine, covering random topics from the shape of wine glasses, to Elphame's chaotic parties.

That was a while ago.

The bottles were now empty and Laec teetered on the edge of dozing. His legs were outstretched, his arms draped over the sides of the chair, hanging toward the floor. His stockinged feet pointed to the ceiling, his boots were… somewhere. He'd slid so far down that his butt cheeks were about to drop off the edge of the seat. The only thing keeping him conscious was the fascinating way the two frozen Çiftas waved back and forth like tall fronds of sea kelp in a gentle current.

At some point, he thought he heard the sound of wings, but it went away.

"Pests," he muttered to the Çiftas. "Pests is what they are. All familiars. Nosy parkers. Meddlesome nuisance…s. All of them."

"There you are!"

Laec jolted as a voice penetrated the silence like a foghorn. Jerking his legs and arms in like a startled bug, he fell off the chair, which made his teeth clack together. He glared up at Kite, looking down her nose at him, the disgust on her face easy to see. Her expression was so familiar it was almost comforting.

"Hello, Fyfa," he said, proud that he could speak so clearly.

Kite frowned with confusion, but with both hands on her hips like that, she looked exactly like Fyfa had when she'd found him in this same state, which made Laec laugh. He couldn't help it.

"What's funny?" She waved a hand in front of her nose. "Phew. You smell like—"

"The r-r-residue at the bottom of a wine barrel?" Laec trilled the r's as he struggled to get to his feet—making it up to one knee before falling over again.

"I was going to say, a bowl of rotten fruit, but that works too." She watched him struggle. "Who's Fyfa?"

He made it to both feet but couldn't seem to take his hands off the ground, and this time, he wasn't quite able to speak without slurring. "Jusht another judgmental female who enjoys looking down upon me from exalted and shuperior heights."

Kite's boots came into view under his nose. "I've been looking all over for you."

"You still don't know where to find me? After all thish time?"

"I know. I'm an idiot for not looking here first. I keep thinking you'll snap out of this… whatever this is, this obsession, that you're in… and return to more productive activities."

"More fool, you." He flung out a hand, marveling at the way it felt, like it was made of rubber. "Help me up, woman."

Kite reached for his hand, but he snatched it away.

"Wait. Tell me what you want first."

She huffed and grabbed Laec by his shoulders, hauling him upright, none too gently. He squeezed his eyes shut, certain that the floor would rush up to meet him and just as confident that there was not a thing he could do to prevent it. Kite brushed the dust off Laec's trouser legs, almost knocking him over again.

"I don't want anything, Stavarjak. It's Bradburn who wants you."

Laec swayed. "The bald jester? What does he want?"

Kite kept him upright and marched him, albeit in a zigzag fashion, toward the door. "I don't know, but I wouldn't recommend calling him that to his face. Especially since he's not even bald." She turned away as he breathed on her. "You really do reek. I'd take you to sober up first, but I'm told there isn't time. Whatever Bradburn wants, he wants it now."

Laec smiled at her, not registering anything that she'd said. "You'd be very pretty if you let down some of those tails running up the backs of your heads. What are they for, anyway?" He tugged a braid before letting his hand flop down on her shoulder.

"Shut it, skunk, and don't touch me."

Laec's smile widened. "You're the one touching me, Kitey-kite."

She growled.

He lost his grin when a serious thought penetrated the fog of his mind. "I forgot about the trial. How's it going for our cotton-headed little friend?"

She muttered something under her breath.

"What did you say?"

She raised her voice. "I said, you're a disgrace."

"What?" Laec pulled back, hurt. He rubbed his nose with the hand that wasn't hooked around Kite's shoulder. "I really want to know… how the trial is going, that is."

She looked up at something above. "Let them know we're coming."

A winging sound passed overhead.

Laec's feet dragged as he leaned on her. "So that *was* Erasmus earlier. I thought I imagined him." Then he stiffened and barked, "Wait!"

She cringed, his voice hurting her ears, then shot him a look of pure loathing.

"Boosh," he said. He paused and tried again. "Boosh. Bootsh. Boo-ts!"

With a long-suffering sigh, Kite left Laec—swaying on his feet—and fetched his boots. She helped him put them on.

"You tell anyone about this, and I swear, I'll take that hair of yours for a trophy,"

He patted her, aiming for her braids but hitting her forehead. "You're so nice. Solanans are so… niiiiiice."

Straightening, she manhandled him toward the door. "March, Fairijak."

Kite got Laec across the palace and into the tradesmen's yard where there was so much activity it made Laec dizzy. The afternoon sun poured over the yard at an angle, its glare slicing into Laec's pupils like arrows.

"Ow." He put a hand over his eyes and let Kite drag him over to Bradburn. He waited, hand still planted over his face, because he could feel the heat from the sun.

"What's this?" Bradburn said in a gruff tone.

Laec opened a crack between his fingers. He closed it again when he saw the look on the captain's chubby faces. The world behind the captain a tilty-whirly blur, like they were having this conversation on a carnival ride.

"It's who you asked for, Captain," Kite replied.

A beat of silence.

"Laec Fairijak," she added, as if uncertain whether the captain was pretending or if he really didn't recognize the flame-haired fae swaying before him. "The Stavarjakian…"

"I know, I know," Bradburn huffed. "He's…"

"Drunk. I know. I'm sorry. I found him like this."

"Has anyone ever told you that you have a talent for stating the obvious?"

Another beat of silence.

Kite let Laec go, and he swayed a little, but overall, he was pleased with his ability to stay upright, especially while blind.

The captain barked, "Sober him up, then!"

"But… I…" Kite sounded bewildered. "How?"

Laec imagined she was looking at him with loathing and was glad he couldn't see.

Whatever Bradburn's answer was, it wasn't verbal.

Kite grabbed Laec and hauled him a few steps further into the yard, then changed direction, entering a shadowy place. Laec dropped his hand from his face but kept his eyes closed. The lids were just too heavy to lift.

Kite, muttering under her breath, transferred one hand to the back of his skull, grabbing a handful of the hair there, like he was a kitten.

"Hey!"

Laec cracked an eye open just as Kite brought him to a standstill in front of a horse trough full to the brim. He took a breath but had no time to yell before she slammed him face first into freezing, filthy water.

## Chapter Twenty-Seven

# Jessamine

Jess woke up with cold feet. Her room was chilly, and the fire had dwindled to coals. Groaning, she rolled out of bed, pulled on a pair of thick socks and knelt before her fireplace. Fresh warmth bathed her face as she raked the coals, then added kindling and logs, blowing until they caught. Now that she was awake, her mind began to tromp its endless circuit, reliving moments of the trial, weighing whether Sasha's chance at an acquittal had been improved or degraded by the most recent testimony.

Every witness the prosecution called had either embellished or outright lied. Sasha's lawyer always objected, but the jury and the citizens were still bombarded by the same message, and Jess worried that it was having Rayven's desired effect. Every enemy witness (as Jess had begun to think of them) postulated that Sasha had incited Rialta to kill the prince. Not every one of them claimed to see Sasha's lips moving, but many did, and Rayven had been thorough, choosing those who had been positioned in different locations but close to the events in the courtyard. Her strategy was obvious; show the jury that, no matter where the witnesses were, they'd all seen the same thing: Sasha calling Rialta, and the dire wolf—who had never killed any fae before in her life—committing murder because she'd been commanded to do so.

To combat this barrage of lies and hearsay, Bertrand called Silverfae who knew Sasha had been with him at court. He peppered them with yes or no questions about Sasha's character, which, he argued, had always been above reproach, in spite of being ridiculed for something Sasha's father had done that Sasha had nothing to do with, and in fact, had been a child when they'd occurred. Forced to stick to yes or no, the Silverfae begrudgingly admitted that Sasha was honorable, obedient to his superiors, took unfair persecution patiently, and never lost his temper. They were forced to admit that while Ruskin had turned on Sasha when the boys were teens, they had never seen Sasha return the prince's vitriol, even behind Ruskin's back. The picture they reluctantly painted made Jess burst with pride. Sasha was exceptional. His own fae said so, even if sullenly and with eyes full of resentment.

Rayven, in an unexpected turn of events, called a fauna fae who was not part of the Fahyli. Domitila was a wiry female with a cat familiar. They worked as pest control in Solana, dealing with rodent infestations in barns and food storage facilities. Jess disliked her the moment she laid eyes on her. Domit, as she was known, had shifty eyes and tugged a little too hard on her familiar's tail as he sat on the edge of the witness box. Domit testified that she and her cat, Tag, had had to develop telepathy for their work. She hypothesized that, were she being beaten bloody by someone—anyone, including someone of high rank or royal blood—she would command Tag to do whatever was in his power to interfere. If the cat somehow managed to kill her attacker, then he'd only done what was asked.

And so it went. Bertrand calling those who supported the truth—that Sasha was innocent and Rialta reacted out of self-defense, understandably, given the circumstances—while Rayven called those who were willing to embroider, to weave a web of doubt over Sasha's true motives.

Sasha sat quietly through every witness account, not reacting. He was calm and observant, showing no fear, no irritation or anger about anything that was said. He was perfect and proved to all—in Jess's opinion—that he was exactly how his countrymen were forced to admit that he was: patient and good, without a malicious bone in his body.

Jess hated the whole circus and just wanted it to come to an end. She started each day with the goal of trying to hide her thoughts and feelings as well as Sasha, but before noon, she'd already failed, getting huffy whenever Sasha was painted in a bad light.

The day that Sasha gave his own testimony, the number of citizens observing the proceedings more than doubled. Sasha was led through his version of events by Bertrand and told them exactly as Jess remembered them. At no point did he ask Rialta for help; in fact, he told the court he had blanked his mind so Rialta would not be incited. She was hunting on the mountainside, and he believed it would be over quickly and his familiar would not be part of the drama. But Rialta was fast, and there was no way for Sasha to hide from his familiar that he was in pain. So she came, enraged, so angry that she could not hear his attempts to calm her, or his cries of NO.

Sasha looked discomfited. He did not want to open Rialta to criticism, but he was oathbound to tell the truth.

Sasha's story was convincing, so Rayven switched focus to the animosity that Ruskin had showed Sasha since they were teens, trying to establish a motive. Sasha expressed bafflement at the prince's sudden hatred of him, relegating it to the same hatred that every Silverfae courtier harbored toward his father, Elvio. Sasha told the court that he did not hold the prince's ire against him because it came from a place of deep loyalty to his kingdom.

When her strategies didn't appear to achieve the desired results—suspicion from the Solanan members of the jury—Rayven pounced on the opportunity to drag Rialta into the mess; telling the jury that even if they had a reasonable doubt about Sasha, his own testimony damned the dire wolf. This made Jess's stomach go so sour that she couldn't eat for the rest of the day. Digit told her that it should make her feel better. It showed that Rayven was getting desperate.

Bertrand objected, of course, reminding the jury that it was Sasha who was at trial. A familiar had never undergone a trial independent of their fae in the history of Ivryndian courts.

Around and around it went, making Jess feel up one minute and down the next. It was exhausting. She couldn't imagine how wearing it was on Sasha.

Yesterday, on the fifth day of proceedings, the trial had come to a close. King Agir stated that the jury had three days to deliberate. When they came to full agreement, the court would reconvene to hear the verdict. If they could not agree by sundown on the third day, the king would make the verdict himself. Rayven objected to the time limit, but King Agir told her that the business needed to be settled quickly, so the Silverfae citizens could go home.

Jess had not slept well all week, so she'd asked Mrs. Tierney for a sleeping draft last night. It had worked, but now that she was awake, there was no way she'd return to slumber. She reached for the metal jewelry box, wedged on its side between a collection of books above her fireplace.

She pulled out her birth certificate and Julian's death certificate, along with one of Julian's baby bonnets. She kept the others in a drawer, wrapped in tissue, but this one was special. Like the others, it had a flourishy name tag, but unlike the others, Julian's baby footprints had been inked onto the fabric. The ink was faded now, and the hem was worn. Jess held it to her heart as she looked at the death certificate, focusing on the handwritten note in the bottom corner that said *death by accidental poisoning*. These words never failed to bring a reaction. Who might have accidentally poisoned Julian more than she herself? She was the one with potentially deadly sweat. She was the one who slept snuggled next to Julian when they'd been infants.

But, if Jess had been responsible, then it would have been Marion who had registered Julian's death, in which case she would have signed her name. And how might Jess have been responsible for Julian's death *after* he'd been kidnapped?

None of it made sense. Based on the testimony of her neighbors, Jess had to conclude that Julian had died after he'd been stolen from Marion's cottage, and the fact that he'd accidentally been poisoned was just a coincidence. Yet the whole thing felt improbable.

Jess thought about Nasyk, and how Tad assumed Marion was from there. But there were no Fontanas on record living in Nasyk. Jess had checked. She didn't know if Fontana was Marion's wedded name or maiden name because Marion never talked about Jessamine's father. Had they been married? Jess didn't think so, but how could she know for sure?

With a sigh, she folded up the paper and the bonnet, tucking them back into the box. They had distracted her from Sasha's situation but reminded her of her own problems. She hoped that Sasha would become her family, but that was uncertain too. They had a daunting hurdle to get over before they could even think about such things. Their relationship was so new. She loved him, and believed he loved her, but how deep did that love go?

A thud and a giggle from down the hall drew Jess from her contemplation. Apparently, she wasn't the only one up. Jess poked her head out the door, looking both ways. The corridor was quiet, the etherlamps turned down to a muted glow. Another giggle—one Jess recognized as Aster's—sounded like it came from Rose's room. Jess wrapped herself in a shawl, and after a glance at Beazle's sleeping form in the rafters, went down the hall.

Rapping softly on Rose's door halted all sounds from within.

"I'm so sorr—" Rose began as she opened the door, then saw who it was and brightened. "Jess!"

She found herself yanked inside the room and the door shut softly behind her.

"Did we wake you?" Aster was beneath the covers in Rose's bed, leaning on two pillows stacked against the headboard. She patted the mattress and Jess got in beside her.

"No." She pulled the covers up to her chest. "I was cold and got up to stir the fire, then I heard you giggling."

At the fireplace, Rose used a poker to shove a large log

back onto the burning pile. "This log fell out of the fireplace. Just about gave me a heart attack. Aster thought it was funny."

Rose made sure nothing flaming would come tumbling out again before hopping into bed with them. The three Calyx huddled together, staring at the flames.

"Do you want to talk about the trial?" Aster asked Jess, her voice low.

"No," Jess replied too quickly. "I really don't." She knocked her shoulder into Rose's. "I want to know how Lady Gillner is doing."

Rose's cheeks flushed, and she hid a smile behind the blanket, drawing up her feet.

"I'm not Lady Gillner yet. Speaking of heart attacks, I thought Ilishec was going to have one when everyone fessed up. If Peony hadn't come clean, I wouldn't have had the courage to either. I still can't believe it's not against the rules anymore. I can't shake the feeling that Artemon and I are being bad."

"Artemon?" Aster snorted a laugh. "That's Lord Gillner's first name?"

"Artie for short," Rose told them. "And he's nothing like what you think."

"Why? What do we think?" Jess called to mind the rather ordinary form and face of Lord Gillner. She'd danced with him many times. He was nice but a little boring and a lot forgettable.

"That he's punching above his weight?" Aster supplied, then laughed again. "*Of course* we think that, because he is. I'm sure he thinks he died and went to heaven."

Rose's look turned dreamy. "He's kind to me and makes me feel smart. He doesn't say anything at all about my looks, never has. No other males are like that. Looks are all they talk about. Did you know he's blind in one eye?"

Aster and Jess looked surprised.

Rose nodded. "He had a fever when he was a child, and it took the sight from one eye. But somehow, it feels like that eye can see into my very soul. He's all that I want, and Bombini loves him too."

Rose was clearly in love, and no matter what Jess and Aster thought of the man she had chosen, she was happy. Her friend's obvious contentment warmed Jess's heart.

"Can you believe Proteas?" Aster gasped. "Getting a servant girl pregnant? Who knew he had it in him? I never thought he'd have the brass to knock up one of the staff."

Rose smothered a burst of giggles. "Do you think they've been doing it in the supply closets?"

Aster grinned. "I can't imagine it. He just seems so… conventional. I never thought he would break any rules."

"Oh! And Gardenia and Regalis?" Rose crowed before stuffing the blanket into her mouth. She ripped it out again. "He's so stable, and she's so… not! How did that even happen?"

"They say opposites attract," shrugged Aster. "They look good together. He's all broody and dark and masculine, and she's all wispy and willowy and feminine. They'll have pretty fae babies if they get that far, but I suspect it won't last."

"Aster!" reproached Rose.

"Just truthing," Aster said, unapologetically.

"I'm more shocked about Peony and Pan," said Jess.

Rose nodded. "I can't decide if I'm more shocked that Pan fell in love with a snob, or that Peony fell in love with someone who is always covered in cat fur."

"Now who's judging?" Aster stuck her tongue out at Rose.

"Hey!" Jess looked affronted. "I love Tully!"

Rose laughed. "I love her too! I'm just saying, he doesn't seem like the type Peony would be attracted to."

"Who *would* Peony be attracted to?" Aster tucked a curl behind her ear. Her hair was a wild mass of spirals. "I thought she'd never go with anyone, she's so dedicated to her work."

"We're gossiping," Rose said with a smile. "We should stop."

It was nice to spend some time with her friends, pretending that everything was fine with the world. Forgetting—even for just a moment—felt like a vacation.

"Oooo!" Jess sat ramrod straight when she thought of the most unlikely couple of all.

"What?" Aster asked.

"Oh, nothing." Jess slumped again. Isabey was a royal, not a Calyx. The consequences were much bigger if her secret got out.

"You can't do that," Rose protested, slapping a hand on the blanket and puffing the air out. "You can't go 'ooo!' then pretend like it was nothing."

Aster nudged Jess. "Yeah, what do you know? Tell us?"

"I can't." Jess pressed her lips together.

"No. Not, you *can't*," Aster said. "You *shouldn't*. It's not the same thing. If it's a secret, we won't tell anyone. We swear. Right, Rose?"

"Of course!"

"Besides," Aster narrowed her eyes. "If you tell, I'll spill who my sweetheart is."

Rose's eyes went round. "You said you didn't have one!"

Aster looked smug. "I lied."

Jess gasped. "That's not fair!"

"It's perfectly fair. Now give," Rose said.

"Spill. We won't tell a soul. You know us."

Both Calyx turned impatient eyes on Jess. They would keep the secret, Jess believed. Besides, she really was bursting to tell someone. She took a breath. "It's Princess Isabey."

"Noooo," Aster whispered.

Jess nodded. "But it's very sad. She was in love with Shade."

The girls looked puzzled.

Rose canted her head. "Shade?"

"A soldier."

Aster's eyes widened. "A Solanan soldier? That *is* juicy!"

"No," Jess rolled her eyes. "A Rahamlar soldier. When would Princess Isabey have had a chance to mingle with Solanan soldiers? Think about it."

"In Syrgana?" suggested Rose. "Or maybe, since she's been here?"

It took Jess a second to process what Rose was saying, and how off she was from reality.

"There was no time for Isabey to get to know anyone in Syrgana, Rose," she said patiently. "She was running for her life, then she watched her sister get murdered by her brother. She was totally distraught. She wasn't about to fall in love with one of our soldiers."

Jess was reminded that her Calyx friends had no understanding of the horrible things that had taken place in the unnamed forest. They'd been told a Fahyli had died, but they'd not known Sy and hadn't been overly grieved by his and Mae's deaths. As much as Jess did not like to admit it, there was a gulf between her and her Calyx friends. She loved them, but when it came to Fahyli doings—and sometimes real life—they were clueless.

Jess explained how Isabey had admitted—secretly, to Beazle—that she'd been in love with Shade and that their affair had gone on for years. His death was the reason she couldn't rouse herself to care about her inheritance. But Jess also relayed how the death of Ander had been the first blow, then the death of her father, the murder of her sister, and finally she'd lost her lover. On top of all that, her brother was setting up to steal a crown that was rightfully hers, since Faraçek had forfeited his right to rule by committing sororicide.

As Jess talked, Rose and Aster grew solemn. The seriousness of Isabey's situation came clear to them and lay over the room like a dense mist.

"That is so depressing," murmured Aster when Jess was done.

Rose stared into the fire. "I don't understand why some people sail through life, getting everything they want, while others suffer tragedy after tragedy. It isn't fair."

"Will she really run away?" Aster shuddered. "That would be horrible."

"I hope she doesn't, but I don't blame her if she does. Faraçek is *highly* motivated to rule," Jess told them. "Even if the princess found the will to fight, I'm not sure she'd have a chance. She's not strong. Meanwhile, Faraçek is totally unscrupulous and willing to do anything because he wants Rahamlar for his son."

Aster looked horrified. "Faraçek has offspring?"

Jess closed her eyes in immediate regret. "No one is supposed to know that. I'm the worst secret keeper ever. Don't say anything to anyone, please."

The Calyx promised, then fell silent. The facts had struck them solidly. Jess was grateful that she hadn't told them that Faraçek wanted to annex Solana's lands too. That would really terrify them, and there was nothing the Calyx could do about it.

Rose looked ashen. "Why is it a secret? And why do *you* know, and not us?"

"A Fahyli mission. They—King Agir and Queen Esha and all the superiors—don't want it to get back to Faraçek that we know. So can we just forget I said anything, please?"

Aster and Rose exchanged a loaded look that made Jess feel uncomfortable and alone. The differences between them were apparent to them now, as well as she.

She brightened in an effort to bring focus back to nicer things. "Your turn, Aster. Who's your secret love?"

Aster shrank down against the pillows, looking reticent. "Promise you won't laugh?"

"Why would we laugh?" Rose said. "We'll be happy for you, as long as it's not Captain Bradburn, that oaf."

"It's not Bradburn." Aster dimpled, looking sheepish. "It's Auvo."

Jess and Rose were delighted. Auvo was a favorite among the Calyx, not just because he had such appreciation for flora fae beauty, but he was funny and sarcastic and passionate. Jess thought Aster and Auvo were perfect for one another.

Jess and Rose cajoled out the story of how Aster and Auvo got together. And while Aster talked, Jess snuggled with her friends, warm in the blankets. She grew sleepy. Their differences faded into the background, and she wondered why she hadn't come to them before, for comfort and conversation. Talking and listening made the world seem less scary.

Nothing had changed. Sasha's verdict was imminent, and Jess didn't have answers about her family. There was still an evil, unseelie prince threatening to take over, but while she was with Aster and Rose, it was easy to pretend, for a little while, that everything was going to turn out all right.

## Chapter Twenty-Eight

# Laec

Laec—in Solanan livery and the military-issued cap that Bradburn's soldiers wore on cold nights—sat atop the city wall facing north, as he had been for the last three nights. The view was beautiful, and the work wasn't so bad. Pastureland stretched toward the mountains—dotted with villages and farms—rising to gentle foothills and forested valleys. Chimneys burped wood smoke in thin streams; owls made their lonely cries from scattered patches of trees; and a dreamy winter mist rose from the ground, gathering in low places and giving the whole scene the look of a storybook setting. The Vargilath range thrust jaggedly into the sky.

Behind him were the sounds of a city at dinner hour. The guards in this post were not coddled, but there was an urn full of hot, honeyed tea, and a nearby bakery donated goods daily: salted twists, loaves with dried fruit, and doughy pockets stuffed with jam or spiced meat.

Further attempts to drink had been waylaid by Bradburn, who'd commanded that no one give Laec a drop of anything stronger than lemon water or tea. His hangover was gone, yet what remained was worse. Not just the craving for alcohol—he'd even snuck a sip of that awful fermented cactus slop the soldiers seemed to like—but a growing sense of shame. He thought he'd gotten over such behavior. He drank at balls and parties, sure, but never overdid it anymore, not since leaving Stavarjak. He'd regressed and could only blame himself.

Bradburn's soldiers wandered back and forth along the ramparts. Those on break chatted amiably, sipping from steaming mugs. Those on duty paced their assigned stretches of wall, attentively observing the countryside, although they usually got a heads up about approaching danger from the Fahyli, whose familiars scouted the surrounding land and mountain range.

The wall looped fully around the city and was guarded by hundreds of soldiers. There were four gates in the wall, but the largest one, which faced west—the gates the rose window looked down upon—was used by the majority of traffic. In peace time, as now, the gates were open during the day. They shut at midnight and reopened at dawn.

When Panther came up the narrow steps and saw Laec, he made a beeline toward him.

"Got roped in, huh? Me as well… obviously." Panther said as he popped his butt up on the wall.

Laec grunted and offered the Fahyli a smile. "Still don't know what I'm doing here. Kite mumbled something about Bradburn's orders, but my ears were full of water at the time."

Panther tugged his collar up to his pointed ears and crossed his arms to keep in body heat. The wind had a bite in it, and if Laec wasn't mistaken, a storm was brewing. Snow clouds had gathered over the city and surrounding area when the Silver queen arrived and probably wouldn't break until she left.

"Sylifke left some of her entourage at the border," Panther explained. "Something about getting stuck in some epically bad weather? Anyway, they're expected to arrive, finally, and Bradburn wants fae at the gate." Panther's expression showed how ridiculous he thought it was. "Said he wanted to make them feel welcome."

Laec snorted. "That shows how much Bradburn knows about fae relations. They'll feel anything but welcome by me, a Stavarjakian."

Panther flashed his teeth. "Elphame's not a fan, eh?"

"To put it mildly."

Laec rubbed his forehead under his woolen cap.

"Itchy?"

He nodded, scratching. "I suspect they pick the roughest wool on purpose, maybe for entertainment. Feels like I have lice."

"Why do you think they issue fingerless gloves?" Panther waved his bare fingertips.

A Fahyli came up the stairs, a female with a sturdy build. She and Laec had never been introduced. She had pink cheeks and an earnest expression. Her hair was like Kite's, in rows of braids, but hers stuck out in tufts. Laec thought she looked like a baby owl: cute, wide-eyed and staring. When she saw Panther, she came over.

"Gitana." Panther nodded to the fresh-faced young Fahyli. "Welcome to the fae contingent. Where's Alan?"

"He's at the courthouse, where I'd like to be too, frankly." She gave Laec an appreciative once over. "You're the import from Stavarjak. Laec, right? Alan is my familiar, the mastiff with the black patch over his right eye."

"Welcome to the wall." Laec grumped. "What's happening at the trial?"

She gaped. "You don't know?"

"If he did, he wouldn't have asked, Git," Panther laughed.

Unfortunate nickname.

"I've been… otherwise occupied," Laec said.

Gitana leaned against the stones opposite, brightening at her chance to share trial gossip. "The jury has been deliberating in a locked room for three days, which was the allotted time Agir gave them, so…" She made a clicking sound, like she wanted a horse to canter. "Time's up. Verdict is due today by sundown. Let's get our boy unshackled."

"You seem confident," Laec said.

She gaped again. Apparently, Gitana was one of those fae whose emotions fully consumed her features. Now she looked like an electrocuted baby owl.

"Have you not been following it at all? How is that possible?"

"Otherwise occupied," Panther repeated.

"Right. Listen." Gitana put both hands out, setting the stage. "Everyone knows Sasha and Rialta were acting in self-defense and that the Silverfae witnesses have been either exaggerating or lying. And Sasha's lawyer, Bertrand? He looks like a jester from a traveling road show, but he's actually razor-sharp."

Panther grinned. "I'm sure Rayven thought she had it in the bag."

Gitana's eyes were sparkling. "Bertrand keeps reminding everyone about the whole reasonable doubt thing. The Silverfae jury members are under pressure to find him guilty because the queen wants to take Sasha back to Silverfall so she can rip them apart there, probably publicly, too. She seems like the type." Gitana's entire body was consumed by a shudder of revulsion. “What a piece of work she is. Anyway, I figure, that’s why the king put a time limit on the deliberations. He’s wise to their game.”

“Not like it’s not totally obvious,” added Panther, blowing heat into his hands.

“When the jury comes out with an undecided result, in about,”—Gitana squinted—“thirteen minutes, then he’ll step in and acquit.”

“The whole charade has just been a formality to appease Silverfall,” added Panther. “The sooner it’s over, the sooner they leave. Maybe then we’ll get some sunshine back.”

“If you’re right about how it’s going to play out,” said Laec, “an acquittal won’t appease them, least of all, Sylifke.”

Gitana shrugged and tucked a stray blond spike behind one pointed ear. “No, but we’ve followed all the rules, even let them take part in the trial. What more does she want? Don’t get me wrong, it’s awful, what happened to her son, but from what I heard—”

“He was a git,” Panther supplied, sounding as callous as Laec felt.

“Hey, watch how you use my nickname,” Gitana mock-pouted. “But yeah, he was a first-class arse.” Her brow wrinkled. “How is the lady who was frozen, anyway? I haven’t heard.”

“No change,” muttered Laec, looking away.

Laec hoped for Jessamine’s sake that it all worked out the way Gitana expected it would, but one thing Laec had learned about himself—and of which he was not proud—was that it was hard to be happy for someone else when he wasn’t happy for himself. Sad, shameful even, but there it was. The ugly truth of Laec Fairijak, selfish brute and whiner. Oh, and let’s not forget drunkard.

Jessamine didn't have to keep her relationship a secret anymore, but what if Laec had done the same? Kazery already disliked him, and Laec was sure the idea of Çifta loving Laec back was laughable to her father, if it had even crossed the merchant's mind.

Laec realized that both Panther and Gitana were watching him. Could they sense the self-pity oozing from his pores, he wondered? Life was funny. Most people were blind to their own flaws. Not Laec. He could pinpoint his failings with hawkish accuracy. His problem was that he was powerless to change them. He didn't want to talk to anyone about what he was feeling, so he gave them a serrated smile, showing his eye-teeth in a feral grin. Gitana blinked, perhaps taken aback, perhaps repelled by his savage expression. He didn't care.

"So," he said, "we'll have an outcome for Sasha in a few minutes. Seems like the rest of the Silverfae retinue should've just stayed in the north. No point in joining their queen now. Not when it's all over."

"True," said Gitana, turning her back to observe the landscape. "They'll leave tomorrow, tails tucked. I almost feel sorry for them. Hey, I think there are riders out there."

Panther and Laec went to stand on either side of Gitana. The three of them peered into the dusky gloom where a pale ribbon of road arched over a series of gentle hills.

"I don't see anything," said Laec, squinting.

"No, there is someone." Panther yelled to alert the soldiers at the gate. "Riders!"

A few seconds later, calls of "Riders, Ho!" echoed along the wall.

Laec spied them; a group of six riders cantering up the road toward the city. They'd come from the mountainside, rather than the king's road.

"Those are Silverfae ponies," confirmed Gitana when the party got closer. "I guess that's the group we're waiting for. Come on. Bradburn wants us to be visible when they enter."

They made their way down the narrow stone steps to the gate and joined the soldiers forming neat lines through which the Silverfae group would pass. The gate was opened, the heavy timbers and iron bracings latched to the stone walls on either side.

Bradburn materialized from somewhere, pink-cheeked and straightening his cap. He caught sight of the fae and beckoned. They let him manhandle them into the places he wanted them, basically front and center. Everyone stood at attention. Laec thought the whole thing was ridiculous, a lot of effort for nothing.

The ponies hardly slowed. Six riders, pale capes billowing behind them, clattered straight through the gate without so much as a side glance. The moment that everyone had been instructed to wait days for came and went in two blinks of an eye.

Bradburn flushed as he watched them go, then snapped, "Why are you staring around like a bunch of idiots? Back to your posts!"

"Sir?" Gitana thrust a hand into the sky like an eager student.

The captain turned weary eyes on her. "Yes?"

"Do you still need us?" She pointed to herself, then Laec and Panther.

Bradburn rolled his eyes. "Get out of here."

Gitana did a little hop and began to jog up the main road.

She looked back at Laec and Panther. "You guys coming? It's sundown!"

Panther shot a questioning look at Laec.

"You go," Laec told him. "There's something I want to see."

Panther set after Gitana, and Laec went back to the top of the wall. There had been something else on the horizon besides riders, but Laec hadn't been sure it wasn't his eyes playing tricks on him. He asked a soldier if he could borrow an eyeglass.

"It's too dark to be of much help," said the soldier, who handed him a heavy cylinder, "but you can try."

Laec put the glass to his eye and scanned the horizon. There was something strange, a line of white and gray. He strained to make out more details until his eye ached. He had to stop and rub his forehead, then once he started rubbing, the itch under his hat came surging back.

"What did I tell you?" the soldier said.

Laec handed him the glass. "Look at the horizon. What do you see?"

The soldier did as he was asked, scanning more slowly than Laec had. "Just a lot of snow. Is that what's got your breekies in a twist? The weather came in with that Silver queen and will leave when she goes. Northern fella like you oughta know that."

"I do know that. But don't you think it looks strange?"

"Strange how?"

"I don't know. Like… thicker, darker than normal, murky and…" He scrunched his eyes up until he fell upon the word he wanted. "Soupy."

The soldier grunted, unconvinced. "There was a storm all along the Vargilath range, a bad one blew down from Kittrell. Not unusual this time of year. Our patrols were called back."

Laec perked up. "There are no scouts out there right now? No familiars?"

The soldier slid the eyeglass into a pouch at his waist. "Not at the moment. Too dangerous." He clapped a hand on Laec's shoulder. "Something's got you jumpy, Stavarjak. I heard you hit the sauce hard recently, must be making you paranoid."

"Must be," Laec muttered.

"Look, Captain Bradburn says you're not needed anymore. Why don't you go home?"

The soldier walked away, leaving Laec standing alone, unable to shake the feeling that something was wrong. He looked out at the mountains again, but it was too dark to see much of anything. Going to the crofter with a hunch was a poor idea. If it turned out to be nothing, Laec would lose even more of the Fahyli leader's esteem. He chewed his lip for a while, feeling tired, wondering if he should ignore his gut and go to the courthouse, be there for Jess. But he'd ignored his gut before and always ended up regretting it, so he decided to find Regalis. The stoic fauna fae would listen, tell him everything was as it should be, and never repeat a word about it to anyone. He should be at the courthouse.

But the guards outside the courthouse told him Regalis was no longer there. He'd been dismissed two hours earlier and had gone to the west keep for rest, apparently not feeling his best. As far as Laec could remember, Regalis had never taken a sick day, or even a sick hour, in the time they'd known each other. And to miss out on the night of the verdict? Concern prodded Laec's mind with chilly fingers as he climbed the long hill up to the palace.

## CHAPTER TWENTY-NINE

# ÇIFTA

THE ICE TOOK Çifta to a new room, but the sculpture of the Silverfall pony and the throne beneath its kicking front hooves gave it away: Sylifke's throne room. A row of tall Gothic arches filled with frost-encrusted glass let dingy winter light into the large space. Fat columns thrust upward to a ceiling so high that the details of the pictures painted there were just a blur.

Sylifke—wearing a pale purple gown, her long white hair intertwined with ribbon and pinned into a pile of curls—sat on the throne, her posture erect. A glittering silver diadem encircled her up do. Her face was almost gaunt, her cheeks hollow, her bones protruding. The combination of her queenly attire and her flinty expression was grotesque. She looked more at home in tawny leathers and tundra boots than she did in this feminine royal costume.

In front of the throne stood Elvio, his hands behind his back.

"Leave us," commanded

Sylifke, lifting a bony index finger tipped with a white talon. "All of you. Soldiers too."

Nobles and courtiers filed from the room, followed by guards. The doors banged shut, and the sound echoed around the pillars.

"You've returned." The queen looked pleased, tapping her talons on the arms of her throne. "And you've been successful, or you wouldn't have such a smug expression. How did you find her?"

Elvio shifted. "I had the help of a fauna fae."

"Well done," Sylifke said quietly, grudgingly.

"But Evelin is not the one you want," the sorcerer told her, looking even more smug. "You were wrong."

The queen canted her head. Shadows shifted across her face. For a brief moment, Çifta thought she caught a glimpse of the skull beneath Sylifke's skin, a fleshless head that never stopped grinning.

"Oh?" Sylifke growled.

Elvio spoke quickly, perhaps having seen the same thing Çifta had. "It was never Salme's daughter that the prophecy spoke of. It is her granddaughter."

Sylifke arched her brows. "A half-fae babe with dark hair?"

"That's right." Elvio watched his queen's expression the way a devoted student memorizes runes.

*He is wondering if she still wants to kill the child,* Çifta mused. *Because he doesn't want to, but he won't ask. Am I right?*

*You give him more credit than I,* the ice responded.

"It's a good thing you have no scruples," the queen told Elvio. "Otherwise, I would worry that you were not up to the task. Not even for Sasha." She lifted her chin, her gaze hard. "What do you propose?"

Elvio hesitated and the queen saw it.

"You may speak freely," she said. "We are alone. Truly."

"May I approach, Your Grace?"

Sylifke made a gesture, and Elvio walked forward until he could almost touch her knee. He had to look up because the base of her throne was three feet above the floor.

"I have a curse," he told her softly, his pulse jumping visibly in his neck. "A powerful one. It can end a life in seconds. I can send the curse abroad without even leaving the city. Over time and space, its potency diminishes, but when it reaches her, it will still be strong enough to kill. The half-faeling will die as an old woman, living her life in hours instead of years."

"How will the curse find her?" the queen asked.

"I have Salme's blood. I can use it to target her granddaughter."

Sylifke considered her sorcerer in silence, talons tap, tap, tapping on the marble. "How will I know whether you are successful or not?"

"I will report the results to you, of course." He dipped his chin in a respectful gesture.

She scoffed, glaring at him from those ghostly eyes. "I am simply to believe you?"

Elvio put on an expression of hurt feelings. "You believe I would lie to you? After all this time that I have served you faithfully?"

"You would absolutely lie to me. Especially when that son of yours is on the line." All the humor went out of her face, and she snarled. "You must think me a fool."

He looked back at the queen benignly, though Çifta saw a fist form behind his back. "Not at all. I will report truthfully, as I have promised."

The queen stood, running her hands down her thighs to smooth her dress. She descended to floor level, coming nose to nose with Elvio, who backed up to make room for her. Sylifke stared at him for a long time, then marched to the row of windows. She turned and crooked a talon at him. Hands still behind his back, Elvio flipped a lock of hair away from his forehead with a jerk of his head and strolled after her. The queen swung open a set of doors and stepped onto a balcony overlooking a garden.

Every tree and shrub was coated with hoarfrost. An iced-over stream wound through the parkland, passing under a footbridge. Beyond the garden, young fae sparred in a frosty yard. The clang of metal on metal carried on the frozen air. Their swords flashed and their exhalations hung in the air, leaving a mist of condensation over their heads.

The queen stood at the railing, her gaze on the fae in the yard.

"You like to be secretive. I understand. I do. Secrecy is inherent in your role. You have magic, there is no doubt of that, but there is power of a different kind to be found in keeping oneself shrouded in mystery. The courtiers fear and respect you because you seem to make impossible things happen—but much of what you do is simply a magician's artifice. Clever sleight of hand. Parlor tricks."

Elvio stood beside her, staring at his queen as she watched the youths fighting. His back was stiff, his shoulders thrown back. One hand gripped the wrist of the other behind him, twisting the skin as he listened to the queen's remarks, so obviously meant to tear him down. But his voice did not tremble.

"May I humbly remind the queen that she would not be in her position if it were not for me?"

She placed the pads of her fingers on the frozen balcony rail, her nails splayed like so many knives. She had yet to look at him, always keeping her eyes on her subjects in the yard.

"You think I will ever forget what we did? Neither of us would be where we are if it were not for the other. I am not your enemy, Elvio, but neither am I a superstitious courtier to be tricked into respecting a hand puppet, no matter how large and frightening a shadow he throws upon the wall." She jerked her chin toward a group of males emerging from a stable. "You see him?"

Elvio looked, sharp eyes scanning faces and forms. It took him a while, but he spotted the subject of the queen's attention. His brows lifted.

*Hirundo*, thought Çifta, recognizing the fauna fae. *He is here.*

He looked like he belonged with the Silverfae males, talking and laughing, pushing each other around, lobbing playful insults, the way males did in every species. Caith fluttered nearby, swooping to his shoulder and alighting before taking off again. Still slender from his fast, Hirundo moved with energy and grace.

*Did she have Elvio followed?* Çifta wondered.

*One of his men also works for her. Elvio just doesn't know it. His tricks are simple when uncovered,* said the ice, *but so are hers.*

"Hirundo." Elvio let out a breath, then cast a sharp look at the queen. "You've hired him to ensure my spell does not fail?"

A joyless smile touched her lips. "Thank you for discovering him. He will be an excellent addition to my personal envoys. Should your spell hit its mark, I shall overlook that you did not alert me to his abilities sooner, knowing I am a collector of such fine fae. I shall assume that you meant to, but had not time, given all that you are responsible for."

"Hirundo won't stay, my queen," Elvio told her confidently. "If I knew he had an interest in being your envoy, I would have arranged an introduction."

"We shall see."

The queen looked at Elvio for the first time since stepping out onto the balcony. To Çifta, it seemed that a subdued look of revulsion passed over Sylifke's features.

"Hirundo is no longer your concern. You have only one focus now, and until your task is complete, I have taken it upon myself to put Sasha under the care of Ruskin's tutors. Rest assured that he and Rialta will be well cared for—as if they were my own."

Her overreach was finally enough to crack Elvio's smooth façade. His eyes lit with fury. "You had no ri—"

"I have every right, Sorcerer. Your son is collateral. I must know where he is at all times; otherwise, you'll spirit him off somewhere, in case your spell should fail. I know you, Elvio Drazek. You parade about like a queen's man, speaking of loyalty and service to sovereign and kingdom, but at heart you are a narcissist and a coward who cannot see past your own hubris. You've only ever been self-serving. If you had not weakened yourself by becoming a father, you'd be pleased to speed this prophecy and see me off the throne."

Elvio looked shocked. "My queen has so little regard for her sorcerer? One can only wonder why she keeps him around. What kind of servant is worth keeping that cannot be trusted?"

"No one can be trusted," she snapped. "Not even family, not fully. I keep you because you are unscrupulous, uncaring of who you harm or what things cost. It is better to have you under my command than under another's. Such as that queen of mud to the east."

Elvio looked even more flabbergasted. "Any blood on my hands is there because of you!"

Çifta wondered at Sylifke's obvious hatred for Elvio. He'd shown himself to have power, but she seemed bent upon insulting him at every opportunity, alienating him, humiliating him.

"Not true," replied the queen. "It was your decision to join me, your decision to serve. I forced you into nothing. You didn't need to say yes to me that day in the gorge, but you did. You betrayed Karinya, your queen at the time, as I am now. Though you serve by my side, I know your true colors."

Elvio gaped. "Blood was shed for you, my queen. For your ascendancy. How can you put full responsibility for the fallout squarely upon my shoulders? It is madness, illogical."

"Mad? Really?" She cocked a fine white brow. "*I* never pretended to be loyal to Karinya. I was forthright with her from the start. But *you,* who were hers before you were mine, are false through and through, loyal to no one but yourself. I needed your help to secure my victory, yes, but had you turned me away, I would respect you to this day." She looked away. "Ironic, isn't it? Some things can only be learned by living them. More's the pity, for I find myself alone. Unable to trust the one who should have been my partner and defender in all things."

Elvio's face was long with incomprehension. He didn't seem to be able to make any sense of what she was saying.

"So… w-what?" he stuttered. "I do this final horrible, unforgiveable act for you, and you will absolve me of all wrongdoing? Give me a place of honor once more? Not just at your table, as I am now, for all to see and think that I am worthy, but in your heart?"

The queen smiled grimly. "No. I find I can hardly bear to look at you anymore, no matter what magic you have, no matter what you are willing to do. If you are successful, you may leave my court forever, with my blessing. Take your son and make a new life abroad. I know you hate me, as I hate you. I know you feel trapped in eternal servitude. I will release you from that. I will release us both from one another's company, and I will sow no foul word against you for as long as I live."

Staring at her in open horror, Elvio opened his mouth but struggled for words. Finally, he could only stutter, "Y-you would release me to your own detriment?"

She shrugged and faced the frosted garden. "It is as I said, Sorcerer. I could not have predicted it. I am grateful for what you did all those years ago, but my regard has turned to loathing. Finish this last task and be gone. Be free. Serve another if you wish. I care not, so long as you lift this evil prophecy from my shoulders before you go. Or lose your son forever."

Elvio closed his mouth with a snap. In the set of his jaw and the flame in his eyes was a new resolve. "I will not fail."

He bowed deeply, though she was looking away. Her eyes glittering with what looked like unshed tears. Elvio stalked away, pale as wax.

The ice kept Çifta there for a time, watching Sylifke after the sorcerer had gone.

The queen did not move from the balcony, only stood with her hands on the freezing marble. Her breath was deep and slow as she watched her subjects, harvesters moving among the trees and young males in mock battle. The cloud cover was so thick that none threw a shadow.

*But he fails,* thought Çifta.

*Yes.* The ice whispered on a drawn-out exhale. *Elvio fails.*

*As you know, your mother stepped in front of the spell that was meant for you. Your father had you out of the house fifteen minutes before the stormbirds circled. Evelin was dead, and you were gone. Hirundo reported Elvio's failure to Sylifke.*

Çifta was quietly amazed. *The stormbirds never saw Kazery, never learned the identity of my father, by a hair's breadth.*

*And you were safely tucked away aboard your father's ship. When he arrived in Boskaya, he even bought a spell to hide your fae ears. You slipped away like a ghost, and a ghost you have been since, as far as Sylifke is concerned.*

*She must have been furious.* Çifta studied the queen's stark profile, the strong nose, the prominent chin. *What happened to Elvio?*

*Ah,* the ice sighed. *All magic has a price, and failed magic exacts the highest price of all. When Evelin took the curse instead of you, there was a rebound, and he became a cripple in one painful instant. He was openly shunned in court, dubbed Elvio the Betrayer. True to her word, Sylifke took Sasha—her consolation prize. As faelings, Sasha and Ruskin were friends until Ruskin was old enough to understand the prophecy and Elvio's failure. Then he turned on his adopted brother and was more than eager to search for you when the Decennial Midwinter Festival came along.*

*How did they know I would be there?*

*They didn't, not for certain. Sylifke has never stopped searching for you, though she never sent Silverfae on these missions. Her reign is unwanted and her citizens long to rebel. She fears that if they knew there was a dark-haired halfling with the power to strike her down, that her own people would aid you. So she hired only outsiders to search for you.*

*Like Hirundo?*

*He made himself available to Sylifke for a steep price, though he never swore allegiance to her. But even Hirundo and Caith's magic isn't enough to cover all of Ivryndi. The lands are too great, and your identity too well protected. When word of Solana's Festival spread, it was Ruskin's idea to search for you there, but not his sole reason for going. He wished to see the lands beyond his kingdom because he'd always been forbidden to go abroad. As he convinced his mother that the Midwinter Festival was worth her attention, he also told her she could trust no one but him with the task. He alone knew what to look for and hand-selected his retinue.*

*Including Sasha.* Images of the Silverfae male filled Çifta's mind. What she recalled most about that moment was the way he'd been looking at Jessamine, both heartbroken and lovesick. It had been an intimate moment between lovers, so personal that Çifta had blushed.

*Yes. Ruskin told only Sasha that he was to watch for a dark-haired Silverfae halfling, someone that was of great interest to the queen, though not why.*

That explained why, when Sasha had seen Çifta, he looked shocked by recognition. He'd known her to be who they were searching for.

How differently things would have turned out had she attended the parties in spite of Prince Faraçek's presence. Instead of being encased in ice, she'd likely be dead. It was unbearably ironic that Faraçek had saved her life just by being there.

*There is so much I never knew... until now.* The ice was her destiny; without it, she would never have learned her true identity. *So many secrets, and so much tragedy.*

*Which brings us to the present,* the ice told her. *Now that you know the truth of your past, the time has come to make a choice about the future.*

## Chapter Thirty

# Jessamine

Agir took the scroll from the juror and waited until she took her place in the jury's box with the others. Sasha stood in front of the accused's box, shackled and bookended by burly soldiers. Bertrand Bedar stood at the defendant's table, and Miss Sabran and her assistant stood before theirs. Queen Sylifke had risen to her feet, resting her hands on the railing and looking down at the room. Every eye was glued to Agir's face. The tension in the room was thick as clay.

The king opened the seal and unrolled the parchment, reading the verdict first to himself, then—with great satisfaction—aloud to the courtroom.

"In the murder of Prince Ruskin of Silverfall, the jury find Sasha and Rialta Drazek…" He looked up at those present, holding their collective breath. "Not guilty."

Jessamine's screams of triumph were lost in the uproar.

The king told Sasha he

was free to go. Jess could read the glorious words on his lips, but his voice couldn't be heard over the din. Solanans leapt to their feet, cheering and clapping, hugging one another. She and Digit—who had sat with her every day of the trial—surged at one another, embracing hard, whacking each other and whooping. Wiping away tears of joy, she looked at Sasha, seeing the relief in his grin as he held his manacled wrists out to be unlocked. She'd never seen a smile more beautiful. He was not guilty. Acquitted. Vindicated. Free.

As his chains fell away, Jess's eyes misted up further.

*CRR-RRA-CK!*

The celebrating stopped abruptly when a sharp retort echoed through the courtroom. It was so loud it make Jess's ears ring and jolted Beazle awake. She looked around, seeing her confusion reflected in the faces of others. There was nothing obviously amiss. Except… except that the Silverfae did not seem confused at all. They looked intently toward the second level, at their queen. Solanan gazes followed the Silverfae ones. Sylifke's long fingers were wrapped around the wooden banister like thin, jointed snakes. The source of the sound was apparent: a long crack had split the wood apart. Frost spread from the queen's touch, crawling across the railing and down the spindles.

For a moment, nothing happened. Everyone stood frozen, looking up at her. Then Sylifke ripped off her veil, and Jess got a clear look at her face for the first time: gaunt, sharp angles, protruding bones, hollow eyes. With her teeth bared, she was terrifying. She glared down at the room, her face a mask of hatred and something else… Triumph? That couldn't be. The Silverfae had lost… Jess shook her head, trying to marshal a proper reaction to the strangeness of it. What was happening?

The Silverfae looked expectant, and it struck Jess squarely

that they had been waiting for this moment. Unlike when Prince Ruskin had gone after Çifta, leaving his subjects shocked and reeling, Sylifke's actions now were anticipated. They knew Sasha would be acquitted, in spite of half the jury being theirs—or maybe because of it.

"Solanans, have care!" someone yelled, though it only served to confuse the Solanan soldiers present. Captain Bradburn was not there, and Ian was somewhere outside. Soldiers and Fahyli had orders only to keep peace. Jess looked at the judge's bench, but King Agir was no longer there. He'd either run, or more likely been shoved by his personal guard, into the judge's quarters. She heard a muffled yell, and a sense of dread closed its grip around her throat.

Her glacial eyes taking on an otherworldly light, Queen Sylifke hissed in a voice that stiffened every hair on Jessamine's body. "*Tydan ar inda. Vas jaras truskeb mi, nyt fulk.*"

Someone yelled, "No!" It sounded like Sasha.

Beazle stirred next to her skull, disturbed as Jess's heart began to thunder. *What's happening?*

Two Solanan soldiers drew blades but were not near enough an enemy to use them. Besides, the Silverfae were unarmed; all weapons had been confiscated at the doors. Citizens recoiled in fear, a few cried out.

*I don't know!* Jess looked around wildly, feeling Digit grab her arm, then let her go again. He moved away… springing over a chair toward…

A Silverfae who *did* have a weapon. A short, crooked blade, whitish and glittering. Ice formed out of nothing. Another Silverfae created a weapon out of nowhere. Jess saw it materialize in his hand, her eyes stretching wide with disbelief.

Jess looked for Sasha, saw him move toward the nearest Silverfae, who turned and lifted his ice-blade.

A sudden roar, like the sound of the whirlpool gorge, rang in her ears. Her vision blanked out as a white-out filled the room with winter. Then screams of terror.

Jess crouched low on instinct. Her hand went to her dagger, but she didn't unsheathe it. She couldn't see anything and risked hurting herself or an innocent.

"Sasha?" she screamed, but the room was full of noise. She could hardly hear herself thinking. Erasmus shrieked from somewhere in the rafters. Heart in her mouth, Jess floundered in Sasha's direction. Immediately, she tripped on something and went down.

*Are you ok?* Beazle asked.

*I'm ok. Stay where you are,* Jess told him. *The Silverfae, I think they're trying to kill Sasha… I can't see anything.*

When she opened her mouth, it filled with snow. It stung her face and hands. She tried to get up, but her boots slipped on the wet hardwood, sending her sprawling again, bruising both knees. It was better to stay down, so she crawled, feeling her way between the rows, completely blind. Pulling the neckline of her tunic up to cover her mouth, she realized she couldn't even see her own hands. She crawled along in the direction she'd last seen Sasha, squinting against the swirling snow. It was freezing. Even the temperature inside her head felt like it was steadily dropping, and a headache blossomed at the back of her head. If this cold got worse, it would soon be unbearable. Already, she struggled to conjure rational thought.

Someone struck her ribcage and fell over her. Someone else kicked her in the thigh as they floundered past. She gasped in pain as her muscles spasmed.

She tried to yell for Sasha, but the sheer volume of noise made it impossible. People screamed and yelled; there was the thunder of magic and furniture falling; plus, her ears felt clogged with snow.

Jess kept thinking about the blades the Silverfae had, how Sasha was so close but so far away. How he'd gone for one of the Silverfae just before the white-out. She huddled on the floor, rubbing her spasming leg and trying to breathe. By the time her thigh muscles relaxed, the hysteria in the room had died down.

Shapes materialized in the blur as precipitation settled. Now she could see figures moving about, wrestling, falling over, crawling on the floor. The snow had stopped swirling, and the mist that remained was clearing. Everything was wet and slippery. Piles of snow had drifted in the corners and topped every surface, including the rafters. People stopped screaming and began helping one another. Jess managed to get to her feet, her face and lips numb, her leg still throbbing. The snow inside her ear canals and on her head melted, trickling down her neck. Her hair was soaked, as were her sleeves and her leggings at the knees.

Beazle peeked out at the room from her hair. *Where's the queen?*

At Beazle's questions, Jess looked up, but the queen was nowhere in sight. In fact, she could see no Silverfae left in the courtroom at all, just a bunch of cold, wet, shocked Solanan citizens, and a few miserable-looking familiars.

*Where have they gone?*

Jess quailed at the thought. The fact that the Silverfae had vanished seemed somehow worse than thinking they were in the room wielding ice-weapons.

*I'll find them.* Before Jess could react, Beazle vanished out the open door.

Reaching the front of the room and leaning on the prosecutor's table, Jess finally found Sasha. Relief flooded her when she saw that he was unharmed. He was near the judge's seat, and there was a body at his feet. A Silverfae body. An ice-blade lay melting on the floor. He saw her and came, handling the slippery floor much better than her.

"Jess." He lifted her and held her tight before looking down at her, eyes clouded.

"What did the queen say?" Jess asked, savoring the feeling of his solidity, of his shoulders, under her hands. "She gave a command, right?"

"Not exactly." Sasha's silvery brows pulled together. "She called for allegiance. She—"

He said more, but Jess didn't hear him through Beazle's telepathy.

*I found her,* Beazle snapped into her mind with an overhead view of the queen. Jess stiffened and gripped Sasha blindly.

"Jess?" His grip tightened on her. "What's happening?"

"Wait—" Jess gasped.

Sylifke was making her way swiftly up a narrow alley. At a turn in the passage, Jess recognized it.

"She is going to the palace," she said.

She felt Sasha go still, letting her see what Beazle had to show her. Sylifke was followed by two Silverfae soldiers wielding ice-blades. They looked like they knew exactly where to go. Citizens dove out of their way.

*Don't lose her,* Jess urged, as her own sight returned. Sasha's worried face filled her vision.

*I won't.*

"Agir has let a viper into the nest," Jess muttered. "Beazle will follow her. We need to find the crofter."

Sasha helped keep her upright as they headed for the door, maneuvering around people and knocked-over furniture. It seemed no one had been badly hurt or killed except for the one Silverfae. As they passed him, Jess saw that he had a broken neck. She looked away, wondering what had become of Digit.

In the hallway outside the courtroom, they found Kite and some of Bradburn's soldiers mobilizing, wet and pale-faced. Etherlight sconces illuminated every shocked expression.

Jess grasped Kite's arm, intending to ask where Ian was, but a vision from Beazle struck her hard, making her gasp. She almost fell. Sasha grabbed her, lowering her onto one of the benches that lined the hallway.

"Jess?" Sasha's lips were close to her ear.

"I'm with Beazle," she told him.

"Still not used to that," he muttered.

Sasha sat beside her as she tried to describe what she was seeing. Sounds around them grew quiet, as others must have gathered in close, listening.

Sylifke was climbing a narrow set of spiral stairs, dusty, with cobwebs hanging beneath the open treads. She was alone. Jess didn't recognize the stairwell, which was frightening all by itself.

*Where is she?* Jess asked Beazle.

*You'll know in a moment,* he responded. *Though, what she's doing here, I don't know.*

As Sylifke mounted the last few steps, a rose-colored light illuminated first her hair, then her torso, then her dress, until her body was engulfed by a gentle pink glow. She turned to face the pride of the palace architecture: the illuminated window, the portal that gathered energy from the ether to power the city.

Jess had never seen the space behind the rose window in person, not even when Digit had been training her. No one needed to go there except for engineers, and even they were rarely needed. If a location had trouble with power, it was usually a local problem—wiring, a frayed cable or a broken tube—not the window itself.

Jess was so surprised that she forgot to relay Beazle's vision to Sasha.

Etherlight was everywhere. Sylifke's body was bathed in it. She stopped on a platform below two thick chains. The chains had to lead to the bell high above the rose window, which marked noon and midnight, dawn and dusk.

"What are you up to?" Jess muttered, her insides cold and shivery. Water still dripped down her skull and the back of her neck.

Sasha's voice came into her ear. "What's happening?"

"She's behind the rose window," Jess told him.

"The… rose window?" he echoed, confused. She sensed him crouch in front of her, look up into her blind face. His breath puffed against her chin. "The… ether portal?"

"Yes," she murmured, transfixed.

Queen Sylifke stood in front of the enormous window and lifted her arms, like she was worshipping its beauty. Her body was dappled with a million shades of pink, rose, faded violet, geranium, magenta, mauve and peach. Jess's breath caught in her throat at the epic scene. Even Beazle, usually unimpressed by things of the fae world, was so affected by the sight that he landed on a rafter and went utterly still, staring.

With her arms high, the queen said, "*Tydan ar inda*."

"She's speaking," Jess whispered, her hands groping Sasha's

shoulders as she did her best to repeat the strange words. "Tydan ar i-inda…"

Sasha translated. "The time has arrived."

Sylifke's talons flexed. "*Vas jaras truskeb mi, nyt fulke. Fynde vuras fjenda os adilaeyec hynda.*"

Jessamine stumbled over the pronunciation.

Sasha translated, his tone growing grim. "Show your allegiance… now, my people. Our enemy is found… destroy her."

Beazle gave a squeak of surprise as the rose window went suddenly dark, as though someone had flicked a switch, shutting off its power. A blast from the queen filled the portal with opaque fog, polluting all the light. Beazle clung to the rafter as the platform and stairs shook. Magic poured from the queen and out through the portal, belching and billowing. Snow and ice pellets gusted from her, filling the air with an intense sound, like a huge snake hissing a warning.

The vision broke and Jess screamed for Beazle, pulse pounding.

*I'm okay!* Beazle sent. *I'm not hurt. She startled me, that's all.*

Her sight returned, but Sasha was just a blur in front of her, his pale hair and face the only thing she could place, thanks to its whiteness. The etherlights were out, and the corridor had fallen into utter darkness. Frightened and confused cries in the sudden black came from not only the courtroom, but outside as well, and beyond. It was a full blackout.

Beazle worked to reestablish their connection, but it came in flashes, snippets broken by darkness. Jess reached for Beazle, straining to grasp what he was seeing.

Between flashes of darkness, Jessamine could make out the shape of the queen. Sylifke's body was bent with sorcery, every muscle straining. Unseelie power streamed from her in a never-ending gush. Winter clogged the rose window, spewing into the sky over the city. Magic flowed from the queen like a living thing, swirling, churning, rushing into the open atmosphere like a writhing nest of snakes. Thunder rumbled as darkness gathered over the city. Snow swirled, filling the sky with skiffs and devils, gathering in the air rather than falling to the ground to melt.

The elegant copper frame around the rose window was coated in ice. Frost crawled along the stones, creeping across the walls, toward the platform and the stairs. More and more winter poured forth, and Jess's mind boggled at it. How long would she go on like this? How long *could* she go on?

"Sasha, she's…" but words to describe what she was seeing would not come.

"I know, Jess," he told her. "I know what Sylifke can do."

Jess felt herself picked up and cradled against Sasha's chest, carried toward the building's alley entrance. Jarred by a crush of bodies, Jess lost Beazle's vision again and saw a sea of shadowy heads following a small flame. Someone had a taper and everyone flocked toward the only source of light.

She told Sasha she could see, and he set her on her feet. They spilled outside. Jess looked up at the sky as they moved along the alley and into the main street, where citizens were gathering. All faces turned upward, to a sky that was no longer a sky but a ceiling. They watched in wonder and horror at the dark clouds that streamed from the front of the palace, pushing across the city, casting a shadow as it went, like some invisible giant was pulling a curtain. It was after sundown, but the sky to the west still had a tinge of grayish light. Against the remnants of the sun, the shadow creeping over them was a stormfront moving steadily across the sky. Soon it would be a suffocating, turbid darkness.

Hand in hand, Jess and Sasha moved further up the high street to a large open courtyard, a public garden where no tall buildings blocked the view of the palace. Jostling their way through the crowd, they craned to look upward. A light snow dusted the tops of the buildings. Jess knew it was just a down payment, a promise of what was to come. Angry, unseelie winter continued to boil from the portal.

Jess shivered. The temperature was dropping. People had mobilized to find old-fashioned oil torches and light them. Small tongues of fire bobbed in the streets, drawing humans and fae to their light. Jess couldn't see any Fahyli.

*Beazle?* Jess probed for her bat. *Come to me, love. It's getting cold, and I'm worried.*

The thick clouds were spreading fast. Torches were held high, but even the torches guttered as precipitation threatened to suffocate them. Without etherlight, the city was staggering, and the temperature was dropping by the moment.

Beazle was shivering too much to form a proper response, but she could feel him nearing, struggling to get to her. He was buffeted by wind and sliced by the cold. Jess strained her eyes for him in the gloom. Relief flooded her as he appeared and went straight for her neck. He crawled under her collar, his claws raking her skin in his desperation to get warm. His little body was so cold that she grimaced. She put a hand over him, pressing him softly into the heat of her neck. Beazle splayed his wings out and lay himself flat against her. He felt like a furry ice-cube.

*Bats don't like cold,* he mumbled, shuddering as he soaked in her warmth.

She squeezed Sasha's hand, and he looked down at her, worry marring his features.

"Why is she doing this?" Jess was beginning to shiver. "Is she so angry over the loss of her son that she'll destroy our entire city? Freeze us all to death?"

Sasha's look was serious. "No, Jess. The enemy she spoke of was not Solana, and she's not even bothering with me. She wants to finish the job Ruskin started. Do you know where they are keeping Lady Çifta?"

Jess nodded. "She's in a small ballroom at the back of the east keep."

"We need to get to her before they do."

The tops of the tallest buildings were no longer visible, shrouded in winter mist. Winter had hit street level now, and snow was piling up in drifts. Jess marveled at the extremes the winter queen was willing to go to.

"Keep us busy floundering in darkness and weather, distracted, while her people look for Çifta," she murmured.

Sasha's gaze flicked over the sky. The magic had spread over the whole city, reached the front gates, and was pushing over the pastureland beyond the city walls.

"Distraction is only part of it," Sasha said, still looking up. "If it was just a distraction, she could have stopped by now. But it keeps coming… she is not letting up."

"So, it's not just a diversion?" Jess's body was seized by a shiver. Her teeth clacked. "What, then?"

Sasha looked down, and she shrank from the look in his eyes.

"I need to free Rialta. It's a signal. Solana is about to be invaded."

## Chapter Thirty-One

# Laec

If Regalis really wasn't feeling well, then he would have either gone to find a nurse or to lie down. Unable to picture the Fahyli wanting the attention of a medic, Laec stopped a servant and asked for directions to Regalis's private quarters. He'd never had a reason to seek out a Fahyli after-hours, and they were almost always to be found either eating or training if they weren't working.

The Fahyli apartments were spread over two floors of a building that divided the upper bailey from the lower and connected the west keep to a watchtower. Gratified to discover that doors were labeled with small metal cut-outs in the shape of the Fahyli's familiar, Laec found Regalis's apartment and knocked. It took a second set of raps before the door opened.

Laec opened his mouth to apologize, then realized it was a female Calyx peeking out at him, a worried expression pleating her otherwise flawless brow. A bright, citrus aroma wafted from her, exquisitely feminine. Her shining eyes were a pale shade of periwinkle, which sent an ache of longing through his heart, because they were so like Çifta's. But not only her eyes were pale, this female was pale all over. Silvery-blond hair, porcelain skin without a mark or blemish, pearl-pink lips, a neck far too long to be practical. Tall, too, willowy, like a sapling. One impossibly elegant hand curled around the edge of the door as she peered out at him.

"Oh!" Laec took a step back. "Hello…" He fumbled for her name but came up empty. He'd only ever exchanged words with Jess's Calyx friends and certainly wasn't enough of a perfume connoisseur to identify her botanical simply by sniffing. As much as he wanted to lean close and take a deep inhale, he resisted.

Regalis's voice came from inside. "Who is it?"

"The Stavarjakian you told me about," the Calyx said over her shoulder in a warm, honeyed voice. She opened the door far enough that Laec could see into the room. She didn't smile, but she said, "My name is Gardenia. Laec, right?"

"That's me. Regalis, I'm so—"

The fauna fae sat wrapped in a plaid blanket near a brazier full of coals. He looked pale and dewy with sweat.

"You're really sick?" Laec stepped inside. "I didn't think you could *get* sick."

Regalis smiled. "Not sick. I—we—were sabotaged. Ferrugin's not feeling her best either. Come in."

Laec entered the quarters and looked around, wishing he'd been given a Fahyli suite since the beginning. Why he'd been stuck in the east keep with all the courtiers, he'd never know. He only hoped it wasn't because Esha thought he had more in common with gilded nobles than with rugged fauna fae.

The bed was large and enclosed with velvet curtains. An elaborate wooden perch—upon which Ferrugin sat, head compressed into her feathers and eyes shut—was situated near a row of windows overlooking the grass of the lower bailey. The suite was as big as his violet one had been, but decorated appropriately for a warrior, a genteel one, but still, a soldier. Blocky furniture in dark, glossy wood. Upholstery in gem tones of sapphire and ruby, trimmed with silver. Tapestries in dark, earthy colors depicting outdoor scenery. The inner wall braced a small bookshelf lined with leather-bound titles and a sturdy wardrobe with a dust-free mirror.

"Looks like a man's room, but smells like a lady's," Laec observed, relieved by the smile on Regalis's face. Whatever was wrong with him, it didn't look too serious. "What's this about sabotage?"

Regalis and Gardenia exchanged a loaded look as she crossed to sit beside him.

"It's my fault," she said in a tremulous voice.

To Laec's chagrin, her eyes welled up. She looked away, a flush rising in her cheeks as she brushed at her lashes.

Regalis pressed his lips together and raised his brows, giving her a look Laec couldn't decode.

"I'm lost," Laec said.

Gardenia smiled and sniffed. "Don't mind me. I'm excessively emotional. A hazard of the trade, and I'm working on it. Regalis"—she shot him the gooiest, most lovesick look Laec had ever seen a female give a male—"is helping me."

"Gardenias are delicate," the Fahyli said, as though that explained it.

"Oh," said Laec, stumped.

"I was complaining to my friend, Azalea..." Gardenia said, cheeks blooming with a fetching shade of pink.

"She was crying," said Regalis, bluntly. "Bawling, really."

Gardenia twisted her fingers around one wrist self-consciously. "Yes, I was crying. It happens a lot, unfortunately, especially when I don't want it to. I was upset because Regalis and I... we don't get much time together, and I've been missing him. Especially since the trial started. It was an overreaction. She should have known that about me by now. Anyway, Azalea loves me. She took it to heart. She was only trying to help."

"Azalea dosed me," Regalis explained with a look of amused irritation. "Made me think I caught a bug; got me dismissed for the evening. Right before the verdict, too. Little turd. Even Ferrugin felt too ill to stay and report how it all turned out."

Laec blinked. "She... poisoned you?"

"She meant well. It was just a small dose of her botanical." Regalis glanced at his familiar, who hadn't moved a muscle or lifted an eyelid.

"Don't tell anyone, please," Gardenia begged, her eyes glassy and as huge as three-ounce coins. "Azalea would be in big trouble. Gardener doesn't have much tolerance for abuse of our raw materials, and Regalis will be fine in another hour."

"I'm already fine," Regalis told her. He stood, still pale, and tossed the blanket on the bed. "Just a little shivery. Can't go back to the courthouse though. Ian will be suspicious." He quirked a smile at Gardenia. "Plus, it worked. We got to share a meal, even though all I could stomach was broth." He lay a hand over his flat stomach, then looked at Laec. "I assume you didn't pop by for a social call. What's on your mind?"

The etherlights guttered, then went out. Shadows swept over the room. The coals in the brazier and the sky outside were the only sources of light, drawing the three of them to the windows. Gardenia's ghostly form hugged in close to Regalis's side.

"What… is… that?" Regalis's words came out on exhales as he wrapped an arm around her.

"I knew it," Laec hissed, his breath leaving a patch of condensation on the window. "Trouble."

"What did you know?" Gardenia asked.

But Laec was struck speechless by the way the sky was morphing before their eyes. A stormfront of boiling iron-gray clouds surged from somewhere over their heads, moving across the city—pulling a curtain of darkness behind it.

"That's not normal," Regalis muttered.

"That's why I came." Laec looked at the Fahyli. "I could see something from the wall, coming over the mountains. It looked,"—he pointed at the storm—"a bit like that."

"But that's not coming from the mountains." The Fahyli bent close to the glass, trying to see as far as possible. "It's spreading over us, stretching toward the front gates."

"I think the source is the same."

Laec and Regalis locked eyes.

"Silverfae?"

Laec nodded.

Ferrugin shook herself, stretched her wings and opened her beak wide. She flapped a few times, moving the curtains around the bed, then hopped to the sill as Regalis opened the window. She dropped into the darkness, then swooped upward and disappeared.

Regalis turned to Gardenia in the gloom, grasping her by the shoulders. His voice was calm, quiet. "What's the protocol for the Calyx in an emergency?"

"Emergency?" Her voice quivered, rising in pitch. "I don't understand. The power is out, but—"

"Think, Gardenia," he prodded. "What's the gardener's plan in case of a problem? A citywide one."

"We, uh, we… in an emergency." She swallowed. Laec could hear it from where he stood. "We muster at Ilishec's workshop and get instructions from there."

"You need to do that, then," Regalis told her, gently pushing her toward the door. "I have to get to the maproom."

"I want to stay with you," she said. "Please don't send me away."

Regalis donned his boiled leather, belted on his scabbard. "You have to, Gardenia, otherwise Ilishec will panic. You must follow the protocol. We have it for times like this."

Laec waited impatiently at the door as Regalis pulled on his boots and debated with Gardenia. They were still arguing—gently, sweetly, like those still in the early days of romance—as Regalis closed his door.

Laec let out a sigh of relief as they finally moved, rushing down the corridor.

"I'll come to the maproom with you," Gardenia said as they struck the flagstones and turned a corner, their footsteps loud and hurried. "It might be nothing, but if it really is an emergency, *then* I'll go to the workshop. I promise."

A small gray raptor swooped over their heads. Something snarled from behind them and suddenly they were surrounded by Fahyli and familiars, all headed to the same place. Regalis gave up, and Gardenia stuck on his heels, falling quiet, probably hoping not to draw attention to herself. The crofter was in the maproom, barking orders. The room churned with animals and fae as they entered, got instructions, then exited. Ian gave Kestrel an order, then looked up.

"Regalis!" Ian looked his Fahyli over from boots to eyebrows and back again, assessing his health. "Are you functional?"

"Better, Crofter," Regalis said, with a hint of a blush.

"Good, because—" Ian looked to the door, and yelled, "Digit, Ilishec's workshop! Category three invasion. Go!"

Laec caught a flash of Digit's hummingbird and a glimpse of a boot heel before the crofter's son was gone.

"Regalis—" The crofter sniffed. "Is there a flora fae in here?"

Laec looked for Gardenia, but she was nowhere to be seen.

"I, uh—" Regalis stalled.

"Never mind." Ian's fierce gaze narrowed on his Fahyli. "Is Ferrugin up?"

"She's up, over the northwest corner. I'd say it's category four, not three."

"Cat four… are you sure?"

"Yes, Crofter," Regalis replied. "They're not exactly pouring over the walls, but there's enough to keep us busy."

Listening, Laec felt winded. Regalis had been receiving information from his familiar before they'd even arrived at the maproom, probably as soon as she left the building. When Jess got visions from Beazle, she was vulnerable until they were over. Regalis had shown nothing, no stress, no interruption of his usual demeanor, a real pro.

"Okay," Ian nodded. "Stick with me until we get to the donjon. I need eyes in the sky. Onyx and moonstone are in the southern queen's parlor, garnet is with them." He noticed Laec for the first time. "Bradburn could use backup at the—"

"I'm on my way to Lady Çifta," Laec interrupted. "Just wanted to inform you."

The last thing Laec wanted was to punch in with Bradburn and the human soldiers. He'd end up too far from the palace, and so far, he'd heard no mention of a contingency plan for the person he cared most about. He had a sinking feeling that there *was* no plan for her. And why would there be? She wasn't even Solanan. *He* was the plan.

Ian blinked, absorbing this. "She's protected by layers of ice. How much risk do you think she's under?"

It was a serious question, thankfully, not laced with the crofter's usual irony, so Laec thought about it seriously. He tried to be objective and found it impossible.

"I don't know," he said, honestly. "But that's where I have to be."

The crofter accepted this without argument. "You're Elphame's man. Do what you have to do. I can't offer you any help. I'm sorry."

He turned back to Regalis to fire instructions using code. Laec realized that onyx and moonstone were Agir and Esha. Garnet had to be the young princess, Kara. Regalis's job would be to reinforce their personal guard and keep them informed, minute-by-minute, as Ferrugin sent him visions. It wasn't the category three versus category four talk that drove home just how much trouble Solana was in—and not just from magical weather—it was the threat to the king and queen.

Laec shouldn't have bothered with the maproom at all, he realized, fear tightening his gut. He should have trusted his instincts back at the wall and gone straight to Çifta. Ruskin had wanted her dead. Ruskin's mother would too.

Without another look at the crofter, or eye contact with the Fahyli coming and going, Laec left the maproom, gripping the pommel of the blade at his side. He almost ran into Gardenia as he turned toward the east keep. He steadied her, then kept going, shaking his head. She should have gone with Digit, but there was no accounting for love, just like there was no accounting for taste.

He picked up speed and was running almost full tilt by the time he hit the final stretch. Sliding around the last corner, he came to a halt, chest heaving. A pale figure hovered outside the ballroom. Just one Silverfae female, slight, and young; no sword, dagger, or any other weapon visible on her person. A scout, then. She had one hand on the door latch and had pulled it open a few inches when Laec appeared, and she looked up.

"Hey!" He barked. "Get away from there!"

She gasped, then peeked through the crack, her eyes widening at what she saw. The scout had found what she'd been looking for. Laec charged. She saw him coming and hissed, then turned and sprinted away, leaving a gust of cold air behind her. He pursued, but she moved like the wind, and he was too breathless now to catch her. He returned to the ballroom, sucking in air and swearing. He stepped inside, then drew up short as the tip of a blade touched the base of his neck.

"Stavarjak," growled the hulking shadow, leveling a scimitar at his throat.

"Boskaya," gasped Laec.

Kazery lowered his sword, his features mostly obscured by the darkness, his eyes dangerous pinpoints of light. A set of teeth showed in the dark.

"Laec. I was beginning to think no one in Solana even remembers my daughter. I'm glad you're here."

"They'll know where she is soon," Laec told him, his heart starting to slow. He glanced at the pillar. There'd been no change. He moved toward Çifta, and Kazery followed.

"I don't suppose anyone else is coming?" the merchant asked without much hope. "Six of mine are stationed at the outer doors, and I'm expecting my best swordsman to join me, but he's late." He paused. "Endyr is never late. I fear the worst."

The sound of yelling and running came from outside the ballroom.

"They're coming," the merchant said, hefting his blade.

Laec unsheathed his sword and Çifta's men faced the doors, side-by-side.

## Chapter Thirty-Two

# Jessamine

THE CITY WAS overrun. Everywhere Jess looked, Solanans fought with Silverfae. Sasha's hand gripped hers, and Beazle snuggled in her hair, as they ran through side streets and back alleys, headed for the west keep where Rialta was being kept. Jess's breath tore through her throat as they climbed to the palace, passing those who'd been frozen solid, unrecognizable blobs inside pillars of ice. She'd faced only a few enemies at a time in Syrgana, but here, enemies—and the carnage they left behind—were everywhere.

*I can help now,* Beazle told her. *I can show you enemies! Let me go up.*

*It's too cold,* Jess argued. *Let's not chance it.*

*I'm fast, though,* he murmured mutinously.

She could feel his reticence. Beazle didn't fancy the idea of flying in this sorcerous weather. He had little tolerance for subzero temperatures, even when they were natural.

As she and Sasha barreled up a set of stairs, her decision to keep Beazle tucked away was galvanized. At the top of the steps, a mastiff with a patch over one eye appeared to tackle a Silverfae, ribcage and hindquarters working as he drove himself forward. But in the next instant, the dog was gone. A block of ice larger than a wine barrel came tumbling down the stairs. Sasha slammed Jess against the wall as it bounced by, crumbling to shards on its way down. From a neighboring street rose a wail so heartrending it made Jess feel like bursting into tears. A fauna fae had lost their familiar, and she knew exactly how that felt.

The Silverfae at the top scrambled to his feet, eyes wild as he caught sight of them.

"You," he hissed, lifting his hands, his fingers turning whiter than white.

"Yes, me," Sasha growled. He pulled Jess up the steps, keeping himself between her and the enemy.

There was a blast of freezing air and a splatter of ice pellets against Sasha's body. They grazed Jess's leggings and boots, but most of her was protected. A crack followed, then chunks of ice spilled down the stairs on either side. The noise was immense in the narrow space.

Jess was yanked the rest of the way to the top, taking the narrow path Sasha cut between piles of ice. Passing the body, Jess saw a ragged white blade embedded in the enemy's chest, his vacant eyes staring up at the sky. There had been no cry of pain. She recognized him. He'd been one of Sylifke's jurors. Sasha had not hesitated to end him, which had implications that Jess couldn't absorb right now.

She reeled mentally as her legs carried her past the corpse, through an alley and onto a dirt path. Following switchbacks up and up, they reached a narrow gate. The sound of battle rose from the streets behind as Sasha slammed the gate shut. They looked at one other, eyes wide, chests heaving.

"You killed one of your own," Jess gasped. Defending himself against Silverfae was one thing. Attacking one was another.

"Would *you* rather be the one to die? Come on. Rialta is frantic." He grabbed her hand.

They ran through the outbuildings of the west keep, weaving between them like shadows. Here there was quiet, a reprieve from the fighting. Jess heard Rialta howling, then the thuds of her body against the walls of her pen reverberated through the chilly air. Just as suddenly, it all went quiet and Jess knew Sasha was speaking to Rialta, likely telling her he was nearly there.

The quiet was broken by a sound of destruction from the other side of the palace, like some powerful force had struck an exterior wall, breaking marble and dislodging stones.

They halted at Rialta's door, gasping for air. Her cell had been guarded, but the guards must have gone running as soon as they realized Solana City had been invaded. Before Jess could search for a key, Sasha took care of the lock by freezing the metal, then kicking the door until it broke.

Rialta came barreling out—a lightning streak of fur, legs, tongue and teeth—straight into Sasha's arms. He fell back as she covered his face with licks. Rialta snaked around, startling Jess by putting her cold nose against her cheek, adding a few licks for good measure. Then she bolted up the path, a white blur with her nose to the ground. Her limp was almost imperceptible.

"Where is she going?" Jess panted.

"Scouting."

A sound rose from the far side of the palace, like an angry wind throwing around sand and stones. Spatters were punctuated by loud cracks and more sounds of destruction. Jess imagined a catapult flinging boulders, breaking mortar apart, putting holes in everything. But the Silverfae didn't have catapults, they had ice. And Sasha had already shown her what freezing temperatures were capable of, even to stone walls.

"Sounds like they're taking the keep apart stone by stone," Jess said, fear rocketing through her. "That's coming from the east keep. The Calyx side of the palace, where Lady Çifta is housed."

Horrible visions rose fully formed in her imagination. Unless the Calyx had Fahyli or soldiers with them, they were defenseless, totally vulnerable. It was obvious the Silverfae didn't care who got in their way, who they froze. The Calyx would be helpless against the kind of sorcery currently wreaking havoc on living beings and walls alike.

Sasha's gaze lifted to the sky, where clouds roiled and snow belched. Within the clouds burst cold flashes of light. Pale white embers of magic swirled through the air, crackling. It might have been pretty, if it wasn't so deadly.

"What's the fastest way there?" he asked her. "Around, or through?"

"Uh, th-through. Underneath. I know the way."

Metal clashing against metal drew their attention to a balcony, just in time to see a figure—encased by ice—tumble over the railing. It crashed at the base of the castle with a horrible crack. Jess shuddered, glad she could not see the mess that resulted. A Silverfae looked over the railing before disappearing back inside, never noticing that she'd been observed. She wasn't even holding a weapon. Panic clawed Jess's throat. How could they combat this? The city was overrun. She didn't know where Ian was, or Laec, or what the Fahyli were doing, or if there was a plan. She put her hands over her eyes, fighting the urge to scream, and pushed out a breath; with it came a moan she was helpless to prevent.

Sasha touched her wrists, gently pulling her hands away from her face. His fingers were warm against her skin, the feeling so stark and surprising that it grounded her, centered her focus on him.

"Listen to me, Jess. I know that you have magic. You're not some helpless little girl." He pulled his hands back and showed her his palms, the pink undersides of his fingers.

"But, if you see this..." Before her eyes, his hands changed. The pink bleached away and became as white as porcelain. The air crackled softly, like the sound of crumpling tissue. His eyes flared along with his magic, bright flecks streaking inside his irises like tiny shooting stars. She could feel the frigid air pouring from his palms.

"White hands." She nodded.

His gaze bored into hers. "White hands. If you see them, do not engage. You cannot win. Most of them cannot do this, but some can, and she'll have brought all of them with her. They have only to get within six feet, and it takes seconds to kill. But we don't just send out cold, we can absorb it too, so I can protect you from the worst of it. Okay? And keep Beazle hidden."

She nodded again, feeling numb. Her poison seemed so little a defense against fae who could throw ice-blades or entomb her.

*I changed my mind,* Beazle told her. *I do like him.*

She half-laughed, half-sobbed in response.

Sasha kissed the corner of her mouth, and together they ran toward the palace.

Jess led Sasha to the maproom, relieved to find that there were hot coals still in the grate to light torches, then through the secret doorway behind the tapestry. Dirt and dust pattered on the floor and the tops of their heads as a shudder shook the palace. The passageway was not quiet, but it was empty, as Jess had known it would be. There should be no enemies down here.

At the bottom of the stairs, the corridor narrowed. Their torches seemed like tiny candles in the blackness, swallowed by the gloom, illuminating only a few feet ahead of them. Following twists and turns, corners and curves, they closed the distance to an exit through a storage closet not far from Ilishec's workshop. Jess begged whatever forces might listen that they find the Calyx whole, unharmed, and, ideally, protected by a contingent of armed guards. She hoped they'd stuck to protocol, but doubt ate at her. The east side of the palace was under attack. What if the workshop was no longer a suitable rallying point? If they'd scattered, it would be impossible to gather all fifty of them safely.

The sound of shoes shuffling against the floor came from around a curve. Jess put a hand on Sasha's arm, but he'd heard it and already halted. There was a quiet hum, which stopped, then went again, then stopped. They listened. The scuffling went on. Not just a few shoes, but many, and breathing. The smell of a rotten bouquet tickled her nose.

Jess called, "Who's there?"

Her question was followed by utter silence. Then the hum began again. Something airborne zipped around the curve, orbited them, then disappeared back the way it had come.

There came a relieved: "Jess?"

"Digit?"

She let out her breath. Of course Digit would use the passageways at a time like this. She moved forward, Sasha almost on top of her, intent on protecting her. They rounded the curve, lifting their torches high, and Jess gasped.

It was not Digit and a few others, it was Digit and a huge group of Calyx crammed into the narrow space like rows of canned sardines. Those carrying torches lifted them, adding to the glow filling the passage. Their collective perfume reeked of fear.

Proteas and his pregnant girlfriend were at the front, hands tightly entwined. Jess could see Dahlia, Peony, Aster, Vanda, Dianthus, Rose, Nympha, Lily, and many more behind, staring from the shadows with huge eyes.

Ilishec called, "Jess! Thank goodness."

Her name echoed down the line as Ania hummed in the air above it. Digit was the only one who didn't look afraid. His calculating gaze swept over Sasha, then back to Jess.

"Aren't you going the wrong way?" Digit jerked his thumb behind him. "There's trouble with the weather back there."

"Is anyone missing?" Jess asked.

"Heath and Gardenia."

At that, Jess gave the tiniest shake of her head, and Digit understood. She was relieved that she needn't explain.

"We need to keep moving." He waved his charges onward.

Jess and Sasha pressed themselves against the wall to let the Calyx pass.

"Come with us, Jessamine," said Peony as she squeezed by. "Leave this fight to the soldiers."

"I'm Fahyli," she reminded her.

"Don't be brave, Jess," pleaded Aster. "Please come with us."

As if to confirm that they shouldn't linger, a terrific crash sounded somewhere far above, followed by the sound of stones falling down steps.

Ilishec said, "We waited as long as we dared."

As though Jessamine would have criticized him for taking those who had shown up to safety. His plan to gather in an emergency had worked, and Jess was beyond relieved.

"Gardenia is probably with Regalis," someone called. "He'll keep her safe!"

Someone else added under their breath, "I hope."

The crowd oozed past them. Aster and Rose sent her pleading looks and squeezed her arm. She kissed them quickly, pecking their cheeks but ignoring their begging eyes. They were frightened for her. She could smell it. But even if she hadn't had Sasha with her, Jess would never choose hiding in safety over standing side-by-side with the Fahyli. Most of the Calyx were safe; once they found Heath, she and Sasha would find the crofter. Jess's biggest fear was that Sasha would be spotted by the Silver queen, even though she'd opted to vanish from the courtroom under cover and leave a minion to end him for her.

Snap squeezed out of line, letting the Calyx brush past him. His eyes were bright, his mouth working as he took Jess's hand. "Take me with you. I don't want to hide. Let me help. I'm not bad with a sword. I've never fought for real, but there's a first time for everything. I grew up practicing with soldiers' sons back in my village. I am not afraid."

"Don't be ridiculous, Snap," said Asclepias as he slid by. "You're not a soldier."

"What are you going to do? Pepper them with snapdragon blossoms?" asked Lily.

"Or blind them with green paint?" someone else taunted.

Jess squeezed Snap's hand, her heart swelling with pride. He had matured since they'd met. She'd just been too busy to notice. He still had those boyish curls that would always make him look young, but he was taller and heavier now, stronger, more capable. He had an impishness and an irreverence that reminded her of Laec.

"I would never take you into harm's way, Snap," she told him. "It's not your role."

"You'd be a liability, Oren," someone called, using Snap's birth name.

Snap ignored them, nostrils flaring. "It's not yours either, Jess."

"It is, though, Snap," she told him gently. "In times like this, I'm Fahyli, not Calyx. You stay with the Calyx and hope they don't need your sword for protection."

"Snap!" Ilishec now pushed through the crowd, his face pale and brow beaded with sweat. "I order you to march."

"Order Jessamine too, then," Snap said, his eyes huge, still holding Jess's hand.

"She's under the crofter's orders now," the gardener replied, with a look at Jessamine that was tinged with sorrow.

"I've got her," Sasha told Snap in a low voice. "I won't let anything happen to her."

Snap continued to protest, but he was pulled by Ilishec and pushed by more Calyx coming up behind. Jess swallowed down the lump in her throat as his grip tightened on her hand before he was yanked away by the force of the crowd. She'd not had a chance to kiss his cheek and hoped they would both live long enough for her to tell him she was proud of him.

## Chapter Thirty-Three

# Çifta

Beautiful shades of spring swept over the land as the ice carried Çifta south from Silverfall. The Vargilath mountain range spread out below, ice-capped rocks thrust high into the sky with thickly forested valleys snaking between the peaks. They passed sparkling mountain lakes, with sunlight glimmering on blue water. Gone were the snow-filled, low-hanging clouds, gone were the flurries that filled the air and dimmed every feature.

Solana city appeared on the horizon, and Çifta's excitement mounted as she recognized the spires and towers of the place she had come to love. When the artist's tower came into view—so many happy hours spent there—her heart lifted. It was like coming home.

Only…

Only, something was wrong.

A stream of thick gray cloud stretched from the central tower, where the rose window was, to beyond the front gates. It crept over pastureland outside the city walls, a stormfront with a serrated edge—an unnatural patch in an otherwise clear sky, and it sat directly over Solana City.

*What's happening? Is this present day?*

In answer, they moved closer.

The city lay in such darkness that it seemed closer to midnight, while the back side of the palace and the land beyond were mostly unaffected by the strange layer of cloud. In the streets, torches and movement drew attention. Scuffles were happening everywhere. Solanans fighting with Silverfae. There were patches of quiet and patches of chaos. And large misshapen blocks of ice, with dark smudges deep inside, lay in the streets.

Çifta had seen blocks like those in the gallery in the palace at Silverfall. She was seized by horror. *There are Solanans inside. Humans and fae. How can they survive?*

*They are already dead.*

*But I don't understand!* Çifta's mind staggered like a drunk, grasping for something, anything solid. *Why is this happening?*

*Queen Sylifke is here, halfling. She is here for you.*

*I have brought this upon Solana?*

Çifta felt consumed by denial. A sensation like quaking took over her being as she hung above the kingdom that had welcomed her. People were cut down in the streets before her eyes. Red and silver blood ran together. Bodies lay on the cobblestones. Images that would be imprinted upon her mind forever. Çifta had never been exposed to such violence. She wanted to turn away, shield her eyes. She couldn't decide which felt worse: the utter helplessness to do anything about what was happening, or the responsibility for it. It was happening *because* of her.

The ice sensed the weight of all she was feeling. *You did not do this.*

They swept close to the palace, then through a door. Inside, they drifted down corridors unnoticed, like ghosts… unseen, unfelt. Even if they had had corporeal bodies, they likely wouldn't have been noticed. Palace residents were either fighting, fleeing or hiding.

Clusters of Silverfae fought with Solanan soldiers, or Fahyli and familiars. A soldier in Solanan livery, the wreathed lion bold against his chest, ran through a Silverfae who had fallen to his knees. Even as he fell, the Silverfae sent a mist up and over the arm and shoulder of the man who had stabbed him, freezing the limb solid up to the elbow. The soldier screamed and staggered back as the fae fell face down, pearly blood seeping across the floor.

They passed another encounter; a Silverfae fought valiantly with two soldiers at once. She cut them down with decisive switches of her ice-blade before launching herself at a snarling dog. The dog's fae followed his familiar, a dagger in each fist, eyes blazing.

If she saw any more, Çifta felt sure she'd go insane. *This is a nightmare.*

The ice did not release her, only carried her onward through the palace. Some corridors were empty and quiet, others clogged with people fighting, or fallen bodies. The dead and wounded were from both sides. Comrades tried to help the injured, binding their wounds, or trying to thaw out body parts while defending from more attacks.

The ice took her toward the rear of the castle, passing more pillars containing bodies and combatants in the heat of battle.

Ahead, Çifta recognized Sylifke as she engaged a Solanan with a spear. She sent a blast of ice to swallow him.

Sylifke, the winter queen, was in Solana. In the palace of the king and queen.

Çifta expected the ice to keep her here, to observe the damage the winter kingdom wreaked upon her friends. But they moved swiftly on.

In the next corridor, the fighting was thicker, and the Silverfae dominated. Left and right, Solanans fell to ice or sword, including a rabid-looking badger who went from snarling to frozen solid in the passing of a moment.

They entered a ballroom that was positively heaving with fighting fae.

It was a melee with a clear division. Behind the Solanan forces, at the very front of the room, before a large empty fireplace, stood a pillar of ice. The sides of this pillar were not rough and opaque, coated with frost. Instead, it was smooth, nearly as transparent as glass.

It was easy to recognize the form inside. It was her form, her face.

*They're fighting… over me.* She thought her heart would burst at the shame and sorrow of it all. She wished more than anything she could stop this. *No. Please.*

The Solanans protecting the pillar of ice were fighting for their lives. And none were fighting with more fury than Laec and Kazery, shoulder to shoulder.

Her father wielded a curved sword so long that Çifta doubted she'd be able to lift it. He danced about like a much lighter man as he thrust and parried, stabbed and killed. She had never seen her father fight, though the stories of his violent past had her imagine it many times. This was the pirate version of her father. Teeth bared, hair wild, he snarled and yelled, even laughed, as he cut down the enemy. His eyes blazed with fury, hatred and something like joy, even though they were clearly outnumbered. He looked like he belonged with a blade in his hand, in the thick of battle, cutting and swinging.

At Kazery's side, Laec moved like a snake, red hair flying and eye-teeth flashing like fangs. He danced forward, someone fell, he danced back, blood flew. Yet he flagged. There were so many bodies on the floor, they drifted like snow. Silverfae poured into the room, some swinging blades they'd picked up from fallen enemies, others blasting deadly magic from white hands. Screams and bellows filled the air. Bodies fell, to be stepped upon or tripped over.

Çifta realized with a sinking heart: *There are too many, and the queen approaches.*

*Shortly, she will come through that door. As brave as your friends and your father are, they cannot withstand her. They have minutes to live.*

*Can you not stop it?*

*I cannot,* the ice whispered. *But you can.*

The sound of fighting faded, and Çifta felt a strange stillness come over her.

*How?*

*Give your life to me.*

*What?*

*I will use your body to save them.*

Çifta's thoughts climbed like a scream, hung there. *What do you mean?*

*This is the moment the prophecy proves true or proves false. You must decide.*

Queen Sylifke appeared in the doorway. She braced two

hands on the doorjamb, observing the chaos. Her pale eyes lifted, focusing on the pillar of ice.

*I give you my body, and you'll save them, but it will be the end of me. Is that what you're saying?*

*Yes.*

*But… I am supposed to be the daughter of winter.*

*No. I am.*

Çifta was crushed and winded by these simple words, but there was no time to even absorb it.

Queen Sylifke entered the room, her pale form slicing through the darkness. She walked up behind a Solanan. With an almost graceful movement of one hand, a thin spear of ice appeared through his chest. He slumped to the floor. He never even saw who had ended him.

*You're the daughter of…* Çifta tripped over what she now knew she should have realized all along. *You're Karinya. You've been Karinya this whole time.*

*Yes.*

Sylifke did not look down, just stepped over the body, her sights set on Laec and Kazery. They were the last bastion, the final barrier between her and what she so badly wanted. She killed another soldier, then another, cutting them down easily. They never even got close to her. Magic came out of her hands like the head of a dragon, on a long sinewy neck.

Çifta's mind lurched. Time was running out.

Karinya smiled into Çifta's mind. *You have given me a chance to set things right. I am sorry to take your life, but it is the only way, and I'll not take it without your permission.*

Sylifke was halfway across the ballroom, closing in on the two men Çifta loved most.

Çifta looked at Laec, sweat pouring down his temples.

*He has been trying to help you the whole time you've been with me,* Karinya told her. *You could not feel the effects of his efforts, but I could. Do not doubt his love for you.*

Çifta felt a wave of both joy and sadness crash over her at these words. Even if she had not been told of Laec's love, she could see it now, as plain as stars on a cloudless night.

There was a cut across his cheek, and a patch of blood blooming on his sleeve. He favored one leg, even as he danced around in combat. In Laec's eyes shone the knowledge that this was where he would die, and that—body and soul—he believed it a worthy cause. He believed she was worth dying for.

*So are you, my darling.* Çifta wished he could hear her. *So are you.*

And her father, the fiercest pirate the Ivryndian Sea had ever seen, yet the kindest man she'd ever known. His beloved face filled her with memories of paternal love and protection.

*I trust you'll be true to your word,* she told Karinya.

*And so I shall be.*

Unable to tear her gaze away from her men, Çifta could feel Sylifke closing the distance, cutting down her enemies. Death was coming, was on the very doorstep.

*After, tell Kazery that no father has ever been adored more by a daughter, and Laec… tell him that he was my dream. He filled my heart with love. I saw my future in his eyes.*

*I'll tell them,* Karinya whispered. *I promise.*

*Do it. You have my permission.*

The scene went fuzzy. Darkness closed in around the edges, shrinking her vision to a tunnel. Kazery's hair became a black blur, but it was the red blur that Çifta clung to, and the last thing she saw before the tunnel closed.

## Chapter Thirty-Four

# Jessamine

Jessamine and Sasha emerged from the stone-throated corridor through the back of a closet. Sounds of destruction had ceased, but the etherlights remained off.

They passed through the workshop, pausing at the door, which sat crookedly on its hinges. A peek into the gardens made Jessamine gasp. Not a living soul could be seen.

The sanctuary that the Calyx and gardeners worked so hard to make beautiful was unrecognizable, coated in an unnatural winter. It almost seemed to glow in the darkness, snow left behind by the world's most vindictive ice storm. Throughout the garden stood pillars of ice, dark shadows barely visible within. Victims of the night, the frozen dead. Not only soldiers, but civilians, too, caught in mid-flight.

Any one of the frozen could be Heath, although their features were too obscured for easy identification. Still, she had to try. Solanan soldiers could be identified by green and blue livery, but plain-clothed citizens were almost impossible to place. Some blocks were whole, some were broken, others were utterly shattered. Jess tore her gaze away from those, grateful that it was too dark to see details.

They moved from block to block, Jess's breath coming fast, dread making her legs feel wooden. Beazle moved against her skull, peeking out to observe the terrible landscape the once beautiful garden had become. Some had tried to hide beneath benches, behind trees, even beneath bushes, but there had been no escape.

They came to a block leaning against a rear wall, tilted at an angle. The top had a crack, through which Jess saw familiar brown hair and part of a frozen brow. She walked around it, and her heart fell when she spied a brown and red moth, a species known as true lover's knot.

Beazle conjured the name like a whimper. *Coco.*

Coco must have landed on the ice after Heath had been frozen, dying instantly, remaining stuck to the surface. A thin coating of ice lay over the tips of her wings but the miniature feathers on her back moved in the breeze.

Sasha put his arms around her, pulling her against his chest. Her shoulders hitched as she fought back a sob. He didn't need her to say Heath's name to know that was who they'd found.

Jess brushed at her eyes. "We joined the Calyx on the same day. His name was Tom Hiller, and his father is a cobbler. He was kind and made beautiful heather. They were innocent, just… in the wrong place at the wrong time."

"I'm so sorry." Sasha whispered against the top of her head. "I wish I could fix it."

A terrific crack split the air, echoing off Mount Vargon seconds later. The mountain was more than thirty miles away, and the repeated echoes were a jarring reminder that the nightmare was not over. Jess thought of Laec, Isabey, the king and queen, the Fahyli, and all her non-Calyx friends. Who else had they lost? In this garden alone, she'd counted eighteen.

There was a shout, then the sound of running feet crushing frozen grass.

*Oh no.*

Jess whirled as Sasha shoved her behind him. She unsheathed her dagger and yanked her fingerless glove off her left hand with her teeth, letting it drop to the ground. Her palm tingled with nightshade, growing cold as wet poison gathered there. Sasha, unarmed, lifted white hands in defense, palms out. Jess peered through the space between his arm and his ribs to see four Silverfae, three males and a female, advancing. Three had weapons, metal ones, not ice. The other had no weapon, but white hands.

*I could have warned you they were coming,* Beazle mourned.

*You stay where you are,* Jess told him.

The white-handed one drew Sasha's focus. One of the armed males stepped onto and over a frozen body lying in the grass like it was a log. Jess hefted her blade, but they paid no attention to her at all. Their whitish eyes were all narrowed on Sasha.

"Here's the traitor's son," the female sneered, her ghostly gaze darting around the garden. "Where's the bitch?"

For a second, Jess thought she meant her, but then she remembered Rialta, a real bitch.

"He's a traitor properly now," added one of the males, spinning a short sword in his flexible wrist. The blade looked just like the ones Solanan soldiers used, likely lifted from a dead body. He jerked his chin at Sasha. "He killed Renfrew."

"Yes, if we didn't know which side you were on before," another said, his upper lip curling, "we know it now. Don't we?"

The female uttered a stream of Silverfae that Jess couldn't understand.

"Renfrew was the one meant to slit my throat in the courtroom, I suppose,"—Sasha moved sideways—"while everyone floundered in the snow. If I'm a traitor, then I was made so by your queen."

Jess lagged behind as Sasha moved, processing what she was hearing and moving too slowly. *Your* queen. Not *our* queen.

Freezing air gusted over her left side—making her fingertips burn—coming from the male with the white hands. It gave her a jolt of reality. Sasha was either absorbing the cold or making some kind of shield. She danced over, keeping fully behind him, where it wasn't so cold she'd get frostbite in the time it took to yelp. She hefted her blade and watched, waiting for one of them to make a move.

"The queen should have known better than to leave my murder up to someone else."

"So arrogant," the white-handed male said, flicking his wrists. Two icy projectiles, misshapen but sharp, flew at Sasha. He batted at one and it crashed into the other, splintering both. Ice chips sprayed across the grass, just as a snarling yip punctuated the air.

Rialta came streaking from the rear of the castle, her limp more prominent than it had been. The Silverfae turned as the dire wolf, teeth bared, hurtled toward them.

Now was their chance. Sasha lunged, thrusting out a hand, and one of the males yelped and went down, one leg swallowed up to the thigh in ice. Rialta leapt at the other male, backpedaling now and screaming. Jess saw him lift his short sword but lost sight of them as she lunged for the female, who spun, raising her weapon in time to fend off Jess's. Frightened that at any moment one of her body parts might be frozen, Jess thrust herself forward, shoving the girl back, driven more by fear than by strategy or training. The female staggered, fighting for balance. Tripping over the same frozen body her comrade had stepped on, she fell onto her back in the grass. Jess stepped over her, shoving her wet palm into the girl's face, leaving a smear of poison across her mouth and up one cheek. The girl spluttered and rolled over, crawled forward on her elbows, spitting and swearing.

Jess turned, her blade up, in time to see Sasha bring an icy longsword, transparent and glistening, in a wide arc. His opponent flicked one wrist and a dagger shot from his palm, slicing Sasha's forearm. But the male's other hand fell into the grass, and pearly blood spouted from the stump where it had been. He fell to his knees, screaming.

Jess gasped as Rialta streaked by, her jaws wet, then flew over her shoulder, bringing another of the males to the ground. Jess could hear the girl vomiting now. Turning to look for any more attackers, she saw two, three, four more Silverfae appear through the archway.

"Sasha!" Jess's voice rose as she backpedaled, trying to keep from spilling her freshly tapped poison.

Sasha saw them, and the look in his eyes filled her with dread. The two of them, and a still-injured dire wolf, no matter how fierce, could not defeat so many. Beazle quivered against her scalp, and she felt his frustration, his desire to help. But even as they came together, Jess behind Sasha's shield again, more enemies poured through the arch. Some were armed with metal, others with ice, others with the worst of all: bare hands.

There was confusion though, arguments in the Silverfae tongue. Some grabbed their comrades, pulling them away.

"What's happening," Jess hissed. A *Datura* chromatype materialized unintentionally from her hand, floating into the air. She blew it so it drifted away from Sasha.

"They have orders that don't involve me," Sasha murmured, eyes on the fae, white hands up and ready.

Rialta was still, half-crouched in the grass, her body ready to spring. Her tongue lolled out, her lips curled up, exposing her teeth. She uttered a soft, constant growl. She looked at Sasha, then the others, waiting for a signal or one wrong move.

From inside the palace came the sound of shattering glass, like a hundred windows had been blown out. A shaft of moonlight touched the garden, drawing Jess's gaze upward. The cloud cover was not nearly so thick anymore, and holes appeared through which the night sky could be glimpsed.

The etherlamps in the garden guttered to life, then went out again. Jess realized that the Silverfae were leaving, some heading to the back of the palace, but most toward the front, the way they'd come.

"What's happening?" she asked again, absorbing some of her poison back into her body.

"Come on," Sasha murmured, and ran toward the front courtyard.

Jess and Rialta followed.

## Chapter Thirty-Five

# Laec

Laec was sure his right arm was about to fall off. It was numb from the shoulder down, yet somehow, the arm still moved, and the sword remained in his grip. The Silverfae were multiplying, but as he fought them, he learned about them. Only a few could produce ice-weapons, only a few had the magic that could freeze in a moment, swallowing an opponent before they realized the manner of their death. Prior to such deadly magic being released, the hand delivering it would turn white. White hands meant get out of the way, fast. Laec learned to navigate this new enemy quickly, but not without cost. The burning sensation on his shoulder where winter magic had grazed him would probably last for hours—the feeling of ice magic was familiar. What worried Laec the most was Sylifke. She was deadlier than any of her people, and she was cutting a path toward them. Already Laec had witnessed her put an ice-javelin straight through a soldier, pinning him to the wooden paneling.

*Crackle. Crackle. Sssssss.*

Laec's ears perked.

***CRACK!***

The fighting ceased, creating a curious tableau. Every eye focused on the pillar where a fissure had appeared, straight through the center of the block, and wide enough to slide a broom handle inside. Laec's heart jackhammered against his sternum. Çifta! The test was over! He gave a yelp of disbelief and excitement.

***CRACK!***

Another fissure split the ice, perpendicular to the first: now there were four narrow pillars. There came a squeak—ice grinding against ice—as the pillars tilted open, away from one another like a narrow tulip. One of the petals leaned dangerously over the merchant's head, where he'd fallen to one knee.

"Kazery, get back!" Laec yelled.

Kazery rolled away like a barrel. Laec danced away from Çifta's ice, shooting quick looks about the room for enemies advancing. They weren't. In fact—he blinked, thinking he must be imagining things—it looked like a few Silverfae had put themselves between Sylifke and Çifta. That couldn't be right, but he had no time to analyze it because the ice-tulip opened another foot.

The petals paused, hanging for a second, creaking and swaying. Mist rose from the opening, obscuring the details of the woman inside. Laec could not see her face but caught glimpses of her torso and long strands of hair. Laec blinked and rubbed his eyes, but yes, it was *white* hair, not black. As white as a swan's feather. Ice clung to her locks, sliding as it melted. Now Laec could see a pink arm, a hand and fragments of ice melting against the skin of her forearm.

"She's alive," Laec gulped in air, then barked a laugh that sounded half insane. "She's alive!"

Kazery was at his side, quiet, still. He stared, as every piece that fell away revealed more and more of his daughter.

Laec raised both arms up, his eyes alight, his sword gripped, now pointing at the ceiling. "She's alive! She's alive!"

Another quick glance at the room revealed the fae really were putting themselves in Sylifke's way, and Sylifke did not try to bypass them, only waited—hatred twisting her features, ghastly talons flexed—her frosty gaze on the pillar. It made no sense at all. They'd been trying to destroy Çifta only a minute ago, now… they waited for her, while she was still vulnerable and so easy to kill. Something else had to be going on here.

Çifta's hand lifted, crossed her torso, and ran down her opposite arm as she swept away slush and moisture. It hit the parquet with a splat. Someone was speaking, but Laec was too focused on Çifta to care, and couldn't understand the words anyway.

***THUD!***

Laec was struck by a battering ram as Kazery shoved him out of the way. The petals opened the rest of the way, smashing into shards that sprayed across the floor like shrapnel. Immediately, puddles gathered as the ice melted. Çifta was shrouded in mist, but she was there, standing on her own, the fabric of her dress stiff but dripping.

"Çifta!" Kazery scrambled to his feet. "I'm here, my minnow! Your father is here!"

She did not respond. The vapor cleared, and Laec's stomach tightened. Something was wrong.

She stepped from the mist, and he got his first good look at her. It was Çifta's beautiful face, Çifta's lovely figure, her glacial eyes… but this was not her. The true Çifta had a sweet and open expression, a woman made to give and receive love. The expression on her face now, the hatred burning from her eyes. She looked… mean… murderous. Unrecognizable.

Kazery grabbed Laec's arm, realizing too that something was amiss. He tried to say her name, but it was just a wheezy whisper.

Laec felt every injury now, and his body grew hot. He began to hyperventilate, unable to stop sucking in air and pushing it out again. His body ached, his skin burned with frostbite, his wounds throbbed. All he could do was stare at her, plead that she emerge. Her lips were still full and beautiful but held a sneer that froze Laec's blood. Her flint-sharp gaze was on Sylifke, and she had yet to acknowledge the presence of anyone else. Her expression was merciless, inexorable and savage rage.

She strode from the remains of the ice pillar, her fingers flexing. Then she halted abruptly. She turned to Laec and Kazery, but it was clear they were an afterthought.

"I promised to save you," she said quietly.

"Çifta, my darling…" Kazery's voice filled with despair. "Look at me."

"You have only moments to get to safety," she replied in an unrecognizable voice. "If you linger, you'll die. You have been warned."

She passed them, leaving them standing in the rubble, stupefied. Laec thought he might throw up.

"Daughter of Winter," Sylifke sneered.

The Silverfae parted, clearing the way between the two females. The expressions on their faces were apprehensive but expectant. *They* knew what was going on.

The answer that came from Çifta's lips made Laec shudder and gasp.

"Queen Karinya to you, traitorous whore." Her voice was as cold as the room, seething with deadly intent.

Kazery recoiled like a man slapped. "What?"

Laec's breathing slowed, but now he was shaking. He and Kazery stared at her back, dumbfounded, as she closed the distance between herself and Sylifke.

"Karinya," Laec husked. In a moment, the light of understanding came into his mind. She'd warned them they would die if they remained, and they'd wasted precious seconds gaping like lost children. There was no time to explain. He sheathed his sword, grabbed the merchant, and dove for the fireplace. Kazery let himself be moved, thankfully, almost tripping as he slid in the water. Had he resisted, Laec did not have the strength to drag him.

The rear wall shifted under Laec's touch, just as Jess had described, and they squeezed through the opening as the temperature in the ballroom dropped violently. The wall closed, muffling sounds of a sudden confrontation, sorcery clashing. Inky blackness engulfed them so completely, they may as well have been miles underground. Their ragged breathing was loud in the small space. Laec felt along the dirty walls and discovered the passage branched off in two directions. He turned left, though he had no idea where the nearest exit was.

"I don't understand," Kazery muttered behind him, seemingly unconcerned at where they'd found themselves or which direction they took. "The ice… it changed her?"

Laec felt his way along, inch by agonizingly slow inch. "Her body has been taken over."

"But… forever?" Kazery's voice broke on the final word.

Laec felt sorry for him, sorry for himself too.

"It cannot be forever," ventured the merchant, his clothing rasping against both sides of the passage, sending years of dust and dirt to the ground. He sounded puzzled and upset, but not angry or panicked. Laec admired his self-possession. "Surely, not *forever.* What kind of strange sorcery is this?"

Laec came to a corner and turned left again. He felt along the floor with his toes, in case there were steps, and kept his fingertips on the walls in case there were torches, curves, or corners.

Kazery groped for Laec. His fingers curled around one shoulder, pulling him gently back. "Explain it to me."

Laec reminded him about the war of the Silver queens, and the claim that Sylifke had used blood magic to defeat Karinya. Kazery grunted to indicate he remembered.

"So, Karinya has come back, in… my daughter," Kazery said. "A parasite, a… possession."

Laec nodded, and the merchant could see the gesture now because a crack of light had appeared ahead. A way out?

"I can't believe she might be gone forever," the merchant said, sounding calm and conversational. "She had to go *somewhere*. She'll come 'round, as long as… that other creature doesn't kill her body."

There were no words to express just how much Laec wanted that to be true.

A crash shook the walls. Light swept suddenly into the passageway, illuminating debris and spider webs. Dust clouded the air, making them cough. Something had knocked stones out of place. Through the hole came strange sounds, like an angry wind. It howled and whistled, gusting freezing air around them, making them flinch and cover their ears. Then, as quickly as it had come, it moved away.

When the air cleared, they picked their way forward to peer through the hole. They hadn't gotten very far, halfway down one side of the ballroom. Except for the dead, the room had been vacated.

The etherlight sconces flickered, struggling to come back to life, and the moonlight coming through the high windows cast strange shadows. A layer of ice coated dead bodies, the floor, and crawled up the walls, where it ended in upward streaks, like long reaching fingers. Many of the stones that had made up this wall were cracked in half and all the glass in the windows had shattered.

"Where did they go?" Kazery murmured.

Sounds of destruction echoed down the hallway.

"Toward the front, from the sounds of it," Laec muttered.

Climbing through the hole, they skidded and slipped on their way to the doors, avoiding the frozen bodies. Pain radiated from Laec's shoulder and knee, but he had no time to dwell on it. There was no one in sight in the hall, but there were shouts coming from the main foyer.

"Come on," Kazery growled and ran in the direction of the noise before Laec could suggest anything else.

Ignoring a powerful urge to collapse, Laec jogged after him. A few steps down the dim corridor, the etherlights surged to full-power. The rose window was functioning again.

## Chapter Thirty-Six

# Jessamine

After slinking through the herb garden, Sasha and Jess hid behind the wisteria boughs that choked the archway to the courtyard. Ice coated the branches, making them sag. The air was laced with tiny particles that glittered. Pretty, but with enough speed, Jess knew, those glitters could rake skin raw.

Sasha peeked into the courtyard. Jess dared a look under his arm. The courtyard was full of the evidence of fighting: frozen bodies, a few that were not frozen, puddles of ice, piles of snow and rubble. But they could see no one alive. From inside the palace foyer, drifting through the broken doors, came the squeak of soles on marble.

Rialta stood behind them, panting and alert, but her tail was up. When Jess looked down at her, she wagged.

Sasha moved into the courtyard cautiously and Jess followed, tense, ready to be attacked. The etherlights in the courtyard guttered, flickered a few times, then the space filled with illumination. Except for a broken step and cracks snaking up the pillars, the palace façade was intact. But every surface was threaded with veins of ice. Climbing plants were broken, ripped apart, and branches lay on the ground, caked with hoarfrost.

Jess looked up toward the rose window, illuminated once more as it drew power. The clouds were breaking apart, and the moon was at its zenith. It was still cold, but perhaps not as cold as it had been.

Etherlight poured through the open palace doorway. They edged their way up the steps and crept to the door. Sasha looked into the foyer first, going still at what he saw. He reached back for Jess. She moved under his arm, and he wrapped it around her as she looked into the foyer for herself.

She sucked in a breath at the scene.

In the middle of the huge marble space, facing off and slowly circling, were Sylifke and… Çifta.

Çifta?

Jess blinked, thinking she must be hallucinating. But no, the woman she and Laec had rescued—what felt like a decade ago—had survived the ice.

"Çifta," Jess whispered, as a thrill raced through her.

The girl from Boskaya had not simply survived, she had been wholly changed by her journey through the ice. Her hair was as white as chalk, yet the most startling difference was her face. She looked more like Çifta's evil twin than the warm, lovely lady that Jessamine had come to know. Except for a red weal across the left side of her neck, she looked unharmed.

It was not just the two females in the foyer that shocked Jess, but the fact that Silverfae citizens had gathered around the perimeter of the room. Watching. All weapons had been sheathed. The audience filled the second level too, looking down at the foyer, their expressions solemn. She and Sasha had been seen, yet no one made any move.

As the Silverfae females shifted around one another, Çifta did glance at them, saw them, but just as quickly dismissed them. She had looked straight at Jess, yet there had been no flicker of acknowledgment or recognition.

Beazle squirmed against her skull, coming out of her hair. He crawled up the back of her head to watch from the top.

Sylifke stood, one shoulder lower than the other, one hand holding her side and the other out in a warding gesture. Blood dripped over the fingers clutching her ribs, soaking her gown, now a ruin of tattered fabric. A patch of blood on her head matted her hair to her skull, knotting her locks into ropes. With her free hand, Sylifke made a claw. Spears of ice hurtled toward Çifta, she but knocked them aside with an effortless wave.

Making those spears had cost Sylifke. She was hunched like a ninety-year-old, while Çifta stood straight and strong.

She took a step toward Sylifke. "Was it worth it?"

The Silverfae were silent as they watched. They had no more presence than ghosts.

Broken and bleeding, Sylifke lifted her chin, her voice filling the foyer. "For more than four decades, the winter kingdom has been restored to the glory of its former years. I, Sylifke of the Outer Darkhan, did that. Not you. History will remember me as a sovereign of the ancient ways. The old magic was mine, for a time."

Jess was confused. What did Çifta have to do with the state of the winter kingdom?

Sasha seemed to hear her thought and put his lips down to her ear. "It's a challenge for power. A fight to the death."

Movement drew Jess's eye upward. The crofter was on

the third-floor balcony, Panther at his side. More Solanans, courtiers and Fahyli came into view, looking down. They were hushed, watching with pale, serious faces. Some shuffled over to make space for Agir and Esha. Even Isabey's grayish face peeked over the railing. No one said a word or did anything to interfere. Jess felt awed, gazing at all those surrounding the room, watching.

"For more than forty years," said Çifta in a voice Jess did not recognize, "the winter kingdom has been enslaved by a usurper and traitor. I, Karinya, the tempest of frozen blades, free Silverfall once more. I shall return it to a kingdom of sunlight and prosperity, where people do not fear to tread their own streets. History will remember you, Fool of the Outer Darkhan, as a traitor, a cheater, and an abuser. A tyrant who defiled herself with blood magic."

Jess shook her head to clear it. *Karinya?*

But there was no mistaking how Çifta had referred to herself. Her voice was strong and reached every ear.

*It's not a fight*, Beazle thought.

*No,* Jess returned. *It's an execution.*

Çifta approached Sylifke, looking down at her unrepentant enemy. When her hand snapped out to the side, and a long, crude axe swept from her white fingertips, razor-sharp and glittering, Jess hid her face in Sasha's chest. The ice-blade cut through flesh with hardly a sound, followed by a heavy thud.

Beazle quivered against Jess. Not afraid, but concerned about what, or who, their friend had become.

Jess looked up as Çifta—no, Karinya—dropped her axe. It shattered on the marble floor.

For a moment, no one moved, no one even dared to breathe. Then Karinya stood straight and turned slowly. As she did, most of the Silverfae citizens who were not already kneeling sank to their knees. Sasha stayed on his feet, though he bowed his head and let out a long sigh through his nose. Rayven Sabran closed her eyes, and Jess swore that the faintest smile lifted the corners of her mouth as she too bowed her head.

They were relieved, Jess realized.

Çifta/Karinya kept turning, looking at each of her subjects, until she faced Sasha and Jess in the doorway. Her glacial-blue eyes landed on Sasha. She looked at him for what felt like forever. Then she raised her hand, palm up, and beckoned.

Keeping Jess a little behind him, Sasha moved forward. Rialta moved up beside him, her nails clicking on the floor. White-haired Çifta rested both of her palms on Sasha's shoulders, looking up into his face. Slowly, she pulled him down and kissed both his cheeks.

"No longer shall you be required to pay for the sins of your father," she said, her voice husky.

Her words, soft as they were, echoed through the room. The Silverfae heard them, and some of them had the decency to look ashamed, including Rayven.

Çifta turned away, having never once looked Jess in the eye, or taken notice of the wee bat on top of her head.

*She doesn't know us anymore,* thought Beazle.

*She went into the ice Çifta, and came out... someone else, their former queen.*

Karinya looked up at those watching from the balcony. The crofter moved to the king's elbow, and they exchanged words.

Karinya put her hand up to someone behind the ring of Silverfae. People shuffled over to reveal Laec, Kazery beside him. They looked as stiff as wax figures, and just as pale. They had eyes only for Çifta. She waited for them in the middle of the floor, with the posture of a queen.

The air was much warmer now, Jess noticed. She had to keep herself from looking at the headless body, silver blood slowly creeping across the marble floor, the blond head… a few feet away.

Laec and Kazery stopped before Çifta, looking at her apprehensively. Her expression was impassive.

Kazery put a hand out toward her, not daring to touch her. "Minnow? Do you know me?"

Laec just stared, his posture bent, blood soaking patches of his clothing. He looked broken, not just in body, but in soul. This was not the woman he loved.

Karinya turned first to Kazery. "She wanted you to know that no father was ever loved more by a daughter,"

The big man fell to his knees, dropping his face into his hands. Laec touched Kazery's shoulder, eyes still on the white-haired Çifta. For the first time, Jess noticed the sharp ears poking from her hair.

"And you, Laec Fairijak." Her voice was as steady as a barge on a windless sea. "She wanted you to know that you were her dream. You filled her heart with love. She saw her future in you."

Laec closed his eyes, his lashes glistened.

"And *I* want you to know," she continued gently, and Laec's eyes opened. "That I, and all of Silverfall, are eternally grateful to her."

A tear streaked through the dirt on Laec's face. Jess felt her own tears welling up, her lips trembling.

Karinya reached for Laec's face. With a soft touch, she wiped away the tear, leaving a streak. "But why do you cry?"

Laec took a shuddery breath. He looked with tormented eyes into the face he loved, belonging now to someone he did not know. And all that he felt, the loss, the heartbreak, the sorrow, filled his face and bent his body.

He opened his mouth, but before he could answer, Karinya said, "There is no reason for tears, Laec." She took in a quiet inhale. "She passed the test."

Then she collapsed.

## Chapter Thirty-Seven

# Laec

Laec dashed forward, his wounds crying out, his vision blurred with tears. He was too slow to catch her, and she landed in a heap. Kazery crawled to her side as Laec cradled her head and torso. Gently, he turned her face skyward and checked for a pulse.

Nothing.

Kazery felt at her wrist. "She was fine," he said. "I see no injury. I don't understand."

Laec did not have an answer. Vaguely, like they were part of a dream, not real life, people approached, Silverfae murmured among themselves. No one seemed to know what to do. Laec brushed the hair away from Çifta's face. She looked like herself again.

He held her, tears streaming down his cheeks. He touched her cheekbone, her chin. Her mouth was open. He put his fingertips under her chin to close it… and met resistance. He blinked, then used more force. Still, her jaw would not close. He put his palm before her open mouth and felt a steady stream of air. It was… cold, and it went on and on, much longer than any final breath should. Cupping his hand over her mouth, the air struck his palm, then curled around it to float upward. Cold air floating *upward*?

"Kazery." Laec looked up at the merchant, beckoning that he should feel it for himself.

Kazery put his big hand in front of Çifta's face. "What is that?"

Laec shook his head.

"Her hair…" Kazery pointed. "Look."

At the roots, Çifta's hair was blue-black again, as dark as ink. Color steadily moved down each hair shaft, slowly, like some invisible artist was painting over the white.

Laec's heart was pounding so hard he could hardly hear anything else. His fingers went to her throat again. He found a pulse, strong and steady under his fingertips. She took a breath.

Her hair was more than half black now. The crowd pressed in close, straining for glimpses of the magic happening before their eyes.

Loath to remove his gaze from her, Laec held her and watched, waited, enraptured. Ink-black reached the tips. When there was no white left, her eyebrows transformed, darkening into the rich Unya shade.

She opened her eyes.

The crowd gasped. Some staggered backward, stepping on others, bumping into them.

Laec studied her, and those beautiful, glacier-blue eyes focused on him. Her brow pinched, then relaxed. A smile stole over her lips, Çifta's smile. Laec felt like whooping for joy, but just smiled back at her.

"Laec." She lifted a hand to his face. "I passed the test."

He bent and kissed her, and his whole being rejoiced when she threw her arms around his neck. He drew her to her feet, mouth on hers, arms firmly around her. He forgot everyone and everything, there was only Çifta, warm and supple in his arms, alive. Returned to him. He kissed her until they were breathless, hearts flying.

Screams and whoops went up around them.

They withdrew and stood forehead to forehead, soaking in the other's love and solidity. Feelings that had only ever been hinted at were now there for all the world to see.

Kazery cleared his throat, and Çifta turned to her father. She hurled herself into his arms and he held her close, his face buried in her hair. When he released his daughter, she stepped back and looked at both her men, eyes grazing them from top to bottom. As she registered patches of blood on their clothing, she lost her smile. Laec wanted to tell her that he couldn't feel any pain, if only just to wipe the concern off her gorgeous face. He'd only just gotten back her smile.

Someone cried, "Hail! Queen of Silverfall!"

Laec looked around, remembering where they were. He felt dizzy watching the Silverfae drop to their knees again. A broken patch in the crush of people reminded him that Sylifke's body lay there. Now there was nothing left of her line. A few big males gathered around the body, murmuring as they bent to deal with it. It seemed that not a single Silverfae wanted to mourn her. Everywhere Laec looked, he saw the eyes of newly released prisoners, full of love and adoration for the one who had liberated them.

Calls of 'My Queen!' and 'Hail the Queen of Winter' rang through the foyer.

"So, are you Çifta or Karinya?" Laec asked, turning to her.

She half-smiled. "I am the daughter of winter."

"What does that mean?"

"It means, I'm me, the same person I have always been, but… I have Karinya's memories, and her magic." She took a breath. "So, I guess… it means I'm both."

Rayven approached, her cheeks wet and eyelashes spiky with moisture. Taking Çifta's hand, she knelt before her and looked up. "You were prophesied, my lady. We've been waiting for you. She tried to keep you a secret, but some of us knew. You survived the ice. You've taken the throne. We need to know what to call you, my queen."

"Her name is Çifta Unya," Kazery told the ex-prosecutor.

Rayven shouted as she stood, "Hail, Queen Çifta of Silverfall!"

Her cries were echoed by all around them, and Laec felt Çifta's hand slip into his. She pressed against him, and he put his arm around her. She looked up, and they could see the question in each other's eyes. What now?

A gust of wind came through the doorway. The air was fresh, but not cold. He squeezed Çifta to his side and lay his cheek on her head. Whatever was next, they'd deal with it together. That much, he did know.

# Epilogue

"WHAT ARE YOU smiling about?"

Jess opened her eyes as Sasha—wearing borrowed work clothes, gloves, and a hat—tossed an armload of rocks onto a wagon.

"You," she murmured. "I'm smiling about you, about… us."

He came close and looked down at her. They hugged, just loving the feeling of being next to one another. She felt his warm lips against the skin of her neck and shivered. They'd been hugging—and kissing—a lot in the two days since Sasha's absolution.

Everyone, from the lowest peasant to the highest ranking courtier—even some Silverfae—skilled or not, had rolled up their sleeves to return Solana, city and palace, to its previous state. The gardens and grounds already looked better without the bodies and rubble. And Jess had seen Isabey earlier, filling cracks in the main foyer.

Solana had lost one-hundred-three citizens, mostly soldiers, but some innocents as well, Heath included. The Silverfae dead numbered only thirty-eight, including the former queen. All traces of Sylifke's malicious weather had evaporated with her death, but a layer of mourning blanketed the city. Ilishec was already planning the memorial, though the Calyx had been seconded to palace restoration, helping where they could with clean up. The carpenters and masons would be busy for a while, fixing the ice damage to walls and features both outside the castle, and inside too.

While most of the Calyx were helping clean the interior and restore the plants that had been damaged, Jess volunteered to work outside with the fauna fae, primarily because that's where Sasha had been assigned. There were whispers that he and Rialta would be invited to join the Fahyli, but Sasha had never broached the topic. They had been working so hard there'd been no time for a private discussion. Jess tried to ignore the fear that Sasha would decide to journey north with his countrymen. There was enough to deal with, and she did not feel that Sasha was in any rush to go anywhere. And Rialta had friends here too, big predators just like her. Rialta and Tully had been seen together a lot in the past two days, igniting smiles with their antics.

She supposed Laec and Çifta would be having a similar talk soon, if they hadn't already. Rayven Sabran had been given charge of the Silverfae who wanted to go home, but they would expect their queen to join them soon. Whenever she'd seen Laec and Çifta, they'd looked like mirror images of her and Sasha. Constantly hugging, never far apart, like they were afraid to lose sight of one another.

Regalis's voice drew Jess from her musings.

"I need order, Gardenia. I like rules, protocol."

Jess's eye was drawn toward the corner of the palace, where Regalis and Gardenia walked together. They were close to one another, and Regalis spoke with his voice low, but it carried on the wind. Jess and Sasha exchanged a look but kept working, looking pointedly away from what was clearly a lovers' spat. Gardenia was trying valiantly not to cry.

"It helps me make sense of the world," Regalis continued. "To have expectations, not just for myself, but for everyone else, too."

Gardenia whimpered. "I've told you I'm sorry. How many times can I say it? I just wanted to be with you. It's where I felt safest. Darling…"

Regalis was struggling to sound calm, but his nerves were clearly fraying. "I get that, but—no, actually, I don't get it. I have a job to do, Gard. Do you have any idea of the danger you put us in?"

Gardenia sniffed. "Yes. Please forgive me. It'll never happen again, I promise."

"I know it won't." Their footsteps stopped, and Regalis let out an exasperated breath. "This won't work, Gardenia. I'm sorry, I really, really like you, but—"

"Like me?" Gardenia's voice broke. "You *like* me?"

They were in their own world, unaware that Jess and Sasha were downwind, hearing everything. Jess squirmed and saw that Sasha felt uncomfortable too.

"We just aren't going to work. We're too different." Regalis's voice was pleading. He obviously didn't want to hurt her.

Gardenia sucked in a deep breath, letting it out in shudders. She began to keen.

"Oh no." Regalis sounded at a loss. "Please, don't… Gard."

Jess caught a scent of spoiled flowers on the wind as Gardenia turned and ran back the way they'd come. It touched her senses and was gone. A whiff of heartbreak.

The shadow of Ferrugin ghosted over the rubble. "I know," Regalis murmured. Then carried on up the road. Only then did he see Jess and Sasha. He froze, misery etched across his face, as their gazes met. Jess felt her heart whimper.

"I didn't see you there," he muttered. "I'm sorry you heard that."

"Oh, Regalis. *I'm* sorry." It was all Jessamine could think to say.

He just nodded and carried on.

"That was awful," Sasha murmured, his eyes on Regalis's shrinking figure.

Jess rubbed her forehead with her glove, smearing dirt. "Ilishec is going to be insufferable now. Poor Gardenia. I hope she wasn't really in love."

Sasha looked confused. "Ilishec? Why?"

Jessamine told him about the warning the gardener had given all the Calyx, canceling the afternoon's schedule just to make sure it sank in. That story led to Hazel, which led to Hazel's condition. The light shifted as they worked, softening everything with a midafternoon glow. Sasha asked her question after question about the Calyx, how she came to join it, about her friends, so many things that they'd never had a chance to talk about.

She stopped midsentence when Snap and Aster came sprinting around the corner, looking ordinary in their work clothes. They headed straight for her.

"Jess!" Snap put up a hand in a wave. Something was clutched in his fist.

"Wait for me, Snap," Aster panted, grabbing at the back of his jacket.

Alarm flooded Jess's blood. "What's wrong? Is it Gardenia?"

Her friends reached her, out of breath. Snap doubled over. Aster shot her a confused look. "What's wrong with Gardenia?"

"I'll let her tell you," Jess said and immediately liked the way it felt to honor Gardenia and Regalis's privacy. It felt more grown up, mature.

Snap straightened, recovering his breath. "Nothing is wrong, not exactly. We—Aster and I—we stumbled across a piece of your puzzle."

"My puzzle?" Jess cocked her head.

"Your *family* puzzle," Aster added.

"We've been cleaning the corridors on the third floor of the donjon. Don't ask me what Silvers were doing up in that tower. Anyway, they blasted some walls, wrecked a few apartments and made a huge mess. There's stuff everywhere, books, clothes, furni—"

"The point, Snap," Aster said, her gaze flicking to his fist.

"We found this." He opened his palm.

A baby bonnet lay in Snap's hand, tiny and wrinkled, familiar yet unfamiliar. It was pale purple, with an embroidered sprig of lavender across the scalloped hem.

Jess went still. She felt Sasha shift closer to her. Aster and Snap held their breaths, watching her, gauging her every reaction. With a surprisingly steady hand, Jess took the bonnet, knowing what she would find. Gently, she flipped up the hem. The curlicued name tag spelled out Julian Fontana. She ran her fingertips over the soft fabric, her heart pounding.

"Where was it?" Jess sounded much calmer than she felt. She was unable to tear her eyes from the nametag. A low hum had begun in the back of her mind, and it was rising, turning into a buzz.

"It was scattered across the bailey below the donjon with a bunch of other stuff…" Snap began.

"Jess?" It was Sasha. He put an arm around her shoulders, and that simple gesture felt like the only thing keeping her from falling apart, crumbling and blowing away.

"I'm okay," she murmured. "Take me there?"

"Of course," said Aster, sounding relieved. She hooked a hand under Jess's elbow and the four of them moved toward the front of the palace.

Jess was glad to be braced on two sides because she wasn't watching where she was going. She held the bonnet, stroking it with a thumb. Her thoughts felt like they'd been sucked up by the vortex of a hurricane. Another bonnet, hidden all this time in a tower of private apartments that Jess had never had reason to visit, even when memorizing the secret passageways. Who lived there? Who could possibly have had her dead twin's bonnet in their suite? She wracked her brains but couldn't name a single resident; they were mostly advisors, counselors of the king and queen, people with power and influence, with nothing to do with the Calyx or the Fahyli. The buzz in the back of her mind had blossomed into a headache. She felt like her head was made of glass and full of hornets.

No one said a word as they approached the main courtyard. Jess could feel her friends looking at her and at one another. They were concerned. Rightfully so; she was concerned about herself.

"Who is that?"

Snap's question drew Jess out of her daze.

Her friends slowed, and she with them. They watched a

male figure shuffle through the front gate, leaning on a crutch, and stop just inside to look around. He had the posture of an old man and was dressed in peasant clothing little better than rags. When he pulled the holey woolen cap off to wipe at his brow, the sun glinted on gold-bronze hair. He was young. Jess shook off her mental fog and studied him. There was something familiar…

She gasped, her eyes springing wide. "Shade," she whispered.

"Who?" Aster sounded exactly like an owl.

"You know him?" Sasha asked.

"Shade!" Jess screamed, and ran forward, shoving Julian's bonnet into her pocket.

At his name, Shade looked over, his brows lifting as she bore down on him. She stopped before him, wanting to throw her arms around him—although she didn't really know him that well—she was thrilled to see him alive.

"You remember me? You… know me?" His eyes skimmed across her face, like pebbles skipping over water.

"Of course I do!" She took one of his hands. Her heart was rocketing around in her chest. He looked thin, exhausted, and cold, but he was alive. Injured, but alive.

"You're… Jess, right?" He squeezed her hand. "Fahyli. The one with the bat…Beazle, was it?"

Jess could feel Beazle's pleasure at having been remembered. "Yes. We thought you died. Fixnix is still searching for you, but they're looking for a corpse. What happened?"

He smiled wearily. "That's a long story. But I can't tell you how good it feels to be recognized."

Jess looked around. At her scream, a few people had trickled into the courtyard to see what was going on. She saw Kestrel and called, "Get the crofter, please! Hurry!"

Kestrel whirled and was gone.

She turned back to Shade, but he was no longer looking at her. His eyes were fixed on the stairs leading up to the front doors. Jess followed his gaze and her body prickled with goosebumps. Isabey stood on the top step, holding a wooden bucket. In trousers, boots and a brown quilted jacket, and wearing a kerchief over her long brown hair, she looked like a servant. She was staring at Shade, unblinking and pale, seeming uncertain of her own eyesight.

"Isabey," Shade whispered, and the name caught in the back of his throat. He took a breath, and his chest hitched. He limped forward, eyes glued to the princess. The tap of his crutch seemed to rouse her from her stupor.

"Sh-Shade?" Isabey dropped her bucket, and it bounced down the stairs. She took one step down, then another.

Shade's crutch tap-tap-tapped on the cobbles. He stopped at the bottom of the steps, out of breath, looking up.

With a cry, Isabey flew down the stairs. She was laughing and crying, saying his name over and over. He threw down his crutch and opened his arms, holding his wounded leg off the ground. She slipped into his arms and buried her face in his neck. He held her close. They both wept. Shade, silently, Isabey crying with her whole body, shuddering as she sobbed against him.

Jess heard him whisper, "Princess. I'm sorry. I'm so sorry. I'm here now. I'm here. I love you. I love you."

Remarkable, Jess thought. Shade had clearly been through hell, while Isabey had been sheltered and coddled and fed. Yet here he was, holding her up, keeping her from falling apart the only way he could, with both body and words.

"That's the soldier you told us about," Aster whispered at Jess's elbow. "He was alive this whole time."

Jess nodded, putting her arm around Sasha's waist. They found it impossible to look away from the couple, and they weren't the only ones. People gathered in the courtyard, whispering about the pair embracing on the front steps, the man standing on one foot, keeping his sweetheart from collapsing. Soon everyone would know. A soldier of Rahamlar, and Isabey's lover—there was no hiding it now—had come back from the dead.

"Look at them," Sasha murmured, squeezing her tight.

"They're *magnificent*," whispered Aster, ever the romantic.

Jess felt Julian's bonnet in her pocket, pressing against her. Seeing the reunification of Isabey and Shade, knowing he'd forged through hell and highwater to get to her, lifted Jess's heart, strengthened her, gave her hope. Isabey had thought she'd lost everyone, but the most important, her soul mate, had returned to her. For Jess, piecing together the mystery of her family would mean peace in her heart. For Isabey, the return of her lover would mean… what? Enough strength to challenge her brother for Rahamlar's crown? Civil war?

They could still hear Shade repeating, "I'm here, darling. I'm here."

Jess's gaze flicked over to the donjon in the distance. She could only see the top of it, with Solana's lion's head pennant flying in the breeze. She felt Sasha look down at her and lifted her eyes to his.

Sasha's arm tightened around her. "I'm here," he told her. "No matter what."

She stretched up to kiss him. She had needed to hear that.

*I'm here too,* Beazle told her blearily. *Since we're doing a roll call.*

Jess smiled and released some of the tension in her body, some of the turmoil in her mind. If Shade's reappearance proved anything, it was that perseverance paid off. If he could forge through hell and high water for a loved one, then so could she.

So would she.

The epic fable is concluded with:

# A Prince of Autumn

## The Scented Court

Book 4

# About the Author

USA Today Bestselling Author, A.L. Knorr is an award-winning Canadian fantasy writer. Known for strong female protagonists, realistic magic, adventure and intrigue, sweet romance, and well-crafted plots that keep you turning pages late into the night, A.L. Knorr is a masterful storyteller. Her debut story, Born of Water, won the Readers' Favorite gold medal for YA Fantasy in 2018, and her stories frequently feature at the top of the Amazon fantasy charts. She lives on the Mediterranean coast with her chef husband and floofy cat, Pamuk. Learn more by visiting www.alknorrbooks.com,, where you can also join her newsletter for updates.

www.ingramcontent.com/pod-product-compliance
Lightning Source LLC
Chambersburg PA
CBHW020522310726
48979CB00014B/2178/J

* 9 7 8 1 9 8 9 3 3 8 5 6 8 *